D0951529

"With its quirky characters and the funny situations they get into, whether they be normal or paranormal, *Nice Girls Don't Date Dead Men* is an amazing novel, deserving of Romance Reviews Today's coveted Perfect 10."

—Romance Reviews Today

"Molly Harper is a premier writer of paranormal romance with an abundance of sharp-edged humor.... Magically believable, imaginative, and brilliantly witty, *Nice Girls Don't Date Dead Men* is an enchanting story of the paranormal."

—Single Titles

NICE GIRLS DON'T HAVE FANGS
RT Book Reviews TOP PICK!

"Hysterical laughs are the hallmark of this enchanting paranormal debut.... Harper's take on vampire lore will intrigue and entertain.... Jane's snarky first-person narrative is as charming as it is hilarious.... Harper keeps the quips coming without overdoing the sarcasm."

—*Publishers Weekly* (starred review)

"Quirky characters, human and vampire alike."

—*Booklist*

"Jane is an everygirl with a wonderful sense of humor and quick sarcasm. Add in the mystery and romance and you have your next must-read novel!"

—*RT Book Reviews* (4½ stars)

NICE GIRLS DON'T BITE THEIR NEIGHBORS

MOLLY HARPER

Pocket Books

New York   London   Sydney   Toronto   New Delhi

Pocket Books
A Division of Simon & Schuster, Inc.
1230 Avenue of the Americas
New York, NY 10020

Copyright © 2012 by Molly Harper White

First Pocket Books paperback edition March 2012

POCKET and colophon are registered trademarks of Simon & Schuster, Inc.

For information about special discounts for bulk purchases, please contact Simon & Schuster Special Sales at 1-866-506-1949 or business@simonandschuster.com.

The Simon & Schuster Speakers Bureau can bring authors to your live event. For more information or to book an event, contact the Simon & Schuster Speakers Bureau at 1-866-248-3049 or visit our website at www.simonspeakers.com.

Manufactured in the United States of America

10 9 8 7 6 5 4 3 2 1

ISBN 978-1-4516-4181-3
ISBN 978-1-4516-4186-8 (ebook)

For Jennifer Heddle,
who helped me bring Jane into the world.

Acknowledgments

Our girl Jane has finally grown up. It's a little sad, writing the acknowledgments for this book, though I know there will be further adventures for the wacky denizens of Half-Moon Hollow. Still, Jane will always be my "firstborn," and I will always appreciate the care and attention of the people who helped me bring her into the literary world.

I'd like to thank my husband, David, and our kids, Darcy and Carter, for accommodating the long hours, "morning zombie Mom," and the weekends on the road. To Mom, Dad, Manda, and Matt, for putting up with public embarrassment, long-winded stories involving obscure publishing terms, and my inability to use voice-mail—I love you guys.

To my agent, Stephany Evans, thank you for . . . well, everything. Signing me, talking me down from the pro-verbial ledge when I need it, and kicking me in the pants when necessary.

And to Jennifer Heddle, I will miss you terribly. That's all I can say.

To Ayelet Gruensphect and Susan Lindsey, my pub-licity team, thank you for all that you do.

A massive thank-you to all of the readers who contacted me, asking, "What happens to Jane next?" Without you, I probably wouldn't have found the strength to drag my rear to the laptop every night.

And to the lovely authors I've met along the way, the most supportive group of people a gal could ask for, knowing that there are others out there, awake at 2 A.M. talking to/for people who don't exist, is always a comfort.

NICE
GIRLS
DON'T BITE
THEIR
NEIGHBORS

1

Whoever said childbirth is the most difficult thing a parent can go through has never dealt with a moody teenage vampire.

—*Siring for the Stupid:*
A Beginner's Guide to Raising Newborn Vampires

Three months after he moved into my ancestral home, Gabriel Nightengale's last box was finally unpacked. The catch was that we could never break up, because I had run out of friends who were willing to help us move.

"I have good news," he said, striding into the library, where I was sprawled on the velvet chaise longue we'd moved into the room only a few days ago. I was reading *Persuasion* again, but this time, I was reading Gabriel's very old, very delicate original edition. It was practically a religious experience.

This was a vastly different library from just a year ago, when it was stuffed with my well-worn paperback versions of Jane Austen and Roald Dahl novels . . . and my creepily extensive collection of unicorn figurines. This was a grown-up library. I'd cleared out quite a bit of space for Gabriel's books and furniture. It wasn't a difficult choice, considering that most of his books were valuable antiques, whereas most of mine were purchased at secondhand paperback shops.

I'd also packed most of my unicorn collection away in the cellar, threatening Gabriel with permanent sunburn if he so much as breathed a word about it to Dick.

As Gabriel moved toward me, my pitifully hideous but lovable dog, Fitz, raised his head from my knee. Gently nudging Fitz aside, Gabriel pressed kisses along the line of my throat and announced, "My VHS tapes now have a permanent home in your entertainment center, alphabetized and divided by genre."

At this announcement, Fitz trotted out of the room in search of some pair of Gabriel's shoes that he hadn't managed to chew yet. I peered up at him over the top of the book, cringing. "So now would be a really bad time to tell you that I don't have a VHS player anymore, right? This is a strictly digital household."

Gabriel groaned and flopped down next to me. "I'm going to have to buy *Casablanca* again."

"You didn't notice the lack of a VCR in the TV cabinet?" I asked.

He shook his head. "You know I don't understand half of the gadgets you have around here."

That was true. The previous week, I'd caught him trying to "reboot" my wireless network by kicking the router across the room. That was a long conversation. I shook my head. "How did I end up in a relationship in which *I* am the tech person?"

He leaned in and kissed me. "When you taught me how

to work my voicemail, I knew I could never let you go."

I giggled as Gabriel crossed the room and selected an older volume from the crowded shelves. I watched him move, unabashedly lovestruck. My human relationships had been few and far between, but they'd been polite, civilized—boring. I craved Gabriel with a bone-deep lust I'd once reserved exclusively for Godiva truffles. I was fixated, not just in the physical sense—although that was an obvious, and occasionally distracting, bonus—but also with what he thought, how he saw the world, how he saw me. It was addictive to see myself reflected in his liquid silver eyes as strong, beautiful, intelligent, and interesting, though slightly exasperating. We each provided a vital service for the other. He made me stronger, and I kept him from taking himself too seriously.

Gabriel settled in next to me, absorbed in a vintage copy of *Jane Eyre*. We sat like that for some time, quietly reveling in not having anything to do, anywhere to be. Crisis-free moments like this had been rare in our relationship.

"*Jane Eyre*?" I asked. "Not your usual selection."

He nodded. "You've only mentioned a dozen or so times that Edward Rochester is second only to Mr. Darcy on your 'Fictional Character Free Pass List.' I want to know what I'm up against."

I smirked, snuggling into his side. "You stand a fair chance. As long as you don't have a crazy wife hidden away somewhere . . ." I stared at him for a beat.

"I don't," he said, shaking his head at me and opening his book.

That may have seemed like an unfair shot, but Gabriel and I had suffered serious relationship issues related to his "careful editing" of his past. Case in point, the fire in my cellar caused by Gabriel's psycho childe, Jeanine, who had stalked me, nearly killed me with aerosol silver, and eventually arranged for our friend Andrea to be forcibly turned into a vampire. I try to resist pointing out that of all this could have been avoided if Gabriel had told me about Jeanine, instead of playing the tortured "I can't tell you because you'll hate me, so I'll protect you by keeping you in the dark" card.

Trust me, that card never works. I ended up with more undead friends and a serious cleaning bill for smoke damage. And then, as the vampire who technically defeated her in a Taser-versus-lunatic-soaked-in-lamp-oil battle, there was the hassle of receiving the proceeds from Jeanine's estate through the Council, then donating them to various charities. I didn't want one penny from her crazy behind darkening my doorway.

"Just checking," I said, smiling sweetly and earning an undignified but amused snort from Gabriel. I returned my attention to poor, persevering Anne Elliot. Once again, I wondered how she managed to go so many chapters without bitch-slapping every single person she came into contact with. I actually wrote a paper about it in college. My professor deducted points for using the phrase *bitch-slap* in the title.

It was totally worth it.

I was just settling into the salons of Austenian Bath when Gabriel muttered, "This is strange."

I looked up to see him pulling a long blue-gray thread from between the nearly translucent pages. My jaw dropped, and I was kneeling on the chaise in a flash. "Is the binding coming loose? No, don't pull it! I can take it to my book doctor tomorrow night."

"Stop hyperventilating, sweetheart. I think it's a bookmark," he said, pulling on the thread until he'd stretched it into my hand. "Here."

I wound the thread around my finger. "What passage was it marking?"

He scanned the page and lifted an eyebrow. "It's an Edward and Jane scene. I know how you love those. Edward's saying, 'I sometimes have a queer feeling with regard to you—especially when you are near me, as now: it is as if I had a string somewhere under my left ribs, tightly and inextricably knotted to a similar string situated in the corresponding quarter of your little frame.'"

I was so caught up in watching his lips as they formed the words that I barely noticed the sudden tension on the fiber wound around my finger. I realized now that Gabriel had slipped a ring onto the thread and was sliding it toward me. I watched as the respectable diamond twinkled in the light of the oil lamp.

"I'm not Edward," Gabriel promised. "I'm not afraid the thread will break and leave me bleeding. Our thread's already been tested. And it will hold up. I'm asking you to make the link permanent. Please, marry me."

I smiled as the ring slid into my hand. I can't say this was a surprise. After the passing of the Federal Undead

Marriage Act a few months before, Gabriel had officially proposed with this very tasteful solitaire. And I'd said no. We'd agreed to move in together because I'd told Gabriel that I wasn't ready to be engaged yet. I was still adjusting to being a vampire. I was still recovering from Zeb and Jolene's wedding from hell. And oh, yeah, Gabriel's childe had just tried to murder me in my own home. I needed a breather.

Gabriel had proposed again a few weeks later, and I wasn't ready. And then again on my birthday, and I still wasn't ready. Then he'd promised not to ask me again until I was ready. And when he'd said that, I'd suddenly felt ready. And then I'd felt like an idiot, because by then, he'd stopped proposing.

This was no ballpark Jumbotron, no ring hidden in a soufflé. It was the right way for Gabriel to ask me to marry him. And this was the right time.

I nodded, mute, and the tension seemed to drain out of Gabriel. He grinned, slid his hands in my hair, and pulled me close. "I struggled with the right passage, you know," he said, sliding the ring over my knuckle and kissing the web of skin between my fingers. "I tried all of Austen's works, but the proposals are all so formal. I thought you would appreciate Edward's passion. And it still involves a Jane, after all. The ring is a copy of my mother's. I took the stone from her engagement ring and had a jeweler place it in a titanium setting."

"Titanium?" I asked.

"Dick knew a guy," he said.

"Of course he did."

"You're a bit rough-and-tumble with jewelry, and I knew it would have to be able to stand up to . . ."

"Nuclear winter?"

His eyebrow lifted. "I never know with you."

I laughed, throwing my arms around him and knocking him back on the seat and straddling his hips. Hovering over him, I nuzzled his neck, kissing and nipping before my fangs extended. I scraped them along his jugular, making him shudder and snake his hands around my waist, pulling me closer. I threaded my fingers through his coal-black hair and tugged his head back. His own fangs snicked out as he grinned up at me. He cupped my cheeks in his palms and gave me my first "betrothed" kiss.

I have to say that if I'd known that was what I had to look forward to as a married woman, I probably would have agreed to the engagement a lot sooner.

He chuckled, pressing his thumb over my right canine, letting it pierce the skin. I nibbled at it as he twisted under me, a sweet little trickle of my sire's blood lending to an equally wet and pleasant sensation elsewhere. Pushing the scoop neck of my blouse away, he trailed his lips over the edge of my bra and snapped the left strap with his razor-sharp fangs.

Your underwear budget triples when you're dating the undead.

"You haven't said yes, by the way," he murmured, snapping the other bra strap with his teeth.

I gasped, and his thumb fell away from my mouth. "I'm sorry! Yes, yes, yes!"

"Should I find it disturbing that it took jewelry to make you cry 'yes, yes, yes' in my presence for the first time?" he asked, nuzzling my throat.

"Nice." I snickered.

"So, who do you want to call first?" he asked. "Your mother? Jenny? Zeb and Jolene? Oh, or I can call Dick, act like I'm sobbing, and tell him you said no. Make him think that he has to take me out for an evening of drinking and not talking about our feelings."

"That's your idea of a joke?" I asked, arching my eyebrow.

He smirked, pulling my blouse over my head. My ruined bra fell to pieces and dropped to the floor. "I find Dick's squirming in the face of emotional vulnerability to be the height of hilarity."

"This is why Dick wins all of your prank wars," I told him, as he pulled me back onto the chaise, my weight settled on his chest.

"Do you want to call your mother first or Zeb?"

I shook my head, cradling my face into his neck. "No."

"No?"

"Neither. First, because I'd like to wait until I can tell Aunt Jettie." I sighed, thinking fondly of my ghostly great-aunt and her equally deceased beau, Gilbert Wainwright. "And I don't know when she'll be back from whatever astral jaunt she and Mr. Wainwright are taking. And second, because I want to lie here with you and enjoy being engaged without being squealed at or hug-strangled or told that I don't want to get married in the spring because it's impossible to get the right mix of seasonal tulips. I just want to . . ." I sighed and rubbed my bare chest against his shirt in a distinctly non-virginal-bride manner. "Bask."

"You never do what I expect you to," he said, kissing the ring on my finger.

"Admit it, that's part of the attraction."

"Yes. Yes, it is." He sighed. "But you will be the one to tell your mother, right? I asked your father for his blessing. But I think you should be the one to deliver the news to your mother."

I snorted. Mama's reaction to our premarital cohabiting included screaming and yelling and threatening us with grounding. Considering that the worst that his own mother had ever done to him was call for her smelling salts, Gabriel was permanently scarred. He had flash-backs for weeks.

"So, I'm thinking . . . Vegas Strip next Friday? We could gamble a little, get married, bail Dick out of jail, and be home by Monday," I suggested.

"We are not going to get married in some dingy chapel by an Elvis impersonator."

"We could get a Streisand impersonator if it would make you more comfortable."

"Jane." He chuckled, exasperated. "Is that really how you want to get married? Skulking off like we're ashamed of ourselves? Was that what little Jane dreamed and hoped for?"

"Little Jane thought she would marry Mark-Paul Gosselaar from *Saved by the Bell* in an English castle. Little Jane was an idiot."

"If you want the English castle, you shall have it . . . minus this Mark-Paul person," he said. "And if you really want the Vegas Strip, you shall have that. I want you to have the sort of wedding that will make you happy."

I countered, "What about the kind of wedding that makes *you* happy?"

"I want to show up in a tux and be told where to stand. That would make me very happy."

I groaned.

"What about wedding planning scares you?"

"All of it. Picking out flowers. The dress. The bridesmaids' dresses . . . no, wait, I'm looking forward to that. Vengeance will be mine. But making all the choices . . . and then having those choices subtly criticized by every woman in my family. And the fact that each of those choices will probably 'ruin the wedding' for someone."

"Ruin the wedding?"

"When my sister wanted to get married at the country club, Grandma Ruthie said the wedding would be ruined for her if Jenny got married anywhere but the Baptist church. Several cousins threatened to boycott if Jenny didn't allow children to attend. Our great-uncle said he wouldn't come to the reception unless she served Pabst Blue Ribbon. People just seem to lose their minds when it comes to weddings. You can't make everybody happy."

"So we won't try," Gabriel said. "We'll do what makes us happy. It's our wedding, after all."

I chuckled, pressing my lips to his throat, the curve of his jaw, as I rolled over him and slipped my fingers around his belt buckle, sliding it open. "Oh, you're so naive. It's cute, really."

We stayed in that happy (naked) secret-engagement bubble until I had to open the shop the next evening. Things had been progressing very nicely at Specialty Books since I'd reopened earlier that year. While we initially depended on special efforts such as the "Bump in the Night" Book Club and meetings of the local chapter of the Friends and Family of the Undead to keep in the black, online sales and increasingly healthy in-store traffic made opening the electric bills and supplier invoices a lot less painful every month.

There were times when I felt like a failure for never leaving the Hollow. I mean, I lived just a few miles from the house where I'd grown up. But there were good reasons for me to stay when I was human—my family, Aunt Jettie, the Half-Moon Hollow Public Library, where I'd devoted most of my adult years to helping kids find books to love. And if I'd left, I might never have met Gabriel. I would probably still be human. And clearly, this was the life I'd been intended for. Big-city life, babies, and aging just weren't my style.

Still, Half-Moon Hollow is a strange place for a vampire to spend her days. The small-town stereotype in which everybody knows everybody, or is at least related to them by marriage, holds true in a lot of places, such as the Hollow. Newspapers and telephones are kept around for convenience, but the real flow of information runs through the kitchens, beauty parlors, and grocery aisles. A visit to town on Saturday morning means the difference between community ignorance and knowing who's in jail, who's knocked up, and whose marriage is teetering on the brink of disaster.

As one of the few "out" vampires living in the Hollow, I was still occasionally the subject of gossip. My neighbors seemed torn between fearing me and remembering me as the goofy band geek who'd babysat their children. You could see it in their eyes sometimes, the initial rush of familiarity and affection, just before they remembered that I was no longer that girl, no longer human. The light in their eyes quickly extinguished, and the outstretched arms that had meant to hug me were extended into a timid handshake—if I was lucky.

But I'd made enough friends in the supernatural community to make up for it. Friends like Andrea and Dick, who'd already arrived at the shop by the time I opened the door. But, considering the noises I heard from the storeroom, I decided to give them a few minutes.

Seriously, I once walked into the office without knocking . . . I was scarred for life. And I'm going to live forever.

I sorted through that day's mail, shelved some newly arrived selections, and replenished the sweeteners in the coffee bar. I fired up the cappuccino machine and found that we were out of two-percent, which meant that my mochaccino had a little less -ccino. I improvised with a little Faux Type O and prayed that Andrea wouldn't hear me messing with her "baby."

"Jane!"

No such luck.

Andrea came rushing into the room, straightening her mussed Titian hair. I cringed. The last time she'd found me turning on the cappuccino maker, she'd thrown a Mayan quartz skull at my head—which, if you think about it, is sort of in poor taste.

"Remember, I am your boss," I said, raising my hands and my bloodyccino in a defensive position.

"What the hell is that?" Andrea demanded, pointing at my hands. Even in her angry, rumpled state, Andrea was one of the most poised and elegant women I knew. I often said she was what Grace Kelly would have looked like if Grace had reddish hair and a propensity for dating redneck scoundrels. And I was going to put her in the ugliest bridesmaid dress I could find.

"Look, I get it. I'm not as good at running the machine as you are. There's no reason to be all snotty about it. Are you going after a raise or something?"

"Not the coffee, you ninny, the rock on your left hand! Did Gabriel finally break you down and convince you to say yes?"

"Did you just call me a ninny? What are you, seventy?"

She huffed, a tendril of her deep red hair fluttering in her face. "Don't ignore the question."

"Yes, OK? I said yes. We're getting married."

I prepared for squealing and a girlie-girlie bonding moment. Instead, she yelled, "Dick! I owe you five bucks!"

I heard a loud "whoop" from the back room as Andrea hugged me.

"You know, you should be a little more considerate of my standing wagers when you make major life decisions."

"You made a bet on whether I would agree to marry Gabriel?" I exclaimed, slapping her shoulder. "And you only bet five dollars?"

Dick walked in and grinned evilly at the sight of us hugging and talking practically nose-to-nose. "Dear *Penthouse,* I never believed something like this could happen to me, but when my super-hot wife asked me what I wanted more than anything else for my birthday . . ."

Andrea sighed and dropped her head to my shoulder in defeat.

"Hey, you married him."

"I have no one to blame but myself," she muttered as Dick left to rummage around in the storeroom.

A mind-boggling mix of fierce loyalty and moral flexibility, Dick used to be the local go-to guy for under-the-table commerce. If you needed an iPod that would only work on European adapters, he was your guy. He lived this way for more than a century, before he fell hard for Andrea, the first woman actually to turn him down in all that time. Andrea didn't find any of Dick's roguish ways remotely charming, which apparently was what he was looking for all along. He managed to make the leap from dating to cohabiting by slowly but surely moving his vaguely obscene T-shirts and *Dukes of Hazzard* memorabilia into her swanky townhouse condo. It was by far the sneakiest thing I'd ever seen him do, and that's saying something.

"Tell her about the other part of the bet." Dick snickered as he reemerged, carrying a bottle of champagne and three glasses.

"How do you always happen to have champagne handy for special occasions?" I asked.

"I hide it in your break-room fridge," he said, popping the cork and pouring generous splashes into each of our glasses, mixing it with synthetic blood for a disturbing mimosa. "None of your employees eats, so it's a safe spot. Now, my dearest wife, tell our Jane the other part of the bet. I'll even help you start off. If Jane said yes to Gabriel before March Madness, you owed me five dollars and . . ."

Andrea sighed. "And . . . you get to decorate the den with your *Dukes of Hazzard* memorabilia."

I winced at the burn of champagne bubbles being channeled up my nose. Dick and Andrea had been battling over the renovations to Dick's family home ever since Gabriel had given the deed back to Dick months before. Gabriel hadn't left the house to rot while it was under his care for the last century or so, but he hadn't exactly kept it move-in ready, either. Using every illicit contact at his disposal, Dick was gathering the manpower and materials to completely modernize the place—indoor plumbing, electrical wiring, lightproofing the bedroom, and adding a "shower big enough for eight" to the master bath.

I chose not to think about why they might need a shower that big.

Having just overseen the completion of his own

home, my human best friend, Zeb, was helping Dick with some of the work. Andrea sat back and prayed that their version of rewiring wouldn't burn the house down while they slept for the day. Other than occasionally suggesting a wall color or picking out tile, Andrea had left the renovations to Dick . . . until he showed her his decorating plans for the den, apparently.

"And this means it is no longer a den," Dick said, nudging her. "It is now a . . ."

"Man cave," she said, wrinkling up her face as if saying the words pained her.

I covered my giggles with another sip of the bubbly. Dick put his arm around my shoulders. "Here's looking at you, Stretch. If Gabriel doesn't make you deliriously happy, I'll kick his ass."

"Be sure to include that in your toast at the wedding." I chuckled.

"Oh, my gosh! The wedding!" Andrea squealed. "When is it? Where will it be? What about your dress?"

I groaned. Andrea considered herself to be the authority on undead matrimony. She and Dick were the first vampire couple to marry legally in McClure County. There'd been an outdoor, nighttime ceremony, the first party Gabriel had hosted at his home in more than a hundred years—and the last one he hosted before officially handing the keys to my sister, Jenny. His gift served two purposes: soothing Jenny's chronically tender feelings after being denied our ancestral home, River Oaks, and giving me a good reason to invite Gabriel to come live with me.

Andrea had worn a vintage confection she'd found online. I'd barely managed to talk Dick out of wearing his "tuxedo" T-shirt, for which I'd been rewarded by not having to wear another damned bridesmaid dress. And now, thanks to her acquired "expertise," Andrea was going to give Mama a run for her money in terms of annoying me.

"Well, Gabriel shot down my Vegas plan, so I haven't a clue," I said.

"You mean, he had a woman *offer* to skip all the wedding crap and marry him in Vegas and he turned it down? I need to talk some sense into that boy," Dick said, shaking his head. When Andrea glared at him, he quickly added, "Not that I didn't absolutely love all of *our* wedding crap, baby. Happiest day of my life. Really."

Andrea sniffed and turned on her heel toward the ritual-candle section. I snickered and taunted Dick. "So much trouble!"

"Shut it, you," he grumbled before pitching his voice into an apologetic whine. "Andrea, baby! I didn't mean it like that!"

Realizing that I'd left my cell phone in Big Bertha, my trusty, weathered station wagon, I made my way out of the shop with a little skip in my step and a tune on my lips. Dick had managed to distract Andrea from her "Our wedding was *special*" tirade with more good news. After reviewing last quarter's sales, he'd found that Specialty Books was actually showing a profit for the first time since my former boss, Mr. Wainwright, opened it sixty years before. Even with the stuff destroyed when his nephew, Emery, repeatedly broke into the shop, we were ahead of our projections for the quarter. Most of the increase was rooted in online sales, a result of Zeb's redesigning the shop's Web site.

And yes, I was letting Dick handle the bookkeeping. It turns out that ruthlessly calculating profits from underhanded back-alley deals actually makes one pretty good with math. And now that I knew where he slept on a permanent basis, I trusted him not to steal from me.

I danced around the front of my decades-old Ford station wagon and saw that Jamie Lanier, our dairy delivery guy, was pulling up to the curb in his Half-Moon Dairy truck. I smiled and waved as I opened my driver's-side door.

"Hey, Miss Jane!" he hollered over the blaring of his earbuds as he unloaded his hand truck.

I cringed at his use of "Miss," which clearly indicated that Jamie still thought of me as the old lady who used to babysit him every summer. Again I say, this is the drawback of living in your hometown. Local hunks have to start off somewhere, and generally, it's as the kid who would only eat smiley-face pancakes from ages five to seven.

And good Lord, Jamie was a hunk. He had the all-American, apple-pie look that they probably used as a template when they made GI Joe dolls. And the color palette wasn't bad, either—warm, tanned skin and olive-green eyes that twinkled at me from under the fringe of his wavy dark blond hair. He loomed four inches over even my tall frame, and I found myself stammering and blushing like a schoolgirl every time he stood less than an arm's length from me.

Did I mention that he was just about to graduate? From high school? Which would make me the dirtiest old lady in the world.

Andrea enjoyed my discomfort each week when Jamie delivered dairy products for the coffee bar, which, again, made me question the value of having girlfriends.

I leaned into my car, searching for the charger cord that tethered my phone. Honestly, it was the only way I could find the damn thing most days.

My head cocked toward the sound of tires screeching. I straightened up to see an old rusted-out black sedan with dark-tinted windows barreling down the street, heading straight for Jamie's truck. Backing out of the rear gate, his hand truck loaded with crates, Jamie had no clue that he was walking right into the path of the oncoming car.

"*Jamie!*" I screamed.

Jamie froze and whipped around just as the car struck him. The force of the chrome bumper striking his knees slammed him to the pavement. Jamie barely let out a yelp as his head made a sick cracking noise against the pavement. I screamed again at the wet thump of the tires rolling over his torso, the snap of breaking ribs.

The car swerved toward me. I felt paralyzed, unable to help myself as Jamie lay bleeding on the street. I stared through the darkened windows, trying to make out any shape or feature behind the tinted glass. But the rapid approach of the car's grille caught my attention. I shoved my palms against the top of Big Bertha's doorframe and launched myself onto the roof, just before the black car smashed into my driver's side. The open door snapped off, flying toward the shop's display window. I landed on my feet as the glass shattered behind me. My heels screeched on the metal roof as I pivoted to watch the strange car speed away.

It fishtailed as it turned the corner to Hesler Street, and although grease and dirt were caked over the plate in a way far too effective to be coincidental, I could just make out a Y and a 7 at the end of the license-plate number.

Dick and Andrea bolted outside, with Dick protectively shoving Andrea behind him as they ran. "Stretch?" Dick yelled.

"Call nine-one-one!" I shouted, leaping off the car and landing near Jamie's crumpled body. His eyes were wild, unfocused. A scarlet slick flowed from his mouth as he gave weak, gasping coughs. His legs were bent all wrong. A thick pool of blood spread beneath him, soaking through my jeans as I knelt on the pavement.

"Jane? Hurts," he whimpered.

"Jamie," I whispered. "Just hold on, OK? We'll get an ambulance here. You're going to be just fine."

Dick, who was kneeling on Jamie's left side, shook his head. "He's lost too much blood. Feel his pulse. Listen to his breath. You hear that wet, sucking sound? There's a lot of internal damage. Even if the ambulance was here already . . . he won't make it."

Dick gave me a meaningful look, and his fangs descended with a soft snick. I snarled and mouthed so only he could hear, "We are not feeding on him!"

"We're going to turn him, Stretch," Dick said, exasperated.

"But—"

"Turn me," Jamie murmured, his voice wet and rough over the crimson bubbles that kept forming under his lips. "Please. Don't want to die."

Turn him? I'd never even seen it done, except in my hazy memories of my own crossover into the world of the undead. I looked to the older vampire. "Dick?"

"No, you," Jamie said, his voice fading with every word. "I trust you. I know you."

"Should I call?" Andrea asked, holding up the shop's cordless phone.

His fingers pressed against Jamie's pulse point, Dick shook his head. He turned to me. "Jane, we need to do something quick."

"I've never turned anyone. I don't know what to do!"

Dick grabbed my wrist and sank his fangs into my flesh. I yowled as the blood poured from the wound. I glared at him as he pressed the gaping wound to Jamie's slack mouth. A cascade of red rolled past his chin onto the pavement with little pattering noises. My eyes popped wide when Jamie latched onto my wrist and drew strong swallows of my blood. I brushed his matted, damp hair away from his forehead and slid my legs under his back to let him rest against me.

I was thankful that Jamie seemed less conflicted than

I had been when I was turned. Not the least bit hesitant, he was taking blood from me as if he'd been born a vampire. With every draw of my blood, Jamie relaxed a bit more, his strength ebbing from his limbs. He was reaching the last phase, the death of his human body.

Hoarse wheezing sounds filled the street as Jamie struggled to draw breath through his nose. He was suffocating, drowning on dry land as his lungs stopped functioning. He broke away from my wrist, gasping, desperately trying to fill them with air. I remembered that feeling. You can't think. You're barely even aware of the pain. All you can focus on is the crushing emptiness in your chest.

"Shh," I whispered, cupping my free hand to his cheek. His fading green eyes searched mine, for assurance, for answers. I gave him a shaky smile. "This part is never easy, but it will be over soon. And when you wake up, you'll be like us."

I pushed my healing wrist against his mouth, letting him take one last weak pull before his eyes fluttered closed. His arms went slack at his sides. His head lolled back against my arm.

Dick squeezed my shoulder gently as we knelt there on the cold pavement and listened to Jamie's young heart beat its last.

2

Welcome to the world of vampire parenting. If you're frightened, confused, and disoriented . . . that sounds just about right.

—*Siring for the Stupid:*
A Beginner's Guide to Raising Newborn Vampires

I sprawled on the couch in the break room, with Jamie's head in my lap, unsure of what to do. I was exhausted, emotionally and hematologically. The blood loss involved in creating a childe takes a lot out of the vampire sire. It's said to be the closest the undead can come to childbirth, which just sounds wrong.

In more than 150 years, Gabriel had created only three children. Two of those children turned out to be evil and went on killing sprees . . . maybe that's why vampires only turn a handful of children in their lifetime.

Crap.

I scrubbed my hand over my face and leaned my head against the wall. Outside, I could hear Dick using a hose to clear Jamie's blood from the street. We hadn't done anything wrong. Dick assured me that we'd followed the Council's protocols for the situation, but it still wasn't a good idea to have a big puddle of blood out in front of the store. It was unseemly.

I reached for the phone several times to call the police, but Dick held it out of my reach and said that we should wait for the Council. We sent Andrea away just after we carried Jamie inside the store. We asked her to drive the delivery truck back to the dairy, then run home. It wasn't that we were worried about Andrea's control. After being a blood surrogate for years, live feeding—particularly on mortally injured minors—didn't hold much attraction for her. But seeing Jamie go through the process brought up bad memories for Andrea, whose turning by Dick's psychotic descendant had been nonconsensual and painful. She wouldn't talk about it. She was so happy to wake up alive with Dick that she didn't make much of it when she was first turned. But privately, Dick told me that she had nightmares about Emery turning her. She dreamed of pain and blood and dark shadows crushing the breath from her. And I wanted to dig up Emery's ashes so I could kill his creepy, milquetoast ass all over again.

Jamie's face was peaceful in death. He looked so young, untroubled. But when he woke, his life would be unrecognizable. He would be angry, confused. I wasn't stupid enough to think that this was my fault. I hadn't made that driver careen down an alleyway and smash into Jamie. And he'd asked me to turn him. But I'd hit a sort of stalemate in life when I'd been turned. I'd been an unmarried, unattached, unsatisfied (recently fired) workaholic.

Jamie still had potential. His was a life that was worth living. He could have grown up, gone to school, gotten a normal job, made some sweet local girl ridiculously happy when he proposed. He could have had babies and gotten into drunken brawls with the other church-league softball players on Sundays. And now he would be frozen forever at seventeen. He would be carded for the rest of his unnaturally long life.

I thought of Jamie's parents, at home, completely unaware that their son's existence had been permanently altered. My parents had celebrated New Year's Eve with the Laniers as long as I could remember. They played cards and ate Chex Mix to the point of garlic overdose while the dads drank toddies that were way too strong. I was usually watching *Dick Clark's New Year's Rockin' Eve* in the den with Jamie and his sister.

They were all going to hate me when they found out what I'd done.

I heard the cowbell tinkle over the front door. Ophelia Lambert, the scary forever-adolescent head of the local panel for the World Council for the Equal Treatment of the Undead, swept into the shop, followed by her panel of ancient flunkies. Ophelia, who had a penchant for themed outfits bordering on jailbait gear, was wearing a lavender poodle skirt with a matching cardigan tied primly around her shoulders.

Ophelia had overseen my prosecution for several random killings and fires the first year I was turned, and she scared the hell out of me—despite the fact that she had found me innocent and chosen not to put me to death. But Ophelia seemed to find my wacky antics entertaining and took a particular interest anytime I ran afoul of the Council's policies.

I managed to focus long enough to register the rest of the panel lining up in an intimidating semicircle around me. There was cool blond Sophie, whose unlined, luminescent face was as unsettling as it was beautiful; the improbably named Waco Marchand, whom one might recognize from the Confederate memorial statue in downtown Half-Moon Hollow; and finally, gaunt and grumpy Peter Crown, who had never liked me . . . or anyone, as far as I could tell.

I stayed quiet, with my hands in my lap. Dick had taken his place at my right, his hand on my shoulder.

"No protests of innocence?" Ophelia asked, frowning at the battered, bloodied teen in my lap. I shook my head. "Very well. Explain yourself."

I sniffed. "This is Jamie Lanier. He's a local kid. He was doing his dairy deliveries, and . . . he came around the truck, and he didn't see—The car didn't even slow down . . ."

Seeing that I wasn't going to be able to provide much more, Dick intervened, explaining about the reckless driver and the extent of Jamie's injuries.

Ophelia's crystalline gaze did not waver from my face. "And what led to your turning him? Did we get a little hungry in sight of the poor bleeding accident victim?"

"He asked me to turn him," I told her, my voice a little firmer than it should have been, given the circumstances. "He didn't want to die."

Ophelia looked to Dick, asking for confirmation. He nodded.

"Dick helped me. He showed me how," I said. "I gave him as much blood as I could before—before he faded out."

The Council members turned to one another and started their silent conversation with lip twitches and various eye gestures. Peter Crown sneered at me, but that was actually friendlier than his usual expression.

I cleared my throat. "So, how much trouble am I in?"

Ophelia gave an uninterested shrug. "No, for once, you seem to have behaved appropriately."

I stared at her, dumbfounded. "Sorry, what?"

Sophie, whom I tried to steer clear of after she'd picked her way through my brain using her special truth-seeking psychic talents, smiled warmly at me. Of course, she smiled that way right before she used said special talents, so I leaned back a little on the couch. "Really, Jane, you should relax. You performed admirably. I would imagine even the human community would appreciate your efforts. We will, of course, contact the human authorities and inform them of young Mr. Lanier's passing."

I nodded.

While Waco, who'd always taken a gentlemanly grandfather stance with me, patted my head affectionately, Peter glared at me. I sat stone-still, unsure how to respond. Where were the not-so-subtle threats? The menu of horrific potential consequences? Ophelia's barbed insults about my spazzery and/or wardrobe?

"This is the part where you say thank you," Ophelia said, lifting an eyebrow.

"Thank you," I parroted back to her.

"We'll work on enthusiasm and sincerity some other time," she said with a smirk.

"Give her a break, Ophelia," Waco muttered. "Under the circumstances, she's holding up very well. I've heard that your first turn as a sire wasn't quite so neat and tidy."

The great thing about people as composed as Ophelia is that when you finally crack them, the brief flash of anger across their features is blinding in its pissiness. Ophelia stood and smoothed her hands over her skirt. "Well, I'm sure you'd like to get home and start 'feathering the nest,' so to speak. You only have three days to prepare for your new arrival."

I nearly dropped Jamie from my lap. "I'm sorry, what?"

Ophelia's lip quirk deepened to a full-on smirk. "Your new childe, he'll be living with you. It's your responsibility to help him make the transition into the vampire world. Didn't Gabriel explain the sire–childe dynamic to you when you rose?"

"Yeah, but I pretty much told him where to stuff it and lived how I pleased."

"And look where that got you," Peter retorted.

"In other words, congratulations," Sophie chirped. "It's a boy!"

"Are you being sarcastic or sincere right now?" I demanded. "Because honestly, I can't tell."

Sophie gave me a sharp little nod. "A little of both."

"Awesome," I grumbled, much to Peter's delight.

Sophie handed me a black gift bag packed with sample bottles of synthetic blood, Blood-B-Gone stain-removing wipes, a GPS-enhanced alarm clock that tracked the sun's movements, SPF-500 sunblock, iron supplements with what looked like a baby vampire on the label, and a copy of *Siring for the Stupid: A Beginner's Guide to Raising Newborn Vampires*. Well, that capped it. No successful endeavor in my life, undead or otherwise, had started with a gift basket.

"Seriously, who do you get to publish this stuff for you?" I demanded, holding up the copy of *Siring for the Stupid*. I looked to Dick, who seemed as perplexed as I was by the events unfolding in the break room. "Is this normal?"

Dick frowned, watching Ophelia warily. "It's not *abnormal*. But, usually, if the Council doesn't feel comfortable with a newly turned vampire's restraint, the representatives take on the job of fostering themselves."

"Well, this was an unusual case," Ophelia admitted. "Jamie's seventeen. He's a minor. He can't live alone unless he's emancipated, which the state won't allow under current vampire rights regulations. And we certainly can't let him return home to his parents. Jamie needs someone who is accustomed to working with children. Jane has that experience from her former profession."

"Jamie aged out of my library program once he stopped reading those Captain Underpants books," I told her. Ophelia shot me one of her patented "why are you still speaking?" looks. I sighed. "For how long?"

"Until he's ready to live on his own," she said, giving Jamie a speculative glance. "Don't worry, I'll be stopping by frequently to check on his progress. As you know, your antics always keep me entertained, Jane."

"I knew it," I ground out. Peter actually chuckled under his breath, which was the first time I'd heard him express anything like humor.

Bastard.

"What about Jamie's parents?" I asked.

"The Council is sending a representative to the Laniers' home to explain what happened. It would be best if they don't know where he is right now. Do not contact them until the Council arranges a supervised meeting with their son."

"You're not sending Peter, are you?" I asked. "Because the news might be better delivered by someone with, um, feelings?"

"Are you saying I'm insensitive?" Peter deadpanned.

"I was going to use the words 'devoid of the milk of human kindness,' but 'insensitive' will do."

Waco snorted but covered it with a cough. "I'll be visiting the Laniers, Miss Jane. Don't you worry, I'll soften the blow."

I nodded. Maybe it would be easier to take such bad news when it came from a guy who looked like Colonel Sanders.

Probably not.

"What about the car?" I asked.

Ophelia shrugged. "What car?"

"The car that hit Jamie. Don't you want to try to find out who caused all this?"

Ophelia gave an uninterested wave of the hand. "It was probably a drunk human, as you said, a hit-and-run driver. It would be a matter for the human police, if you care to report it. But as I recall, you and the local law-enforcement agencies don't play well together."

I had to concede that. The last time I'd had contact with the Half-Moon Hollow PD, I'd asked one of the officers if it was uncomfortable to have his head jammed so far up one of his own orifices. Filing a missing-persons report on Andrea was considerably more difficult after that.

"Jane?" Gabriel came crashing through the store and into the break room.

"Ah, the lover's dramatic entrance," Ophelia drawled.

"What's happened?" Gabriel exclaimed, obviously confused to see the adolescent draped across my legs. "Are you all right? Were you hurt?"

I started to sniffle at the idea of having to explain the situation *again*, and Ophelia rolled her eyes. She muttered instructions to Dick, and the rest of Council swept from the room.

"We'd better get them home, Gabe," Dick told him as he lifted Jamie from my lap. "I'll explain later. Jane's holding it together so far, but she's about this close to a tirade like we've never seen before."

I felt Gabriel shudder beside me, and despite myself, I felt my lips twitch as I elbowed him in the side. He

slipped his arms under mine and led me out of the shop.
Dick carefully laid Jamie in the back of Big Bertha and
ran around to the driver's side. I saw him instinctually
reach for the handle of the driver's-side door that was
lying crumpled on the concrete. I giggled at the absur-
dity of the gesture. A wave of nausea and fatigue surged
over me, and that giggle melted into an all-out hysterical,
bent-over-my-own-knees guffaw.

Sensing the tirade unraveling, Gabriel ushered me
into his own car. He tucked me into the passenger seat,
and I tilted back against the seat, swiping at my eyes.

"I didn't mean for this to happen," I murmured as he
turned the ignition. "I never mean for any of it to happen, but something always seems to sneak up and bite us
in the ass, doesn't it?"

He pulled me close and kissed my temple. "This time
around, let's just assume the best of each other and go
with the flow," he murmured. "It would save a lot of
time . . . and Tasering."

With that, my fiancé drove me home, my head cradled on his knee.

This was what happened when you dated a guy who
saved you from a gunshot wound in a muddy ditch.
There's a certain amount of drama expected in your relationship.

Gabriel and I had the opposite of a meet-cute. We
had a meet-casualty. The short version is that when I
was (unfairly, unceremoniously) fired from the library,
instead of getting a severance check, I got just enough
of a gift certificate to get rip-snorting drunk at Shenani-

gans. I met Gabriel, sobered, and flirtation ensued. My car died halfway home. I was spotted walking home by the town drunk, Bud McElray, who mistook me for a deer and shot me. I was left in the ditch to die, only to be found and turned by Gabriel.

But when I tell the story in public, Gabriel had to turn me because of wounds I suffered rescuing blind orphans from a flaming, totaled van.

Gabriel eventually tracked Bud McElray down and exacted ironic revenge on my behalf, forcing Bud from a deer stand and then shoving a tree on top of him to make his death look like a tragic hunting accident. Bud's death and the ensuing dirty, naked argument we had over it is one of the darker episodes in our relationship. Not many couples can say they consummated their love after crashing through a coffee table.

We put Jamie in the guest room, the same room where Andrea had lain while we waited for her to rise. I hoped this wasn't becoming a habit. I didn't want to start a B&B for vampires in chrysalis.

Having been beaten, bled, concussed, and repeatedly electrocuted, I was unconscious during most of Andrea's transition. I didn't realize how mind-numbingly boring it was. Other than avoiding contact with my family and stocking up on bottled blood and comfortable clothes for my new charge, there hadn't been much to do other than paint my toenails. And Dick's. That would teach him to fall asleep on the couch.

Zeb brought by a selection of comic books and video

games from his personal stash to keep Jamie entertained post-rising. Andrea and Dick ran the shop, because it seemed wrong for me to be away from home at the moment. Gabriel and I paced a lot.

By the second night, we were all going a little nuts. To help pass the time, Jolene dropped by with the twins, Joe and Janelyn. They'd become quite the fixtures at River Oaks since Gabriel and I had been appointed the only trustworthy babysitters Jolene and Zeb knew. (Andrea and Dick served as alternates.) Mama Ginger was bumped after she got baby Janelyn's ears pierced without discussing it with her parents. And then there was an unfortunate episode involving Jolene's pack, which a tight-lipped Zeb would only refer to as the "Greased Pig Incident."

Our apparent willingness to supervise their offspring, combined with the fact that they lived on the edge of River Oaks's acreage, meant that they were frequent visitors. It was nice to have kids running around the old house, considering that the opportunity for the pittering and pattering would be scarce over the next few centuries. There weren't many routes around the whole "vampires can't have babies" rules. Plus, it was always entertaining to watch Gabriel with my godchildren. He was always all stiff and formal with them, until we left the room and we heard suspicious raspberry noises and baby talk. Of course, when we returned, we usually found him reading them the stock report as if it was the Brothers Grimm.

It was fascinating to watch the new parents at work.

Jolene and Zeb maneuvered like a well-oiled machine. If Joe needed a bottle, Zeb already had it mixed and un-capped before Jolene could reach for it. If Janelyn needed to be burped, Jolene had the cloth over Zeb's shoulder before he could get the baby into position. The synchro-nized diaper changes had a graceful, if stinky, ballet quality to them.

Some nights, I felt as if they were in some sort of military maneuver, them against the babies. *You will not drive us crazy. You will not beat us. We will have sex again someday.*

Jolene had relaxed a lot. The little things that used to wind her up didn't bother her anymore. I think that once a woman has pushed two watermelon-sized objects out of her body, sans drugs, the prospect of her in-laws not liking her doesn't matter so much anymore.

We were settled, as so many people were when they reached their thirties. It had just taken Dick and Gabriel a while to get around to it. We spent weekends at my house, watching movies, the babies asleep upstairs in the old nursery. You'd think a bunch of supernatural crea-tures would find this boring as hell, but after two years filled with blood, heartache, hostage crises, and death, a quiet movie night seems downright decadent.

Sometimes I marveled at how grown-up we'd all become, and then Dick would recite a sixteen-stanza penis-based epic poem, and I'd take it back.

While the kids played on the living-room floor, Jolene compared this endless stream of empty time to waiting for a baby to be born. Everyone was excited and on edge, but the details were uncertain and out of our hands.

"Have you and Gabriel discussed what's going to happen when Jamie rises?" Jolene asked, tossing her hair.

Once again, I wondered why I surrounded myself with women who were much prettier than I was. Surely, there was some sort of self-defeating psychology at work here. Jolene was gorgeous in an exotic way that had almost intimidated me out of getting to know her when she first started dating Zeb. She had a perfectly oval face, with high cheekbones and wild curls that were a dozen different shades of auburn. My only consolation was that when she parted those lush pink lips, she sounded like Lulu from *Hee Haw*.

To be honest, not many guys cared about that.

"Mostly, we've been staring at each other, wondering what the hell we've gotten ourselves into this time," I admitted.

"Well, you're basically becomin' parents. And let me tell you, that's a relationship changer."

"But you had two kids at once. Your perspective is kind of skewed. I mean, how much trouble could one teenager cause?" Jolene stared at me for a beat before I yowled, "I'm so screwed. Damn it, Jolene!"

"I thought you wanted my opinion!"

"Well, not if you're going to bring reality into it!" I glared at her as I reached for the ringing phone, knowing that it was my mama before I picked up the receiver.

"Oh, honey, did you hear what happened to poor little Jamie Lanier?" Mama asked without saying hello first.

She'd returned to her "no greetings" method of phone communication since Andrea ratted me out about turning down Gabriel's first proposal. "He was minding his own business, delivering his dairy, and he was attacked by a vampire. Carol Ann Reilly said they pulled him from the truck, drained him dry, and turned him."

I huffed out a breath. "That's not what happened!"

"What?"

I cleared my throat. "I mean, that's not how it happens, Mama. Vampires don't attack random strangers and turn them."

"Oh, honey, I know, and I told Carol Ann that with bottled blood and willing donors, y'all don't really have to attack people and drag them from their vehicles like in the movies. Really, I wish that woman would go to a couple of FFOTU meetings with me, she's so close-minded."

I bit my lip. But with Jolene's wolfy hearing, she laughed freely.

"Your vampire Council sent someone over to tell poor Rosie and Jeff what had happened. And the worst part is that the Council won't even tell them where he is! Their own son, dead, and they're 'not allowed' to see him."

I felt a lump grow heavy in my throat. *Please, please, please, don't let Mama notice that I've stopped talking,* I prayed. *That's always a tip-off that I'm not telling her something.*

"They're so torn up over it," Mama continued. "I went by to visit them, of course, to take them a casserole and tell them about Friends and Family of the Undead. And

you wouldn't believe the throng of people over there.
It was like a funeral without the body. Anyway, I was
thinking maybe you might go over there to visit them,
Jane, and show them that this isn't the end of the world.
They've always thought so much of you, honey. I think it
would help them a lot."

I felt that same hot, oily rush of guilt that I always
felt when I was about to lie or omit very important details to my mother. How was I going to face her, tell her
what I'd done? After her initial shock over my turning,
she'd always written off the bloodier aspects of vampirism as something I had to do. Would she still think that?
Would she fall back to her old ways and think I'd just lost
control of my bloodlust and made Jamie into a snack?
I cleared my throat, willing that huge breath-hindering
lump away.

"I don't know if that's such a good idea right now,
Mama. Technically, they're in mourning. And they probably won't want to see any vampires until they see their
son."

"I don't think you're giving them enough credit,
Jane—"

"Mama, trust me on this one."

"Fine." With a sigh and an FFOTU platitude about
family and acceptance, Mama moved on to breezier topics. My sister Jenny wanted to know if I wanted to join
the scrapbooking class she was teaching down at her
new paper-craft shop. And this time, she meant it in a
friendly, nonmocking way. My grandma Ruthie and her
ghoul-beau Wilbur were preparing for a weekend away

in Hot Springs, which was a scenario I didn't want to imagine, ever. My father had finished a draft of a book on historically notable vampires of Half-Moon Hollow, which he'd written with Gabriel's and Dick's help.

After a few attempts to extract myself from the conversation, I finally convinced Mama that Fitz was choking on a baby toy and I had to rescue him with the doggie Heimlich. I hung up the phone and buried my face in my hands.

"If you keep doin' that, you're gonna get wrinkles," Jolene said. I smirked at her. "Oh, I forgot, you're never gonna get wrinkles. Bitch. But you could get some serious scratches from that rock. Wow! This is the first time I've had a good look at it." She yanked my hand closer for inspection. "Very nice work, Miss Jameson. So, why isn't your mama here right now, drillin' you about wedding details?"

"Um . . ." I realized that it was the first time I'd spoken to my mother since getting engaged, and I hadn't even thought about telling her. I hadn't thought about anything beyond my immediate future. Suddenly, my engagement news didn't seem so earth-shattering.

More than anything, I wished that Gabriel had taken me up on my elopement offer, because we'd be married by now. I had a feeling that I wouldn't want to think about wedding plans for a long time to come. Of course, if we'd taken that impromptu trip to Vegas, that crazy driver would have hit Jamie without vampires nearby to help him. We would have come back from our honeymoon to attend his funeral.

As I mulled that over, Dick and Gabriel loped into the kitchen, with Zeb and Andrea at their heels, all with a strangely uniform "We need to talk" expression on their faces. I arched an eyebrow, but that was mainly because of the way Dick was dangling Joe by his ankles, while the baby giggled hysterically. Jolene sighed, retrieved her inverted offspring, and smacked the back of Dick's head.

"This is why you're an alternate," she told him.

Gabriel cleared his throat. "Jane, I know that you're still a bit in shock from Jamie's turning, but we were hoping you might be ready to talk about a few things."

His formal tone brought a ghost of a smile to my lips. "Such as?"

Gabriel and Dick exchanged uneasy glances, making me cry, "Stop doing that! I swear, I liked it better when you two were conspiring against each other, not me. Out with it!"

"Jane, you were nearly hit by a car today. Maybe it was an accident, but I think we can agree that there's a ninety-percent chance that it was intentional," Gabriel said.

"Ninety percent?"

"I did the math," Andrea assured me. "The number of occasions in which you have been injured due to accident or miscalculated practical jokes, versus intentional injury."

"The point is, we're not going to wait around for trouble to find you this time," Gabriel said. "This time, you're going to let me use every resource at my disposal to seek this person out and stop him."

"Agreed," I said, nodding.

He arched an eyebrow. "You're not going to protest?"

"No, I think you have a really good grasp on the problem. I'm not going to do anything that pushes us apart or drags the problem out. If you need to stay with me at the shop while I'm working, we'll set up office space for you there. Hell, I'll get you your own fax line. If you think we need to close the shop for a while, we can do that. Let me know what I can do to make this situation easier for you."

Frowning, he sighed. "Now is not the time for sarcasm, Jane."

"I'm not being sarcastic!"

"Then I have no idea how to respond."

"You kiss me and tell me everything is going to be OK."

He kissed me. "Everything's going to be OK."

"OK."

"I think I just threw up in my mouth a little bit," Zeb griped.

"Stretch, you have any idea who might have been behind the wheel of that car?" Dick asked. "You said it swerved toward you after it struck Jamie. Do you think it's possible that you were the target and Jamie was just collateral damage?"

"Yes," I said. "That's actually been buzzing at the back of my brain since Jamie took his last breath. And after the last couple of years, I actually have a system for narrowing down a list of suspects when something like this happens. But honestly, I don't think I have any enemies left at this point. I mean, I haven't done anything to anyone lately. And I don't think I have anything that anyone else would want. That's generally what gets me in trouble. First, there was Missy, the insane real estate agent who wanted to take my house and turn it into a tacky vampire condo development. Then Esther Barnes, the psychic who tried to scramble Zeb's brain and prevent his wedding to Jolene. And of course, Jeanine. But those were all cases of my actually doing something to piss someone off."

"What about the ladies in the Chamber of Commerce?" Zeb asked.

"Well, yeah, they're plotting against me, but Nice Courtney says their plans are of the 'make Jane a social pariah who dies pitiful, penniless, and alone' variety. I think it involves getting all of my advertising changed to say 'Specialty Hookers.'"

"Local vampire haters?"

"Nah. I can't see one of them having a beef with me specifically. If anyone, they'd go after . . ." I pressed my lips together and gave Dick a speculative look.

"What?" he demanded.

"Oh, nothing."

"Former employers?"

"Mrs. Stubblefield is drying out in a rehab center in Bowling Green."

"Gabriel's other errant vampire children?"

"He promises me there are no others," I muttered, narrowing my eyes at him.

Gabriel elbowed Dick in the gut. "Jackass."

Dick chortled and ducked a second blow from his childhood best friend.

"Have you noticed how many people don't like you?" Jolene asked. "Your grandma Ruthie, my aunties, Mrs. Stubblefield, old lady psychics."

"Ooh!" Zeb exclaimed. "What about all those girls you insulted-slash-made-cry in high school? We just saw them at the reunion. That probably stirred up some feelings."

"I don't think you're helping there, Zeb," Dick said, patting Zeb's shoulder.

"And I didn't 'make' those girls cry. In general, I was responding to bitchery in kind. I was provoked!"

"Every time?" Andrea asked.

"There weren't that many times," I insisted.

Andrea looked to Zeb, who was nodding. "Yes, there were," he said.

"What about assassins paid by your grandma Ruthie?" Jolene suggested.

"That is . . . surprisingly plausible," I grumbled. "Look, over the years, my unique sense of humor and perverse grasp of honesty may have led to some hurt feelings and long-held grudges. But overall, I'm a pretty likable person."

They all seemed to bite their lips simultaneously to keep from snickering.

"I hate you all!" I exclaimed.

"I'm glad y'all are takin' this so seriously," Jolene said in her best motherly tone.

No one had the decency to look sheepish.

"OK, so the suspect list is long and somewhat vague,"

Andrea said. "The question is, how do we keep Jane—
and by extension, her loved ones and colleagues—from
getting shot, stabbed, poisoned, beaten, Tasered, burned,
maced, or otherwise slapped about by anonymous yet
incredibly determined forces?"

"We don't let her work alone at the shop," Gabriel
suggested.

"We put her in a hermetically sealed plastic vampire
habitat," Dick said.

"We hire one of my nicer cousins to come over durin'
the day and keep an eye on the place," Jolene added.

"We keep her from handling guns, knives, poison,
Taser guns, fire, or mace so she doesn't injure herself,"
Zeb said.

"These are all good suggestions," I said. "Except for
putting me in a vampire hamster cage. But Gabriel's
right. I'm tired of waiting around for trouble to come
to me. I'm tired of dreading a ringing phone because it
could mean that one of you has been hurt. I'm tired of
keeping my head in the sand. So I'm going to take a more
proactive approach."

"We," they chorused.

"Instead of sitting around, waiting for the next incident, I—"

"We," they corrected me again in chorale, which was
a little creepy.

"We are going to try to find the person driving that
car. The plate was obscured, but I got a partial number.
Jolene, do you have any cousins who work in the DMV?"

"I'm insulted that you even have to ask." She snorted, bobbing the baby on her hip. "I have three."

I scribbled out a description of the car's make and model and the partial license plate and handed it to Jolene.

"Can we get a whiteboard, like on *Law and Order*?" Andrea asked.

Dick nodded. "I was thinking official 'Keep Jane from Being Murdered Task Force' T-shirts."

The team seemed ready to "break" to take on their individual tasks, when Gabriel raised his hands. I gritted my teeth and waited for the inevitable speech that could be summed up as "I think we should keep Jane locked away and ignorant for her own protection." Instead, Gabriel said, "I would like to lodge a formal objection to the 'go looking for trouble' plan. I think it's ill advised and very likely to get at least one of us hurt. But I'm also smart enough to recognize that it's an empty gesture, and since you're going to do it anyway, I might as well get onboard."

I cooed. "Aw, you know me so well." I pressed a kiss against his tensed, frowning lips. "You know, you'd think I would be used to someone trying to kill me by now, but it still hurts my feelings every time."

3

Newly risen vampires are unpredictable. Handy items to have nearby: Bottled blood, silver chains, and a Snuggie.

—Siring for the Stupid:
A Beginner's Guide to Raising Newborn Vampires

On the third day, I insisted that Jolene, Zeb, and the kids stay away. In fact, I asked them to leave their home at the edge of my property and visit Jolene's pack for the night. Not all vampires wake up, well, sane, and I didn't want Zeb's family to become collateral damage to Jamie's newborn thirst.

Dick, Gabriel, and I sat in the kitchen, staring up at the ceiling, as if we could peer up into the room where Jamie was resting. Sometime around midnight, there was a buzz along my spine. It was as if I could hear Jamie's body picking up its pace, the ripple of energy that would animate him, since blood and electrical impulses had waved bye-bye about three days ago.

"You feel that, too?" I asked Gabriel, who was staring up at the ceiling with trepidation.

He shook his head. I frowned.

"Is this a sire thing?" I asked. "Could you feel me when I rose?"

"It's a one-time privilege," Gabriel told me. "It ensures that you're present when your childe rises. In some cases of particularly troublesome charges, such a tracking device would be handy in the long term."

"I'm going to pretend that you're not talking about me," I retorted.

Dick put a hand on my shoulder. "Stretch, go slow, OK? Be careful. Newborns are tricky. And he's a newborn teenager. It's like a hormone double whammy. Imagine what Ophelia must have been like when she first rose." Gabriel cleared his throat in that "Shut the hell up" manner he'd mastered so many years ago. The look on my face had Dick scrambling to reassure me. "I'm sure it will be fine. Nothing to worry about. Go on up."

Rolling my eyes, I quietly took the stairs two at a time with my boys close behind. Jamie's body was still and cold on the bed, but you could feel the undercurrent rippling along his skin. I sat on the bed carefully and began unbuttoning my blouse so he could pull the collar aside.

"What are you doing?" Gabriel demanded, while Dick seemed torn between laughing and desperately searching for meaning in the crown molding.

"He's going to want to feed," I said. "I don't want him making a buffet out of the townsfolk."

"And why does that involve taking off your shirt?"

"I'm not taking off my shirt. I'm making it easier to access my neck," I said. Gabriel frowned. "What? The first feeding I had was with you. I thought this is how it works."

"But he can have bottled blood," Gabriel protested.

"I thought you said the first feeding was a sacrament."

"That was before it was coming from *you*."

"Seriously?" I exclaimed. "Is this like the vampire version of the breastfeeding debate?"

"What if he fed from your arm instead?" Gabriel said. "It's a little less . . . personal."

"Gabriel, I'm trying really hard to understand your point of view here, but you're a few syllables from pissing me off."

Gabriel raised his hands in a defeated gesture. "Fine, I'm just going to stay back here. Watching. Intently."

I shushed him and felt Jamie stir next to me. His eyelids snapped open, and he jerked as if coming out of a bad dream. He blinked a few times, his eyes adjusting to the sharp, startling clarity of vampire vision. He slowly sat up, stretching his re-formed muscles.

The undead are, generally, more attractive than before we've turned. Even vampires who weren't conventionally attractive in life have a certain sensual sparkle after death. As long as they keep up with basic hygiene, they will stay that way. Jamie, who was already blessed in the looks department, now had a distinctly unfair advantage. The eyes were more jade than olive now, standing out starkly from his creamy skin. His full lips parted over unnaturally white teeth. The boyish charm was still there but layered over something more dangerous, more compelling.

Suddenly, I felt Gabriel's eyes on me, and if I could

have blushed, my cheeks would have been beet-red. I cleared my throat and kept my voice low, smooth. "Jamie, how do you feel?"

"Like I got hit by a car," he muttered. He jerked again, realizing that the feminine voice from his bedside was not, in fact, his mother.

Jamie grabbed the sheet and pulled it to his chest. "Miss Jane?"

"Jamie."

He scanned the room quickly, saw Gabriel, and scrambled across the bed. He almost toppled off onto the floor, but his reflexes helped him stop just before his weight shifted over the edge. He did a sort of tuck-and-roll thing that landed him on his feet. His eyes took on a sort of panicked glaze, and he started gasping for breath. I could see the comprehension cross his features.

He didn't need to breathe.

"Jamie, I'm going to need you to stay calm."

"Calm? What's happening to me?"

"What's the last thing you remember?"

He chewed on his plump bottom lip. "Uh, I was working. I drove the truck up to your shop. You waved hello and smiled at me. I remember thinking how much I liked that sweater on you, cause it made your, uh"—Gabriel cleared his throat, Dick threw Jamie a warning look, and Jamie immediately recognized his subbasement position on the room's totem pole—"eyes stand out. You screamed my name, and I turned around, saw the car headed for me . . . And that's it."

"That car ran you down. It was a hit-and-run. You

were bleeding, and there was a lot of internal damage. You were dying, and you asked me to change you."

Jamie rubbed at his Adam's apple and swallowed, a sign of the thirst building in his throat. "I don't remember. I remember a feeling of not wanting to die, but that's pretty much it. So, I'm a vampire now?"

"Yes."

"Cool."

My brow furrowed. "Really, that's it? That's the sum total of your response?"

"Yeah." He shrugged.

"We're talking a total change in lifestyle here, new hours, new diet, new rules, new lifestyle. And your response is 'cool'?"

"Do I get a long black coat like that Angel guy? Ooh, or Spike. My sister loves that show."

"All that MTV and Twitterfacing has seriously dulled you kids to emotional response, you know?"

A note of genuine fear, of concern, crept into his voice. "Wait, do my parents know I'm a vampire?"

I nodded. "Someone from the Council, the governing body for vampires, went to your house the night you died."

"What do you mean, 'the night I died'? How long have I been out?"

"It takes three days for a vampire to rise."

"I've missed three days of school?" he yelped. "Unexcused? I'm going to be kicked off the baseball team. Aw, man, my dad's going to kill me!"

"I'm pretty sure calling in dead counts as an excused absence."

"Were they pissed?" he asked. "Am I grounded?"

"Noo. They were upset that you were hurt. But they weren't angry . . . at you."

"Can I see them?"

"Not for a few days. We need to make sure that you're, uh, safe, to be around humans. It's sort of dangerous for you to be around people right now. And I know you would hate to hurt someone. You're going to need to get used to feeding and the whole bloodlust thing, before we can let you around innocent bystanders."

"Aw, man, why'd you have to bring up food? I'm starving." He groaned, rubbing his washboard abs. "Well, not starving, really, but, thirsty, really thirsty. Like I've been stuck out in the desert for days. Is that normal?" he asked, voice garbled as his fangs stretched out and bumped his lip. "What's that?" He slapped his hand over his mouth. "What the hell is that?"

"Those are your fangs," I told him. "It's a perfectly normal response to your hunger."

"Oh, my God, this is so embarrassing! I feel like I should walk around with a big notebook over my face."

I laughed, but Gabriel asked, "Why is that funny?"

"How do I make them go away, Miss Jane?"

"Well, right now, you need them. But we'll work on the whole retracting issue. We're just going to stay nice and calm, and I'm going to walk you through your first feeding, OK?"

"Is it going to be gross?"

"It takes some getting used to," I told him. "But it's no big deal. Were you embarrassed when I used to serve you smiley-face pancakes?"

"I'm embarrassed that you're talking about it now," Jamie said, shooting a pointed look at Dick and Gabriel.

"Well, this is just like that. It's just breakfast. Now, I'm going to put my wrist up to your lips, and you just do what feels natural, OK?"

"Is it going to hurt you?" he asked, eyeing my arm fearfully.

"Not if you don't want to hurt me," I assured him. "Now, just put your fangs into the skin and bite down."

"I can't, it feels . . . I don't want to."

"Maybe we should just try the bottled blood," Gabriel offered.

I shot a glare at him. "Are you going to helicopter-grandsire him, or do we want a fully functional vampire who won't be living in our basement thirty years from now?"

"What?"

"Here, Jamie, I'm going to help you this once, but the next time, you have to do it on your own." I bit through the thin skin over my veins, shuddering at the weird wet crunching sound it made, and offered it to Jamie. He tentatively ran his tongue along the wound and lapped at the cool rise of blood welling up from my skin. I could hear Gabriel growling behind me. Jamie latched onto the bite and pulled blood from the wound in earnest. His hands wrapped around my arm, and he leaned into me, nestling his back into my side. He relaxed, nuzzling the skin of my arm in a way that was distinctly not "platonic."

Chewing my lip, I looked up to Gabriel and Dick. My fiancé seemed to be debating whether to let me handle the situation or throw Jamie out a window, while Dick was struggling against hysterical giggles at my plight.

"Jamie, that's enough, now," I said, using what I hoped was a good impersonation of my mother's "Jane, be reasonable" tone.

Jamie grumbled and tugged my arm possessively. He shifted his hips toward me, and my eyes widened. Jamie had a little problem. Well, not a little problem. It was a perfectly average "notebook-worthy" problem.

He opened his eyes and followed my eye line to the tent in his sweatpants. He immediately pulled away and grabbed a pillow to cover himself.

I was woefully unprepared for living with a teenage boy.

"Sorry," he said, grimacing.

"It, uh, happens," Gabriel acknowledged, moving ever so subtly closer to the bed to help me rise from it. "Just don't let it happen around Jane. It's not appropriate."

"Who are you, again?" Jamie demanded of Gabriel.

"Did you want to try some of the bottled now?" I asked, pretending the embarrassment away by sheer force of will. "You need to get used to feeding both ways. If you want to feed on humans, that's your choice. But as long as you're living with me, I'm going to ask you to stick to a nonviolent diet."

Jamie accepted the offered Faux Type O, took a sip, and blanched. "I'm good—Wait, I'm living with you?"

"Yes, I turned you, so I'm responsible for you. Like a foster parent. If you screw up and eat a busload of nuns, I am in some serious trouble. So, if I ever come down on you or seem like I'm being unreasonable, it's just because you don't quite get the rules yet. And I'm trying to keep us both from getting the Trial—the vampire version of ironic/painful capital punishment."

Jamie's eyes scanned the room, checking out his new digs. Considering that it was my room when I stayed with Jettie as a kid and still sported peppermint-striped wallpaper and a lacy canopy bed, I didn't think he was terribly impressed. "How long will I be here?"

"Until you're ready to live on your own."

"But what about school?" he demanded, his voice cracking Peter Brady–style. "And work? Baseball? College?"

"I honestly don't know. Maybe, when you're ready, we could have Ophelia arrange some home-school lessons so you could still graduate with your class . . . assuming that they're willing to have a nighttime ceremony. And as for college, maybe in a few years, you could try it. Since the Coming Out, more schools have been adding night classes to their schedules. I know you were probably counting on baseball scholarships, but I can help out with tuition. I feel sort of responsible for this. I'm so sorry, Jamie. I know this is a lot to take in. Trust me, I've been there. The thing you have to focus on is that you're alive, technically speaking. And that once you stop thinking about everything you've given up, being a vampire is pretty awesome."

"Like what?" he demanded.

"Well, you're superstrong, for one, like athletes on illegal substances times a thousand. And that thing you did to keep yourself from falling on your face? Doesn't compare to what you'll be able to do, balance- and agility-wise. You can run faster than you ever imagined. And some vampires get extra bonus talents."

"Like singing?"

Dick snickered and muttered something about "karaoke," which was clearly a reference to the last time we'd gone to the Cellar as a group and I'd performed a particularly sad rendition of "Love Is a Battlefield." Gabriel tried to cover his laugh by clearing his throat but failed. I scowled at them both.

"No, like Gabriel can alter human memories. It's a handy skill when you're feeding off your neighbors and need them to remember falling neck-first on a barbecue fork."

"Wow," he marveled. "What can *you* do?"

"I can read minds."

Jamie looked stricken, which made me wonder what he'd been thinking in the last few minutes.

"Only human minds," I told him. "But I try not to go sifting around in other people's brains. It's just rude. I still can't get the hang of reading vampires, unless I'm feeding from them. And that's generally when Gabriel and I are . . . never mind."

"I want to see," Jamie said.

I frowned. "Gabriel and I are not doing that in front of you."

"No, I want to see how fast and strong I am. Can you take me outside? I just, I want to run or something. Please? I feel like I've been sleeping for days."

I looked up and saw Gabriel shaking his head.

"I'm not sure that's a great idea, Stretch," Dick added, casting nervous glances at our young ward.

Jamie gave me the big green puppy-dog eyes, and I felt a strange melty sensation in my chest. I groaned. This was not a healthy precedent to set, him persuading me by being adorably pathetic.

"Please," he begged. "I have some questions for you, and they're kind of, um, private."

"What kind of questions?" Gabriel asked.

"The private kind," Jamie shot back.

Unsure, I gave Gabriel the classic eyebrow lift, meaning, *For the love of God, please tell me what to do.*

Gabriel shrugged. "It's up to you. You're the sire now."

"That is decidedly unhelpful," I told him.

"Douche!" Jamie fake-coughed into his hand.

I turned on my young charge and gave him a withering glare. "Seriously, did you just douche-cough my fiancé? What's next? The dreaded slut-sneeze?"

Dick laughed under his breath. I whirled on Dick. "I so should have let you turn him." I turned toward Jamie and poked a finger into his chest. "OK, but the first sign of you bolting for that busload of nuns, I break your ankles like Kathy Bates in *Misery*." He gave me a blank look. I sighed and tried to think of a more modern cinematic torture reference. "I'll go Jigsaw on your ass." He laughed. "I am completely serious. You will do what

I say, when I say it, or you won't be able to walk for a week."

He looked frightened for a moment, then nodded. "Believe it or not, my mom used to say that right before she'd take me and Daisy into Walmart."

"Nice." I snickered as I tossed him a T-shirt extolling the virtues of the Southern Festival of Books. "Take it easy. It's your first time out."

We trotted down the stairs with Gabriel and Dick close at our heels. I stopped on the front porch, sniffing the air, trying to sense any humans who might stumble into our path. Jamie was staring up at the sky, shielding his sensitive eyes from the light of the moon. He flexed his hands, marveling at the way the sinew and bone moved under his skin. He smiled, looking to me like a baby taking his first steps.

"You ready?" I asked.

Jamie was stretching his arms behind his shoulders in that jocky way that clearly communicated that he did not consider me athletic competition. "What happened your first time out?"

"I tried to eat my best friend."

His arms froze over his head, and he frowned. "Oh, well, I'll try not to do that, then."

I laughed and took a few quick steps toward the pasture. Jamie quickly caught up to me. My new childe running was a thing to behold. How someone so bulky could be so lithe and light on his feet was a mystery. We ran across the width of my land, leaping high over the grassy hills for no other reason than that we could. Jamie whooped as he landed, a little unsteady on his feet, and then bounded over an old shed my great-grandfather used to use as a deer blind.

"This is great!" he crowed, flipping back into a handspring and walking on his hands on the tall silvered grass. I sat down on a fallen log and watched, a bemused smirk tilting the corners of my mouth. "I can see everything, every crater on the moon, every branch on every tree. I can smell everything, the grass crushing under my feet, the smell of your skin. Did anyone ever tell you that you smell just like peaches and cinnamon?"

"Easy," I told him sternly.

"No, it's just that the smell sort of sticks out in my mind, probably because it was the last thing I smelled as I was dying. That smell means safe, it means home, which is probably some weird vampire instinct thing, huh?" he continued as if I hadn't just admonished him for inappropriate sire harassment. "How come we never hear about this stuff when they talk about vampires on the news? It's all 'Be respectful and cautious when you're approaching the cranky undead.' No one ever says, 'Vampires are like superheroes. Ask one of them to leap over a tall building in a single bound!'"

"Because vampires would get extremely annoyed if humans did that," I mused.

"Whatever. If I get to go back to school, I'm going to convince the coach to let me keep playing baseball. We could totally win state with my new skills," he said, springing back to his feet and executing several backflips. "We'd have to play at night, though."

"Well, they might let you on the cheerleading squad, either way." I laughed as he tumbled across the moonlit clearing.

"Hey!"

"I'm just kidding. If they let you back in school, I will go to every game and wear one of those big embarrassing pins with your picture on it."

His face split with a huge, toothy grin. "Really?"

"Really. Someone has to keep you from snacking on the outfield. The Half-Moon Howlers couldn't stand the loss if you were staked by angry spectators."

"Funny." He frowned, finally coming to a stop so he could sit beside me. "So, you said something about rules earlier? You should probably tell me about those now. Nothing that's this awesome can come without some serious drawbacks. Like steroids or dating a hot chick with a crazy dad."

"How much do you know about us?" I asked. "Like our origin stories, the reason we came out of the coffin, that sort of thing?"

"Well, I was in elementary school during the Great Coming Out, and my parents wouldn't let me watch the news because they were afraid it would give me nightmares."

"Thank you for reminding me again of how young you are." I sighed. "OK, no one knows where vampires come from. Almost every culture has some sort of vampire creature in its folklore. I could bore you to tears describing how the most popular beliefs originated from the Slavic traditions, probably spread by Gypsies as they traveled through India and Egypt. But it's your first night, and I'll spare you. There are plenty of books in the library that you should study, anyway."

Jamie blanched at the mention of assigned reading but maintained a respectful silence.

I continued, "Vampires had it pretty good for about two thousand years, lurking in the shadows, drinking their fill, looking all pretty and ageless. And then this doofus tax consultant Arnie Frink gets turned and sues his boss for nighttime work hours, citing the Americans with Disabilities Act. After the courts determined that Arnie was not, in fact, crazy—or breathing, for that matter—Arnie got his night hours, a handsome settlement, and an interview with Barbara Walters. Vampires were out, whether they wanted it or not. You probably remember everybody running around panicking, buying Vampire Home Defense Kits at Walmart, and making crosses out of tent stakes. Vampires were panicking, too, forming the World Council for the Equal Treatment of the Undead, making tentative agreements with the governments of the world, trying to keep the angry mobs at bay. But I realize that you'll find all of this equally boring coming from me, so I'm just going to refer you to the *Guide for the Newly Undead*. It's basically the survival guide for newly turned vampires. You need to memorize it, maybe carry portions of it around in your pocket."

Jamie groaned at the thought of homework, so I moved on to more interesting topics. "The rules are pretty simple. The most important thing you have to remember is: Sunlight is bad. It will kill you. No arguments, no bargaining. You will be a little pile of dust. I tried using SPF-500 sunblock once but ended up with severe burns on my hands because I forgot to protect the creases between my fingers. The pain I can't even describe. I would avoid it altogether to the best of your ability."

"OK, but what about stakes and crosses and silver bullets and all that? 'Cause I'm thinking a silver-bullet gun would be pretty awesome for self-defense. It would go with the black coat."

I sighed and made a promise to myself to keep Dick and Jamie separated as much as possible. "We're allergic to silver. Imagine sticking your hand into a hornets' nest and being forced to listen to the Wiggles while the little bastards repeatedly sting you." He shuddered. "Yeah, it hurts. And if you get dosed with too much of it, your healing abilities are overwhelmed, and you can have the vampire version of anaphylactic shock."

"Huh?"

I sighed, reminding myself that I was dealing with a young person. "Anybody at your school allergic to peanuts?"

He nodded. "Tiffany Scott's face swells up and turns purple if she gets near a PB and J. She has to sit at a special table in the cafeteria."

"Same principle."

"That's kind of cool."

I harrumphed. "Let's see, wooden stake to the heart, beheading, and setting us on fire—all fatal. We can see our reflections. Crosses aren't a big deal, unless you and

God have some unresolved issues. We can go into homes uninvited, but we could be criminally charged if we do, so let's not try that."

"Can we turn into bats?"

"Sadly, no."

"Garlic?" he asked.

"Stinky but not harmful."

"What about sex?"

I tried to maintain the most neutral expression possible. "What about it?"

"Will I be having it?"

"That's sort of up to you."

Jamie moved toward me and put his hand on my thigh. I shot to my feet and backed away to a distance that wouldn't get me put on some sort of watch list.

"No, no, no. That's not how this works at all."

"But you said Gabriel was your sire, and you're . . . with him."

"I'm with him because he's my boyfriend, well, my fiancé now."

"Seriously?"

I mulled over whether he was more surprised that I was getting married or that I was marrying Gabriel. I nodded. "He just happened to become my boyfriend after I was turned. It has nothing to do with the sire thing."

"But what if I want to date?"

I shrugged. "After you're settled, you can date whoever you want, as long as they're a consenting adult and you don't do anything anatomically compromising in my house."

Given the gleam in his eyes, I was suddenly very thankful that Jamie couldn't get anyone pregnant. There wasn't enough latex at Goodyear to contain that gleam.

"You have to be careful around humans, Jamie," I said, my tone gentle. "Daddies who wouldn't be happy to find you rolling around the backseat with their daughters aren't going to be happier about it now that you have fangs. And while getting hit with a shotgun blast won't kill you, it will sting like the dickens. And you don't want to hurt the girls, either. You're a good-looking guy. You could break a lot of hearts."

He grinned at me and put his hand on my knee.

I groaned.

"I misread that again, huh?"

"Yes. And your hand's still on my knee." I sighed. "That settles it. We're going to have to keep you away from Dick Cheney."

"The vice president?"

"Oh, we need to talk."

4

There will be outside events that can distract you from your duties as a sire. Only leave your childe with other vampires whom you trust. Do not under any circumstances leave your childe alone with a human, unless you enjoy settling wrongful-death suits with large amounts of your money.

—*Siring for the Stupid:*
A Beginner's Guide to Raising Newborn Vampires

Jamie proved to be as energetic and fretful as any newborn baby on his first day home from the hospital. None of us got any rest until the very last dregs of night sky had been burned away by sun and he collapsed in the guest room.

After precious few hours of fitful sleep, I was having a very strange dream. First, a burly man with wild, curly dark hair was standing in front of River Oaks, screaming and shaking his fists. I reached out to his mind, but all I got were rolling waves of hate, grief, anger, and regret, in alternating shades of red and orange. I pulled away, recoiling from the angry mass of thoughts. My weird dream brain shifted to inside the house, and my grandmother was standing in the corner of the room, and she was angry, hissing horrible things to me. I was a disappointment to my family. I was a thief. I was a usurper. Her voice was a cold fog that slithered across the floor, over my bed, wrapping itself around my head as the insults struck closer to home. I was unnatural and wrong. It should have been me who died. I was a whore, sullying my family's home with my vile dead lover.

Sadly, it was pretty much the same speech I got last Christmas.

The very moment the sun slid behind the horizon, the phone rang. Gabriel groaned and rolled away from it. Still groggy, I reached for the receiver and clicked the remote for the sunproof curtains to rise. Lovely purplish twilight poured in through the windows as my eyes adjusted. Blinking blearily, I picked up the receiver and heard a ragged sniffle from the other end of the line.

"Jane, sweetie, I have bad news."

Slightly more awake, I pushed the receiver closer to my ear. "Mom? What's going on?"

"Jane, your grandma Ruthie passed."

I sat up, taking the quilt with me and knocking Gabriel out of bed. "What?"

"Ow," Gabriel muttered into the floor.

"Your grandma died this afternoon. I'm so sorry, honey."

"No, no, I'm sorry, Mom. Are you OK? What happened?"

My mind immediately went to Grandma's boyfriend, Wilbur, whom I'd never trusted. Grandma Ruthie's four husbands and her previous fiancé had all died under suspicious circumstances, involving a speeding delivery truck, a brown recluse bite on the inside of the throat, a previously unknown allergy to Grandma Ruthie's famous strawberry-rhubarb pie, a golf-related lightning strike, and a miscalculation of a Viagra dosage. So, when she paired up with a ghoul—a sad version of vampirism so weak that they barely qualified as immortal—with a similar marital history, I'd stated (loudly enough for the entire family to hear me) that it was only matter of time before one of them ended up dead. Although Wilbur was basically the Splenda of vampires—a weak, ineffectual imitation of the real thing—my money was on Grandma Ruthie. I'd placed a small wager with Dick relating to the possibility of her being dosed with botulism.

Wilbur and Grandma Ruthie seemed very happy together, although I guess that when you never know when your lover might facilitate your release from your mortal coil, it adds a certain amount of adrenalinated spice to the mix.

Shudder.

"Your grandmother had a stroke at the Garden Club meeting. She was screaming at Bitty Tate about having the gall to put marigolds in the sponsored planters in front of City Hall without permission. And she just keeled over."

That didn't sound "natural" to me, but I didn't think it would help to point that out. It struck me that for once, my mother had a legitimate reason to be overwrought, to make demands and have hysterical hissy fits. But she seemed so calm. Her voice hadn't cracked once in our conversation. She hadn't commanded me to construct a salad from bacon, cream cheese, and gelatin and get myself to her house to receive well-wishers. She wasn't even asking what I planned to wear to the visitation. I was more than a little worried.

"How are you doing?" I asked.

"I'm fine, honey. I've been preparing for this for a while."

"That's weird."

"You know me, Jane. I've got to handle all the details now, focus on that. I'll fall apart later. Don't you worry."

I nodded. When Mama finally wound down, Daddy would be there for her, to pick up the pieces. He was better at that than people gave him credit for. But I would be standing by with industrial-grade sedatives, just in case.

"Now, your grandma had her service preplanned—"

"Of course she did," I said, rolling my eyes and imagining the eulogy Grandma had most likely typed, highlighted, and delivered to Reverend Neel.

"But there's no rule that says we have to have the funeral services during the day. We could push it back until after sunset," Mama offered.

I smiled. "Ruthie would roll over in her casket if she knew you were doing that."

"Jane!"

"Right, sorry. Too soon. I'll be fine, Mama, honestly. I sort of said my good-byes when she, you know, declared that I was a soulless monster and no longer her grandchild. And really, most of the town knows about my condition now; they won't question why I'm not there. And really, I don't think Grandma Ruthie would want me there with her friends, anyway."

"Well, at least come to the visitation."

I was ashamed at the sheer length of the pause.

"Janie, I need you there, please." Her voice rose a couple of octaves, and my resolve crumbled.

"All right, Mama, for you, I'll be there."

We discussed logistics and food. Turns out I was expected to prepare a macaroni salad, a cheese platter, and corn relish, despite the fact that I couldn't eat any of it, and we both knew that Grandma Ruthie's church-lady friends were going to bombard Mama with enough casseroles to sink an armada. But it was the gesture that counted. If I showed up to the service empty-handed, it would be seen as thumbing my nose at Grandma one last time. And even if I was inclined to use an entirely different finger, I wouldn't subject Mama to whispers from the church ladies about how heartless her child was.

For once in my life, I was going to get through a situation with a little dignity. OK, I probably wasn't, but I would fake it as if my life depended on it.

I hung up the phone, and for the first time in my life, human or undead, my first instinct was to pick the receiver right back up and call my sister.

Weird.

Gabriel climbed back into bed, burying his face in a pillow. Shell-shocked, I leaned against the headboard. "My grandma died."

Gabriel raised his head, his brow crinkled. "But I thought you said meanness was a preservative."

"Clearly, I was wrong," I sighed as he twined his fingers through mine. "I'm OK. Really. I'm a little sad that she died with things so bitter between the two of us, but I'm also smart enough to recognize that was never going to change unless I magically transformed myself into the person she wanted me to be. I didn't owe her that just because she happened to be related to me. But I do owe it to my mother and my sister to help them through whatever mourning process they're going to go through."

Gabriel put his arm around my shoulder and tucked my head under his chin. "What do you need from me?"

"I need you to be well rested, so when this all comes crashing down on my head, I have a safety net," I said, nuzzling his neck.

"Excellent. I can do that," he said, closing his eyes and seeming to doze off in a sitting position.

I listened for sounds of movement in the house but heard nothing. Apparently, the phone didn't wake Jamie. Carefully unraveling myself from Gabriel's grasp, I went downstairs and found that my childe had not risen for the evening, which wasn't surprising. But the trail of empty synthetic blood bottles scattered from the kitchen to the stairs told me that at some point during the day, he'd managed to get out of bed and drink the last of our Faux Type O supply. I never heard of a newborn doing such a thing. I'd practically been comatose during my first few days as a vampire. But I supposed all bets were off when you were dealing with any food source and a teenage boy.

"It would be wrong to kill my childe," I muttered, sorting through the debris to try to find some semblance of food. I settled on a half-empty bottle of Sangre left over from a party a few weeks before, hidden at the back of the fridge. "It would be wrong to kill my childe."

My teen-o-cidal thoughts were interrupted by a knock on my door. I still had the bottle to my lips and was mid-swig when Jenny burst through the door and wailed, "Jane!"

I nearly choked on the fancy dessert blood, reminding myself once again that giving Jenny a spare key to the house had been a gesture of good faith. Taking it back now would be a leap in the wrong direction. "Jen?"

I'd never seen my prim, polished sister look so disheveled, and that includes the time we got into a mud-wrestling match at last year's Chamber of Commerce Fall Festival. Her dark blond hair was scraped up into a limp little ponytail. Her eyes were red-rimmed and swollen. And she was wearing a raspberry-colored track suit. I wasn't even aware that Jenny owned a track suit.

Jenny sniffled and threw her arms around me. Gabriel came downstairs and saw Jenny sobbing quietly into my neck. He lifted his eyebrows in amazement. I shrugged. When he moved back toward the steps, I mouthed, "Coward!" silently to him.

"Jenny, calm down," I said, awkwardly patting her back. "Let me make you some coffee."

"OK." She whimpered soggily as she dropped into one

of the kitchen chairs. "I just couldn't go by Mama's house and worry her, so my first thought was that I should go to you."

"Really?"

"I know, I was a little surprised, too," she admitted as I set up the coffeemaker. "I mean, I know she wasn't perfect. I know the two of you never really got along, but it's still hard, you know? I hate that we were so close for most of my life, but at the end . . . we were barely speaking."

A little pang of guilt twinged in my chest. Grandma Ruthie had been such a divisive force for the two of us. I was Daddy's clear favorite. We operated on the same wavelength. As much as I thought Jenny was Mama's favorite, our mother's loyalties had always been divided. While she asked me why I couldn't be more like Jenny, she was constantly fussing to Jenny about how worried she was about me. Jenny was just looking to be someone's favorite. Grandma was more than willing to provide her the kind of attention she wanted, if Jenny was willing to jump.

As Jenny and I started to mend our fences over the past few months, she and Grandma Ruthie spent less and less time together. Grandma couldn't understand why Jenny was "wasting her time" with me. And Jenny lost patience with Grandma's continued criticisms and complaints about me. It felt terrible to be the wedge that drove the two of them apart, but I had to admit that Jenny was more relaxed, more human, without our grandmother's influence.

I was glad that Zeb and Jolene spent so much time at the house and occasionally required sustenance. Otherwise, I would only have the creamer and the sugar left over from my human days to offer Jenny. I poured her a cup of coffee and sat down across the table.

Jenny smiled as a thank-you and sipped. "Mama said for the visitation, we should come up with our favorite memory of Grandma. In her notes to the pastor, Grandma said she wanted us to show what a kind, loving woman she was. I thought I'd talk about all the times she took me on special little shopping trips or when she'd take me to the Teeny Teas to show off the dresses she'd made me. What about you?"

Hmm, a nice, sweet story about Grandma Ruthie. The happiest memory I had of her was when she and my ghostly aunt Jettie had a screaming match through a dry-erase board. The memories of her dragging me kicking and screaming to the Teeny Teas would hardly qualify as memorial material. Nor would her disappointment with my low placement in the one Little Miss Half-Moon Hollow pageant she'd managed to force me into. Or the time she refused to speak to me for an entire summer because I wouldn't date some mouth-breathing cretin grandson of one of her bridge club friends. (Best summer of my life.)

"Jane?"

"I'm thinking," I muttered.

The tantrums, the scoldings, the faked medical emergencies, the many, many reminders that I was not what she expected in a grandchild. I can't say they made for warm, fuzzy Grandma memories.

"There has to be something, Jane. I mean, you weren't always at each other's throat."

"You know, in some cultures, the bereaved hire mourners to make sure it looks like the deceased is beloved and missed. Maybe I could hire someone to do my special memory?" I suggested. Jenny frowned at me. "Look, Jen, I didn't measure up for Grandma Ruthie. She didn't make any effort to hide that. Why pretend now? If I get up in front of a crowd of people and wax poetic about my poignant, life-affirming moments with Grandma, everyone will know I'm lying. So why do it?"

"Because at least you've made the gesture?"

"Jenny."

"Funerals are for the living, Jane, not the dead," she said, right before realizing how inappropriate that statement was and starting to giggle. She rolled into all-out guffaws and sat there, braying like a donkey, with tears streaming down her cheeks, until I handed her a wet paper towel to wipe down her face.

"You done now?" I asked, bemused.

She sniffed and nodded. "It was worth a shot. I don't even know why I'm saying this stuff. My therapist says it's a coping mechanism. I think I can control or fix the situation by making comments like that."

"Whoa, back up, did you say 'therapist'?"

"Yeah, Kent and I actually started a few years ago after he threatened to move out. He said my need to organize was crushing his will to live."

"There's been a lot going on with you that I never knew about, huh?"

"Yep," she muttered, sipping her coffee.

"Is Mama in therapy, because that would be—"

"No."

I sighed. "Too good to be true."

Jenny nodded.

Jamie came sauntering into the kitchen without a shirt. He was yawning and stretching his arms over his head, his ab muscles flexing for all they were worth. My sister spewed a mouthful of coffee into her cup.

"Hey, Jane, we're all out of blood."

In the upset over Grandma Ruthie, I'd completely forgotten about the undead teenager sleeping upstairs. My eyes darted from my flabbergasted sister to my young ward. I decided to play it off as if nothing was wrong. Maybe Jenny would assume that she'd had some sort of nervous breakdown and was hallucinating.

I frowned. "Yes, some mysterious force swept through the kitchen last night and sucked up all the available sustenance."

"Yeah, I got a little hungry." Jamie gave me his most charming smile, which did less for my motherly instincts than it had the day before. "Oh, hey, Miss Jenny."

I internally snickered at the fact that he called her Miss Jenny. She was just as old and frau-ish as I was. It was hilarious, right up to the point where the warm, rich scent of Jenny's pumping blood wafted toward him. His nostrils flared, and I could see the muscles in his jaw working as his mouth watered. His eyes darted toward me, panicked. I shook my head. His fangs snicked down with a click, but he slapped a hand over his mouth to cover them.

"Gabriel!" I crossed the kitchen, putting my body between Jamie and my sister. I pressed the bottle of Sangre into his hand and, in the best persuasive voice I could muster, said, "Jamie, you're going to go upstairs and drink this. You don't want to drink from a human, especially a friend of your family's. You're going to stay up in your room until you hear Jenny's car start, do you hear me?"

Jamie seemed to be calculating the distance between us and the table. I could practically see him mapping the acrobatic leaps it would take to get around me and sink his fangs into Jenny's tempting jugular. I curled my fingers around his biceps and pushed him back with all my strength.

"Jamie," I growled. *"No."*

The tension in his arms was immense, as if he was struggling against me and himself. I saw the tiniest smidge of saliva pooling at the corner of his mouth. I shook his shoulders, and he seemed to snap out of his predatory haze.

"But she smells so good!" he cried.

"Jamie, no!"

"Please!" he begged.

"Jamie, as long as you're living under my roof, you're going to follow my rules. And that means not feeding on my family members," I told him.

"I hate you!" he yelled, stomping toward the stairs. Gabriel appeared at the kitchen door and grabbed Jamie's arm, leading him from the room as gently as he could. Gabriel was murmuring soothing, mildly threatening words to my grumbling childe as he marched him upstairs.

"I have turned into my mother." I sighed. "Stake me now."

I turned to find my sister staring at me with a horrified expression on her face. "Oh, Jane, you didn't!"

"What?"

"You and Jamie? What about Gabriel?"

"You just saw him. And it's been great. Frankly, I need him around to control Jamie."

"Ew! You mean, he was with you when it happened?"

"No, Dick was with me when it happened," I said, my brow scrunched in confusion. Jenny's jaw dropped, and she let out a little squeak. "What? Oh! *Ew!* No! I didn't sleep with Jamie, I just turned him!"

"You turned him?"

"I had to."

"I'm—I don't know what I'm going to do. But I think I have to tell Mama!"

"You're telling on me, seriously? Are you five? I didn't have a choice, Jen."

"No, I don't mean I have to tell her because you did something wrong, but you know what happens when I'm around her. She senses something's up with weird mothering ESP, corners me, and the next thing you know, I'm spilling my guts. How do you think she found out about that time you and Zeb stole the garden gnome from Mrs. Turnbow?"

"That was you?"

Jenny ignored my indignation. "You know I'm going to end up spending a lot time with her with all this funeral stuff, and she's going to want to latch onto anything non-funeral-related to focus on. Damn it, Jane, how could you put me in this position?"

"You're right. How could I be so thoughtless?" I deadpanned.

"OK, fine, that was bitchy of me. But still."

"Can we go back to the sad state of mourning for our grandmother?"

"No way, sister. I've gone years without a legitimate reason to grill you—"

"And yet you did it anyway." I snorted.

"Right, so now's my chance to put those skills to good use."

"Argh."

"So, you turned Jamie. How does this work? Did you have to drink all of his blood? Why is he staying with you? How does Gabriel feel about all this?"

"OK, first, no, I didn't drink all of his blood, because he was hit by a car and was basically bleeding out before I could even get to him. He did drink a little of mine, though."

She sighed. "Poor thing."

"Yeah, he was pretty banged up."

"No, I meant you," she said, grimacing sadly at me. "That had to have been scary."

I arched an eyebrow and waited for the punch line in which I was a horrible, immoral monster. But Jenny just reached out and squeezed my hands. "Thanks, Jen. It was. And now, because I'm the one who turned him, Jamie has to stay with me while he trains to be a grown-up vampire."

"So it's a mommy sort of relationship?"

"No! He's my young ward. Like Batman and Robin."

"Wasn't Batman's relationship with his young ward—"

"Don't start," I grumbled. "There was never conclusive proof."

"And does young Jamie always wander around the house shirtless?" she asked, trying to sound nonchalant and failing miserably.

"Jennifer."

"What?" she asked, the picture of innocence. "I'm just curious."

"Can we go back to rarely speaking?"

Jenny snorted. "Hell, no. If I'd known your life was this entertaining, I would have wrestled you into submission years ago."

5

Feeding schedules are important. While your newborn childe shouldn't wake up during the day, he will wake up far less whiny if he feeds just before sunrise.

—*Siring for the Stupid:*
A Beginner's Guide to Raising Newborn Vampires

On the night of my grandmother's funeral, two strange things happened. First, someone threw a recently detached deer head onto my front porch. Second, well, I'll get into that in a bit.

Fortunately for me, Zeb came by the house during the day to retrieve a blankie left behind by the twins, and he found the deer head flung against my front door like a taxidermist's Valentine. He disposed of it and hosed off the porch before Fitz could start rolling on it. He also called me to try to explain the situation and his theory that the venison delivery was the handiwork of the driver who had hit Jamie, but because daytime leaves vampires less than, well, conscious, I told him, "Take your muffins to Boston and shut it, Terrance." And then I hung up on him.

As the sun set, I snuggled into Gabriel's back and tried to hang on to those last dregs of sleep. Anything to keep me from the evening looming over me. I was supposed to drop by my mother's house in about an hour to visit with the last of the well-wishers. There was a little part of me that felt guilty for not being there for my mom while she buried her own mother. But Mama had assured me that she would be fine as long as I did my time at the visitation.

She may have phrased it in a different way.

Gabriel had been my rock for the last few days, which made up for the fact that he and Jamie had been driving me to empathize with those crazy housewives who flip out and poison their whole church congregations. With three women in the family, it had been like a war zone in my parents' house for one week a month. And we still weren't as whiny as those two little wenches.

Gabriel complained that Jamie got Fitz too riled up when they played. One of their more memorable escapades resulted in Fitz dragging Jamie out through his doggie door and knocking off a chunk of the doorframe. Jamie complained that Gabriel watched too much History Channel. Jamie drank all of the Faux Type O in the house and left his empties in a pyramid formation on the porch. I will not describe Gabriel's reaction when he walked in on Jamie watching *Jersey Shore*. I couldn't tell whether it was because of the age difference or the generational difference or the fact that Jamie figured out that appearing to flirt with me in any way made Gabriel's fangs grind. Either way, it was annoying as hell.

I'd promised them both that one more fight over whose turn it was to take out the garbage would result in my drinking a dozen of Andrea's espresso concoctions, enabling me to stay up after sunrise and rip their fangs out as they slept. That had managed to keep them quiet for about twenty-four hours.

Drawing on experience with her werewolf relatives, Jolene told me that this was very normal pack behavior, particularly in a pack where the males perceived limited resources. In this pack, the resource was my time and attention. It helped to try to see both points of view. Gabriel had finally gotten me to agree to marriage, to long-term commitment, and our lives had settled down a little, only to have the rug yanked out from under him and a new disruptive family member added to our household. And poor Jamie, he just recently had normal body parts arrive, and then suddenly he's dead, drinking blood, cut off from his family, and having to entrust his well-being to his former babysitter. Plus, because the school board considered him dead, he was being home-schooled through the end of his senior year. No baseball. No prom. And the board wouldn't budge on a nighttime graduation ceremony.

Overall, we were lucky that he only blew up at us and screamed, "You're not my parents!" once every few hours or so. I'd asked Jolene for advice on how to bring down the tension in the house, but most of her suggestions involved rolled-up newspapers. Rolled-up newspapers are not a universally applicable solution.

Jolene's information from her cousin at the DMV was

equally unhelpful. There were no plates in that sequence registered to a rusted-out early-model black sedan. There was a very similar plate registered to a pickup truck that had been sent to a car cuber in Monkey's Eyebrow three years ago. So, my proactive bent to find the driver who ran Jamie down was at a temporary standstill. At least until I could get my own crime lab and analyze the paint samples scraped down Big Bertha's body.

Why now? Why would someone want to hurt me now? It had been months since I'd had trouble with anyone. And the deer head on my porch was a troubling development, especially when combined with the dream about the angry guy on my lawn. I couldn't help but feel that I was missing something. Something important. If I could just connect all of the pieces, I could fix it. Car accident . . . deer head . . . Gabriel . . . angry redneck.

And that was the moment when my brain pushed through that final layer of sleepy awareness and came fully awake.

Damn it.

Rubbing at my eyes, I reached toward the nightstand and grabbed my cell phone. Jenny had been texting me updates throughout the day. Most of it was stuff like "Aunt Maisie threw herself on top of the casket. Again." Or "Mama saw what Cous. J. is wearing and said the f-word. Wish I had video cam."

Scrolling through her texts, I smiled, although I was sorely disappointed to have missed Mama dropping the f-bomb. Jenny had, however, had the presence of mind to use her phone to snap a photo of Cousin Junie's ensemble—what looked like a low-cut backless black top and a leopard-print wrap skirt better suited to the poolside than the graveside. I burst out laughing, which made Gabriel stir beside me.

Shaking my head, I texted back that I was sorry I had missed it and would see her soon. So far, the mourning process seemed to have brought the three of us closer together. Heck, Jenny and I had actually shared a couple of bemused smiles at the visitation, when Junie showed up with her signature "Hot Dog Bake" and insisted that Mama have some to keep up her strength. And Mama was deeply appreciative when Jenny distracted her long enough that I could dispose of the offending mix of hot dogs, crushed Ritz crackers, and cream of mushroom soup.

Yack-worthy casseroles aside, the visitation had been surprisingly pleasant. In Half-Moon Hollow, visitations were held on the evening before the burial, giving the community the chance to offer condolences to the bereaved and help them consume the overflowing buffet of condolence foods. It is believed that the deceased soul will not be able to pass over to the Great Hereafter unless all humans in attendance are stuffed to the gills with grits casserole, deviled eggs, and funeral potatoes. These foods are to be present at every stage of the mourning process, from comforting family members immediately after the death to the luncheon after the burial. If at any time an empty plate or serving platter is spotted, the shabby, halfhearted treatment of the deceased will be the talk of the town for months.

So, when the sun had set the night before, I had showed up with the requisite buffet offerings, although the very smell of homemade pimento cheese had made Gabriel roll the car windows down just so the ride would be bearable. I'd taken my place at Mama's side in the receiving line, which, as Southern Funeral Law dictated, included anyone who had ever met Grandma Ruthie or anyone she was related to by blood or marriage. And a few people had actually shaken my hand, despite the fact that it obviously made them uncomfortable.

As a human, I'd done everything possible to avoid these situations. And other than being seriously wearing on my mental shields, it had been downright tolerable. Maybe it was better simply because Gabriel had been there. For the first time in my life, I didn't have to attend one of these things alone. It had been almost disorienting how sweet it was to feel his hand at the small of my back as I walked across the room. I didn't get the pitying "you poor spinster librarian" looks. There were no pointed questions from Mama's friends about when I would settle down. Bessie Paxton didn't even make a snarky remark about the "stress" I'd put my poor grandmother under, something she did regularly when Grandma Ruthie was still alive.

Then again, I imagine that sort of thing tends to diminish when your scary vampire boyfriend is standing right behind you.

As sick as it was to think of a funeral visitation as a night out, it had been nice to be out of the house and childe-free for an evening. Andrea and Dick had stayed home with Jamie, which he'd bitterly resented. He'd said he didn't need to be babysat. But then Dick had offered to show him how to hot-wire my car, which I'd bitterly resented. The trick had been getting through the visitation with my poker face intact whenever a mourner mentioned "that poor Lanier boy" and how torn up his parents were over his being turned. Jenny had—surprise, surprise—managed to keep my involvement in the situation to herself. I think she was using a combination of meditation and internally chanting her sorority's secret motto to keep from spilling the beans.

For my part, every time Jamie had been mentioned, I'd turned back toward the open casket and looked at Grandma Ruthie. She would have been very pleased with the delicately tinted peach suit Mama had found hanging in her closet in a garment bag marked "Visitation Attire." At some point, one of Whitlows was going to have to change her into the black bombazine gown that had been marked "Burial Attire." She'd even attached little bags with matching shoes and accessories.

It was strange that Grandma was making her final appearance at Whitlow's Funeral Home, where she'd been mourning husbands since 1957. I had a sneaking suspicion that they would name the room after her in memoriam. She'd left very specific instructions for how the room would be laid out, the flow of traffic through the receiving line and around the buffet, and the spray of white roses and gardenias on top of the dignified maple casket. And true to form, she had actually written her own eulogy for Reverend Neel. Mama had given the good reverend her blessing to wing it, once she saw that it was thirty-seven typed pages.

So far, the only real sore spot in the planning had been Wilbur, who had pitched an unholy fit and made a dramatic exit from the funeral home when he found out that he had not, in fact, been included in Grandma's will. His indignant fury that he hadn't been left "with so much as a red cent," confirmed my long-held suspicions that Grandma Ruthie had been another installment in Wilbur's Retirement Through Inheritance Plan. But at least Grandma Ruthie had died of natural causes, unlike the suspicious exits of Wilbur's previous lovers.

Shuddering at the thought of Wilbur being anyone's lover, I glanced at the clock and realized that I had about twenty minutes to get to Mama's house, or she'd start to think I wasn't showing up. Shaking Gabriel's shoulder to wake him, I climbed out of bed and padded into the bathroom for my somewhat extensive daily dental regimen.

I turned on the shower, letting the room slowly fill with steam and desperately trying to remember the deer-head conversation with Zeb. I looked in the mirror and saw that my hair was actually doing something seminormal, so at least I wouldn't have to wrestle it into submission during my limited grooming window. Yes, vampires could see themselves in mirrors. And doing so post-turning was a much more pleasant experience. I basically got the bookworm's dream makeover package. My skin was clearer. My hair had changed to an actually desirable color found in the brunette spectrum. My eyes, formerly an unremarkable muddy hazel, were now a clear and compelling hazel. My teeth were whiter, but I did have to maintain the aforementioned brushing and flossing routine.

I didn't expect to wipe the steam away from the glass and see the bluish, shadowy figure of my grandma Ruthie standing behind me, glaring at my reflection.

"What the fack!" I yelped, turning and scrambling away from the ghastly apparition of my grandmother in the buttery yellow pantsuit she'd worn to her last Garden Club meeting. My feet slipped out from under me, and I landed against the closed bathroom door with a loud *thump*.

"Language, Jane." Grandma sighed, peering down at me with that familiar disapproving curl to her lip.

"Jane!" Gabriel called from the other side of the door. "Are you all right?"

I pressed myself hard against the solid oak, eager to put more space between my grandmother's sneering specter and myself. For the first time in my life, I was honestly afraid of Grandma Ruthie. Alive, she'd been a judgmental and intimidating presence in my life. Now she was just scary. Her mouth was an angry faded slash across her face. Her eyes were shadowed, opaque, and dark. I could see every bad thought she'd ever had about me reflected in them.

"Grandma Ruthie, what the hell?" I yelled as Gabriel pounded on the other side of the door, rattling the knob. "What are you doing here?"

She smirked at me and turned toward the mirror to

adjust her smoky wisps of hair. "I honestly don't know. I was yelling at that simpering idiot Bitty Tate, and the next thing I knew, I was standing in the foyer here at River Oaks. You were sleeping, lazy little snip that you are. So I made myself at home, and don't think that I haven't seen how you've been running things around here over the last few days, Missy. You should be ashamed of yourself, turning your ancestral home into a den of iniquity."

"Didn't you see a tunnel of light?" I asked. I reconsidered, then added. "Or maybe a large warm pit opening up beneath you?"

"I'm not dead, Jane."

I snorted as the knocking on the other side of the door stopped. "Which is a shame, since they buried you this afternoon."

"No, I'm not dead. Obviously, the good Lord has another purpose for me, Jane. And it's quite clear why I'm here," she said, sighing happily. "It's finally my time to be mistress of River Oaks."

"Um, first of all, that's a really creepy way to put it. And second, I'm already the mistress of River Oaks."

"Not by right." Grandma sniffed. "The house should have gone to me. You're just a usurper, a pretender. Jettie must have been out of her mind to leave it to you."

"Well, it's too late now, because you're dead."

"So are you."

"Yeah, but I have a physical form; you don't."

"You have a choice. You can accept that I'm here to stay and stay out of my way. Or you can move out and leave the house to my judgment, as you should have in the first place."

I stared at her. "You mean it, don't you? This house means so much to you that you'd rather it sit empty and cold, a shell for you to wander around in for eternity, than for me to stay here and fill it with life."

"Well, you're not exactly filling it with life, are you?" she asked, sneering nastily and looking to my middle, to the womb that would never produce future Earlys. "Better that it be maintained by someone who appreciates the family history, who will care for it, love it. You'll only turn it into a tomb."

"You're insane. I used to joke around about how you were crazy, but death has honestly pushed you over the deep end, hasn't it?"

Her misty form undulated toward me like some sort of psychotic sea creature. Her bitter, twisted face leaned uncomfortably close to mine as she spat, "You've had it entirely too easy, Jane. All your life, I've never understood what you thought was so special about you. You expect everything to just fall into your lap as it always has. Well, no more. I will be making life here at River Oaks very unpleasant for you, from here on out. How would you like to go to your death-sleep one morning only to wake up with the full sun shining on you because I've thrown open all the curtains?"

"You can't." I laughed. "You're not strong enough to move objects yet. It took Aunt Jettie months to figure it out. And by the time you do, I'll have figured out some sort of exorcism ritual to toss your flat, disembodied ass out of my house!"

With that last syllable, the door behind me suddenly gave way. Grandma Ruthie's spectral form dissipated as the shower steam billowed out of the doorway. I flopped back against the fallen door, my head striking the wood with a dull thud.

"Ow!"

Gabriel and Jamie were standing over me with crowbars in their hands and confused expressions on their faces.

"Aw, man!" Jamie cried, throwing his crowbar down in disgust.

"Explain," I said, arching my eyebrow at him.

"Gabe said we could kick the door down if we couldn't pry it loose from the hinges," he grumbled. "I was really looking forward to it."

"Well, why don't you go down to the root cellar and kick through a cabinet door," I told him. "There should be plenty of the old ones left over from the kitchen remodel."

"Really?" He beamed at me before scampering down the stairs. "Thanks!"

"Do you really think encouraging wanton destruction is the best way to foster him into a mature, responsible vampi—*umhpf!*" Gabriel exclaimed as I launched myself at him, throwing my arms around him. "Jane, what's the matter?"

"Grandma Ruthie is here with us," I whispered, knowing that in all likelihood, Grandma's invisible self was hovering somewhere in the room, watching the havoc she was wreaking.

"Oh, sweetheart, of course she's still here with us. I know the two of you didn't part on the best terms, but you'll always carry your memories of your grandmother with you. The fond memories will outshine the bad."

"No, I'm not stuck in the depression phase, Gabriel. I'm saying Grandma Ruthie is *here* with us, haunting the house. She was in the bathroom with me just now, basically declaring open war against us if we don't move out. I sent Jamie away because I didn't want to scare him."

"The same boy who wanted to watch the *Saw* marathon the other night?"

"Enjoying exorbitant movie violence isn't the same as knowing there's an angry septuagenarian poltergeist hanging around the house."

"What do you want to do?" Gabriel asked.

"Well, I don't want her in the house, that's for sure. Do you think Dick knows a guy who could do an exorcism?"

"Of course he does," Gabriel said. "Whether that will involve paying his guy with a case of stolen car batteries, that's the real question. I'll call him. Why don't you get dressed and go to your mother's? I'll stay here with Jamie and try to sort this out."

"I wish you were going with me. You've made this whole process so much easier," I said, kissing him deeply. He gave me a quizzical smile. "Hey, you're forgetting how many grandparents I've buried. Even with the haunting issues—comparatively, this has been a cakewalk."

"I wish I could go with you, too."

I bit my lip and stifled a giggle. "I would believe you're only saying that to be nice, but I am leaving you here with an undead teenager and a dead senior citizen."

"I'm stowing away in your car."

I slipped into the black pencil skirt and pewter-colored cardigan I'd picked for the funeral "after-party." I was still strapping on my black heels when I came out onto the porch to find Jamie doing scissor kicks through a series of cabinet doors he'd set against the foundation of the house. I shook my head at him, feeling a rush of genuine maternal bewilderment.

"If I catch you buying ninja stars from Dick, we're going to have a problem."

Jamie grinned up at me and, without looking, toed a door up from the ground and punched through it, midair. His enthusiasm for destruction was contagious. I barely contained a snicker as I accused him of being a show-off.

Hearing a faint engine noise in the distance, Jamie and I turned to see a black pickup roll down the driveway, spitting dust and gravel in its wake. Instinctively, I moved closer to my childe, positioning myself between him and the unknown driver. Jamie seemed mesmerized by the truck as it moved toward us. I cast out my senses, and I could feel the chaotic tumble of red, angry images. Whoever was in that car wanted to rip me to shreds.

"Do you know who that is?" I asked quietly as I took off my heels. I'd learned from experience that trying to fight in pumps got you nowhere.

Jamie's mouth flapped open like a guppy's. The passenger door popped open, and I saw Jamie's mother jump out. I saw now why Jamie was so paralyzed by the approach of the truck. Hell, seeing the look on Rosie Lanier's face, I was a little afraid.

Apparently, Ophelia had informed Jamie's parents who had sired him.

I remembered Rosie Lanier as one of those impeccably dressed moms who managed to traverse a muddy soccer field without dirtying her Naturalizers. Her once carefully maintained mane of blond was dull and stringy, sticking to her red, blotchy face. It looked as if she hadn't removed her mascara in days. And as she stormed across my lawn and lunged at me, I could see that not only were her shoes muddy, but they didn't match.

"How could you?" she demanded, slapping me across the face. "How could you do that to him?"

My cheek stung from the impact, but I accepted it. I was inclined to think that I deserved to be hit, whether I'd saved her son or not. I couldn't bring myself to lift my hand to stop her, even as she shook me so hard my earrings clattered to the gravel.

This was just not my day. Night. Whatever.

"You killed my son!" she screamed, rearing back for another blow. Mr. Lanier stepped out of the truck. He was staring at Jamie, watching his son with a mixture of horror and uncertainty. I was yanked inside his head before I could stop myself. His thoughts were a dizzying tidal wave of love, horror, relief, regret, and overwhelming fear. He'd never thought he would see his son alive again, and, well, he wasn't really, but he was moving and talking and staring right at them. And while he wanted to run to him and throw his arms around Jamie, he was struck still by fear. Would Jamie hurt them? Try to bite them? He knew that I was a vampire and that I'd never hurt anyone. But did that mean that his son was safe? Should he be moving closer to protect Rosie from us?

At this point, I wanted someone to protect us from Rosie.

Gabriel came rushing out of the house just as Rosie backhanded me.

"Mom, stop!" Jamie cried, grabbing at Rosie's wrists.

"Rosie, please," Mr. Lanier said softly, stepping closer.

Mrs. Lanier shook off Jamie's hold. He let her shove him away as she seethed. "You killed my boy, you monster!"

"Mrs. Lanier, I'm so sorry. I didn't have a choice."

"Don't you talk to me about choice, you murdering bitch!"

As she stalked closer to me, Gabriel stepped between us and took hold of the arm that she was swinging at me. "You need to calm down, ma'am."

"Hey!" Jeff yelled. "Get your hands off my wife!"

"Gabriel, go inside," I said in a low, even tone. He hesitated, but I leveled a "don't argue" gaze at him. "I can handle this myself."

"I'll be right inside," he said. He looked toward Mrs. Lanier and added, "Watching."

"Mom—Mom, I'm standing right here!" Jamie cried. "Can you at least look at me?"

"Mrs. Lanier, you've known me since I was a little girl. Do you honestly think I would have hurt Jamie? Would I have bitten him if it wasn't absolutely necessary?"

"I don't know who you are since you became this *thing*!" she shouted at me.

"This thing is just like your son. Jamie's the same sweet kid he always was, just a little different now. You have an amazing opportunity here. You almost lost your son, but you can still talk to him. You can still hold him. And tell him you love him. Can you honestly say that you don't want that?"

"I don't know!" his mother shouted.

"You don't know?" Jamie and I chorused.

"What do you mean, you don't know?" Jamie demanded. "I'm your son!"

"You're a vampire," she shot back. "You drink *blood*. You're dangerous. We weren't even allowed to know where you were until today, 'for our own protection.' Did you think we were going to bring you home with us? Did you think we'd let you near your sister?"

And by the look on Jamie's face, I realized that yes, Jamie did expect to be taken home. Even though we'd explained that he was staying with us for the time being, he'd expected to go home with his parents. And he couldn't comprehend that it wasn't going to happen that night. It might never happen.

Suddenly, I realized that my mother was not so bad.

"Mom," Jamie said, his voice dangerously close to a sob as he stepped forward and took her hand. "Please!"

"You stay away from us!" she yelled, stepping back toward the truck.

"You can't just cut him off like that!" I exclaimed.

She yanked the truck door open. "I can do anything I need to do to protect my family."

"He's your son!" I cried.

Rosie slammed the truck door, but Jeff gave Jamie one last sad look. Quietly, he said, "Our son is dead."

The engine roared to life, and the truck thundered back out of the driveway. I watched the taillights dim in the distance, mesmerized by the fading color. Jamie sat down on the porch steps with a thud. Although he was naturally quite pale, his face seemed ashy gray.

"Well, I don't have to worry about school anymore," he said. "Or baseball or college."

"I'm so sorry."

He sighed, running a hand through his hair. It was a manly, though weary, gesture, and he might have pulled it off, if not for the faint bloody smudges of vampire tears around his eyes.

"It's OK to be upset, Jamie. There's nothing wrong with being hurt when your family rejects you. And it could have been worse. Gabriel's family tied him to a tree and left him out for the sun."

"Yeah, I guess."

"My mom keeps trying to force-feed me pot pie," I added.

"What's wrong with that?"

"Have I not mentioned the 'solid foods make us vomit' thing?" I asked, cringing. "There's a whole thing with our enzymes—well, a lack of enzymes. The bottom line is that all human food will now taste like wet dirt and gym socks to you."

"I've been too thirsty to think about it," he said, his brow furrowed. "But now it makes a lot more sense that you don't have any food in the house . . . Well, this day just keeps getting better and better."

I smiled at him sympathetically. "It's OK. You know, you've adjusted to this new life pretty well, considering. You haven't had a big freak-out moment. I had several when I was first turned. You haven't tried to run away. You haven't tried to attack a bus full of nuns. As your sire, I'm very proud of you."

He groaned. "What is your deal with the busload of nuns?"

"It's an interesting visual," I said, shrugging and pulling him to his feet. "Come on, we'll go inside, and I'll warm you up a bottle of blood."

"What about your mom? Weren't you supposed to go over there tonight?"

"I'll call her and tell her I can't make it. She'll be fine."

Unfortunately, Rosie Lanier managed to call my mother before I did. Mama took time out of her busy grieving schedule to call me and yell like I haven't heard since that time she found the belly-button ring I'd sported for a grand total of three weeks in college.

"Oh, Jane, how could you?" Mama cried, so loudly that I had to pull the phone away from my ear. "You were doing so well, not eating people."

"I didn't eat him, Mama, I was saving his life. It was either this, or he was dead. It was the same sort of situation I was in, injured and not likely to get medical attention in time. Jamie asked me to turn him, just like I asked Gabriel to turn me. Would you have rather Gabriel just left me alone to die because he was afraid of upsetting you?"

"No, honey, you know that. It's just—Oh, how am I going to face Rosie?" she fretted. "This is so much worse than that time Jamie threw that water pistol at your head and left you with that little divot in your eyebrow."

The aforementioned dented eyebrow winged up to my hairline. I'd completely forgotten about that. Jamie's mom had made him pay for my emergency-room deductible with his piggy-bank savings and birthday money. But he never pitched another tantrum while I was babysitting him. I was so bringing that up later.

Mama's insistent voice jerked me out of my thoughts. "Aren't you worried about what people will think?"

"When have I ever worried about what people will think?" I asked.

"That was before you owned a business that depended on the goodwill of your neighbors."

Dang it, she made a good point. My vampire and werewolf customers wouldn't care much about my emergency sire status, but a sudden exodus of walk-in human customers would hurt business. I would have to talk to Andrea about increasing our online sales presence, just in case.

"I'll be fine, I promise."

"Well, what does Gabriel think of all this?" she demanded.

"He's fine with it," I said, my voice rising to an octave only Fitz could hear. From across the kitchen, Gabriel gave me a sardonic little frown.

"Honey, you have to be careful. You're in a very delicate stage in your relationship right now. You're living together. Gabriel's finding out about all of your annoying little habits."

A little huff of outrage escaped my mouth. "What annoying little habits?"

"You're discovering things about each other every day, not all of them good. Most of them not good," Mama continued without pause. "And you're not married, so Gabriel practically has an escape hatch built into the back door. And then you add an attractive younger man to your household—he's practically an adorable baby bird with a broken wing. This is going to add stress to your already fragile relationship."

"Fragile?"

"It's like you're trying to chase Gabriel away." Mama sighed. "You're not getting any younger, you know, honey."

"I'm not getting any older, either." I snorted.

"You know what I mean!" she exclaimed. "It's like you're trying to sabotage your relationship. Don't you want to get married? Don't you want to make a commitment to Gabriel?"

And suddenly, we were right back to the sort of conversation human Jane would have had with her mother. Obviously, Grandma Ruthie's death had sent Mama into a regressive tailspin.

"Actually, I'm not worried about making a commitment to Gabriel, because we're already engaged. Have been for a couple of weeks now. 'K 'bye!"

I hung up the phone, despite Mama's overjoyed shrieks, and banged my head against the countertop.

"I'm going to kill Ophelia for this. I don't care how many intimidating quips she throws at me. Her adolescent ass is mine."

A word about romantic relationships between sires and their children. That word is "complicated."

—*Siring for the Stupid:*
A Beginner's Guide to Raising Newborn Vampires

For the record, exorcisms are not as easy to perform as you would think.

For one thing, when you cast a spirit out of the house, you have to be very careful to name a specific spirit, or you could bar other ghosts, namely Mr. Wainwright and Aunt Jettie, from ever coming near the property again. And second, if you do the rite with enough conviction, you can cast those spirits into the next plane whether they're ready to move on or not. So, in other words, if I messed with forces I didn't understand, I could accidentally send my most cherished relative to that big University of Kentucky basketball game in the sky.

Researching the various ways to evict my lifeless freeloader gave me something to think about, besides the gigantic pile of wedding-planning books Mama had left on my front porch that afternoon.

The Vegas route was looking better and better.

I already knew a little bit about ghosts, thanks to my experiences with Mr. Wainwright and Aunt Jettie. For instance, spirits are not confined to specific places. They can wander as far as their energy can take them. Aunt Jettie had always had the energy of a hyperactive kindergartner at naptime, so it was no wonder that it took her six days after the passing of her sister to touch down finally at River Oaks. Since Grandma Ruthie's spectral presence had been popping up all over the house and generally making a nuisance of herself, I wasted no time in breaking the bad news to her.

Aunt Jettie responded by cackling. "Oh, sweetie, I know!" she crowed. "That's where I've been the last few days. All of Ruthie's exes got together as soon as they heard, and they've been throwing a party like you wouldn't believe down at the cemetery."

"Nice," I muttered as Mr. Wainwright shared a commiserating glance with me and shook his head at my dead aunt's doing the cha-cha around the parlor. Gabriel and Jamie appeared in the doorway. Gabriel chuckled at Jettie's antics, but Jamie, who didn't quite understand why there were transparent people in the living room, rolled his eyes and went to the kitchen for a bottled blood.

Aunt Jettie stopped two-stepping long enough to smirk at me. "There are a quite a few men around this town who have been waiting for this day for a while now, Jane."

"So, if you knew Grandma Ruthie was here, why did you stay away for so long?" I demanded.

Aunt Jettie's misty form stopped in its tracks. I would say that her face went pale, but ghosts pretty much corner the market in pale. I guess spirits turn sort of bluish-gray when they're shocked to the point of vomiting ectoplasm. "That's not funny, Jane."

"Oh, I'm not laughing. Grandma Ruthie has decided that she's going to haunt me out of the house."

"Oh, hell, no. Ruthie!" Jettie yelled. "You get your skinny ass down here!"

I waited, but Ruthie didn't respond.

"Ruth Ann Early, I'm calling you! Don't pretend you don't hear me!"

"Can she just ignore her?" I asked Mr. Wainwright, who nodded sagely.

"Absolutely. We don't have to answer one another," Mr. Wainwright said. "Though certain humans with necromantic or medium abilities can call upon the dead and compel them to answer, spirits do not have any authority over one another."

"Though it's pretty damn rude for someone who claims to be such a paragon of good manners!" Jettie yelled, glaring at the ceiling.

The windows and the china-cabinet doors began swinging back and forth. A clay handprint I'd made Jettie in third grade tumbled from a shelf and shattered. Gabriel crossed the room, prepared to protect me from flying objets d'art. Jamie came rushing back into the living room.

"The fridge door came open and smacked me in the face," he said indignantly. The purpling bruise on his forehead was already receding, but I could tell that Jamie was more afraid than hurt.

"Does it seem odd that she's advancing so quickly?" Gabriel asked. "At this point, most spirits haven't accepted their passing yet. Doesn't it take weeks to build up this kind of kinetic energy?"

"Well, she always did succeed by being a pain in the ass while she was alive. Why not now?" Jettie called out.

There was an increased burst of activity. The curtains flapped like linen flames leaping from the windows. The cabinet door slammed against the wall so hard that the glass shattered. Figurines danced on the trembling shelves. And then, suddenly, nothing. Absolute quiet. Jamie seemed to relax instantly at my side, mirroring my movements like a nervous puppy.

"That hit a nerve," Jettie said nastily.

"What happened?" I asked. "Why did it die out so suddenly?"

"I would say her tank ran out of gas, so to speak," Mr. Wainwright said. "You said she appeared to you before, Jane? That she was able to speak to you for several minutes? She managed to seal a door shut? She made you uncomfortable by changing the atmosphere of the room?" When I nodded, he said, "For a new spirit, that would take a lot of energy. I would imagine she will be quiet again for a few days after this display."

"It explains why we hadn't heard from her again until now," I mused. "So, she's just lurking around in the ether, watching us and saving up her energy?"

"Essentially," Mr. Wainwright responded while Jamie declared that it was "über-creepy."

"I have a few books on the subject at the shop."

I had the urge to kiss Mr. Wainwright on top of his balding, insubstantial head. "Of course you do. Any chance she could decapitate a deer and leave the head on my front porch?" I asked. They gave me twin expressions of confusion and concern. "Probably not. Hey, can't you just kick her out of the house?"

Jettie grinned at me. "You mean, a ghost fight?"

"It's the opportunity you've been waiting for all of your life."

"It doesn't work like that, honeybunch," she said, her vaporous white hand caressing my cheek like a cool breeze.

"But you touch objects around the house all the time," I insisted. "And you and Mr. Wainwright touch each other in ways I don't even want to think about." Beside me, Jamie shuddered.

"Yes, but I choose to touch those objects. I choose to allow my energy to interact with Gilbert's."

"Hold on a second," I said, holding up my hand. "Deleting that mental image from my memory . . . and done. Please continue."

Jettie sighed at my emotional immaturity and said, "If I took a swing at Ruthie, she'd just let that punch flow through her like water. And the same goes if she tried to hit me. We'd just be swinging back and forth until the end of time. And as much fun as that might be, I don't want to devote my afterlife to a catfight with your grandma."

"Oh, fine," I grumbled halfheartedly.

She crossed her scrawny arms over her chest and gave me her best impression of a stern look. "Now that the excitement is over, would you mind telling me who this handsome fellow is and what the hell you're doing wearing an engagement ring?"

"I ask myself that, too," Jamie muttered. I smacked him on the back of the head while Gabriel glared.

"Aunt Jettie, you remember Jamie Lanier. Jamie had a little accident a while back, and I had to turn him. He's staying here with us until he learns the vampiric ropes," I said, condensing the tale considerably. Jamie shot me a grateful glance, as if he was glad not to have to live the whole tragic mess again. He gave Auntie Jettie a winsome, though fanged, smile. She winked right back at him.

"And the ring?" Mr. Wainwright demanded.

"Oh, we're engaged," Gabriel said, his tone playfully dismissive.

Aunt Jettie squealed loudly enough to make those of us with superhearing clutch at our ears. She threw herself at me, attempting a hug without concentrating, and went through me. I shuddered against the clammy "got into the shower too soon" sensation. "I'm so happy! Oh, Gabriel, honey, I told you she'd say yes eventually!"

"I just had to wear her down," Gabriel conceded.

"Well, I'm just as pleased as I can be," Jettie crowed, sitting down on the couch as Mr. Wainwright's ghostly form hovered near and bussed a frosty path across my cheek. Jettie demanded all of the details of how Gabriel "wore me down." She cooed and "awwed" appropriately over Gabriel's choice of proposal mediums, while Jamie rolled his eyes and made little "cracking the whip" noises under his breath.

"You do realize that I'm sitting right here, yes? That I can, in fact, hear you?" Gabriel asked him.

Jamie nodded. "Yeah, pretty much."

Gabriel growled. "Look, you—"

"Guys, not right now, all right?" I sighed. "I can only handle so much family dysfunction in one evening. Grandparent hauntings trump irritable male vampire posturing, hands down."

"I think Jane could use some air. Dealing with Ruthie always did take the wind out of her sails. Why don't you two go for a nice little walk, while we get to know Jamie? We'll pop over if there's any trouble."

Jamie seemed distinctly uncomfortable at being left alone with two dead strangers. "Um . . ."

"Sweetheart, I hate to break it to you, but you're the closest thing I'm going to get to a great-grandchild," Aunt Jettie said as Jamie awkwardly settled next to her. "You'd better get used to me. Besides, I can give you all of the dirt on your dear sire. Humiliations galore."

Jamie rubbed his hands together in gleeful anticipation.

"Oh, yeah, well, when we get back, we can talk about my dented eyebrow," I retorted as Gabriel pulled me from the room. Jamie blanched. "That's right, Mama reminded me of the water-gun incident. Vengeance will be mine, Lanier!"

Gabriel dragged me out the front door, toward a path through the woods to the old cow pond. The words "cow pond" may not evoke images of the world's most romantic spot. But with the night birds chirping and the stars winking softly overhead, it was a pretty pleasant place. Gabriel demanded all of the details of the water-gun incident. He was simultaneously entertained and indignant on my behalf.

"Your childe should have more respect for you, Jane, even more so if he damaged your head in his human life," he chided.

"I think we can agree that my head was bound for damage, with or without Jamie's help," I retorted.

"You know what I mean. Your guilt has kept you from being strict with Jamie. You're trying too hard to be his friend, not his guide through his perilous first year as a vampire."

"Have you been reading Jolene's parenting magazines again?"

"Yes, and that doesn't mean that what I'm saying is untrue. You need to keep a firmer hand with Jamie."

"Oh, like you kept with me?" I snorted.

"That was different," he insisted.

"How?"

"Well, my interest in you was romantic. I didn't want to push you away, though, in the end, I guess I did that anyway. If anything, you should learn from my mistakes as a sire, not repeat them."

"Look, I know it's been different since Jamie moved in. I know it's an adjustment. We just have to make the best of it. Sure, Jamie can be an annoying, hormonal, self-centered, stubborn, lazy, sarcastic . . ."

"Where are you going with this?"

I frowned. "I'm not entirely sure. I know that deep down, he's a nice person, but he does the most ridiculous, thoughtless, boneheaded crap. He pulls this whole 'Oh, you can't be mad at me because I'm winsome and adorable' thing. Sometimes I honestly think I'm going to kill him. It's just so freaking dysfunctional. He wants me to take care of him, but he resents my treating him like a child. He's scared of growing up, but he clearly doesn't want me taking care of him. I'm having a really hard time finding the line to walk here. And the last thing I need is you chiming in, telling me that the little progress I've made isn't healthy. Can we just not talk about this right now? Can we enjoy the fact that we're together, out of the house? I miss being alone with you, having you all to myself."

Gabriel looked the slightest bit ashamed and pressed a kiss at the corner of my mouth. "You miss being able to have sex in the living room."

"During which I am alone with you," I said.

He chuckled. "Think of this as a premarital cooling-off period. We've been living together for a while. Having Jamie around keeps us from taking each other for granted."

I stopped in my tracks. *Cooling-off period?* What were we? That sounded like something you did for frenzied gun-shop customers or couples mired in divorce mediation. It did not sound like the foundation for lifelong marital bliss. I tugged at the hem of my shirt and kicked off my shoes. "Oh, screw this, now we have to have sex."

"What, here?" he asked, motioning to the grassy, leaf-strewn ground, which, I had to admit, didn't look like the ideal spot for a tryst.

I pushed his shirt over his head and yanked at his belt. "Yes! I have had it with teenagers and unstable dead family members. We deserve a little time to ourselves. Naked."

Gabriel cleared his throat as I started shimmying out of my jeans. "But isn't it a bit . . . exposed?"

"Yes, which means that we probably have a maximum of ten minutes before someone figures out that we're actually trying to enjoy ourselves, so they must put an immediate stop to it . . . so drop your pants," I commanded. His eyebrows bobbed. "Sorry, I know this isn't very romantic."

He bit his bottom lip, the upper quirking into a dirty little grin. "Actually, it's working for me."

I barely had time to get out a laugh before he had both tails of my shirt in his hands. There was pressure at my shoulders and the sound of fabric rending. I looked down to see him holding the scraps of my shirt in his hands. He smirked and shrugged. "If you get to be bossy and demanding, I get to be bossy and demanding, too."

I hooked my foot around his ankle and shoved him back, straddling him as he landed. He threaded his hand up my side, plucking at the nipple before stroking my collarbone. He gasped as I ground down in little circles. He moaned and bucked up under me, sending me sprawling to the ground. He slid over my back, pressing kisses along my spine as he raised me to my knees. He knelt behind me, tugging my panties down.

His hand skimmed around my hip, pulling me back against him. He ground into my ass, cupping his fingers around my pulsing warmth.

He nipped and bit at my neck. I vaguely registered the sound of a zipper lowering. He guided his head between my folds and surged up as his fangs sank in to my neck. I cried out at the sudden sensation of fullness, of being stretched and molded to him as he thrust inside me. I sat back, balancing against his thighs as his hands roamed my stomach, my breasts, settling over my throat as he pulled the blood there. I pulled his wrist across my mouth, caressing it against my cheek before sinking my fangs into his skin.

Love. Full. Love. Love. Love. Mate. Happy.

This was pretty typical of Gabriel's thought stream during sex. The irony was that this was the only time I was privy to those thoughts, so my only window into my erudite mate's soul was when he was reduced to a horny, happy, monosyllabic mess.

He pushed my shoulders forward until my palms rested on the dirt. He wound my hair around his fist, tilting his head to the side so he could continue to feed. The other hand snaked between my thighs to stroke and tease.

My whole being seemed to tense up as he timed his hand, his fangs, and his thrusts in tandem. When one sensation struck, the next was on its heels. I was unbearably full, the coil of winding pleasure tensing inside me until I cried out.

He withdrew his fangs, licking at the wounds gently, before sinking them in again. I arched up, screaming. He shuddered against me, his fingers threading through my hair to drag me closer as he released. I sank to the earth with a sigh, his weight settling pleasantly on top of me. Breathing deeply, I pressed my cheek to the cool ground, enjoying the tickling sensation of the blades of grass against my skin. I closed my eyes, winding Gabriel's arm around me as I listened to the cicadas chirp and the mosquitoes drone. I could have very easily, and happily, fallen asleep right there. But there was an unaccompanied teenager in my house . . . and leaf bits sticking where leaf bits just didn't belong. I smiled, bussed Gabriel on the cheek, and stretched my arms over my head in a languid "holding on to the last moments of peace we'll have in who knows how long" gesture.

"You know, I have to say, for our first 'outdoor adventure,' I think we performed admirably." I sighed.

"This isn't our first outdoor adventure," he said, trailing his fingertips across my collarbone.

"I think I'd remember the leaf-bit issue if we'd done this before," I countered.

"We've had sex outside before, behind your shop," he reminded me. "It was a semi-enclosed area, but I think it should still count."

"Hmm. That does count. You're right."

"I usually am when it comes to reminiscing about sexual encounters with you," he said, smirking. "Because I remember every. Single. One." He punctuated each word with a biting kiss across my throat.

"Really?" I drawled.

"Vividly. It's hard to forget a woman who manages to seduce you while spouting odd literary trivia and anatomically specific threats."

"Still think having Jamie around is going to force a 'cooling-off period'?" I asked him smugly as I wrestled my way back into my bra.

He helpfully adjusted the strap over my shoulder and snapped the clasp for me. "Yes. Or it could drive an insurmountable wedge between us, so that we end up heaving the bric-a-brac at each other—*uff*." He chuckled as I elbowed him in the chest.

"That was one time!" I laughed as he slid his arms around me and kissed my hair. I shrugged him off, grinning cheekily as I plucked grass and leaf bits from his hair. "And it wasn't bric-a-brac. It was a book . . . Wait, are we referring to our first fight or our last fight?"

"It's sad that you have to ask," he said, swiping at the mud on my cheek.

"You throw one little paperback at a guy, and he gets all sensitive."

He retorted, "It was the *Lord of the Rings* trilogy! In hardcover!"

Somewhere in the distance, I heard a *ping*.

"What the?" I turned toward the noise, only to have

Gabriel wrap his arms around me and throw me to the ground. I heard his breath explode from his lungs as if he'd been punched in the back. I felt an odd sharp object poking me in the chest. I looked down, unable to comprehend the red flower blossoming on Gabriel's chest.

There was an arrowhead poking through Gabriel's shirt.

7

Do not allow your childe to subsist on bottled blood
alone. Newborn vampires need the nutritional
support of live blood, or at least donor blood if the
childe has qualms about violence. A bottled-only
diet would be like allowing a human kindergartner
to live on Jujubes and Mountain Dew.

—*Siring for the Stupid:*
A Beginner's Guide to Raising Newborn Vampires

"Ow," Gabriel said dully, as if he'd just stubbed his
toe. He slumped against me and passed out.

Seeing the red-tinged grain of the wooden shaft
sticking out of his skin, I felt a surge of panic. Did an
arrow count as a stake? I realized that the arrow was
lodged in the wrong side of his chest. He'd been shot
about four inches too far to the right to do any permanent
damage. But obviously, it still hurt like a bitch, because
Gabriel was completely unconscious, the skin around his
lips white and tense.

Fighting down my panic, I closed my eyes, focused
my senses, and opened them to search for any signs of
a human or a vampire nearby. There was no scent. No

movement in the distance. I could hear a skittering heartbeat, moving away from me quickly. I could hear the faint crackle of tree limbs as the human archer ran from the havoc he'd caused. His mind was racing, so scattered and hyped up that I couldn't grasp at a single thought stream.

Should I chase him or help Gabriel? Considering how much Gabriel was bleeding and the likelihood of being skewered myself if I caught the human, I decided to stay. I cupped my hand over the wound, thick red blood welling around my fingers and the arrow as I applied pressure.

I thought back to all of the bad Kevin Costner movies I'd seen involving dancing with wolves and Robin Hoods without the proper accent. When the hapless sidekick was skewered, Kevin would snap off the feathered end of the arrow and pull it out. I gently pulled Gabriel toward me and saw that there was no traditional feathered end to the arrow. It was a plain old sportsman's arrow, like most of the deer hunters in the area would use.

I opened Gabriel's shirt and saw that the flesh around the protruding arrowhead was withered and crackling. A reaction to the wood?

I reached over his shoulder and snapped off the notched end as close to his back as possible. Waking, Gabriel winced, leaning heavily against me.

"Ow," he said again, sounding more annoyed. I took this as a good sign.

I wrapped my fingers around the arrowhead. "I'm not going to lie, this is going to hurt."

"What?"

Without further preamble, I yanked hard. Gabriel yelped as the arrow slid free and clattered to the ground. The jolt of pain seemed to help him focus. His eyes narrowed, snapping to my face.

"Someone shot me with an arrow!" he exclaimed.

A nervous laugh bubbled up through my chest. "Yeah, sweetie, that's why there was a narrow wooden cylinder sticking out your back."

"Well, now that the initial panic is over, I find I am really pissed about it!" he grumbled.

I laughed, running my hand over my face. "Let's get you into the house before he tries it again, OK?"

"You know, this is your fault, Ms. Spontaneous Outdoor Sex," he grumped as I hauled him to his feet.

"Actually, you're right. I should have known better," I admitted, tucking his arm around my shoulders and supporting his weight as we walked. "Nothing good comes from us having sex outside. I just now recall Taseing you after the shop incident and then creepy Jeanine sending me pictures of our activities afterward."

"We just need to do more thorough perimeter checks from now on," he muttered.

"Why are you limping?" I demanded. "The arrow didn't hit you in the leg."

He stopped, his shift in weight pulling me to a halt, too. "I don't know. It just seems like the thing to do after you've received an arrow wound."

I sighed as he straightened his gait and walked normally. "You are so the guy for me."

The wound had closed by the time we reached the

front door. Gabriel kept repeating, "Who the hell shoots an arrow at someone? Doesn't anyone have any respect for the recent advancements in firearms?"

"What happened?" Jamie called as we passed the parlor door. Jettie had him ensconced on the couch with a bottle of Faux Type O, playing a video game while she showed him my high school yearbooks. Where was the loyalty? Honestly.

"Just a little mishap with a stray arrow," I said through gritted teeth as I steered Gabriel down the hall to the guest bath, where we kept the medical supplies.

Jamie dropped his controller and followed us. The potential to see real carnage was more appealing than killing digital zombies, or whatever he was doing.

"Do you think it could have been a hunter?" I asked Gabriel. "They've strayed onto my land before. I try not to get too grumpy with them, because, well, they're armed."

"We could go look in the woods," Jettie offered, appearing at my elbow. "See if there's a suspicious character hanging around." I nodded, and my ghostly friends disappeared through the front wall of the house.

"It's nowhere near bow season," Jamie said.

"So, you're familiar with bow-hunting, are you?" Gabriel asked, his tone suspicious.

I smacked his good arm. "If you're going to be accusatory, at least man up about it. Jamie, did you shoot Gabriel in the back with a bow and arrow?"

"What, am I going to get sent to time-out if I did?"

"That's not really an answer," Gabriel noted.

"No, OK, I didn't shoot you. I was showing Jettie how to play *Madden NFL 11* on Wii."

"When did we get a Wii?" I asked.

"This is what's disturbing to you in this situation? Heretofore unaccounted-for gaming equipment?" Gabriel demanded.

I shrugged. "How am I supposed to take away privileges if I don't even know what privileges he has?"

"Damn it, I knew I shouldn't have told you!" Jamie exclaimed.

"Can we focus the conversation on my nearly being killed by a flying stake?" Gabriel asked, his pallor getting more ashen by the second.

"Jamie, could you grab Gabriel a couple of packets of donor blood from the fridge? Dick brought some by a while ago," I asked, pulling out my cell phone. "I'm calling Dick."

"Jane. Wait."

"Gabriel, I know you're probably kind of embarrassed. I'm not sure what to do here. Of everyone we know, I'd say it's most likely that Dick has survived something like this."

"I don't feel very well," Gabriel said, his voice strained as moisture pooled at the corners of his eyes.

Jamie scoffed. "I thought we don't get sick. Aw, come on, Gabe, tears? I'm gonna find your man card and rip it—"

Suddenly, blood was streaming down Gabriel's cheeks. Our tears had traces of blood in them, leaving rusty pink streaks on our faces if we cried. Gabriel looked as if he was starring in a PSA about the Ebola virus.

"Jamie, shut up," I commanded in a tone even Jamie couldn't argue with. "Gabriel, what's wrong? What hurts?"

Gabriel opened his mouth to answer, and a tidal wave of dark crimson poured out of his mouth and onto my hands. Jamie shrieked and scrambled back. I let Gabriel sink to the hallway floor and cradled his head in my lap. He coughed, spraying red streaks across an ancient family carpet.

Grandma Ruthie's tinny, disembodied voice fluttered at my left ear, screeching, "Don't let him bleed on my rug!"

I ignored her, concentrating on the blood that seemed to be seeping from Gabriel's very pores. I sniffed at the arrow wound. The skin was starting to re-form around it, although blood had started to gush in waves from the puncture, soaking through his shirt and seeping onto my legs. I'd almost forgotten that Gabriel was still holding on to the arrow. I took it from his hand carefully. It smelled funny, bitter and metallic, with an undertone of sickly sweetness. The wood seemed spongy and weak, as if it had been submerged in water for a while.

"This is what you get when you lie down with a monster." Grandma Ruthie sighed at my ear, clucking her tongue. "Nothing but blood and death and ruined carpet."

"Shut the hell up, old woman! You laid down with more men than I ever could!" I screamed as Gabriel retched against me, spilling blood over my jeans. "Gabriel, please, tell me what you need me to do."

Jamie was kneeling beside me now, holding Gabriel's legs as he thrashed and twitched. "Do we call an ambulance?"

I shook my head, bit my wrist, and pressed it to Gabriel's mouth. "We have to flush out his system with new blood. It will help him heal. Same thing happened when I got silver-maced last year. Get my cell from my purse. Call Dick, tell him we need blood, any kind he has. *Now!*"

When Gabriel didn't draw from the wound, I opened his mouth and dripped the blood past his lips. I could hear Jamie on the phone with Dick, his young voice pitched by panic. Gabriel's eyes dropped closed, but I saw his throat working to swallow. This was a hideous feeling. The helplessness, watching as he suffered. This was what Dick had felt when I'd been sprayed last year. This was what Gabriel had felt on the side of the road when I was shot in the back and he came to my house to find me bleeding.

My blood seemed to help. Gabriel's legs stopped twitching. His fingers wrapped around my arm, holding it to his mouth. I stroked his forehead and asked Jamie for a wet cloth to clean the rust-colored tears from his cheeks. Minutes passed silently, without comments from Jamie or Grandma Ruthie. My limbs were starting to feel heavy, cold. I could feel my body functions slowing down as the blood left my veins. I tried to remember the last time I'd fed and couldn't. Clearly, my siring schedule

was a little more hectic than I'd thought. "He's going to
need more blood than what I can give him."

Jamie shrugged as if he couldn't figure out why I was
telling him this. "OK." I smacked his arm and glanced
pointedly at his wrist. "Fine. I can't believe this," he
grumbled, biting into his arm. "Ow! That hurts!"

"Be nice. I gave you my blood when you needed it." I
helped him bring Gabriel's mouth to the freely seeping
wound. This feeding was more detached, clinical. Jamie
was leaning away from Gabriel as if he was afraid that
someone would burst into the room and accuse him of
being bromantic with his grandsire.

I was momentarily sidelined, with less blood circulating around my brain, and the panic was seeping in at
the edges of my consciousness. What more could I do?
Should I call the Council? What could they do for him?
Vampires healed on their own. There were few medical
treatments for us other than blood.

Suddenly, Gabriel broke away from Jamie's arm, spew-
ing all of the blood he'd just ingested over Jamie's shoulder
and onto the floor. Jamie cursed and wiped frantically at
his clothes. Gabriel's skin was cold and gray as I pulled him
across my legs. I slid my hands down his cheeks, trying to
wipe away some of the sticky crimson from his skin. His
eyes wheeled frantically, searching the ceiling behind me.
He couldn't seem to focus on my face. I leaned close to touch
my forehead to his. His chest gurgled as he panted against
my cheek. His fingers plucked frantically at my sleeve, pulling me closer. My eyes burned with unshed tears.

"Just hold on, please?" I begged him. "We're going

to get married. I want to spend the rest of my undead life annoying the living hell out of you. I can't do that without you."

Dick and Andrea burst through the front door, blanching at the sight of Gabriel curled in my lap. Dick murmured, "It looks like a Tarantino movie in here."

Recognizing a starving vampire when she saw one, Andrea rolled up her sleeve and took my place by Gabriel. She cradled his head with a practiced air and had him latched onto her wrist before I could blink. Reluctantly moving away from him, I felt the hysteria I'd been tamping down clawing its way up my chest to my throat. My knees gave out, and Dick caught my elbows to keep me from collapsing bonelessly onto the floor like a rag doll. "Easy there, Stretch."

"I don't know what happened," I said, wiping at my wet cheeks with shaking hands as Dick led me to the couch. "We were just walking outside. We were talking, laughing, and then there was this noise, a *ping*. And Gabriel had an arrow poking out of his chest—"

I sprang off the couch and grabbed the arrow from the floor. "Dick, who do you know who might work in a lab? A hospital, blood bank. Hell, I'll take a high school chemistry teacher if they know what they're doing."

"Why? Don't you think we should focus on Gabriel right now?"

I gingerly held up the arrow fragments. He leaned over to sniff the wood and made a sour face. "I want this tested for poisons, contaminants, drugs. I want to know why Gabriel reacted this way to this arrow."

"We can be poisoned?" Andrea exclaimed. "Why didn't I know this? I think that should be in the *Guidebook* somewhere."

"I'm serious, Dick. I want to know what's wrong with that arrow," I told him.

Dick snickered. "Well, sure, I'll just scoot on down to my crime lab and fire up the gas chromatograph."

I glared at him. He grimaced. "Inappropriate humor is how I cope, Jane."

"Don't tell me you don't know a guy."

He shrugged. "I know a guy."

"Of course you do. You think you can get me results quick?"

"For a price."

"There's emergency cash in the library, stuffed inside a copy of *The Great Gatsby*. Take as much as you think you'll need." Dick lifted a brow. I squeezed his arm. "I trust you, Dick."

"Shouldn't I take my turn feeding him?" Dick asked, his forehead creased with concern for his old friend.

"I'll take another turn before we take him upstairs," I said, shaking my head. "It would be better to know what we're dealing with now. Just go."

Dick gingerly wrapped the arrow bits in a plastic kitchen baggie and told me to wash my hands, just in case whatever poison the arrow contained could be absorbed through the skin. He kissed Andrea on the top of her head as she continued to feed Gabriel, and slipped out the front door.

"You know, it's at times like this that I'm really glad I'm

friends with Dick Cheney," I said as Andrea squeezed my fingers with her free hand.

"He is handy to have around when you need favors of a secretive and dubious nature," she acknowledged.

"Honey, I don't want to know what kind of favors he does for you."

"See, you made a lame little joke," she said, nudging me. "Everything will be just fine now."

When Andrea was starting to feel woozy, we poured the donor blood Dick had brought over down Gabriel's throat. I took another turn feeding him, hoping that somehow there was enough of his own blood left in my veins that it would be like getting an infusion from a compatible donor. He finally stopped throwing it back up, which I assumed meant that he was getting better. Andrea helped me lift Gabriel and carry him upstairs. I stripped off his bloody clothes and tucked him into bed. Andrea went downstairs to work over the bloodstained carpet, which she seemed to think she could clean with some club soda. When I suggested kerosene and a match, she was horrified.

Stroking his hair back from him his gore-covered face, I pressed a kiss to his temple. Jamie came through the bedroom door with a bowl of clean water and a rag.

His expression was sheepish. "Sorry I freaked out down there. I've just never seen anything like that. I mean, I've seen horror movies, but that was . . ."

"Real life, Jamie. There's no shame in being scared. I was terrified. I'm just better at covering it up."

Jamie's brow furrowed as I cleaned Gabriel's face. "You really love him, huh? Not just the sweet 'oh, we met in high school and just couldn't seem to find someone else' sort of love, but the epic, desperate, 'move mountains and cross oceans' sort of love."

I chuckled. "I think that would be an apt description. When you realize that someone would do anything for you, even if it means separating themselves from you, risking that you'll never love them again, just to make sure you're safe and well . . . There's no coming back from that. You'll do whatever it takes to be with them. You might want to kick their ass a few times along the way. But when you find that, you don't let it go."

Jamie shuddered.

"Too mushy?" I asked.

"I'll survive."

Gabriel grumbled in his sleep and shifted against me. I bit into my wrist and let the blood drip into his mouth.

"Hey, you've got to stop doing that. You've fed him twice already. Dick said you could drain yourself dry."

"Look who's the voice of reason all of a sudden," I muttered.

"If I was the voice of reason, I would have kept you from giving Dick cash."

I laughed, an honest-to-goodness bark of sincere laughter, and he grinned at me.

"I mean, seriously, I get why you're with Gabriel, as much as it pains me to say it. He has that whole sophisticated-older-guy thing working for him. But what's with Dick? He's fun for me to hang out with because he's a total dude. But the old Jane, the Jane I knew growing up, wouldn't have looked at that guy twice."

I smiled fondly at him, because I knew he was painfully correct, and nodded to the trunk at the end of the bed. He sat down and folded his long legs under his butt, like a child waiting for story time. "Did I ever tell you about my first night out as a vampire?"

He shook his head, and I felt very remiss in my duties as a sire. Mine was a cautionary tale that should be printed and handed out as a "how-not-to" pamphlet for young vampires as they entered the undead social scene. He said, "You've mentioned something about freaking out and trying to bite Zeb."

"Well, there was that. But I'm talking about my first night *out* as a vampire, out on the town. Back when Andrea was human. She took me out to this vampire sports bar, the Cellar. It was a completely respectable, nondangerous place. So, really, we should have been fine. Andrea had a little too much to drink. I ended up pouring her into my car and running back for my purse, only to find that the bartender was getting roughed up."

"By Dick?"

"By some lowlife who thought that being a vampire was a good excuse to shake money out of food-service workers, as opposed to getting a job."

"So, it *was* Dick," he said as if I was missing his point.

I glared at him. "Would you let me tell the story?"

"Said lowlife, whose name was Walter, by the way, turned his less-than-honorable intentions toward me. We ended up brawling in the parking lot. I held my own until Walter tried to crack my skull like a walnut with his bare hands. I kicked him in the nuts. And Dick stepped in to chastise me for unsportsmanlike conduct. That's how we met."

"So, the point of this story is . . . don't go out drinking with Andrea?"

"No. Well, actually, yes. That's a pretty important life lesson. But the point of the story is, after the fight, I ended up being accused of Walter's murder. After meeting me just once, Dick was willing to speak up for me to the Council, to help me clear my name. Even though it was clearly in his interest to stay far away from any sort of law enforcement. That's just the kind of guy Dick is. Once you're his friend, there's nothing he won't do for you. And yeah, I do trust him. Because I know exactly how sneaky and underhanded he's capable of being, but he's never lied to me—even when it would have been better for him if he had. That matters."

"You're happier now, aren't you?" he asked, sort of squinting at me as if he was seeing me for the first time in a long time. "You weren't ever this . . . settled before, content, I guess would be the word. You were always sort of sad and stressed out whenever your mama would drag you to church or family stuff. I always figured it was because, well, you were with your mama."

I snorted. "You weren't wrong."

"But you were sad, as a human."

"I don't know about sad. But I was lonely. There were things in life I was missing, and I didn't even know it. My life is more now. I have more. And yeah, I had to give up some things, but in the long run, it's not so bad."

He took a sip of bottled blood. "I feel like I should be different, somehow. I never really liked baseball all that much. I mean, I was good at it, and my dad wanted me on the team, but it wasn't like I woke up in the morning excited because I got to play. And now it's not really an option, and I just don't know what I'm supposed to do with myself. But I'm scared to try anything new, in case, you know, I go all crazy and evil."

"I was afraid of that, too. But that's not really the way it works," I assured him.

"Are you the same sort of person you were when you were human?"

"That's a good question. I don't think my essential makeup has changed. I still believe in heaven and hell. I still believe that a person should do whatever they can to prevent hurting someone else. Then again, I've killed someone. I've nearly been killed myself. I've got blood . . . or dust on my hands. And that changes you. But you're so young, you were bound to change, whether you were human or vampire."

He frowned. "So, it's OK if I don't want to be Mr. All-American Jock anymore?"

I put a hand on his shoulder. "OK, but you should be warned, if you start wearing guy-liner and go all Prince of the Undead on me, I'm going to pull embarrassing mom stunts, in public. Calling you 'sweetie' in front of your peers. Discussing your showering habits and questionable stains in public. I'll put my heart and soul into your humiliation."

"Why would you do that?"

"To amuse myself. Seriously, do you pay attention when I speak?"

He rolled his eyes and ignored the potential "moming" of it all. "You think I'll be happy?"

I shrugged. "What do you want me to say? 'Be a good boy, say your prayers, eat your vegetables, and everything will turn out fine'?"

"Obviously, the vegetables are a no-go, but I wouldn't mind a little smoke blown up my shorts," he deadpanned.

I ran a hand over Gabriel's forehead. I sighed. "Say your prayers. Drink your blood. Be nice to your sire. And everything will turn out fine. Was that enough smoke?"

"Yes, thank you."

"What are sires for?"

8

Take the time to get to know your childe. What were his interests before he died? What were his hobbies? Knowing how to reward your childe goes a long way in raising him to be a responsible, nonhomicidal member of society.

—*Siring for the Stupid:*
A Beginner's Guide to Raising Newborn Vampires

I considered it a sign of how much I loved and trusted Dick that nearly twenty-four hours had passed, and I hadn't automatically assumed that he had absconded with my cash. Gabriel was resting comfortably, only waking every few hours to feed, smile weakly at me, and then fade back into sleep. Dick returned the next night. He strolled casually through the door with a cooler full of blood and made it look as if he wasn't scrambling up the stairs to check on his old friend.

I was sitting on the window seat, watching Gabriel sleep, and reading *Jane Eyre* while I wound the gray "heartstring" around my finger. Andrea was running the shop. Jamie was downstairs, considerately playing a quiet game of *Madden* on our unaccounted-for Wii with

Zeb. Jamie was chugging bottled blood as if it was getting ready to expire, but so far, he was handling his first prolonged vampire–human interaction like a champ. My ghostly surrogate grandparents were roaming the property, thoroughly upset with themselves for not being able to find any sign of the arrow-slinging hunter in the woods. It was bizarre. There wasn't a footprint or a broken twig to be found.

"My buddy at EKU says thanks for the fiver," he said, waving a manila envelope as he came through the bedroom door.

I snorted. Eastern Kentucky University was the site of the only forensic science program in the state. The idea of Dick waiting around in a college lab while a graduate student in an ironic T-shirt did our dirty work made me giggle. "Your buddy did this for five bucks?"

He smiled indulgently, kissing my head as he handed me the envelope. "Five thousand."

I closed my eyes and reminded myself that Dick had just done me a huge favor. And that I would have to replenish my "the end is nigh, run like hell" cash stash in the library.

"Was there change?" I asked. Dick smirked at me. "Never mind."

Zeb walked into the room, nursing a sore gamer's thumb. "Oh, good, I was afraid you'd already explained it to her." I shot Zeb a confused look when he gingerly sat on the foot of our bed. "What? If I miss stuff, it takes me forever to catch up."

"I'll spare you a night spent poring over that expensive, not-user-friendly report. My buddy Denny said the arrow's shaft was soaked in concentrated amounts of liquid caffeine, aspirin, and warfarin, none of which was listed on the arrow's manufacturing label."

Dick and Zeb looked at me expectantly.

"What?"

Zeb gave me a "hurry up" hand gesture that looked alarmingly mimelike. "This is normally the part where you tell us what that means. It keeps us from having to look stuff up."

"We hate looking stuff up," Dick added.

"I don't know *everything*. I'm not omniscient."

"Well, she knows what 'omniscient' means, which still puts her ahead of us." Dick snorted. "Fortunately, Denny attached a note to the report. Warfarin is an anticoagulant, once commonly used as rat poison. Large doses can cause damage to capillaries, increasing their permeability, causing diffuse internal bleeding. Combined with aspirin, which would increase the effects of the anticoagulant, plus caffeine to dilate the vessels and speed up the process. Soak a porous wooden arrow in that stuff for a few hours, fire it at an unsuspecting member of the undead community, and you've got yourself a recipe for a scary stigmata vampire. Gabe's body couldn't metabolize the blood because it was too thin. His own blood vessels were practically dissolving; it had no place to go but out. Eyes, nose, and mouth were the most convenient exit."

"Is there anything we can do for him?" I asked.

Dick shook his head. "Replacing his blood is a good

first step. The next step is fresh-frozen plasma, which I happen to have stashed in my car, and massive doses of vitamin K are another. I brought enough for all of us to take so he'll absorb it when he feeds from us. The fact that he's not rejecting the blood anymore is a good sign. Give him a day or two; he should be up and around. Have you called Ophelia?" he asked.

"Not yet. I wanted to know what exactly we were dealing with before I called," I said. "I have no doubt she will come by with her trademark sarcasm, and we'll all feel less than placated."

"You know she'll ask you who you think did this. Any clue?"

"I'm not even sure whether the happy archer was aiming for me or Gabriel. He covered me at the last minute, so the arrow could have just as easily hit me." I shook my head. "And the DMV lead was a bust. Have you heard anything about a rusted-out black sedan getting repairs at any of the local shops?"

"I put an ear out at all of the junkyards and body shops that specialize in junkers. None of them saw any car with the kind of damage that would have come from ramming Big Bertha."

"I know I said I was going to be proactive about finding who hit Jamie, but I just haven't had time. Clearly, leaving it alone for even a few days was a mistake."

"Well, it's not like you haven't had other things going on."

"No excuse," I said. "I'm not going to let this escalate like I have with all of the thundering loonies I've encountered in the past. This bullshit stops now."

I picked up my phone and dialed Ophelia's number. She didn't pick up, sending the call to a pretentious voicemail message about subjecting her consciousness to stuttering, incoherent messages that amount to nothing. I rolled my eyes and shut my phone.

"You know where Ophelia lives, right?"

He groaned. "Jane."

"Dick," I shot back in the same exasperated tone.

Dick squeezed my shoulder. "You know, I've noticed that you're OK when someone comes after you. But someone threatens your boyfriend and your dog, you go a little nuts. It's scary as hell."

"I am fiercely protective of the people . . . and canines I love," I said. "You know, that circle includes you."

"I know it, Stretch."

I gave him a pointed look, to which he responded with a cross-eyed grimace. He sighed. "I'll take you there, but if she asks, you're holding me hostage." When I laughed at him, he exclaimed, "She's scarier than you!"

There was no small amount of mockery as Dick drove me to a little two-story ranch house on County Line Road. I had always pictured Ophelia living in some super-mod, black-leather-and-chrome-filled condo. Martha Stewart could have lived in this house. There were flipping geraniums in the window boxes on the front porch.

I knew that Ophelia was going to be annoyed by my intrusion, but there was nothing to be gained from waiting. I needed to involve Ophelia now, to ask for her help before anyone else got hurt. I got out of the car and bounded up the neatly swept steps. I had raised my hand to knock on the door when it opened and swung away from my outstretched hand.

In front of me was a beautiful little girl. Her cheeks were as white and smooth as ivory. She was wearing a little red cardigan over a pleated plaid silk skirt. She was literally the girl with the golden curl, one adorable little ringlet that hung in the middle of her forehead. Her eyes were ice and fog combined, gray and cold and calculating.

I leaned back and checked the house number to make sure I was standing at the right address. I turned to ask Dick if this was his idea of a joke, but he was sitting in the car, avoiding eye contact with me.

Coward.

"Is your mommy home?" I asked, lifting an eyebrow.

"Georgie!" I heard a voice call from the rear of the house. "How many times do I have to tell you not to answer the door without me?"

That was Ophelia's voice—Ophelia sounding like an actual teenager, for once, instead of the jaded, annoyed Council official. I gawked openly at the little girl and then at Ophelia, who appeared at the door in jeans and a plain white T-shirt. It was the first time I'd seen her in an outfit that didn't feature a theme. She didn't make eye contact with me, focusing instead on the little girl, who, I now realized, did not have a pulse or breath. This wasn't a normal kindergartner. This was a tiny vampire.

"That's insulting," the little girl drawled, sounding quite bored. "I would be perfectly safe, no matter who was at the door."

"I'm more concerned for the person knocking," Ophelia said, her tone dry. "Jane, looking disheveled. What a surprise. Please stay right there without stepping inside my home."

"Ophelia, what the—?"

"Ophelia, you're being horribly rude. Where are your manners?"

"Oh, I'm used to it," I assured the little girl. "She doesn't like me very much."

"She doesn't like anyone very much," she shot back.

"Jane, this is my sister, Georgie," Ophelia said, her hand curling protectively around the girl's shoulder.

"And how old are you, Georgie?" I asked, instinctively slipping into the voice I used on the kindergarten students who visited the library.

"Old enough to be insulted by that tone of voice," the little girl deadpanned. "Ophelia said I was her sister. Do the math, woman. Do you have any deductive-reasoning skills at all? Honestly, Ophelia, is this what passes for a vampire these days? Why do the newbies always insist on treating me like one of their pwecious preschoolers? If I'm offered one more juice box, I'm going to be forced into drastic action. It will be Oslo all over again."

"Oh, Georgie, calm down." Ophelia sighed. "You barely got away with Oslo the first time. And where would you find a crate of plague rats in this day and age?"

"Are you challenging my resourcefulness?" Georgie demanded.

"Does someone need a nap?" I asked, patting her head.

"Does someone need to be defenestrated?" she retorted, whirling on me.

I have to admit that having those little china-doll eyes narrowed at me sent a chill down my spine. So I did what any sensible person would do when confronted with a miniature killing machine . . . I leaned closer and provoked her.

I smiled in that saccharine way that drove Jenny nuts. "I don't know what sort of low-rent vampires you're used to dealing with, but I know exactly what 'defenestrated' means. And if you think you're strong enough to push me out a window, bring it on, Pocket Vamp."

Georgie's lip curled up as she ground her tiny baby fangs together. The tension in her face suddenly snapped, and she turned to Ophelia.

"I like her," Georgie said as Ophelia handed her a handheld game unit. She skipped out of the room and settled on top of the kitchen table to play.

Ophelia waited for Georgie to clear the hallway and whirled on me. "Perhaps I've made the boundaries of our relationship unclear. We're not friends. We do not pop over to each other's house for a cup of sugar and gossip. If you do not walk right back out that door and forget that you ever saw Georgie, I will make your life so miserable it will make your sad spinster librarian existence a blissful memory."

I frowned, screwing up my lips while I shook my head. "Nope. I don't think you will."

She blinked incredulously, as if she thought she had heard me wrong. I smirked at her.

"Because Georgie likes me," I added. "And I get the feeling she hasn't met a lot of new people in the last couple of . . . centuries. Imagine her shock and disappointment if you dismembered the first friend she'd made since moving here."

Her face shifted from its unamused stone setting with the slightest ripple of muscles. For a split second, she actually looked defenseless and human.

"You know, I've heard a lot about you. Ophelia, the badass head of the local Council. Ophelia, the brilliant schemer. I've never heard anything about Ophelia, the undead babysitter."

"Why would I possibly share personal information with you, the vampire equivalent of Jerry Lewis? She who accidentally destroys all she touches?"

"I think you're thinking of Steve Urkel," I said. When she didn't respond, I grumbled, "Fine. If you satisfy my curiosity, I will give a full report on the latest buffoonery to befall Gabriel and me. It will help you get ahead of whatever weird-ass catastrophe is heading my way. Consider it a professional courtesy."

Ophelia pursed her lips. "It's not in Georgie's best interest, or mine, for locals to know about her. It would make both of us too vulnerable. She's well known to the international Council. But Dick's the only 'civilian' in Half-Moon Hollow who knows about her, and that's only because of our . . ."

"For the love of God, just say 'history,'" I said, shuddering.

"Fine, because of our history, Dick is one of the privileged few to have met Georgie," she said.

"I don't understand. Aren't there rules against turning children into vampires?"

She sighed and motioned for me to sit on the sweet little blue corduroy couch in the living room. I could have been sitting in any family room in any home in the Hollow. The walls were painted a soft, warm caramel color. There was a throw rug that blended the tans and the blues with a contrasting turquoise. Pictures of Georgie and Ophelia through the ages lined the walls, starting with oil paintings and working toward freshly printed photos. There was a Wii console over the TV and a neatly arranged stack of games. There were several broken controllers tossed into a nearby wastebasket, next to a half-dozen still-in-the-package replacement controllers. Apparently, Georgie got frustrated when she lost. Vampire strength and childlike impulse control must have been murder on Ophelia's Visa bill.

"I'm only telling you this because I think it will be of value to you. If you use this information to turn on me . . ."

"Yes?"

"I'm trying to come up with a description of what I'll do to you that won't give Georgie nightmares," she said, frowning. "And she saw a good part of the Salem witch trials . . . and the second season of *Desperate Housewives*."

I shuddered as Ophelia cleared her throat. "Our parents brought us over on one of the crossings just after the *Mayflower*. They always were quick to jump on bandwagons. You can't imagine the conditions on the ship. Hot, cramped—and the smell. It makes me shudder even now. At night, I would go aboveboard just to get a breath of fresh air while everybody else was asleep. And one night, this white face emerged from the shadows, and I was sure I was seeing some sort of ghost. Instead, I met my first vampire. His name was Joseph. He was nearly five hundred years old, and he wanted to see the New World. He'd stowed belowdeck in the hold, behind crates and barrels, feeding on rats to avoid being noticed. Now I realize that he must have been lonely and starving, but he didn't try to bite me. He wanted to talk to me. No one had ever really talked to me. People didn't have much use for girls back then, you know. It wasn't just 'be seen and not heard.' It was 'you have one purpose on this planet, and while you're not serving that purpose, you don't exist.' But Joseph, he was probably the most polite, most genial man I'd ever met. And every night, we talked. About the world, about the people on the boat, about my family. I never told my parents about it. I knew they'd either lock me in the brig or decide I was mad. So I kept Joseph my secret.

"There were problems almost as soon as we reached what would become Massachusetts. The land of promise and plenty was not as advertised. My family fared as well as any of the others, which was not well at all. Everyone was so sick. Food was scarce. We had to work constantly just to scratch out the barest of existences. My vampire friend hovered nearby, watching to see if I was strong enough to survive the fevers and the pox. I wasn't. Two weeks before my sixteenth birthday, he turned me before I could die of what was probably the flu."

Ophelia absentmindedly rubbed at the crook of her neck, as if she could still feel the sting of her sire's fangs at her throat. "I rose just in time to find that Georgie had taken ill after I did. I couldn't stand the idea of letting her be buried in an unmarked grave. My friend, my sire, tried to talk me out of turning her. He ordered me not to, as a matter of fact, but she was my sister. I wasn't close to my mother or my father. Parenting, as it was then, didn't exactly foster a warm and loving relationship between parents and children. As far as I was concerned, Georgie was my whole family. My sire was furious with me for what I'd done. He took me before the group of vampires that ruled us at the time, the precursor to what is now the Council. They decided that they would let Georgie live but that I would be responsible for her for the rest of my days. My sire left me in the care of the Council for my first three hundred years, to help foster a better respect for the order of the vampire world. And I wouldn't be able to turn another soul until I was a thousand years old."

"But what's so terrible about a vampire child?" I asked. "Other than that she's incredibly creepy? And she's obviously hard on gaming equipment."

Ophelia frowned at me but gave a small smile when Georgie grunted and chucked the game unit against the wall. The fragments skittered across the floor as Georgie crossed her arms over her chest and stuck out her bottom lip.

Ophelia sighed. "It wasn't so bad at first. She was always such a sweet, smart girl. She could figure out what was expected of her, where she couldn't cross the lines. But imagine being a teenager in a little girl's body. Or a forty-year-old. You've got all the thoughts and feelings of an adult, but you're trapped in childhood. Georgie will never grow up. She'll never fall in love in a way that doesn't break several laws. Other vampires will never see her as anything but a disturbing liability. I've doomed her to this."

"But it's better than being dead, right?" I asked as Georgie amused herself by balancing on the very edge of the kitchen counter while standing on her hands. "How much worse would it have been to watch her die?"

Ophelia smiled fondly. "Exactly. There will always be drawbacks, little dramas and problems. But having her with me, being her guide through this life, is worth it. I try not to question my decision, because I know I did what was right. I will not feel guilty for it."

"I get it, I get it," I said, chuckling at the bright blinking neon hints she was dropping about the similarities between our situations. "Incredibly transparent message received. And still, you managed to rise in the Council ranks, even though they were pissed at you."

She snorted. "I was given a thousand-year ban on turning another vampire. The Council's theory was that I probably wouldn't live that long, so I would be kept from causing any more damage. No matter how high up I am in the vampire hierarchy, I will always have that hanging over my head."

"Well, that explains Waco's comment about your first turn as a sire not turning out so well."

"Yes, Waco does enjoy his little jokes," she deadpanned. "Now, what buffoonery were you referring to earlier?"

"I see personal share time is over."

"Indeed."

I took a deep breath and explained about the arrow, the poison, and Gabriel's current state of coma. I was rather proud that I managed not to tear up or get all quivery-voiced as I spoke, even when I described the torrents of blood Gabriel had thrown up while we tried to force-feed him.

"And you suspect foul play? You don't think it's possible that a hunter stumbled onto your property and accidentally shot Gabriel?" she asked.

"As in, 'Oops, I accidentally let a dangerous wooden arrow fall into a solution that could poison a vampire and then wandered onto the property of one of the few out vampires in town, only to lose control of said arrow and fire it three inches to the left of the heart of that vampire's fiancé'?"

"Yes, it is an unlikely sequence of coincidences," she admitted. Behind her, Georgie had moved on to standing on the very tips of her toes while balancing on the back of a kitchen chair. I was torn between telling Ophelia and marveling at Georgie's equilibrium.

"Besides, Jamie says it isn't bow season."

Ophelia smirked at me fondly. "I take it that you're acclimating well to life as a sire?"

"I wouldn't say 'well,' but I am acclimating."

"And the dynamic between Gabriel and your young

charge? What was Jamie doing while Gabriel was bleeding and vomiting?" she asked.

"Being a teenager," I responded, controlling the urge to roll my eyes. "He was pretty grossed out and upset about the stains on his jeans."

"Too 'grossed out' to have been involved in the poisoning?" she asked, her brows knit in an expression of irritated confusion.

"Gabriel asked the same thing. But I don't think Jamie has this in him. Besides, he was playing video games in the house while we were outside."

"Do you have any other suspects?" she asked.

"I honestly don't know. Jamie's parents were so angry with me over Jamie's becoming a vampire. His dad's a hunter. Do you think it's possible he was angry enough to take a shot at us?"

She nodded. "We'll look into it. And we'll have trusted vampires do the occasional security sweep by River Oaks."

"How occasional?" I asked.

"Are you questioning the generosity of your Council?" she asked, one eyebrow raised. I shook my head, all innocent eyes and guile. "It was good that you brought this to our attention, Jane, rather than waiting until the situation escalated out of your control. It showed an unusual amount of common sense on your part."

"Thanks, I think."

"It wasn't necessarily a compliment."

"I'm aware of that."

9

Although vampires are seen as lonely, brooding creatures, all of us, whether young or old, need socialization. Vampires who spend too much time alone lose their humanity, and with that their ability to safely attract and feed from their human prey.

—*Siring for the Stupid:*
A Beginner's Guide to Raising Newborn Vampires

My first day back at the shop didn't go as I'd hoped. I pulled into the space in front of the shop to find Andrea scrubbing furiously at the window.

"Uh, sweetie, I think we've talked about the fact that our customers don't really care about the cleanliness of the front window. They sort of like the idea that no one can see them from the outside," I called as I climbed out of Big Bertha.

Andrea ignored me, continuing to swipe at the soapy glass. Her sleeves were rolled up, reddish bubbles slipping down her arms. There were words slashed across the glass, half-disintegrated by Andrea's efforts. I could make out the top half of an M, a U . . . R . . . D . . . E . . . R . . . I . . . N . . . G . . . B . . . I . . . T . . . C . . .

"Aw, hell." I sighed. Andrea kept her eyes down and focused on her task. Scanning the window, I saw the slightest traces of older paint in different areas of the glass. "This isn't the first time, is it, Andrea?"

She heaved a heavy breath out of her nose. "No. Every night since the Laniers were informed, the same message. 'Murdering Bitch.'"

"Well, that's just hurtful. And inaccurate."

"Sometimes it's in different colors," she offered. "I have a feeling that the Laniers have been telling their tale to whoever will listen. Because the handwriting has looked different on a few nights. I didn't want to tell you, because I didn't want to worry you. But it's been pretty strange around here lately. Stranger than usual. The Tuesday Night Book Club has suspended its meetings indefinitely, because the humans don't trust the vampires enough to attend for the time being. The Chamber of Commerce called to reiterate that they don't want you to be a member. Several of your old friends from the library called to cancel holds they had on books on order. Between hate mail and people calling to tell us that they'll never shop here again after what you did to 'that poor Lanier boy' and the people coming in and begging us to turn them, too, the only store traffic we've had lately has been of the crazy variety. We haven't had an in-store sale in days."

"What about online?"

She shrugged. "Same, with the exception of an influx of orders for werewolf relationship guides out of Alaska, which is weird. We're not so infamous that Mr.

Wainwright's old customers in Cornwall don't want their *Field Guides to Pixies and Fairy Folk.* That will sustain us, but if we can't lure back the locals, we're going to feel it in a few months."

"As in?"

"As in, that raise I was hoping to ask you for—I won't even bring it up," she said, frowning. I slapped my hand over my face. "It will work out," Andrea assured me. "Once Jamie's allowed back out in society and the truth comes out. The scandal will die down. Somebody will wander into the Piggly Wiggly drunk and topless, and everybody will forget all about you and your whole scarlet woman persona."

"Scarlet woman?"

"Seducer of young men, ruiner of lives, danger to the morals of American youth."

"I got it, thanks."

Andrea hosed off her handiwork, and I dragged the soap bucket into the shop. She followed, rolling down her sleeves as I sorted through the disturbingly large stack of pink "While You Were Out" slips.

"I sorted them into piles: 'Please turn me/my chronically ill parent/my dying cat into a vampire' and 'You're an evil whore, rot in hell,'" Andrea said helpfully.

"The 'rot in hell' people actually left their call-back numbers?"

"Well, I did ask politely. I think it caught them off guard," she said, wiping down the coffee-bar counter. "How's Gabriel? Dick said he was staying at your place tonight to keep an eye on him and Jamie."

"Still sleeping. But his color is getting better. He actually has a skin tone found in the spectrum of human shades. Dick thinks he might wake up in the next day or so."

"Sounds promising."

"Yep. OK, enough of this brooding crap." I grunted, throwing the "rot in hell" stack into the wastebasket. "You are going to mix one of your evil high-octane coffee potions for me. We're going to call Ophelia and tell her about the hate mail and window graffiti. We're going to set up a video camera to train on the front door to get proof that the Laniers and their friends are defacing the shop, then hand the tapes over to the human and vampire authorities."

Andrea made a wincing face.

"What?"

"We're going to pull a sting operation on the grieving parents?" she asked.

"The grieving parents who are defacing my shop and maybe playing toxic William Tell games with my fiancé? Yes."

She winced again.

"What?" I demanded.

"It's just that, archery shenanigans aside, if they're just painting the shop window, I kind of understand why they're doing it. They're angry and confused, and the only target they see to lash out at is you."

When Andrea saw the incensed look on my face, she changed conversational lanes abruptly.

"Which is obviously an inappropriate way to channel

their grief, and the sooner we guide them toward professional help, the better."

She ducked when I slung a copy of *The Guide to the Newly Undead* at her.

"And you need to find more appropriate ways to channel *your* anger! Aren't you supposed to be planning a wedding right now?"

"Really?" I gaped at her. "My fiancé has been poisoned into a coma, and you think picking out monogrammed napkins and color-coordinated Jordan almonds is going to make me feel better?"

She scoffed. "Well, no, Jordan almonds are so 1980s . . . I can tell from your expression you're not going to have much of a sense of humor about this wedding thing, are you?"

I groaned. "I don't even know where to start. I should just admit defeat now and turn the whole thing over to Mama."

"So, you're OK with the ribbons on the invitation matching the aisle runner, the bridesmaids' dresses, the table linens at the reception, and your garter, all of which your mother chose because she thought sea-foam green would complement Gabriel's eyes?"

I shuddered and thunked my head down on the counter. "I should have done a better job of selling elopement."

"What you need is Iris Scanlon," she said, digging through her purse for her wallet.

"Is Iris Scanlon an Internet-ordained minister who

doesn't ask questions?" I asked, sidestepping when Andrea chucked the *Guide* at my head.

As it turned out, much to my disappointment, Iris Scanlon ran Beeline, a new daytime concierge service for vampires. She was a combination event planner, notary public, and contractor. While many changes had been made to society overall to accommodate vampires, there were still some things that had to be handled during the day. Government buildings, for one, were still only open during daylight hours. And it was rare to find contractors and service people willing to come out to a vampire's house at night.

Because vampire marriage was still a new phenom-enon, the wedding industry was still very much daylight-oriented. One of Iris's specialties was assisting in planning vampire weddings. It said so right on the business card Andrea fished from her purse. Iris was exactly what I needed—an indifferent, but committed, outside third party to handle the little details that would drive me nuts but that I couldn't trust to Jolene, Andrea, or Mama with-out their personal tastes influencing their decisions.

"She does great work," Andrea assured me. "She just started up, so I wasn't able to use her for our wedding. But she helped out with Hadley Wexler's wedding last month and she's planning Sophie's commitment ceremony to her longtime girlfriend."

"Sophie from the Council?" I said, raising my eyebrows. "I didn't see that one coming."

"Call her, make an appointment, make your life easier," Andrea said, sliding the card to me.

"Yeah, 'cause that always works." I snorted. "This still feels weird, planning a wedding while Gabriel is so sick."

"Consider it a hopeful gesture," Andrea said, rubbing my back. "Think of how happy Gabriel will be when he wakes up and sees how much progress you've made toward marrying him."

"Really?"

"Ask Dick how thrilled he was when I neglected to ask his opinions on flower arrangements. He commissioned a T-shirt in my honor: 'My Girlfriend Kicks Your Girlfriend's Ass.'" When I squinted at her, confounded, she said, "In Dick's way, that's the highest compliment you can pay a woman."

"I will never understand your relationship."

Andrea grinned at me. "Right back atcha, sweetie."

I did make the appointment with Iris. And by the time Gabriel woke up two days later, sore and grumpy and not entirely sure what had happened to him, Iris had already sent me fabric samples for the dreaded linens, aisle runner, and napkins. And there wasn't a speck of sea-foam green in sight. From her e-mails, Iris seemed competent, no-nonsense, and completely unsentimental about this wedding stuff.

Iris was quickly becoming my favorite person. Ever.

Gabriel wasn't entirely pleased with me for going to Ophelia, but I think it was more a matter of male pride than anything else. I came home to find him propped up on a stack of pillows, sipping blood through a crazy straw (because it amused Zeb) and wearing *Star Wars* pajamas (because it amused Dick). He was pale and drawn and still had purplish bruises under his eyes, but he was awake. And he was smiling at me.

"I love you, I love you, I love you," I babbled, kissing him over and over until Zeb pleaded that we were grossing him out. Gabriel smiled blithely up at me as I hovered over him and then flinched as I grabbed a pillow and whacked him over the head with it. "And don't you *ever* do anything like that again! I am the one who ends up in the stupid life-threatening situations. You are the levelheaded, responsible one in this relationship. Got it? This is how this whole thing works. We have to stick to our designated roles, or there is chaos!"

Dick snickered. "It's true. If Zeb suddenly starts being all dashing and sexy, what am I going to do?"

Zeb took offense to this. "Hey, I can be dashing and sexy! Jolene says I'm like the human Wolfman."

"Jolene lies," Gabriel told him, his voice slightly hoarse from disuse.

Dick agreed. "A lot."

"I'm going to play *Madden* with Jamie. He respects me, at least," Zeb grumbled.

"No, I don't!" Jamie called from downstairs.

"So, Dick says I've missed quite a bit while I was out. He says you paid Ophelia a visit?" he said, threading his fingers through mine. I pulled myself onto my knees and glared at our big-mouthed friend.

"It's called heading a problem off at the pass," I said.

"Is that a euphemism for emasculating one's betrothed while he's unconscious and unable to defend himself?" Gabriel asked dryly.

"No, it's a euphemism for accessing resources that we don't have by alerting the Council to our problem, rather than playing junior detectives ourselves. They've already installed a camera outside my shop door that is so scary and official-looking that the locals stopped painting my front window. Plus, this particular choice of directions doesn't involve Ophelia suspecting me of hurting others for personal gain."

"Unless Ophelia finds out that you're Gabriel's beneficiary on his life-insurance policy," Dick said, snickering.

"I am?"

Gabriel seemed insulted that I didn't think he would provide for me in the event of his staking. "Of course you are!"

"How do we even *get* life insurance?" I asked. "We're dead."

"Well, not according to the paperwork I filed with State Farm," Gabriel said.

"But somehow, my reporting to Ophelia skirts an ethical line."

"OK, so it was a smart thing to do," Gabriel admitted. "When did you arrive at this 'resources' conclusion?"

"When I realized that I'd given Dick five thousand dollars and asked him to drive halfway across the state to a college crime lab for tests that may or may not have detected the poison in your system in a way that may or may not have helped us treat you," I said, glad that I couldn't blush.

"Clearly, your judgment goes out the window when I'm unconscious," he said, managing to hide his smirk as he slipped an errant tendril of hair behind my left ear. "And how is Jamie doing?"

"Fine. He seems to be spending a lot of time in the shower," I noted quietly, my voice so low that even Jamie's superhearing couldn't pick it up.

Dick chuckled, followed by Zeb and Gabriel.

"What?"

"Remember that summer I turned thirteen and my mom complained that she couldn't ever get me out of the bathroom?" Zeb asked.

"Yeah, but that's because you were—" I slapped my hand over my mouth. *"Oh!"*

"Welcome to the world of parenting," Zeb said. "It's one big, horrifying miracle."

"Augh!" I grumbled.

I tried to defuse my embarrassment by talking about Iris and the progress she was making with the wedding. Although I was loath to admit it, Andrea was right. Gabriel was thrilled that I'd made the effort to call a wedding planner. He was so heartened by my apparent interest in wedding planning that he immediately perked up, called Iris, and arranged a meeting the next evening to be followed by an appointment at a wedding-dress shop in Murphy.

My stomach sank at the words "dress" and "shop," and I searched my memory banks for my list of plausible reasons I could not go shopping. I hadn't had to use them against Mama in so long that they'd receded from the tip of my tongue. "Wait, how did she manage to arrange that so quickly?"

"She said she has her ways," Gabriel said. "Also, she's been warned about what Andrea called your 'unhealthy aversion to trying on clothes,' so she will accompany you to the shop to provide hard liquor and moral support."

"I think I love her a little bit," I admitted.

"Hell, if she can sneak booze into a bridal store, I may love her a little bit," Dick said.

"You know, it strikes me as sort of useless to be planning a wedding when we haven't decided when the wedding will be," Gabriel said, toying with the engagement ring on my finger.

"Actually, I had an idea about the date, but I didn't want to do anything until you woke up," I said. "What do you think of July eighth?"

"As dates go, I believe it's a perfectly respectable one."

"It's Aunt Jettie's birthday. I think it would be nice to get married on her birthday."

"Aw, that's sweet," Dick said. "She'll love that."

"And it will be so close to July Fourth weekend that most of the relatives on Mama's side will still be hungover, so maybe they won't be able to make it."

"That's less sweet," Gabriel conceded. "But I think it's a good, strong wedding date."

"And now that the wedding date is settled, you know what that means," Dick said, gleefully rubbing his hands together in a way that made me distinctly nervous.

Gabriel's voice was just as uneasy. "We can order those embossed matchbooks I love so much?"

"I can start planning the bachelor party," Dick said, giving his best impersonation of an evil supervillain laugh. Or maybe it wasn't an impersonation.

"This is not going to end well for me, is it?" Gabriel asked me.

I sighed. "Remind me to exchange some cash for pesos in late June. I don't think they'll accept American money when I have to bail you out of jail in Tijuana."

Gabriel chuckled. "Still, July eighth. I'm very excited. It only gives us a few months to plan, you know."

"If we don't get it done by July eighth, it doesn't need to be done," I assured him.

"Be sure to explain that to your mama." Dick snorted.

I laughed and smoothed the hair back from Gabriel's forehead as he eased back onto the pillows, exhausted. My hand froze over his temple as the temperature just over my shoulder dropped by ten degrees. I could feel frosty breath on my cheek as my grandma Ruthie's voice slithered into my ear.

"Keep making plans, little girl. This wedding will never happen," she hissed.

I immediately glanced over to Dick and Gabriel, who didn't show any sign of having heard the voice. I rolled my eyes. It would appear that my dear departed grandmother was choosing not to reveal herself to them, targeting me for her "loving" messages. Grandma Ruthie's spectral presence around the house seemed to have diminished since her outburst with Aunt Jettie.

There were little flare-ups here and there. My car keys would disappear. The windows would rattle. Random trash would appear on the counter, but I think that was Jamie. Jettie said that Ruthie was probably rebuilding her strength for another big blow-up.

But every once in a while, while I was lying in bed, I would hear her voice whispering over my ear. She knew exactly what to say to keep me from drifting off to sleep—that Gabriel was going to wise up and leave me standing at the altar, explaining to my family why I would spend the rest of my unnatural life pathetic and alone. Or variations thereof.

"Why would anyone want to marry you?" She had a sneer in her voice. "I never understood what you thought was so special about you. You're not all that pretty. You have the figure of a linebacker. You don't have any real talents. The only thing you've ever been good at is reading. A first-grader can do that."

"Shut up, old woman," I grumbled, refusing to let my lip so much as tremble.

Gabriel leaned toward Dick and quietly asked, "Is this a new endearment that became popular while I was unconscious?"

10

Iris Scanlon was everything I'd hoped for. She was a cross between gypsy and pixie, a tiny, compact body topped with a wild, curling mop of sable hair. She wore a knee-length black skirt and a pretty ice-blue eyelet blouse, paired with no-nonsense black pumps. She was constantly scribbling notes in a small pad tucked into her leather folio embossed with the signature Beeline logo of a determined little cartoon bee.

Gabriel was wearing nonpajamas for the first time in almost a week and sitting on the couch, firing questions at her. I had no idea he cared so much about cummerbund colors and DJ playlists.

Personally, I wanted to gauge exactly how much

weirdness she could take, so I asked Iris about the weird-
est request she'd ever handled for a client.

She sipped her iced tea and suppressed a smile. "I'm
going to have to say being called at dawn to arrange for an
animal-wrangler-slash-cleaning-crew-slash-contractor
to restore a vampire's living room. Said vampire didn't
know that tigers make terrible house pets, until the tiger
destroyed his couch and tried to chew through a wall.
As a human, he loved cats. He figured he was bigger,
stronger, and scarier now, so he needed a house pet that
was bigger, stronger, and scarier . . . Apparently, he'd
never seen a single episode of *When Animals Attack*. But
the good news is, now I know how a tranq gun works."

"Good, then you're prepared to deal with my mother."

"I don't understand. She sounded perfectly nice on
the phone," Iris said, her brow creased.

"On the phone?"

"Yes, she called me this morning to talk about your
preferences for the flowers. She's planning to meet us at
the bridal shop later. Your sister is planning to be there,
too."

I groaned, covering my face with my hands. "Isn't
there such a thing as planner–client privilege?"

"Well, no, not unless you warn me of meddlesome
relatives beforehand. Also, she called me, so I assumed
that you had already talked to her about my involvement
in the wedding plans."

"Well, I didn't. I don't know how she finds these things
out. She just does. It's her evil power."

Iris seemed to sense my panic and that we weren't

off to a great start to our relationship. She squared her shoulders and made another little note in her folio. "I've dealt with difficult family members before, Jane. It won't be a problem. From now on, we'll have a password. Any changes to wedding plans or meeting times will require the password before I give anyone the information. Also, I'll let the vendors know that any changes require password confirmation."

I tried to make my patronizing smile a bit more pleasant. "We'll talk on the way to the bridal shop. Once you have the background information, I think you'll agree that a password's not going to do you much good."

It might have seemed odd to drive more than an hour to Murphy with Jolene and Andrea in tow, but there were very good reasons that I could not go to the only bridal shop in the Hollow, the Bridal Barn. Those reasons were that it was (a) hopelessly stuck in the 1980s, with scary shoulder pads and neon-colored layered chiffon creations, and (b) run by Jolene's aunt Vonnie, who had hated me since my involvement in Jolene and Zeb's wedding. I didn't think it would be wise for me to get anywhere near her while she was holding scissors or pins . . . or large-gauge sequins.

On the way, I gave Iris a sort of highlight reel of Mama's most memorable antics. It wasn't that my mother didn't love me. Sure, it had taken her a while to get used to the whole vampire-daughter thing. And for a while, after she realized that I would never give her grandchildren, she took to her bed. But she soon snapped out of it, joined the FFOTU, and tried to force-feed me pot pies for my own good. The problem was that she'd seen my wedding in her head for so many years that I knew that any deviance from that vision would just not be accepted. She honestly believed that my opinions were just weak protests, cries for help for Mummy to come along and fix everything. Then again, Mama thought I would be marrying Zeb—best friend since babydom—someday, which showed how much she knew.

"So she washed all of the dirty clothes in your luggage, then decided that the clothes in your closet weren't clean enough and washed them, too?" Iris marveled as Jolene described Mama's response to my returning from vacation with Gabriel last year.

"And then she ironed all of her jeans." Andrea hooted.

"With starch," I added, turning Big Bertha on to Yancy Street toward the Bridal Dreams Boutique. The name of the shop alone was enough to have me looking for U-turn options. I was not one of those women who dreamed of poofy designer silhouettes and exotic beading. I was a realist. My pale skin didn't look good against white. Mermaid skirts made me look like a snowman. And butt bows made me break out in hives.

It was nearly two hours after the shop's closing time, but Iris had arranged for us to have the place to ourselves, for a handsome "viewing fee." Through the front window, I could see that Mama and Jenny had arrived before us and that someone had given Mama one of those rolling racks, upon which she had already hung a half-dozen frou-frou princess nightmare gowns.

"Andrea." I whimpered, lowering my head to the steering wheel.

"Yes, Jane?"

"There's a stake Velcroed underneath your seat. I want you take it out and shove it into my chest. Tell Gabriel I died bravely, in defense of democracy and fluffy kittens."

Andrea snorted. "That seems a little dramatic. You're a dog person."

"Why do you have a stake Velcroed under your seat?" Jolene demanded. "We agreed that you would tell us when you have concealed weapons."

I felt a gentle nudge at my shoulder. Iris was holding a flask in front of my face. A flask completely encrusted with pink crystals save for the little yellow crystal bee on the front. She flipped the cap open, and I could smell the vodka fumes rolling over the lip.

"This is not my first rodeo," she said, shaking her head.

"I think we've just been replaced as best friends," Jolene muttered to Andrea.

If the liquid courage didn't secure her place as my newest closest companion, Iris's masterful handling of my mother sealed the deal. The first thing Iris did as she came through the shop door was exclaim over my mother's wonderful taste in dresses. Then she managed to whittle down Mama's selections by asking if she preferred the A-line skirt with the floral motif or the ball gown with the ribbon sash. Did she like this full tulle skirt or the cathedral train? Before Mama knew it, she'd been talked out of half of her picks, seated in one of the uncomfortable little tea chairs by the dressing rooms, and eclipsed as the organizer of this gathering.

Jenny just sat back and marveled. "Where was she when I was planning *my* wedding?"

Iris wandered around the shop selecting dresses that were a little closer to my taste. I didn't know how comfortable I was mixing my supernatural friends and my family. I mean, sure, my parents had hosted a beautiful baby shower for Jolene. But at the time, they didn't know that she was a werewolf. And Andrea had been human then. Now that my family was aware of my friends' "unique" nature, I expected it to feel different.

I hadn't counted on them bonding over their mutual exasperation with me. My clumsiness, my stubbornness, my ability to injure myself or others just by walking across a room. It was all the stuff of instant sisterhood.

"I never thought I'd see the day Jane would voluntarily go shopping," Mama said, sipping the tea provided by a harried shop assistant named Claire. "I thought poor Andrea would have to use her vampire strength to hog-tie Jane and put her in the trunk."

"I haven't read many books on vampire wedding etiquette, but I think hog-tying the bride is rude in any culture," I noted.

Andrea ignored me and said, "I practically have to force her at gunpoint to go with me to shop for jeans. She always finds cute stuff, with my guidance, but she acts like I'm torturing her."

"Well, to be fair, she has flashbacks," my sister added,

winking at me as she handed me a fluffy full-skirted gown.

"Jenny," I said in a low, warning tone.

Mama looked at me quizzically and then burst out laughing. "Oh! I'd almost forgotten about that."

Jolene and Andrea exchanged glances, silently debating whether the potential hilarity could be worth suffering my wrath. They grinned simultaneously.

Shit.

"I hate you guys," I mumbled as I strode into the dressing room and took the first of Mama's dresses off the hanger.

As I wrestled my way into what felt like miles of tulle, Jenny was telling the story of Homecoming dress shopping with me my sophomore year. Jenny was nominated for the court, so Mama was insisting that I go to the dance to support her. Jenny, of course, had already picked out her gown before she was even nominated. But it was three days before the big event, and I was still lobbying to wear jeans and combat boots. Mama and Jenny had frogmarched me into the Tot, Teen, and Tween Shop downtown to find something "that won't make you look like a motherless hobo," as Mama had so gently put it. After a dozen ruffled, bow-covered nightmares, I'd decided I'd had enough. I yanked a dress over my head, forgetting about the zipper. The zipper got caught in my hair. I felt as if I was being attacked by the ghosts of evil prom queens and fought back. And because the dressing rooms were framed with curtains instead of doors . . .

"She came stumbling out of the dressing room into the shop with her panties bared and her dress over her head," Jenny said, hooting.

Andrea and Jolene were falling all over each other laughing.

I glared at the lot of them. "I think I remember why I hate shopping," I said, my hands on my hips.

"Oh, honey," Mama murmured, her eyes misting. "It's so beautiful!"

I turned toward the mirror and flinched. "I look like a bad meringue hallucination," I said.

The skirt seemed to explode from beneath the bodice, making my hips look a mile wide. The hem was hovering about an inch off the ground and revealed my white gym socks. The sleeves were those padded "belle" sleeves, but they'd long since deflated and hung from my biceps like droopy balloons. Iris had stopped in her tracks across the shop and dropped the tiara she'd been holding.

"You look like Cinderella," Mama cooed. Behind her, Iris, Jolene, and Andrea were shaking their head in sync.

"If she was doing the walk of shame home from the ball," Andrea muttered. Jolene and Jenny snickered. I bit my lip to keep from joining in.

What? Even I can appreciate a good snark at my own expense.

"You couldn't have worn nicer socks?" Mama asked. "Well, baby, I'd say you have a winner first time out."

I shrugged. "Mama, this is not the dress."

"But you look so—"

"Mama, I want you to close your eyes. And for just

one moment, forget how excited you are about me finally getting married and how excited you are about finally seeing me in an actual wedding dress. Close your eyes, and really think about my body type and what looks good on me."

Mama complied.

"Now open your eyes," I said.

Her eyelids popped open, and she scanned me from head to toe. She blanched and made her "I smell something" face. She shook her head, as if that would make the image go away. "Oh, honey, no."

I nodded, my lips tucked into a humorless grimace. "There we go."

"That is not the dress."

I shook my head slowly. "I would like this off of me now."

Claire helped me wrestle the skirt back into the dressing room. "Don't feel bad, Miss Jameson, this dress has been here since 1992. It's been forced on countless brides by their mothers. It's still here. That should tell you something."

I thought of all of the women who had worn this dress before me and shuddered.

"We have it cleaned a few times a year," she assured me.

The rest of the evening was a blur, as my friends and family argued over which silhouette suited me best. Jenny and Mama went to search in the back room, where the owner stored the dresses for brides with "problem areas." Iris had begun making notes on which manufacturers she could call for special samples.

"What's that?" I asked, pointing to the light blue-gray dress hanging on a rack near the register.

Claire laughed. "Oh, that's a dress for the costume shop down the street. Our seamstresses do repairs and alterations for them all the time. DeeDee Wilkins-Reed dressed up as Elizabeth Bennet for some charity costume thing a few weeks back and split a seam. That just goes to show that dress clothes and a few dozen sausage balls don't mix."

Andrea, Jolene, and I shuddered collectively.

I stepped closer to the dress. I lifted the plastic bag protecting the material and smiled. This was the sort of dress an Austen character would wear . . . in a highly sanitized, beautifully lit movie adaptation. And unlike every other dress in this shop, I could actually see myself marrying Gabriel in it.

I turned over the tag and saw that the dress was my size. Obviously, the wedding-dress gods were smiling on me.

"Can I try it on?" I asked Claire.

"I don't see why not. Just avoid any sausage balls."

"Not a problem."

"It's been dry-cleaned, right?" I heard Andrea ask as I went back into the dressing room.

I slipped the dress on, and it seemed to caress me like water sliding down my skin. It was light and comfortable. There was a smattering of beadwork along the empire waist, emphasizing the elegant bell of the skirt. The hem was scalloped with lace and beadwork. The sleeves were short and capped and actually made my arms look long and graceful.

I wanted to be married in this dress. That special feeling that all brides talk about? Finding "the one"? This was it. I ripped the curtain back and stepped out. Andrea and Jolene squealed. *Confirmed!*

"Oh, my gosh, it's so beautiful," Andrea gushed as Jenny clapped her hands over her mouth.

Jolene's face fell from its usually luminous smile. "But wait, it's a rental gown. People have worn it before you. It's used."

"It's vintage," I corrected her.

"It's icky," she mewled.

"I wore vintage at my wedding, and you didn't say it was icky," Andrea said, her brow lifted.

"I did, you just didn't hear me," Jolene retorted, wincing when Andrea punched her arm. "Ow! This is what I get for hanging out with vampires. My aunts tried to warn me."

"Your aunts are vicious bitches," Andrea shot back.

Jolene shrugged. "You're not wrong."

"Hello, can we refocus on my bridal hotness?" I demanded, gesturing to the long, slender lines the dress somehow "magicked" onto my body.

"Jane, I think we need to go with a ball gown and a long-sleeved jacket," Mama was saying as she emerged from the back room. She stopped in her tracks when she saw me and tilted her head, her expression confused. "Oh, well, that's nice."

"Nice? Mama, that's gorgeous," Jenny said, stepping closer so she could examine the beading. "Really, really beautiful, Jane, and so completely you."

"It's so nice to hear you say that and know you don't mean it as an insult," I told her. She nodded as she bent to examine the hem.

"But it's gray," Mama said. "And it's not a wedding dress."

"But it's an Austen period dress," I objected.

"We could definitely build a theme around the dress," Iris offered.

"But it's so plain," Mama whined. "And I'm just not getting the 'bridal' feeling from it."

"But I *am* getting a bridal feeling from it."

"But why gray? Why not white?" Mama asked.

I smirked. "Mama, if you really want to have that discussion, I will give you a detailed explanation. For once, I have details to give."

"I do not want to hear this," Andrea said, shaking her head.

"I think I do," Jenny said. When Andrea and Jolene turned toward her, surprised, she lifted her hands in a defensive gesture. "I don't think curiosity is out of line."

"But Jane, everyone will think—"

"No one's going to think anything. It's not like it's possible for me to be pregnant. I'm a vampire. All of the traditional planning rules have been drop-kicked out the window. Besides, wedding dresses weren't traditionally white until Victoria made it popular. It's not an authenticity stamp or anything. So, tell me, forgetting that this is supposed to be virginal white. Do I look pretty?"

Mama took my face between her hands. "Absolutely gorgeous."

I made a quick, very persuasive phone call to the owner of the costume shop. I offered her what was easily three times the cost of the dress and made sure to give Claire a healthy commission. It wasn't her fault that she sold me something that wasn't part of the stock. Since she wasn't paying for the dress, Mama insisted on having it repaired and thoroughly dry-cleaned and then bought me a pretty pair of gray ballet flats and a little beaded comb for my hair.

Since I'd managed to stumble into a theme for the wedding, Iris said I'd actually made her job a little easier. She rattled on about period-appropriate flower choices and food, about little touches we could add to the ceremony to make it more Austenian. Andrea made me promise that we would try to wrestle Dick and Gabriel into cutaway coats and beaver hats. It seemed to help our short time frame that my choices were narrowed. My color schemes were limited to what would go with the pewter-gray gown . . . except for the bridesmaids' gowns. I'd already decided that they were going to be a distinctly nonmatchy lemon yellow that Jolene's aunt Vonnie would have to special-order. The kind of yellow one would find on takeout menus or particularly urgent Post-it notes.

In fact, if the outdoor lighting failed, we could use the color of their dresses to illuminate the ceremony.

And yes, I had to use a vendor who hated me, because Vonnie held the only pattern left in the continental United States for the "Ruffles and Dreams," the very dress I'd had to wear in Jolene's wedding. Revenge would be mine, for a few months, until I revealed the dove-gray bridesmaids' dresses I actually planned for them to wear.

As we were loading our purchases into Big Bertha, Mama pulled me aside and stage-whispered, "What's this I hear about not having Jenny in your wedding party?"

I was caught like the proverbial deer in the headlights. My eyes went wide, and my mouth seemed to lock shut. I cleared my throat. "Oh, well, I know Jenny and I have been getting along better lately, but I'm still not comfortable—"

Mama huffed. "Oh, don't be silly, Jane. How do you think Jenny is going to feel if she's not at least a bridesmaid?"

I thought Jenny would be just fine with it. In fact, when I had talked to her about this very subject, her response had been, "I'm fine with that." But of course, instead of saying that, I said, "I wasn't a bridesmaid in Jenny's wedding."

"Well, Jenny had so many friends she had a hard time choosing from them. You said you understood."

"Yes, because I didn't want to wear the foofy pink dress she'd picked out. I think I'm doing her a favor in return," I said.

"What will people think if you shut your sister out of your wedding?"

"They're going to think, isn't it nice that Jenny came to the wedding to support Jane instead of going through with that pesky lawsuit?"

Mama waved my concerns away with a flick of her wrist. "That's just silly talk. Jenny, sweetheart, Jane needs to talk to you about finding shoes to match your bridesmaid's dress."

Andrea and Jolene turned to me, twin expressions of confusion and shock on their faces. Having expected some maneuver like this from Mama, I tried to calculate the impact of futilely objecting to the bridesmaid shuffle versus future machinations. I decided to let Mama win this battle if it meant that she'd stay off my ass in other more important wars. So I bit my lip and said nothing. Jenny scurried around the car, followed by Jolene and Andrea.

"I thought I wasn't going to be in your wedding party!" Jenny exclaimed.

"That's what I thought, too, but Mama's insisting."

"Insisting that I wear that hag rag of a dress you picked out? Gee, thanks, Mama."

"Hag rag?" Andrea repeated.

Jolene sighed. "I'm sure I had that comin', considerin' the color of peach I made you wear."

I did my best to look contrite. "I'm sorry."

"No, you're not," Jenny muttered.

Andrea raised her hand hesitantly. "Can we go back to 'hag rag'?"

"Just remember, I will be responsible for planning your bachelorette party," Jenny told me.

I snorted. "Anything you do won't be nearly as scary as what Jolene's cousins did."

11

At some point, your childe may challenge you
to a fight. Try not to beat the childe too badly.
Imagine having your mother knock you into
unconsciousness. It would be emotionally scarring
on several levels.

—*Siring for the Stupid:*
A Beginner's Guide to Raising Newborn Vampires

I knew that Gabriel was feeling better when he threw
Jamie through a wall.

Tension in the house had been increasing since I went
back to work. I think Grandma Ruthie was making her
presence known by moving cell phones and checkbooks
and anything else we needed. She would hover over us in
our sleep, whispering. She'd pop up behind us in mirrors
and corners of rooms. Aunt Jettie was spending most of
her time patrolling the grounds with Mr. Wainwright, but
every time she sensed Grandma Ruthie materializing,
she'd pop into the house. The amount of energy she was
expending left her exhausted.

Gabriel and Jamie were increasingly cranky with
each other. Gabriel's recovery from the poisoning was

slow. We figured out that several small meals of donor blood throughout the night healed him a lot faster than bottled synthetic, but he was still pale and weak. He was able to get out of bed, but he hobbled like a man who was nearing his bicentennial birthday. Feeling weak, dependent, brought out the worst in him. He was still loving and appreciative of me, but everything about Jamie set his fangs on edge.

Little disputes over dirty laundry on the floor and sorting the recycling became screaming matches. Gabriel would corner me and complain about my "inconsiderate bratling" of a childe. Jamie would pout in his room until I came to investigate his absence, then make forced confessions of how much easier life would be without Gabriel living with us.

Things at the shop weren't much better. Once word got around that I was back to work, every other person who came through the door asked me to turn them. I heard every sob story possible, from terminal illness to needing a few extra decades to pay off student loans. Oddly enough, my vampire clientele increased. It was as if I'd passed some sort of test. I was a "real" vampire now.

The vandalism had dropped off completely with the installation of the security cameras. The only glimpse we'd caught of the perpetrators was a hunting boot as the person stepped just a tiny bit into the frame, saw the camera, and ran away.

I lived on edge, fearful of what each evening would bring. I was afraid of walking to the door every night. I was afraid to let Gabriel get too close to the windows.

I tried to devote my attention to wedding details, to something hopeful, but with Iris on the case, there wasn't much for me to do. After deciding on the Austen theme, she'd pretty much run the show, sending me daily progress reports and e-mailing pictures of the invitations, linens, and other items she'd arranged. And then Jamie got a look at the old-fashioned morning coat Gabriel would be wearing and nearly fell over laughing—which started another argument, which sent me running for work early that night.

So when I came home and heard the commotion from the driveway, I gritted my teeth and stomped up the front porch steps. At this point, I was hoping that the happy archer had broken into our home for a rumble, because I didn't think I could put up with much more step-sire drama. How could Jerry Springer not have featured this on his show yet?

I opened the door to find Gabriel growling as he pinned Jamie to the wall by his throat. Panic rippled up my spine. I knew there had been an edgy tension between the two of them, but I never thought Gabriel would lose control of himself like this. He looked like one of those angry stepdads you saw in domestic-violence PSAs.

"What is going on here?" I yelled.

Gabriel's eyes darted toward me, and Jamie took advantage of this and punched Gabriel in the jaw. He followed through the swing, clipping Gabriel's chin with his elbow.

Gabriel's hands closed over Jamie's throat and squeezed. Jamie clawed at his hands, finally breaking the hold by punching him in the chest. Gabriel dropped to the ground, sliding his feet against Jamie's legs, knocking him forward. He hooked his hands under Jamie's arms and tossed him as he rolled onto his back. Jamie yelped as he flew through the air and flopped bonelessly against the wall, which buckled under the impact. Jamie's legs flopped through the drywall. From my vantage point, I could see his feet resting in the parlor and his torso stretching into the hall.

"Gabriel! Jamie! Stop it, this instant!"

"Hi, Jane!" Jamie said brightly. Gabriel took advantage of this lapse in attention and socked Jamie in the mouth.

Aunt Jettie materialized at my elbow. She looked amused but sheepish. "We tried to stop them, sweetheart, but it was too entertaining."

Mr. Wainwright appeared next to her and added, "Did you know that Jamie used to wrestle with his friends in his backyard and upload the footage to YouTube?"

"Y-YouTube?" I spluttered. "What?"

"Jamie's signature move was getting hit in the back with a folding chair," Jettie said, a gleeful glint in her eyes. "I tried to find one in the garage, but I think your grandma Ruthie came over last year and 'borrowed' the card table and chairs for her bridge club."

"Wait, wait—Gabriel, Jamie, what in the name of SpongeBob are you doing?"

"Gabriel was just showing me some moves," Jamie said, elbowing Gabriel in the gut. Gabriel grunted and punched Jamie in the kidney. "We were watching *Underworld*, and Gabriel said Selene's movements were 'preposterous and tactically ill advised.' " The accurate yet slightly exaggerated pomposity in Jamie's imitation of Gabriel sent a little shiver down my spine.

"Given the latex catsuit she was wearing, I tend to agree," I mused.

Jamie grinned at me. "He tried to show me how one of the fight scenes would look in the real world."

"And that ended in the partial destruction of a house that survived the Civil War, how?" I asked.

"Everything after the first hammerlock gets a little hazy," Gabriel confessed, shaking his head as if there were something loose inside.

Jamie grinned and helped Gabriel up off the floor. Gabriel slapped him on the back and chuckled. They seemed to have bonded over beating each other senseless. I moaned and scrubbed a hand over my face. For the first time, I felt truly outnumbered in my own home. I thought perhaps I was better off when they were pointedly ignoring each other. Still, it seemed like a step in the right direction for Gabriel. He hadn't had this much exercise in weeks. His face was no longer the color of overboiled oatmeal, and he was moving as if he had cartilage in his joints.

"Call the contractor to get this fixed. And try to stay away from the load-bearing walls, OK?" Jamie struggled up from the floor and tossed Gabriel into the kitchen by his ears. "On second thought, why don't you take this outside?"

I turned toward Aunt Jettie and Mr. Wainwright, who

were already phasing through the door to check the woods around the house for intruders.

"I'm going to get a snack. I'll be right out," Jamie called, jogging into the kitchen. Gabriel met him at the doorway, elbow-checking him as he walked out, and then turned his attention to me.

"You worry me," I told Gabriel as his arms slipped around my waist. "You worry me so much." Gabriel slipped his hands under my shirt, tracing my ribs with his fingertips.

"I take it you're feeling better?" I asked him.

He gave me a lopsided grin as he brushed kisses along my jaw.

"We can't," I whispered as he nipped at my earlobe and did that thing with his tongue that made my eyelids flap like window shades.

"We can't what?"

"We can't . . ." I made a meaningful eye gesture that in feminine circles meant "sex" or maybe "over there." "Jamie's just down the hall . . . and he has superhearing."

"He's a big boy, Jane. I'm pretty sure he knows that we have intimate relations."

"Oh, why did you say it like that?" I groaned. "That's what my grandma called it."

Gabriel shuddered, dropping his hands away from my breasts and scooting away from me. "Well, bringing up your grandmother effectively prevented all future erections, so thank you."

"I'm just uncomfortable with the idea of him being

in the house when we're having . . ." *Don't say "intimate relations." Don't say "intimate relations."*

"Happy Naked Fun Time?" Gabriel suggested.

"Exactly." I nodded.

"So, what's your suggestion?" he asked. "Are we going to resort to outdoor sex for the duration of his stay?"

"Not with Gabriel-hating archers waiting outside our door."

"Is that supposed to be funny?" he asked.

"I thought it was pretty funny!" Jamie yelled from the kitchen. "And yes, I can hear you. Every word. And I do not want to be anywhere near Happy Naked Fun Time."

Gabriel's jaw went slack with horror, and I burst out laughing.

"Sinners!" Jamie yelled.

I backed toward the door, giving Gabriel a positively sinful smile. I'd closed my hand around the doorknob just as a knock sounded on the other side. Gabriel was at my side in a flash. He looked through the peephole and pulled the door open. Ophelia was standing on the other side. In place of her usual outfits, she was wearing khaki capri pants and a cute red-checked summer blouse with cap sleeves. Her thick brown hair was smoothed back with a little red headband, for goodness sake. She looked as if she was heading to a church picnic.

I wondered who, if anyone, stayed with Georgie while Ophelia was out. She was often running around on Council business. Did she pop in a DVD for Georgie and hope for the best? Would a four-hundred-year-old child be offended if you got her a babysitter? Given her reference to plague rats, I would guess yes. But I knew that referring to Ophelia's baby sister in front of Gabriel would not improve my tenuous rapport with my local Council representative. So, for the first time, I kept my mouth shut in front of Ophelia.

"You seem to be healing quickly enough," Ophelia said, her tone dry, as she eyed Gabriel's arm slung around my shoulders.

Gabriel cleared his throat and immediately became prim, proper, public Gabriel, which he always seemed to do when Ophelia was around. "Yes, I am."

"You know, it's customary to invite someone in when they're standing on your doorstep," she said, smiling sweetly.

"Won't you please come in, Ophelia?" I asked, making an exaggerated sweeping gesture with my arm, like a game-show hostess on crack.

Rolling her eyes at me and looking very much her physical age, she strolled past me. She caught sight of the mangled interior wall and turned. "Remodeling?"

"Male bonding," I responded, at which Gabriel nudged me in the ribs.

Ophelia chuckled. "Yes, that's why I stopped by. I wanted to see how you and your young charge are getting along. I was a little concerned after our conversation. Between your siring duties and your usual personal peccadilloes, I would hate for you to be overwhelmed."

"Peccadilloes?" I parroted. "That's a bit unfair. Troubles? Sure. Drama? Certainly. But peccadilloes makes me sound like something out of a Wilkie Collins novel."

"Jane is doing a fine job with Jamie," Gabriel told her. "Considering."

"Considering?" I turned toward Gabriel to give him a scathing glare.

"It's a figure of speech," he assured me.

"An insulting figure," I grumbled. "I'm doing just fine. Our discussion the other day helped put things in perspective for me."

She gave me a small smile, then turned that frank, disconcerting gaze on Gabriel. "I understand that congratulations are in order. I was a little insulted that you didn't tell me earlier. You know that the Council tracks all vampire marriages."

"Well, we have been a little busy, what with the parenting and the poisoning and all," I said.

Ophelia's smile widened. "Yes, I received Dick's test results, which were quite impressive, by the way. The array of toxins used can leave no doubt about what the archer intended. Waco and Peter were somewhat concerned that yours was a test case, a dry run, so to speak, for attempts on other vampires. So, if nothing else, we can use connections with local businesses to watch for humans buying large quantities of rat poison and aspirin. Forewarned is forearmed and all that. I only ask that you let the Council handle any lab testing in the future. We know you're very resourceful when you need to be, but if there was a deeper investigation into the matter, we would want to be able to prove that the samples were not tampered with."

"I will definitely take advantage of that in the future. I don't think I can afford frequent access to Dick's connections."

"I know what you mean," she said. "Do you have any idea how expensive children's footwear from the 1930s can be, even with the 'Dick Cheney discount'?"

"I can honestly say, no."

"Why would you need—" Gabriel began to ask.

"Never mind," Ophelia and I chorused.

"Did you know that Bud McElray had a brother?" Ophelia asked, watching me carefully.

I subtly shifted my gaze toward Gabriel, whose hand closed over my shoulder in a comforting squeeze. "It's all right, Jane."

"How does she know about Bud?" I asked. It wasn't exactly a secret among our friends, but I thought we'd been able to keep Gabriel's tree-pushing tendencies off of the Council's radar.

"I had to tell her," Gabriel assured me. "When she was investigating you for murder, she demanded the complete story of your turning. I named Bud as the hunter responsible for your shooting. When he turned up dead, she connected the dots."

"And you're not in trouble for it?"

"He was given a rather large fine," Ophelia conceded. "The only thing that saved him from the Trial was that Mr. McElray wouldn't be missed by outspoken family members, and Gabriel had managed his little bit of revenge without stirring up much public interest."

"Is that why you asked about Bud's brother?"

"Did you know him?"

"His name's Ray McElray," I said, shrugging. "His grandma went to church with my parents, so the only information I have is from 'prayer concerns' about him and his brother."

Ophelia's confused expression prompted me to imitate my mother's voice. "Please pray for poor Velma as she had to sell ten acres to pay for Bud's fourth stint in rehab. And please pray for Ray as he begins his community service for assaulting a meter reader."

Gabriel shuddered. "We've talked about that voice, Jane."

Ophelia snickered. Rolling my eyes, I added, "He was a big-deal football player in his day, took the Howlers closer to state than they'd ever been, before or since. He actually went to college for two semesters before he blew out his knee and his scholarship got pulled."

"Do you know where he is now?"

"Yeah, he's in jail," I said, trying to remember the last bit of gossip Mama had shared with me about Ray. "He has been since about two years before I was turned. You know those big reels of scratch-off lottery tickets they have at the front of convenience stores?" Gabriel nodded. "Well, Ray kicked in the front of the Quickie Stop and stole one of them."

"That's . . . surprisingly clever," Gabriel said.

"It would have worked out, too, except that when you claim scratch-off winnings of more than six hundred dollars, you have to present valid identification. He was smart enough to redeem his winning tickets at different stores around the area, but the lottery board noticed when one man claimed more than seventy thousand dollars in scratch-off winnings within a twenty-mile radius of where a reel of tickets had been reported stolen. Still, it's far more respectable than Bud's antics, which included peeing in a public fountain during a Memorial Day service."

Ophelia's lips twisted into a disdainful moue. "And if I told you that Ray had recently been paroled? And hasn't reported to his parole officer in two weeks?"

"So, wait, you think the arrow has something to do with Gabriel's pushing the tree on top of Bud McElray?" I turned to Gabriel. "You mean, they really are after you, not me?"

"It's possible," he conceded.

"Oh, OK, then."

Gabriel scowled at me. "And by OK, I'm sure you mean, 'Oh, my love, whatever will I do if you come to harm?'" he said dryly.

"No, it's just that I'm so used to people coming after me, it's kind of a refreshing change of pace."

Gabriel pinched his nose as if he was trying to ward off a headache.

"It's my ability to find the silver lining in any situation that endears me to you," I reminded him. I turned to Ophelia. "I don't suppose you've taken Ray into custody for questioning and this whole thing could be wrapped up tidily in the next few days?"

Ophelia gave me a patronizing smirk. "Of course not. We haven't been able to track him down, either.

He has no family in the area, no property. It's like he stepped out of the facility in Eddyville and disappeared. And considering that he's being tracked by creatures with supernatural hunting instincts, that's quite the accomplishment."

"It makes sense. Mama said Ray . . . went a little survivalist after the college-dropout thing. He lived in these little hunting shanties he'd built out in the woods behind his grandparents' place, till the house was repossessed and he sort of became a permanent camper out at the state park. When he went to jail, his camper was towed to an impound lot, and Bud got his pickup truck."

"How could you possibly get that many details from gossip your mother mentioned in passing years ago?" Ophelia asked.

"Wacko survivalist lotto thieves tend to stand out in my memory. The human grapevine works just like the vampires' gossip circuit," I said. "It's just a little more oriented around coffee and cake."

She cleared her throat. "Yes, we'll be seeking Ray McElray for questioning. I think it should go without saying that you should stay on your guard."

"And yet you're saying it anyway," Gabriel muttered. I snorted, surprised that Gabriel was actually sassing the one person who seemed to intimidate him.

Clearly, I was a bad influence on him. Or maybe Jamie was a bad influence on him.

Ophelia pointedly ignored his insolence. "Don't go wandering around your property willy-nilly. Use caution while you're at your shop. We'll continue to have Council representatives discreetly drop by there and here. And please, please, do not try to track Mr. McElray down yourselves. You've proven how well you handle these confrontations on your own. We don't want a repeat of the Missy situation or the Jeanine debacle."

"I handled them fine," I mumbled.

"What was that?" she asked.

I shook my head, smiling blithely.

"You know, I've had vampires doing random checks of the woods surrounding your property off and on for days, and they haven't turned up so much as a suspicious scent. Frankly, they're getting a little bored. You're not very interesting to watch, you know. They'd heard all these wonderfully scandalous stories about you, and you're hardly living up to the hype."

"I suppose I have you to thank for telling those scandalous stories," I muttered. Ophelia had the good grace to cover her snicker with a cough.

"Have you given any more thought to who might have shot at you?" she asked.

I snorted. "No, it's not like I've devoted every waking thought to it since the night it happened. I mean, what's a debilitating poisoning between friends?"

Gabriel opened his mouth, but my wayward childe chose this moment to jog back from the kitchen, his torn T-shirt slung over his shoulder.

"You ready to be beaten on some more, old man?" he asked. Jamie's skin still held the faintest flush of his predeath tan, and the muscles he'd gained from years of baseball rippled as he moved. He shot Gabriel one of his million-watt grins, the white of his teeth somehow making the green of his eyes stand out even further. He noticed the sweet-looking teenager standing to my left and ratcheted up the power of his smile.

For her part, Ophelia was staring openly at my childe, barely restraining the drool that threatened to drip down her chin. My motherly instincts found this to be somewhat offensive, considering that I was standing three feet away, but I bit my tongue and stored it away for future blackmail material.

"Does he always walk around without his shirt like that?" she asked, the last syllable cracking slightly. Behind her, Gabriel choked on a chortle.

"No," I said pointedly. "Jamie knows better. In fact, after introducing himself politely, he will be going right upstairs and changing into something that covers his manscaping."

"I'm Jamie," he said, reaching out to shake Ophelia's hand. "Nice to meet you. And I don't manscape. But Gabriel does."

Gabriel punched Jamie's shoulder, and Jamie smacked him back. He gave Ophelia a good-natured wink, and I cringed a little. Jamie had no idea how ancient Ophelia was or her position of authority. In Jamie's mind, Ophelia was fifteen, two years younger than he was, and not quite a dating candidate. He was giving her the polite sort of charm he'd probably bestow on a friend's cute younger sister, friendly but nothing too promising.

Ophelia seemed to be caught in some sort of force field. She couldn't move. She couldn't speak. She couldn't look away from Jamie's goofy, sunny face.

I cleared my throat. "Jamie. Shirt?"

Jamie chuckled. "Right, sorry."

He took the stairs two at a time, with Ophelia's eyes glued to his back. I waved my hand in front of her face, and she seemed to shake out of her stupor. Her eyes focused on my smirking face, and she fell right back into business mode.

"We'll take care of this, Jane," she said, leveling me with those ancient eyes. "This is what we do, protecting the safety and interests of our vampire constituents. You were wise to bring this to our attention. Now, continue that line of rational thinking, and let us handle it. It will save me so much paperwork."

I sighed. "I promise."

"You promise what?" she asked. "I need specifics."

"I promise not to put myself in a situation I have to be rescued from," I grumbled as Jamie trotted back down the stairs wearing a wifebeater that showed off his arms. It was the dude equivalent of a low-cut halter top and booty shorts. My childe was a hussy.

"Good girl," she said, patting my head. "Gabriel, it was lovely as always. Jane, stay out of trouble. Jamie, it was a pleasure." She smiled demurely at him and gave a little wave as she sauntered out of the foyer.

"She seems cool," Jamie said, peering out the front window to watch Ophelia climb into her car. "How old is she?"

I found my right pointer finger raised and hovering two inches in front of Jamie's nose. "Jamie, no."

"What?" Jamie demanded. "She seems like a nice girl. You said that if I date, it has to be another vampire."

"Not *that* vampire," I insisted. "And she's not a nice girl. Nice girls don't threaten innocent librarians with dismemberment on a regular basis."

Jamie's face was puzzled, but he was still eyeing the door as if he was considering chasing Ophelia down the driveway and asking for her cell-phone number. Honestly, where was his loyalty? Clearly, constantly belittling and threatening one's sire was nothing compared with the overwhelming influence of male hormones.

"She's four hundred years old!" I blurted out.

Jamie did a bit of a double take. "Really?"

"Yes. That doesn't make her a cougar, that makes her a saber-toothed tiger."

Jamie grinned. "That's kind of hot."

"You're going to ask her out just to spite me, aren't you?"

"Maybe."

"Why couldn't you have been a girl?" I groaned.

12

There will be nights, just before dawn, when you will wonder, what has happened to my life? What happened to staying out all night and drinking the blood of the innocent? The answer is simple. You became a sire.

—*Siring for the Stupid:*
A Beginner's Guide to Raising Newborn Vampires

Of course, I immediately started looking into Ray McElray's whereabouts. I didn't plan to confront him. I just wanted to find him, so I could point the Council in the right direction.

I meant no offense to the Council and its resources, but I had a lot more faith in my own research skills. Do not mess with a librarian with a history of cyber-stalking her vampire sire and various step-grandparents.

Unfortunately, those skills got me jack squat. The house where Bud and Ray grew up had burned to the ground right after I left for college. None of the neighbors remembered anything about the family after their grandma Velma died. The Half-Moon Hollow Library hired a new youth librarian who realized that the library's passwords to state databases hadn't changed since I was fired, so that cut off my access to birth and death records. I had to use Google like everybody else. It was demoralizing.

As I was entering my credit-card information into PeopleFinder.com, I welcomed the distraction of Zeb and Jolene dragging the twins through my front door. Well, technically, Jolene had a baby under each arm. Zeb was loaded down with the ridiculous amount of paraphernalia required to sustain two babies.

Jolene huffed a breath out as she dropped the combined weight of three people on my couch. "My cousin down at the DMV says Ray hasn't come in to renew his driver's license, which did expire while he was in prison. Also, you owe him a ham, the expensive kind, from Italy."

I took Janelyn from her and nuzzled her head of strawberry-blond hair. "I feel like I should be doing my own meat-based negotiations. Parma ham isn't cheap."

"Well, to be fair, he is risking his job to help you track the guy who could be trying to kill your fiancé," Zeb pointed out as I jiggled Janelyn on my knee.

"Oh, fine, put it in perspective, why don't you?" I sighed.

"What about tax records, voter registration, magazine subscriptions?" Jolene asked.

"He can't pay taxes on wages he doesn't earn. I don't think he's legally allowed to vote. And I don't think I want to know what kind of magazines he likes," I answered.

"I think you're going about this in the wrong way,"

Zeb said. "You're looking in all the right places, all the places the Council's going to check anyway. You need to get down and dirty. You need to check all the places the Council won't think of. You know things about the people who live here, the weird Hollow underbelly, that some ancient pencil pusher wouldn't even consider a possibility. You need to embrace the Dick factor."

Jolene opened her mouth to comment. I raised my hand and put a finger to her lips.

"So, what does that mean?" I asked. "Bars? Bingo halls? Parking lots of shady roller rinks?"

"Well, I haven't heard a bad idea yet," Zeb said. "But I think you need to think outside the coffin, so to speak. Where is he getting his money? Where would he spend his time? He just got out of prison. What's his favorite food, the first place he'd head for a pig-out?"

"I don't know. It's not like I can find enough information on him to create a dossier. I have secondhand gossip from my mama."

"Do you think she knows anythin' else?" Jolene asked. "Maybe you should call her?"

"I'm doing pretty well keeping Mama off my back with all the wedding stuff, thanks to Iris's brilliant maneuverings. I don't think I should tempt fate—"

"Hi, sweetie!" I turned to find that my mother was bustling through my front door, carrying an enormous three-ring binder covered in pink Chantilly lace.

"What have you done?" I hissed at Jolene.

"Maybe a million dollars should drop out of the sky?" Jolene said, peering at the front door.

"Oh, sure, for that, your evil powers don't work," Zeb muttered.

Mama kissed my cheek and set her binder on the coffee table with a thud. Gabriel and Jamie had emerged from the kitchen to say hello to Zeb and Jolene, but seeing my mother, they simultaneously turned on their heels and used their vampire speed to disappear. I definitely liked it better when they weren't getting along.

"Mama, what are you doing here? With binders?" I waited for her to look down into her binder and said, "I thought Iris had all this stuff at her house to protect it . . . er, keep it in one place."

"Oh, I found her address and dropped by earlier to pick up some information I needed." Iris had an unlisted number, lived in the middle of nowhere, and regularly took four different routes home to keep her clients from finding her house. Clearly, I had underestimated Mama's resourcefulness. Again.

Maybe I should have asked Mama to find Ray McElray. She'd have him hog-tied in the back of her car in time to go home and watch *Law and Order*.

"You didn't break into her house, did you?"

Mama ignored the question, instead wedging herself between Jolene and me on the couch and plopping a sheaf of magazine pages onto my coffee table.

"Sweetie, I have a very important question for you," she said, her tone solemn. For a brief, horrifying moment, I thought for sure she had figured out the whole "Grandma Ruthie haunting" problem and was going to ask me just to play nice with Ruthie for eternity, for the sake of family harmony.

Mama took a deep breath. "What are you thinking as far as wedding favors?"

"I have to say, I haven't been thinking of them at all, really."

"Well, I think those little packs of Jordan almonds are becoming sort of passé. And no one does the tiny bottle of bubbles anymore. I was thinking little white plastic caskets filled with candy."

"No," I said, shaking my head very slowly. "Not a chance."

Jolene added, "One of our fancier cousins was really into Frisbee golf, so he and his wife had nice monogrammed Frisbees made up and gave them as favors."

"You want to put Dick next to an open bar and then hand him something he can throw at us?" I asked.

"Well, we can table this discussion until we get some better ideas," Mama said. "Oh, and I wanted to go over the menu for the reception with you. I know you don't eat, but you know how your uncle Dave can be if his blood sugar gets low. So I think we need to double the variety of appetizers distributed during the photos."

I sighed, reminding myself that photos were the only traditional wedding folderol that Mama was absolutely insistent on. She figured that this was the only wedding she was getting out of me, so she wanted it to be well documented. And serving appetizers while people waited around for us was just the polite thing to do.

"By his blood sugar getting low, do you mean he has too many beers and starts griping about Aunt Vi's addiction to QVC?" I asked.

"Exactly," she said, pulling a page ripped from a bridal magazine out of her binder and handing it to me. "What do you think of these?"

"Mini-cheeseburgers?" I asked, passing the burger pictorial to Jolene. "Are we going to let White Castle do the catering? That's an idea I can actually support."

"Don't be silly." She chuckled, pulling out another spread on the virtues of mini-quiches. "But your daddy would be thrilled. He just wants to make sure we have Swedish meatballs."

"Why is all the food miniature?" Jolene whispered, clearly horrified. Werewolf metabolism ran ridiculously high to help fuel their change. They had to scarf down calories all day just to sleep all night, like a little hibernation. Thanksgiving in a werewolf clan was like a full-on farm livestock massacre. And major celebrations like weddings were the sort of horrifying tale that barnyard animals might whisper to their children to keep them in line.

Zeb muttered. "There's going to be a full dinner afterward. Calm down."

"Look, I don't think you need to worry about all this," I said. "Pick whatever's going to make you and Daddy happy." Jolene cleared her throat, so I added, "And Jolene."

"But honey, you know what a nightmare it can be to make your aunts happy, meal-wise. Aunt Lyla's on Atkins again. Aunt Gladys refuses to eat anything but tuna from the can—"

"I really don't see anybody from the family coming to the wedding, Mama. I haven't spent any time with them since I came out. I don't think they're going to be comfortable around me."

"Oh, Jane, now you're really being silly," she said. "You spent Christmas with the family this year."

"I spent Christmas with you and Daddy this year, after the other relatives left for dinner at Aunt Tootsie's."

"Well, that's because you couldn't join us for lunch!" She sniffed. "Now, let's be serious, Jane. About these mini-quiches—"

Rather than face a cheese-versus-spinach debate, I blurted out, "Hey, Mama, do you remember Ray McElray?"

Mama made a clucking noise in her throat and claimed Joe from Jolene. She sighed and nuzzled the head of the closest thing she'd ever get to a grandbaby. "Poor Velma never could get those grandsons of hers straightened out. It just broke her heart, right up until the end. I'm just glad she passed before that no-account Bud had his hunting accident."

Jolene raised her eyebrows at me, questioning. I gave an imperceptible shake of the head, and she pressed her lips shut.

"And then Ray being sent to prison over something as silly as lotto tickets? I say, if you're going to go to jail for thieving, be a man about it and rob a bank. Go big or go home."

"Sometimes your mom is freaking brilliant," Zeb marveled.

Mama preened. "Thank you, Zeb."

"But no one's heard from him since he got out of prison?" I asked.

"Not really. I mean, I know he went by Margie Nash's florist shop to make sure the flowers on Bud and Velma's graves are changed every two months. Margie mentioned it at the quilt shop the other night. She said he seemed really torn up over Bud dying while he was in prison."

"I don't suppose he left a billing address?" I asked.

Mama shook her head, a perplexed expression creasing her brow. "You know, it's funny, Margie said he refused to give her one."

"Credit-card information?"

"Jane, what on earth is going on with you? Why are you asking all of these questions about someone you barely know? Oh, my Lord, is this another one of those vampire things? When did Ray get turned?"

"No, Mama, Ray's not a vampire. Did Margie say she saw him during the day?" I asked. When she nodded, I said, "OK, so he's still alive. I just need to talk to him. And I'm having a hard time tracking him down. That's all."

"Talk to him about what?" Mama demanded.

Shit. I was drawing a total blank. Why had my verbal incontinence chosen this moment to abandon me?

"She owes him money," Jolene piped up. I shot her an incredulous look. Jolene, proud of her quick thinking, added, "Well, actually, she owed Bud money. He did some yard work for her right before he died, and she was never able to pay him. She's felt guilty about it, and she wants to pay Ray instead."

OK, I had to admit that was pretty impressive. Zeb beamed at her.

"You gave Bud McElray work, Jane?" Mama asked, her head tilted at me with this strange, unfamiliar expression on her face—pride. "That was very sweet of you. I hope he didn't take advantage."

"Oh, no," Zeb said, grinning. "Bud's work really blew Jane away."

I glared at him and mouthed, "Too far."

"So, if you see him, Mama, could you call me?" I asked. "Right away? And don't approach him or anything. I'd like to talk to Ray about it myself, with him being so torn up about his brother and all."

"Sure, baby," she said, smoothing my hair back from my shoulder and patting my head fondly. "Oh! I almost forgot. I need to see your dress."

Mama bustled out of the living room, leaving me to chase her up the stairs to the master bedroom. I abused my vampire speed to get around her and clean up any incriminating items that might have been lying around our room. "I just want to match the ribbons to the gray of your dress, honey. I think you'd call it Colonial Pewter, but Iris thinks it's more of a Silverstreak."

"What in the hell are you talking about?" Mama held up a color wheel from the ribbon manufacturer, and I groaned. "You have to be stopped."

"Just get the dress out of the closet, smart-ass."

"Mama." I gasped, downright proud that she'd called me a mildly foul name. I pulled the garment bag out of the closet. I knew that something was off the moment I pulled it free. The bag's weight was distributed in a weird, bottom-heavy fashion, and the zipper was undone. I was paranoid about Gabriel sneaking a peek at the dress. There was no way I would leave it open like that. "That's weird," I muttered, carefully taking the hanger out of the bag.

Mama gasped. I was holding what looked like a burial shroud. The bodice of my dress was just a central location for the fluttering wisps of gray silk, the scraps left of the sleeves and skirt. It hadn't been cut, it had been torn, viciously, over and over, until all that remained were shreds.

On the closet floor, amid the pile of gray scraps, I saw a pair of long silver sewing scissors. They'd belonged to one of my great-aunts, who'd been a quilting enthusiast. I'd hidden them from my grandma Ruthie when I was ten, after she'd made me one too many sailor dresses. I'd spirited them away to the attic and stuck them behind a loose panel in the wall. Clearly, Grandma Ruthie had found them.

Just behind my right ear, I heard it. Cold, hissing laughter. My grandma's laughter. Disembodied laughter was probably all she was capable of, considering the effort she'd put into tailoring my dress.

My head swam as the slips of silky material fluttered through my fingers. My dress. My dress was destroyed. The only thing I'd actually liked about this whole wedding thing, beyond spending eternity with the man I love and all that hoo-ha, was the dress, and now it could have been used as a costume of a particularly slutty zombie.

"Jane?" Mama said apprehensively. I heard her step out into the hallway and call for Gabriel.

"That is it!" I screamed. Gabriel never told me exactly what I yelled after this, because it was sort of a high-pitched audio blur that made Fitz come running into the room. But in Jamie's estimation, from two floors away, it was something along the lines of "Damn it! That is the absolute limit! It's not enough that I have a teenager running around my house, drinking all my blood and reminding me how old I am. I have a crazy person trying to turn my fiancé into a pin cushion. I've got to pick out food I can't eat to feed people I don't like and pretend that I'm some sort of sacrificial virgin just so I can sleep with someone who's already living with me. And now I'm not even going to be well dressed while I do it, because some crazy-ass spirit decided to play Edward Scissorhands with the only bridal dress in the state of Kentucky that doesn't make me look like a desperate hooker!"

My legs went to jelly, slipping out from under me as I collapsed onto the floor. I heard Mama calling my name, her voice muffled as if my head were underwater. Gabriel walked into the room, and some strange instinct had me wanting to hide the dress. Since it would be bad luck for him to see it. And then the fact that I was trying to shove ribbons of unrecognizable fabric behind my back made me giggle, and then I was all-out laughing hysterically as my vision blurred and my eyes rolled up.

* * *

I didn't know that vampires could black out, but there I was, lying on the floor in my parlor with Andrea and Jolene standing over me, tutting sympathetically. Andrea helped me sit up, while Jolene handed me a warm cup of O-negative. Aunt Jettie and Mr. Wainwright were standing in the corner, Jettie wringing her hands and wiping at her cheeks while Mr. Wainwright stewed. I blinked hazily as my eyes adjusted to the lights, and I saw the pile of rags that used to be my wedding dress.

And I started to cry, like a big old hysterical bridezilla. Mama dabbed at the streaks of blood on my cheeks with a tissue. "I haven't really cared about any of this wedding stuff. That dress was the one silly wedding thing I was really excited about. Why'd she have to take that away? What the hell did I ever do to her?"

"What is she talking about?" Mama asked. "Is she hallucinating? I don't think she hit her head when she passed out."

"Where's Gabriel?" I asked, sniffing.

"Pacing outside the door," Mama said. "I called Andrea, and we convinced Gabriel that this was more of a lady issue. I didn't think you'd want him to see you like this. Also, Jamie heard you screaming and ran for the root cellar. What were you saying, anyway? You were talking so fast I couldn't understand you."

Huh. My mother had actually done what was best for me. Based on what I needed. I think that's one of the seven signs of oncoming Armageddon. But instead of being a jerk about it, I said, "Thanks, Mama."

"Jane, I am so sorry," Jettie cried, while Mr. Wainwright patted her shoulder. "She's gotten so good at hiding from us, operating under the radar. I had no idea what she was up to. If I'd had any idea . . ."

"I can't believe she did it," Andrea said. "Imagine the energy it took to shred your dress like that."

Jolene growled. "This is it. We're takin' this dead bitch down. I don't care who she is, Jane, you don't go messing with a girl's wedding dress."

"What are you two talking about?" Mama asked. "Why are you calling Jamie a 'dead bitch'? I know he can be a little disagreeable sometimes, but all teenagers are."

"What does Jamie have to do with this?" Andrea asked.

"Well, he ran for the cellar, so I assumed that he destroyed Jane's wedding dress in some sort of adolescent snit. Jane did it to one of Jenny's pep-squad uniforms when they were in high school."

"It was her away uniform. And she tore down my wall-sized collage of Keanu Reeves pictures. She had it coming."

"Agreed," Andrea said.

"But if Jamie didn't do it, who did?" Mama asked. "You said 'she.' What did you mean?"

I tried to picture telling Mama that her own mother was (a) hanging around the earthly plane and (b) spending that time threatening/annoying the bejesus out of me. I didn't see that going over well. So, of course, I was preparing a completely plausible story about further retaliation from the Chamber of Commerce, when Jolene said, "She means the ghost of—"

"The ghost of River Oaks!" I exclaimed, shaking my head at Jolene.

"Honey, that's silly. The house isn't haunted. River Oaks has been in our family for generations, and we've never heard anything about a ghost, much less a ghost that goes around cutting up dresses. Besides, there's no such thing as ghosts."

"Mom, your daughter's a vampire, and you can't believe there's such a thing as ghosts?"

She frowned. "Good point. OK, if it's a ghost, who is it?"

Jolene, ever freaking helpful, said, "Oh, it's—"

"A poltergeist," I ground out, glaring at her. "A poltergeist with absolutely no backstory or personality whatsoever. It was most likely attracted by the chaos of Jamie's adolescent energy. We only call it a her because it does such petty, teenage, dirty, vicious, bitchy, hateful—"

Andrea cleared her throat. "OK, Jane, we get it."

"Yes, and I'm going to get something, too. An exorcist, do you hear me, old woman? I don't care who else you take to the next plane with you. You're out."

"Well, I didn't understand any of that," Mama said. "And right now, I think we need to focus on your dress. Is there any part of it that can be salvaged?"

I held the two largest scraps. "As a formal blindfold, maybe."

"Save that for the honeymoon." Andrea snickered.

"Really? You've got jokes?" I muttered.

"We'll just call the costume shop and see if they have anything like it," Mama said. "And if they don't, we might have to go back to the bridal shop."

I groaned.

"I'm sorry, Jane, honey."

"No you're not," I shot back.

She nodded. "You're right."

I barked out a soggy laugh and swiped at my cheeks. "Well, at least you're honest."

Mama hitched her purse over her shoulder. "I'm going to call Iris, honey. Don't you worry about a thing. Mama's going to take care of everything."

With that, she kissed me on the forehead and walked into the hallway.

She called over her shoulder, "And you might let Gabriel know you're OK, because he's out here pacing a hole in the carpet."

Gabriel came rushing into the room and threw his arms around me. "I've never heard you make a sound like that before. It was terrifying. Please don't do it again. All screaming in this room should be of the pleasant variety."

"Ew," Andrea muttered.

"We are exorcising Grandma Ruthie," I growled. "Tonight. She's gone too far this time. Call me names, fine. Move stuff around, OK. But this is where I draw the line, do you hear me, Ruthie?"

I heard an indignant hiss behind me, but Ruthie wasn't able to do much more than move a few strands of my hair. She was exhausted by her efforts. Now was the best time to strike.

"I just happen to have pulled out your 'Exorcising Grandma Ruthie' file while you were, er, indisposed," he said, handing me the stack of papers I'd collected on exorcism rites. "You circled the ritual you thought would work best. I sent Dick out to collect a virgin goat."

"You are so the guy for me." I sighed and stood on my tiptoes to kiss him thoroughly. "Aunt Jettie!"

"Yes, honey, I'm standing right behind you," she said gently.

I turned around to find her and Mr. Wainwright eyeing me as if I were one of those performing bears that turned on their owners. "I need you and Mr. Wainwright to get as far away from here as possible. I don't really know what I'm doing, and I don't want to accidentally send you into the white light."

"If we go, we go," Jettie said. "I don't want you to keep her hanging around the house because you're afraid of hurting me."

"What's existence without the risk of the unknown?" Mr. Wainwright said, stroking his cool, misty hand along my cheek.

"We're not leaving you until the time is right." Jettie's cold arms embraced me, sending shivers down my spine. "We'll come back tomorrow night, unless, of course, you jettison us into the great beyond."

"That's very helpful, thanks," I said.

As the pair of them faded away, I turned to my favorite werewolf.

"Jolene, honey, I love you, but you and Zeb need to take the kids and go home. I don't want some sort of creepy accidental possession thing to happen to the twins."

Jolene opened her mouth to protest but quickly shut it. "You're right. I know you're right. And I hate it. I'll find some other way to help. Be careful."

Zeb and Jolene gathered up their brood and headed out. Dick arrived with the goat. I didn't ask questions about where he got it or why he chose to load it into the backseat of Andrea's car, rather than his El Camino. While Jamie and Gabriel helped him wrestle it off of the half-devoured backseat, Andrea asked, "Are you sure that you're not rushing this?"

I shook my head. "No."

"Do you have any clue what you're doing?"

"No."

"Are you sure this is going to work?"

"No."

She wrapped an arm around my shoulder and clapped me on the back. "Excellent. It will be just like running the shop, then."

13

There will be times when you will have to discipline
your childe. Remember, a fair sire is a sire who
doesn't wake up chained outside at dawn covered
in suntan oil.

—*Siring for the Stupid:*
A Beginner's Guide to Raising Newborn Vampires

Four hours.

Four hours spent chanting and dancing around that
stupid goat, surrounded by protective sea salt. And not
one peep out of Grandma Ruthie. Nothing. Nada. Zilch.
For all we knew, Ruthie was lurking in the attic, sharp-
ening a stake. The only good news was that we hadn't
accidentally sent Jettie and Mr. Wainwright into the
next plane. Mr. Wainwright was hard at work searching
through the inventory, trying to find ways to determine
whether the exorcism had worked and, if not, how to
perform a far more effective one.

I will admit that I'd sort of gone into the whole
thing half-cocked. There were all these warnings about
meditating and centering oneself before the ritual that
I'd completely ignored, because I was pissed. Given

my half-assery and my shaky emotional state, I was lucky that no one had gotten hurt during the exorcism. Although Dick might never forgive me if the footage Jamie surreptitiously shot with my cell phone showed up on YouTube.

Even with a few clarifying days' worth of hindsight behind me, I still had occasional crying jags when I realized how much animosity Grandma Ruthie had to feel toward me to do something like that. The very woman who had been after me my entire life to be more feminine and traditional had taken my wedding dress and turned it into confetti. Iris had already sent me pictures of dress designs that were similar to the one I'd found. I'd tried looking through them a few times, but then I would start thinking about shopping for another dress with only a few more weeks before the wedding. I would start crying at the very idea. Gabriel would get uncomfortable with my blatant and heretofore unprecedented show of girliness and call Jolene. Jolene would bring over dessert blood and a Jane Austen DVD. Gabriel and Jamie would hide somewhere in the house.

My young ward had been suspiciously quiet lately. I wasn't sure whether it was because he'd heard me have a complete nervous breakdown. Or whether the snippy antics of the little-old-lady ghost in our house had scared him. Knowing my luck, he was having some sort of Internet romance, and I'd come home to find some sixteen-year-old Goth chick from Kansas City sleeping on my couch.

I didn't even know how to begin to approach him.

What if it was some guy problem that would gross me out? What if it was some adolescent vampire problem I was completely unprepared for? I'd asked Gabriel to step in and talk to him, and although the conversation was cordial, Gabriel said Jamie hadn't coughed up any information about what was bothering him and kept trying to distract Gabriel with discussions of Civil War history—clearly a desperate measure on Jamie's part.

Unable to help Jamie, I found that distracting myself with work helped. It made me feel like a guilty, harried working mother, leaving him with Gabriel all night, but it was better than sitting around the house, staring at Jamie . . . which seemed to upset him.

At the shop, I could search for exorcism tips. I could search for information about Ray McElray without Gabriel breathing down my neck, trying to assure himself that I wasn't about go all solo vigilante on some menacing redneck. Apparently, he wanted to be with me when I went all vigilante.

Andrea sat at the end of the coffee bar, going over the books for the quarter. Sales were looking up this week, as rumor had spread about the wedding because of Mama's caterwauling about her "youngest girl *finally* getting married." It seemed that local vampire and human gossip worked much like celebrity politics. Sure, my neighbors and acquaintances had accused me of everything short of hog-tying Jamie in the back of Big Bertha and turning him against his will, but all of that could be forgiven and forgotten if a big, splashy wedding was on the horizon. Even if that wedding was neither big nor splashy. People

I hadn't spoken to in years came into the shop, asking about the wedding. High school classmates, even the ones who wrote "sucks" after my name on the Key Club posters, stopped by to make sure they got an invite. Mama's friends dropped by with engagement presents, mostly cookbooks and crock pots, which was sort of ironic if you thought about it.

I responded by looking up the cost of airline tickets to Niagara Falls.

On the plus side, between the wedding looky-loos and the nutters who wanted me to turn them, the increased shop traffic resulted in more sales, which was starting to tilt the accounts a bit more toward the black side. This made balancing them a little less of a chore for Andrea, who preferred vaguely positive news to "we're going brooooooke" news.

Andrea hit the total button on the calculator and cleared her throat. "Well, we suck as ghostbusters, but we're pretty fair book salesmen. If we continue like this for the next six weeks, we can turn around the damage done by your Jamie escapade."

"I think 'escapade' is a slightly unfair description, but that is good news," I said, closing the cash drawer with a final jangle. "You know, it's been kind of nice having a boring night at work. Even if Mary Beth Cartwright, whose name I could not remember at our tenth reunion, did come in and tell me she didn't care when or where my wedding was, she was coming because it was that important to her."

"Aw, honey, weddings bring out the weird in people,"

Andrea said, waving her hand at me. "Remember how pissed off my parents were that I didn't invite them to mine? I mean, they disown me for consorting with vampires, and then they have the nerve to be 'deeply hurt by my selfish actions' when I don't let Daddy Dearest walk me down the aisle?"

"You did send them a wedding announcement."

She snorted. "I did that to give me closure. And to give them one last flip of the proverbial middle finger. I did not expect terse and passive-aggressive e-mails about how hard-hearted and ungrateful I am to exclude them from my life."

"You know, sometimes I worry that we've been a bad influence on you," I told her. "You were such a nice girl as a human."

And again, she snorted. "Please, I'm ten times happier as a vampire. My only regret is that I can't track down a boyfriend or two and use my evil vampire powers to hypnotize him into stripping naked and dancing the Highland Fling every time he hears the word 'hello.'"

"But he would hear it several times every day," I told her.

"What's your point?"

I shook my head, wondering where my classy, demure friend had gone. "That's just wrong . . . And still, even with that disturbing image burned into my cerebral cortex, this is still more fun than being at home."

"Jamie still having teenage angst?"

"Like an episode of *Dawson's Creek*." I sighed.

Gabriel and Dick came moseying through the front door, arguing over Dick's illegal parking habits. Dick had driven Gabriel into town so we could take Big Bertha home. Since Gabriel's injury, the guys were adamant that we not drive home or close up the shop on our own. And frankly, I can't say that I blame them. Equally bad things had happened to the two of us when we'd closed up solo.

"And the menfolk arrive to escort us defenseless females to the safety of our keep." Andrea sighed.

"You have got to stop giving her Jane Austen books," Dick told me.

"Did you have a good night?" Gabriel asked, nudging my hair aside so he could kiss the nape of my neck.

"We had an uneventful night, for which I am thankful," I said. "And I am ready to go home. Who's with Jamie?"

"Actually, I thought it would be OK to leave him alone for an hour. He's been behaving so well lately, it seemed sort of insulting to keep treating him like a baby."

"Look at you, being all reasonable." I chuckled, grabbing my purse from under the counter. I paused and gave him a speculative look. "You locked up all the liquor in the house before you left, didn't you?"

He shrugged. "I would have set the parental controls on the cable channels, but you've never shown me how."

I laughed, waiting for Andrea to lock and gate the front door before we split for our respective cars. I sniffed the air, wrinkling my nose at the roiling scent of burning plastic. "Do you smell that?"

I caught sight of Gabriel's horrified expression and turned to where he'd parked Big Bertha, nearly a block away. A small spear of flame spiked up from under the hood. The fire seemed to spring to life, sucking in air as it spread over the hood and bubbled the windshield with the force of its heat.

"No!" I exclaimed, running toward it, but Gabriel and Andrea dragged me away. Dick sprinted past with the shop's fire extinguisher in hand. As he sprayed the engine compartment with foam, a sickening golden glow spread inside the car. The upholstery lit up like a wick, sucking the flames into the cabin of the station wagon. Even from a distance, I could see the windows buckling under the pressure of expanding hot air.

"Dick, get back!" I yelled, just as the windows exploded, sending shards of glass hurtling our way. Dick yelped, covering his face with his hands as he collapsed to the ground. Gabriel forced me to the concrete, then tackled Andrea to keep her from running to Dick. The fire extinguisher clattered to the ground and rolled under the flaming wreckage of my car.

"Get inside, now!" Gabriel yelled as he pulled Dick away from the fire.

I helped Andrea unlock the shop gate and crawl to the safety of the door. I heard the siren of a fire truck squealing down the street toward us. By the time Gabriel fireman-carried Dick into the shop, I was in full-on meltdown mode.

"He killed Big Bertha!" I seethed. "He killed my car."

"And I'm just fine, thanks," Dick mumbled as his cheeks expelled dozens of splinters of glass. The tiny cuts healed over, leaving Dick handsome, pale, and whole.

"Sorry, Dick, are you OK?" I asked, feeling selfish and

guilty as Andrea pressed a warm cloth from the coffee bar against Dick's bloodstained cheeks.

"Fine," he said, swiping at the bloodied, torn "Beer— It's What's for Dinner" T-shirt with disdain. "Ruined my favorite shirt, but I'm fine."

Behind him, Andrea mouthed, "Thank you, God."

"I can't believe Ray did this," I growled. "I thought he was angry with Gabriel. With the exception of trying to run me down, he hasn't done anything to put me in danger. Why would he go destroy a car that is clearly not something Gabriel would drive?"

I saw a guilty, furtive look flash between Dick and Gabriel.

"What?" I demanded.

"There was a note on the hood," Gabriel said, pulling the paper out of Dick's back pocket. "It was pinned to your grille with a wooden stake."

" 'Stop hiding behind her or she gets hurt,' " I read aloud. "Well, that's sort of misleading. You're not exactly in hiding. You've been recovering from his arrow wounds. And he hasn't been all that proactive, either. I mean, we're just sitting there like dead ducks all day, and he hasn't even made an attempt to break into the house."

Cue another guilty, furtive look between Gabriel and Dick.

I sighed. "You two should never play poker. Come on, out with it."

Gabriel cleared his throat. "Erm, the reason he hasn't tried to break into the house during the day is that I contracted with a company Dick recommended to install a comprehensive security system at the house. The contractors worked during the day while we were asleep and finished before we woke so you wouldn't notice the changes. Everything they installed complemented the renovations you'd already done. The window panes were replaced by bulletproof glass. The sunless shades now bolt from the inside with a magnetic lock that will only release when triggered by outdoor UV sensors. The doors were bolstered with reinforced steel. And the doorknobs emit an increasing electric shock to whoever tries to use them without a key."

"But why didn't you tell me any of this?"

"Because I didn't want to panic you into thinking that McElray had us running scared. And you tend to get a little crazy when anyone suggests changes to the house," he said. Dick nudged him, and he added, "And you would have objected to the cost."

My eyes narrowed. "How much would I have objected?"

"Remember last year's tax bill? The one that made you hyperventilate into a paper bag?" he asked.

"That much?"

Gabriel winced. "Triple it."

"Triple!"

"Between the secrecy and the rush job and the measures they had to take to keep it from being noticeable, it added up," he said sheepishly. "I suppose it's too late to say it was an early wedding present." He tried to fake a winsome smile.

I glared at him. "What happened to not keeping things

from me anymore?" I demanded. "What happened to no more leaving me out of the loop? And how the hell has Mama been able to get into the house during the day to drop off wedding stuff if the doorknobs are electrified?"

Gabriel cleared his throat and very softly said, "They're electrified if you try to open the door without a key."

"You gave my mother a key?"

Dick nudged his wife toward the door. He whispered, "Run."

Fortunately for Gabriel, a lady in a fireman's uniform knocked on the shop door at that very moment, and I was unable to carry through my plan involving a more thorough smacking with Tolkien. Anna Mastrofilippo, the only female assistant chief with the Half-Moon Hollow Volunteer Fire Department, stepped through the door with a bemused, frustrated look on her round, cherubic face. Anna was one of the first graduates of my after-school program for advanced readers.

"Miss Jane," she said. "Would you care to explain how a half-gallon tank of gas got lodged next to your engine block with a rag wick hanging out of the spout?"

"Anna—"

"Look, I know weddings are expensive, but if you're going to set fire to your own car to collect the insurance money, you're going to have to come up with a less obvious way to do it. I've got to report this to the police as arson! My mama's going to have a fit when she finds out. You know she loves you. All she talks about is that Tuesday Night Book Club that meets down here. She can't wait for it to get started up again, even if it means that Rosie Lanier never speaks to her again. And now I have to tell her that I got you arrested and her book club shut down."

"Anna, I did not set Big Bertha on fire for the insurance money. For one thing, I wouldn't get that much money. And for another, you know I would not do that to anything that belonged to Aunt Jettie. There's this person who's been leaving us threatening messages. The car is just his latest note. So far, we've let the vampire authorities handle it. There are reports, if you'd like to look them up."

I handed her the note from Ray. "Down at the Council office, right?" she asked, scribbling on her clipboard. "I'll ask Ophelia for the paperwork."

"You know Ophelia?"

"Oh, sure, we, um, handle a few vampire-related fires every year," she said, looking a little uncomfortable. She cleared her throat. "So, Mama wants to know why you haven't called the bakery to order your wedding cake."

Thrown by the sudden shift in conversational lanes, I stuttered. "W-well, that's one of the things the wedding planner hasn't booked yet."

To be honest, I hadn't really thought much about the cake, since I wasn't going to be eating any of it. And I really hadn't thought of it in the last few minutes, what with the "burning car" scenario playing out. But Mrs. Mastrofilippo worked at one of the best bakeries in town, so it made sense to order from her . . . even if I found the idea of a three-layer Italian cream cake that

I couldn't enjoy extremely depressing. And since Anna had her finger on the "Jane gets charged with vehicular arson" button, I decided it was prudent to play along.

"Well, tell her to call," Anna said. "I think Mama's feelings are a little hurt that you haven't come by yet. When is the big day, anyway?"

"July eighth."

"This the fella?" she asked, nodding toward Gabriel. He smiled and shook her hand as I murmured introductions. "Well, I'll be expecting my invitation," she said, offering me the clipboard. "I need you to sign here. We'll have your car towed to the scrapyard. You'll have thirty days to claim it before they stick it in one of those cubing machines."

Dazed, I signed the release form. Anna bid my friends good-bye and left the shop, calling for her colleagues to "haul it!"

I turned to Andrea and Dick. "What just happened?"

When Gabriel and I arrived home, I was frustrated, sick, and tired. I knew that Big Bertha was only a car. I knew that she was just a hunk of metal and badly repaired paint. But she was also Aunt Jettie's car. Big Bertha was the car she'd used to teach me how to drive, the first and only vehicle I'd ever owned. And now she was a pile of scrap metal. I wanted nothing more than a long, hot bath and a long pull off the bottle of Hershey's Blood Additive Syrup. But the moment I stepped through the front door of River Oaks, I could tell something was wrong.

The house was too quiet. There was no jumbled mess of sneakers by the door, no video-game noises coming from the parlor. There was no life in the house.

"Where is he?" I murmured, before calling, "Jamie!"

"What's wrong?" Gabriel asked as I sped up the stairs.

"He's gone!" I shouted from the landing after I'd searched Jamie's room. "There's no sign of him. What if he's hurt, Gabriel? What if Ray McElray came here before setting my car on fire? What if—"

Gabriel gripped my arms as I tried to sprint past him toward the front door. "We can't think like that. Let's just calm down and try to think clearly before you go running off into some bizarre redneck trap. Also, your aunt Jettie is hovering behind you, trying to find a way to break into the conversation without startling you."

I turned to find Jettie, wringing her hands. "Honey, I couldn't stop him. Nothing I said made any difference. He wanted to see them so badly. I think he's been waiting for an opportunity like this for weeks, and Gabriel leaving was just the excuse he needed."

"Wanted to see who, exactly?"

"His family," Aunt Jettie said, cringing.

I sighed. "How long ago did he leave, Aunt Jettie?"

"About thirty minutes ago," Jettie said. "I stalled him for almost an hour before he took off. I had to play the pleading-grandma card to the hilt to keep him that long." She frowned, adding, "Ruthie might have been able to get him to stick around."

"I have to go after him." I turned on Gabriel. "We can't let him get near his family. He could lose control.

He could hurt one of them. He'd never forgive himself if he did."

"I'll come with you," he said.

I nodded and leaped off the front porch and took off at full sprint toward the Lanier place on Melody Lane. As I ran, pushing myself faster than I could possibly have driven there, I thought of the horrors that could be waiting for us at Jamie's house. What would I do if he'd hurt one of his family members? Could I blame him, after the things his mother had said to him? Would I be able to turn him over to Ophelia?

"You realize, of course, that we could have driven my car," Gabriel said as we skidded to a stop at the end of Jamie's driveway.

"About half a mile ago, yes," I said, resisting the urge to pant. I scanned the front yard of the Lanier home. Jamie was nowhere to be seen, but I could sense three very active minds inside the house. The thoughts weren't happy, exactly, more contented and relaxed, certainly not the thought patterns of a family being terrorized by their former son. I crept around the side of the house and found Jamie standing there, in the shadow of an elm tree, tracks of blood tears streaming down his cheeks as he peered through the lit window. He stood on the edge of that golden patch of light, barely visible even to my keen eyes. I approached him slowly. His ears perked up, and his eyes shifted toward me, but he didn't move. I carefully closed my fingers around his arm.

In the gentlest voice I could manage, I said, "Jamie, we've talked about this. You can't leave the house alone.

And you definitely don't want to make contact with your family when they've told you to stay away."

Jamie looked through the window and watched as his family sat around the kitchen table, eating pizza. They were talking about their day and laughing. It was hesitant, soft laughter, but they seemed to be enjoying themselves. Jamie's jaw worked as he ground his teeth.

"Jamie—"

"I'm sick of this," he whispered. "I'm sick of being locked away like I did something wrong. Look at them! They're just carrying on with Pizza Night, like I'm not even gone. Like I was never there in the first place! Why did this happen to me? What did I ever do? This isn't fair! I didn't ask for this."

I looked over my shoulder, where Gabriel was waiting. I thought of my own postexistential crisis, when I'd clung to the ceiling like a cartoon cat and accused Gabriel of slipping me a roofie so he could have his way with me and then turn me. So far, Jamie's outburst was less accusatory but more heartfelt. He was far more levelheaded than I had been as a kid, YouTube antics aside. I thought back to all of the arguments I'd had with my mother growing up and how I'd hated it when she told me I was overreacting when I dared to express my feelings. So, instead, I nodded and said, "You're right."

Jamie did a bit of a double take and spluttered, "Wh-what?"

"No, you're right, this sucks. I'm sorry this happened to you. I'm sorry I was the one who did this to you. If I could go back to that night in front of my shop and move just a little bit faster, do more to warn you about the car—I would do anything to keep you from getting hurt, Jamie. You deserved a normal human life. Going to the prom. Finishing high school. Accidentally knocking up your girlfriend your sophomore year of college. Getting a nine-to-five job, so you can support her after your shotgun wedding—"

"You know, you're not making human life sound all that great."

"Huh." I chuckled. "I guess I'm not."

"Probably better off as a vampire," he admitted, dropping to the ground and leaning against the tree.

"Probably." I sat down next to him.

"It's not fair," he said, his voice suddenly calm and clear. "It's not fair that they can just kick me out of the family. It's not right that parents can just decide not to love their kid anymore."

"You're right," I told him. "You are absolutely entitled to be pissed right now. But the thing about family is that you can't control what they do. Trust me when I say that. If I could control my mother, the world would be a good and decent place. You can only control how you respond to it. And if they never come around, if they shun you for the rest of your life, it's their loss."

Jamie nodded, his head bent so low that his chin was practically touching his chest. Slowly, inch by inch, he leaned his head toward me until his temple was touching my shoulder. Blinking furiously, I slipped my arm around his shoulder.

"Your life is never going to be the same, but it can

be so much more interesting," I told him. "I would hate
for you to miss out on it because you were scared or too
hung up on your past to look to your future."

He groaned. "Did Tony Robbins write that?"

And thus endeth the poignant siring moment.

"You are such a pain in the ass sometimes," I told him
as I helped him to his feet. "Look, I'm all for letting these
emotional breakthroughs breathe, but we've got to get
out of here before your family looks out the window and
sees our pale asses lurking outside their window like a
pair of undead Peeping Toms."

In the distance, I could see Gabriel's whole body relax
as we moved away from the house.

"What even made you run off like that? I know you've
been quiet and a little withdrawn lately, but I thought
we've been getting along better."

Jamie shot me a sheepish look. "For the last few weeks,
I've been hearing this voice in my head, whispering.
While I was trying to sleep. While I was playing video
games. While I played with Fitz. It was telling me how
I didn't belong at River Oaks, that my family missed
me, that my mother probably wanted to see me. How
much I was hurting them by staying with you. And I just
couldn't take it anymore. Gabriel left, and I thought it
wouldn't hurt anything if I just ducked over to see them.
And then I got here and saw that they weren't exactly
pining away for me."

"This voice that whispered to you, was it male or
female?" I asked.

"I don't know," he said. "It sounded all hoarse and whispery, kind of like that Voldemort guy in the Harry Potter movies."

"Yep, definitely Grandma, then," I grumbled.

"But I thought you did that exorcism thing," he said.

"The more time we spend together, the more you'll see that I fail miserably at about half of the things I try."

"Really?"

"Really," Gabriel said, taking my hand and settling between us as we walked toward home, putting a brotherly arm around Jamie's shoulder. "In fact, her failures are far more entertaining than her achievements. Have I ever told you about her foray into the local Chamber of Commerce?"

"Actually, my mom told me about that," said Jamie, who was conspicuously not throwing off Gabriel's proffered arm. "Didn't you and your sister end up wrestling in the mud at the Fall Festival?"

"Yes, we did, and that's why I don't consider it a failure, because Jenny and I get along much better now that we've knocked some sense into each other," I said, glaring at Gabriel. "I learn something from all of my failures, so it's not something to laugh about, really."

"What about the time you tried to move me into your house in the dead of night, so your mother wouldn't know that we were premaritally cohabiting, only to have her show up on our lawn, screaming her head off? What was the lesson there?"

As Jamie guffawed, I ground out, "That when I tell

you to take a twenty-mile detour around my parents' house while moving your stuff, you should do it, even if it sounds silly?"

Gabriel snickered. "What about the time—"

"Oh, my Lord, when will you run out of stories?"

"Never, I hope." Jamie chortled.

Gabriel feigned offense. "So, you're saying that I'm like your drunken, senile auntie?"

"Pretty much," Jamie agreed. "So, tell me some more Jane stories. Is it true that right after she was turned, she ended up dancing naked in the fountain outside the library?"

I grumbled, "I definitely liked it better when you two weren't on friendly terms."

14

There are rewards to being a sire: companionship, passing along your knowledge, and keeping up to date with the more modern generation. And the added bonus of having someone who will honestly tell you, "Do not leave the house in that outfit."

—*Siring for the Stupid:*
A Beginner's Guide to Raising Newborn Vampires

With the household's teen crisis averted and the research into Ray McElray and exorcism at a standstill, I went about trying to solve the wedding-dress problem in a way that did not involve further shopping.

For one thing, I resisted shopping whenever possible. And for another, I didn't have a car. The reports had been dutifully filed with the insurance company and Ophelia, who, mysteriously, had come to the house to collect them. If she kept up with the visits, I was going to have to buy Jamie a case of that stupid Axe stuff.

Jamie, for his part, was trying to make up for his scampering off by being more helpful around the house. Even his room was less of a pit. And when he heard the faint whisperings of my grandmother's voice, he either told her off or came to me to tell me what she'd said. Grandma Ruthie was becoming quite the slippery little specter. Neither Jettie nor Mr. Wainwright could seem to catch up to her when she made her appearances in the house. She was always one room away, just a little bit too fast. She was the freaking Hamburglar of the ghost world.

Big Bertha was a total loss. Even Dick's numerous contacts didn't have the power to resuscitate a car from the dead. Her carcass was sitting at the Half-Moon Hollow Scrap 'n' Salvage waiting to be cubed. Gabriel had offered to let me use his car. Heck, he'd even tried taking me down to an all-night dealership in Murphy to pick out a new one as an early wedding present. But I wasn't ready for another car yet. And I was sulking a little.

So, Friday night found me in front of the mirror, trying on every dress I had, trying to salvage some sort of wedding outfit that would keep me out of the bridal shops. My choices so far had included a navy-blue church dress with a sailor collar that my mama had purchased for me in high school and a vintage red dress of Aunt Jettie's that I'd worn to a Christmas party here at River Oaks. There was also a strapless black number that I'd worn to Jolene's engagement party, only to be found by Zeb's mother, rumpled and pantiless in a parking-lot clutch with Gabriel.

Wearing the black dress, I stood in front of the mirror, considering the red. It was perfect—fabulous, even. Cinched at the waist with a scarlet sash, the luscious, floaty material fell in a perfect bell around my knees. I even had a pair of sassy pomegranate-dyed pumps to match, thanks to my many turns as a bridesmaid. It was sort of sweet to have something of Jettie's to wear as my wedding dress. And the idea of a vampire wearing a blood-red dress down the aisle tickled me. But it wasn't the gray dress.

I sighed. With a couple of quick phone calls, Iris could do away with the whole Austen theme. Hell, she could probably work with this dress and turn the wedding into some mod 1960s masterpiece. I was just going to have to suck it up and make the best of it.

Jolene came into my room, hefting a white garment bag. "Hey!" she sing-songed, laying the bag on my bed and kissing my cheek.

"If that's your bridesmaid's dress and you're here to kick my ass, I will remind you that I asked your aunt to leave off the butt bow this time. Consider it a gesture of goodwill."

"No, believe it or not, I am not here to avenge myself for the radioactive yellow you picked out," she taunted. "I am a good friend, you jackass. And I have two surprises for you tonight."

"Isn't that what Marley told Scrooge?"

"Jane," she huffed. "And by the way, it was three ghosts. Yes, I have read that book, so suck it. The first surprise is this. I didn't want to get your hopes up until it was finished."

Jolene unzipped the garment bag and whipped it away. She was holding my wedding dress, re-formed. The beading, the color, and the shape of the dress were all the same.

"How?" I asked, hesitantly fingering the water-soft material as if it would evaporate into smoke.

She grinned impishly. "The women of the pack re-created it from a picture of the original dress. I had some shots on my phone from the bridal shop, and Aunt Vonnie still had your measurements from the bridesmaid dress fittings. It turns out my aunts can make clothes that are actually flattering."

"But your aunts hate me."

She cringed. "Well, you're not their favorite person. But my mama doesn't hate you. And she's the alpha female, so she told them to pull their heads out of their tails and do something nice for a girl who's been such a good friend to me."

My eyes stung, and I felt my nose tingle, a sure sign that I was about to burst into tears. Instead, I threw my arms around her and tackled her into a hug. She lost her footing, and we landed on my bed, my dress fluttering safely to the side as I sobbed.

Andrea came wandering through the door and made an ugly snorting noise. "Please, for the love of God, don't let Dick see you doing that. He already writes too many imaginary letters to *Penthouse* without the help of visual aids."

I giggled, sniffing as I helped Jolene up. I held the hanger up for her inspection. "It's my dress!"

"I know," Andrea said, grinning. "I helped with some of the basting."

"You knew?"

"We didn't want to get your hopes up, just in case it didn't come out."

"Can I try it on now?"

"Actually, my mama's going to do a fitting with you on Monday. In fact, Zeb is taking the dress to a safe, undisclosed location across town, so certain scissor-happy ghosts don't get their bitchy mitts all over it." Jolene yelled the last bit, just in case Grandma Ruthie was listening. "We've already called Iris to tell her to call off the dress search."

"Does *everyone* know my wedding planner's cell number?" I wondered.

"I think she sees you as a special case," Jolene told me. "She needs all the help she can get."

"What's the second surprise?" I asked. "Did you get 'N Sync back together so they could play the reception?"

"No, I think we can agree that it's for the greater good that they stay separated," Andrea retorted, patting my head. "The surprise is that we're going out tonight. It's your bachelorette party. We are going to distract you from the chaos of your everyday life by dragging you to several bars, getting you blind, stinking drunk, and making a public spectacle of you. There may also be an obscene lollipop bouquet involved."

"You're going to take me to the Meat Market, aren't you?" I groaned, thinking of the only all-male, nearly nude revue in the tristate area, where we'd subjected Jolene to similar premarital humiliation. Once again, this confirmed my theory that bachelorette parties were less about celebrating the end of a girl's single days and more about friends getting revenge for what the bride put them through during the planning process.

Jolene threw her head back and laughed. "And Jenny's waitin' downstairs. Surprise."

I went to the mirror to give my hair a quick brush and slap on a little lip gloss. "Is my mama downstairs, too? Because that would really ramp up the yikes factor."

Andrea shook her head. "No. I thought about it, but I'd like to be able to look your mama in the eye again."

This was my own fault, really. I'd insisted on having the bachelorette party long before the wedding. Because I'd gone on girls' nights with Jolene and Andrea before, and I didn't want to start my married life feeling like something recently scraped off Lindsay Lohan's shoe. Gabriel was not happy with the idea of us going out alone. In fact, he'd done his best to talk Andrea and Jolene out of any bachelorette shenanigans. But they'd convinced him that it was wrong to stop living our lives, just because some crazy redneck had turned my car into barbecue. They wanted to give me the full bridal experience, they said, which made me think that they were still holding grudges about their own bachelorette soirees. I have to learn to practice restraint when it comes to bachelorette accessories. Making Andrea wear the penis tiara all over town was probably going a bit too far, but she had made me tie perfectly square bows on more than fifty lawn chairs for her outdoor ceremony. It felt justified at the time.

I sighed and slipped on some black kitten heels. "Let my bachelorette quote-unquote fun begin."

"Aren't you going to change?" Andrea asked.

I looked down at the little black dress I was wearing. "What's wrong with this?"

"Jane, you are not wearing that dress," Andrea told me. "You do not make good decisions in that dress. Remember Jolene's first girls' night out after the babies? You tried to get a tattoo, but your skin kept healing up."

"That tattoo would have been really cute," I insisted.

"It was a full back piece composed of flaming skulls!" Andrea exclaimed.

"Which is why I don't drink tequila anymore."

Thank God she didn't know that this dress was also a contributing factor in the engagement-party parking-lot incident.

"A little help here?" Andrea begged Jolene.

"Don't look at me," Jolene said. "I love that dress. Bad Decision Jane is a hoot."

"You suck," Andrea countered.

"Well, you're the vampire, so that means *you* suck."

"I'm leaving now," I told them, grabbing my purse.

Andrea and Jolene bickered as we descended the stairs to find Zeb and Dick helping Jamie set up some sort of *Call of Duty* mega-tournament.

True to Jolene's word, Jenny was waiting downstairs in the living room. She was wearing black skinny jeans and a slinky red beaded top, a far cry from her usual twin sets. As I rounded the corner into the living room, I could see her twisting her hands in her lap, a clear Jenny sign of discomfort. Jamie was on the end of the couch, fiddling with a controller and chugging a Faux Type O. Jenny was sitting as far away from him as possible, eyeing him warily. Gabriel was sitting close by, pretending to read the newspaper but keeping a close watch on our charge for signs of bloodlust.

"Ready to go, Jen?"

"Yep!" she cried, her voice cracking as she sprang to her feet and practically ran across the room. I rolled my eyes as she fluffed my hair. "You look nice. Doesn't she look nice, Gabriel?" Jenny tittered in a high, panicked pitch.

Gabriel put his paper down. "Yes, I love that dress. I have very fond memories attached to that dress."

Jolene whispered, "I told you so," and realization dawned on Gabriel's face. ———

"I don't think I want you wearing that if I'm not going with you," he said.

"It will be fine," I told him.

"Do you need a cardigan?" he asked. "Those bars can get rather chilly. Maybe a parka or a snow suit?"

"Aw, come on, Gabe, she looks hot," Jamie protested.

I crossed the room to kiss Gabriel. "Thank you, Jamie."

"Pretty maids all in a row," Dick said with a grin, giving us a wink. "Well, not quite maids—"

"Watch it," we chorused.

"Zeb, don't you think Jolene would be much more comfortable with an overcoat?" Gabriel asked, motioning to the blue-jeans miniskirt that exposed a good deal of Jolene's leg.

Zeb shrugged. "What do I have to worry about? Wolves mate for life."

Jenny's eyebrows arched. "What does that mean?"

Whoops. This was the danger of mixing new, nonsupernaturals into the group. This was the first solo outing my sister had ever taken with me and my supernatural friends. I was interested to see how it would pan out. I don't think Jenny was completely comfortable around Andrea yet. And since werewolves were still very much a secret from the human world, she had no idea what to think about Jolene, a gorgeous semi-feral-looking girl who'd just had twins, ate like a horse, and never gained weight.

"It's just an expression," I told her as Jolene nudged him in the ribs and informed him that mating for life only counted if the male wasn't smothered in his sleep.

"You have your pepper spray?" Gabriel asked me. I nodded. "And your silver spray?"

Jamie scoffed. "I don't get it. If you're that worried about her, why not just give her a gun?"

Everyone in the room stopped and stared at Jamie in horror, even Jenny.

"Do you really think releasing an armed Jane into the public is a good idea?" Zeb asked.

Jamie frowned, mulling it over. "Good point."

"And on that note, having had my own childe turn on me, we're leaving," I muttered.

"Don't do anything I wouldn't do," Jamie called as we walked toward the front door. Over my shoulder, I heard him say, "Don't worry, Gabe. My cousin Marnie had a great time at her bachelorette party, and she came home perfectly safe. Of course, she was pregnant by a stripper dude who called himself Marcus the Matador, but she was perfectly safe."

"Jamie," Gabriel groaned.

"The wedding was called off," Jamie added.

Dick chided, "Not helping, Junior."

We piled into Jolene's SUV. Our gal werewolf was serving as the designated driver, since she was still nursing. I turned to Jenny, who was trying to swat several stuffed sheep into the twins' car seats so she could buckle her seatbelt.

"You know you don't really have to be nervous about Jamie, right? He's never fed on a human. He's been on bottled or donor blood since he was turned. He won't hurt you . . . probably."

"That's not what I was nervous about," Jenny insisted. "It's just—I mean, have you seen him? I mean, he was cute when he was a kid, but now it's just—I mean, it's not fair! For him to have sexy vampire charm on top of being so good-looking . . . And now I feel like a sex offender for even saying that out loud."

I patted her shoulder. "Oh, Jen, it's not a big deal. I had those same thoughts after I turned him, and that doesn't make me the biggest pervert in the world."

She sighed. "Oh, thank you."

"You're the biggest pervert in the world, because you're three years older than me, and that makes you just a tiny bit sicker than me," I said, grinning evilly.

She groaned, covering her face with her palm. "Thank you, Jane."

Jolene snickered as she turned her land yacht toward town. "Aw, hell, Jenny, don't worry."

"Yeah, those feelings of shame and guilt generally melt away after the second cocktail," Andrea added. "Add to that, watching your sister carry this around all night, I predict you'll be feeling just fine in about an hour."

With a flourish, she whipped out a bouquet made of Tootsie Roll Pops with a long, obscenely pink ribbon stamped with "Last Chance for a Suck!" in bold black letters.

I shook my head. "I knew the penis tiara was going too far."

She handed me the bouquet. "And I told you I'd get back at you."

We argued about the various pranks and humiliations of our bachelorette parties and how they might influence the level of havoc played out that night. We argued and giggled and accused, while Jenny listened. And I felt a little bad that Jenny probably felt left out of the conversation.

"You know, I'm kinda glad this is the last weddin' our group is going to have," Jolene said. "I'm not sure if our friendships will survive too many more of these."

"Aww, you're having our last wedding, Jane!" Andrea exclaimed, her eyes welling up.

"If you start to cry, I will slap you," I warned. "We will not make it through this thing if you cry when you're sober."

"Nobody likes a girl with streaks of blood down her face," Jenny said, gently patting Andrea's arm. "Think happy thoughts, like how much fun it will be making Jane stick singles down a couple of the dancers' banana hammocks."

"B-banana—Where did you even learn the expression 'banana hammock'?" I demanded.

Jolene cackled as we pulled into the parking lot of the Meat Market. "Jane, I have a feeling you're going to learn a whole lot about your sister once we get a couple of drinks into her."

I groaned. "Jolene, we have got to get you out of the house more often. Ever since the twins were born and your life became sex-free, you've gotten all aggressive with your girls' nights out."

"Zeb and I have sex all the time," she protested. "We had sex right before we left the house tonight."

I arched an eyebrow at her. "So, I have a teenager in my house, and I'm lucky to get a handshake. But you have infant twins, and your house is a den of desire?"

She nodded. "The women in my, um, family tend to bounce back into our sex lives pretty quickly. Hell, four weeks after the twins were born, Zeb was cuddling me and kissing my neck and telling me how proud he was of me and how I was handling the kids. And next thing you know . . ."

Jenny made the "bow-chicka-wow-wow" music.

Jolene chuckled. "I've never been inhibited or anything, but once Zeb saw me give birth and lived through it, there wasn't much about my body that could gross him out. I didn't worry so much and just enjoyed myself. Basically, the twins were the start of our own sexual revolution."

"That really doesn't help me, because I'm never . . .

ever giving birth. But Gabriel has seen my body do other weird stuff. Third-degree burns. Gunshot wounds. That sort of thing."

"It's comparable," Jolene promised me.

"Ugh, this would be so reassuring if I wasn't thinking about you having sex with my best friend right now."

Oh, the butt-cheek bacchanalia of the Meat Market. How I had missed it. Jenny watched bug-eyed as three men in strangely ill-fitting sailor uniforms shook it to "In the Navy." Andrea had a roll of singles the size of a softball and kept waving them around so the dancers would constantly circle our table. Jolene, having suffered through her own phallic-themed bachelorette saga, was kind enough not to make the whole night about humiliating me. She limited herself to exclusively ordering me drinks with extremely sexual names. I don't even want to know what goes into a "Screaming Sex with a Bartender." I just know said bartender was really happy to even hear her say the words aloud.

And then I realized that I had had sex with the other bartender on duty. I'd dated Joe Tilden in that regrettable summer after my sophomore year of college when I discovered low self-esteem and tequila. Joe had gotten my hair caught in his watchband mid-thrust and mistook my yowls for cries of pleasure and continued toward an unremarkable end. Of my handful of partners, he was memorable but not for a good reason. I turned on my heel, directing my body entirely away from the bar, and

prayed that the strobe lights had damaged Joe's eyesight
over the years.

"Oh, my gosh, is that Joe Tilden?" Jenny whispered, her
face flushed and red. I prepared an elaborate justification
for her staying in her seat and not embarrassing me in
the interests of sisterly love and devotion. But Jenny
ducked behind my chair and hid her face in my shoulder.

"You OK, Jen?"

"Don't let him see me!" she whimpered. "Oh, my
gosh, I'm so embarrassed!"

"Jennifer, what is going on?" I demanded.

Jenny's blush stained her cheeks even brighter. She
relaxed as Joe turned his back and began working the
opposite side of the room. "Well, you remember before
Kent and I got engaged, he went on a spring-break trip
with a few of his friends from chiropractic school, and I
got upset? We had that huge argument about his goals
and where I fit in on his five-year plan?"

I nodded. "It was the only time Mama ever came to
me because she was concerned about where *your* life was
going."

"Well, we took a little break to see where our relationship was going. And I may have gone on a one-
woman tear through most of the bars in the Hollow,"
Jenny said, covering her face with her hands. "Joe and I
went back to his apartment after last call. I didn't even
enjoy myself because I kept getting my hair caught in
his stupid—"

"Watchband!" I gasped.

Jenny's eyes went wide. "You, too?"

I clapped my hands over my mouth as a hysterical cackle burst from my throat. Jenny paled and looked vaguely ill.

"I told you that you'd find out all kinds of new stuff about your sister!" Jolene crowed. I scowled at her.

"Oh, this is just wrong," Jenny moaned.

"I wonder if he went after cousin Junie as some sort of family hat trick?" I said.

Andrea smirked at me. "You know, they say that you have sex with every person your partner has had sex with. So . . ."

"Andrea, I appreciate your burgeoning puckish sense of humor, but this is just like that time you wanted to wear the 'Team Jacob: Because Vampires Shouldn't Sparkle' T-shirt at the shop," I said, shaking my head. "It's funny but not the time or place."

"Jolene, since you seem to be one of the few people here Joe Tilden hasn't slept with, could you go to the bar, please?" Jenny pleaded. "We're going to need drinks, lots of them."

About five cocktails in, I realized I'd forgotten the girls' bridesmaids' gifts out in the SUV. I was giving them little clutch bags and shoes to match their dresses, which was actually a gag gift. Their real gifts were framed photos of the three of us on the porch swing at River Oaks. My sister was getting a picture of the two of us in matching Easter dresses when we were three and seven. She loved that sort of thing.

I know I yelled my car-seeking plan loudly enough for

the girls to hear me, but they were distracted by Marcus the Matador taking his whirl on the stage. I teetered out to the car, wishing I could trade my ice-pick heels for a pair of bunny slippers and pondering why I'd thought that alcohol and stilettos would be a good mix.

I was a few steps away from my car when I heard the gravel crunch behind me. I sniffed and picked up the scent of motor oil and tobacco. I turned and saw a dark figure outlined against the lights of the bar. He was wearing overalls and a ski mask, which was unusual for June. And in general, people in ski masks are up to no good.

"Oh, did you pick the wrong girl to mug," I said, rolling my eyes. "OK, Skippy, we could do this the easy way, you going home with both testicles intact. Or there's the other way. I sort of gave away the ending there."

He whipped a canister out of his pocket, and I could see that it was silver spray. And that's when it was confirmed that I was dealing with Ray McElray. How many muggers carried vampire self-defense spray around just in case they mugged the undead? Having been sprayed directly in the face by the stuff last year, I knew I didn't want it anywhere near me. I caught his hand and wrenched it back.

I felt my fangs extend, and I was this close to snapping them right into his jugular. I shoved him away.

"Listen to me, asshole. I've never killed a human before. I've never even bitten a human in anger. And you're not going to screw up my record." I grunted, shoving him against the truck in the next space.

He howled as the bone stretched toward snapping.

With his other hand, he punched my cheekbone over and over until I released his wrist.

Ow.

I shook off the pain radiating through the entire left side of my head. Unfortunately, I shook a little too emphatically and ended up head-butting him . . . which just hurt worse. The pain gave me a sort of mental distance from the fight. I reached out to his brain, and the first layer of emotion was surprise. He didn't expect this kind of fight from me. He felt foolish for thinking that I would be docile. Female predators were always the ones you had to watch. His brain was a tangled red mess of rage . . . and reluctance? He wasn't angry with me. He was just using me for something. *Message.* That was the word he kept thinking. *Message.* I was his message. Hurting the vampire wasn't enough anymore. Gabriel Nightengale had to be taught a lesson.

I saw two little boys, running in a field. I saw dog tags. I saw a house, a burned-out shell overgrown with weeds and long abandoned. I saw a tree, splintered and fallen. I saw a trailer parked in the middle of the woods. In the distance, I could see the Half-Moon Hollow water tower silhouetted against the full moon.

He shoved me back, slamming my head against Jolene's SUV so hard it shattered the side window. Just as my knees hit the ground, the headlights of all of the cars in the next row popped on, illuminating my masked friend, who I had to assume was Ray McElray. Two vampires in black SWAT uniforms hopped out of the vehicles as if their polyester pants were on fire. Gabriel and Dick came running around the end of the row, sprinting toward me.

Ray shoved his hands into his pockets and pulled out what looked like two air horns. He held them out and pressed down on the triggers, releasing a curtain of silvery spray. Jamie and the uniformed vampires fell back, instinctually shying away from the noxious liquid. Gabriel and Dick ducked through it, their skin sizzling and smoking. I looked up to see Ray sliding behind the wheel of the truck I'd shoved him into. He'd fired up the engine and started pulling forward before Dick managed to throw himself onto the hood.

"Dick!" I shouted as Ray's truck screamed out of the parking lot. The vampire SWAT guys jumped into their SUV and followed. "What do you think you're doing?"

Gabriel looked torn between following them and helping me. Finally, he and Jamie pulled me to my feet. "What are you doing here?" I asked as Gabriel swept me into a bone-crushing hug.

Jamie patted my shoulder awkwardly. He backed away and went to stand next to Ophelia, who was wearing another church-picnic outfit—a white and yellow sundress that tied with a big pretty bow on the back of her neck.

Ophelia said, "We thought Mr. McElray might be watching the house. He'd see if you left without any of the men. He would see you as being vulnerable and might follow. We wanted to see how far he would take the 'stop hiding behind her' sentiment."

"And the two-man SWAT team?" I asked, feeling

rather dizzy now that the head wound was catching up to me.

Ophelia's nasty smile was a slash of white against the obscene red of the neon lights. "I thought it might be a good opportunity to meet with Mr. McElray and inform him of the proper etiquette of dealing with our undead citizens. I didn't expect him to be quite so well prepared."

"So you turned my bachelorette party into a sting operation?"

Ophelia shrugged. "It was either that or the wedding ceremony. I thought you would appreciate preemptive action."

"I am sorry, Jane. This is not an effort to leave you out or keep you in the dark," Gabriel said, glaring at Ophelia. "Had Ophelia not pulled rank and threatened me with certain anatomically specific punishments should I tell you about her plan, I never would have allowed it."

"Well, that explains why you didn't try to veto the party. How did Ophelia even know about it?" I asked.

Ophelia smiled. "Jolene invited me."

I groaned. "I have got to talk to that girl about boundaries."

The SWAT vampires came back empty-handed but for a scraped-up, sullen Dick. Ray McElray knew the roads of the Hollow better than they'd anticipated, they explained, and after throwing Dick off of his hood in a driving maneuver that would have made Dick's beloved Dukes of Hazzard proud, he'd turned off his lights, sped through the treeline, and taken some winding, barely graveled path through the woods off County Line Road.

"What is going on with your super troopers?" I demanded. "How can one half-crazy human elude you for so long? What happened to 'vampires are expert trackers'? Can't you just get a scent on him and follow his trail?"

"Jane, I understand that you're upset, but you need to adjust your tone before my patience wears thin," Ophelia said, her own tone cold. "We don't know how Mr. McElray was able to stay off of our radar for so long. My only guess is that he knows the backwoods of this area much better than we ever could, and it is giving him a distinct advantage."

Ophelia yelled at the SWAT guys in several languages, and they slunk into the bar to scrape my drunken bridesmaids off the floor and hustle them outside. Andrea was confused by Dick's appearance in the parking lot but was in no state to ask too many questions. Jenny was singing an eardrum-altering version of "Hot Stuff" at the top of her lungs. And Jolene was confused about why Ophelia had arrived so late to the party.

My wedding party, ladies and gentlemen.

The SWAT guys escorted us home and were instructed to keep watch over the house until dawn. Zeb had apparently lost the Wii tournament and therefore had to clean up the mess from the party while the others went on their strip-bar stakeout. He was more than happy to take his tired, sober wife home, while Dick had to carry tipsy but cheerful Andrea to their car. Jenny passed out on the couch, and we didn't have the heart to do anything but put a wastebasket and some Advil near her head.

"I gotta say, as far as bachelorette parties go, the arrival of SWAT personnel was still more fun than Jenny's party," I murmured as Gabriel walked me up the stairs. Jamie was on our heels, recapping all of his favorite parts of the evening. Most of them involved me getting my ass handed to me by a masked redneck.

"Well, did you live the last moments of your single life to the fullest?" Gabriel asked, grinning wryly at me as Jamie split off to his room. "Is your last wild oat sown?"

"Hey, don't get all superior with me. I happen to know for a fact that Dick plans to kidnap you into some poker night gone wrong this weekend. You're the one who hasn't bid good-bye to singleness."

"Darling, I bid good-bye to singleness the moment I met you," he said, before kissing me hungrily.

"Oh, if there wasn't a mini-vamp with superhearing sleeping thirty feet away, that line would get you lucky," I said, shaking my head in mock sadness.

"Thank you!" Jamie called. "And don't call me a 'mini-vamp'!"

Establishing dominance early in the relationship is key. Vampire children are like human children in that they can sense weakness. They will wait for you to be busy or too distracted to realize that you've given them permission to feed on the pizza guy.

—*Siring for the Stupid:*
A Beginner's Guide to Raising Newborn Vampires

Wedding planning and personal security seemed to take up most of my time for the next few days. Jolene's amazing wedding-dress save allowed Iris to devote her attention to finalizing the details. The fitting went well, because Jolene's mama had forbidden Aunt Vonnie from speaking directly to me. And it may have been a panic-based delusion, but I thought the werewolves' copy was even prettier than the original costume. This was a good thing, because, surprise of all surprises, all fifty guests we'd invited had RSVP'd yes, including my cousin Junie, who hated me. I suspected that my mother's friends and family just didn't want to miss the spectacle.

Ophelia's badly trained goons—Thing 1 and Thing 2— still lurked in the woods outside my house, hoping that Ray would show up. Jamie amused himself by trying to track them while they were trying to track Ray. Because my childe was apparently too damn dreamy for Ophelia to get annoyed with, she declared that this was good practice for a baby vampire and that the goons weren't to hurt him or allow themselves to be tracked too easily.

In an attempt to be supportive, I sat on the porch with Fitz and watched as he stalked them. I got a look at Thing 1's face when Jamie jumped out of a tree and tackled him. He did not look amused.

We managed to talk Ophelia out of a full security escort when Gabriel finally convinced me that Big Bertha was never coming back and that we needed to return to the all-night car dealership. I grumpily agreed to purchase a Honda Ridgeline because it was comfortable to drive but had a truck bed big enough for Dick's connections to install a full-sized hidey hole. The salesman, Marty, annoyed me by directing all of his questions to Gabriel, even though it was my check paying full sticker price. But given that I still wanted to be driving Big Bertha, I was probably going to be annoyed by the situation anyway.

I decided that drinking Marty dry and leaving his body draped over his desk would probably be bad form.

Because there were a few other accommodations, such as superstrength sunproof tinting, that we needed from the dealership, we left my new truck in Marty's care. Gabriel drove us home in his car. I used my night vision to read the owner's manual and brochures for my new truck.

"Is it wrong that I'm actually considering pulling over so we can have sex without worrying about being heard?" he asked as we turned on County Line Road.

"Not as wrong as the fact that I'm considering it," I said. I looked out the window for a suitable make-out spot and found none. All I could see out the window was the county's water tower, silhouetted against the full moon.

"Stop the car!" I yelled.

"Jane, I was only kidding. I know that having sex in a car in the middle of nowhere violates your 'How to avoid being killed like a dumb-ass second-string character in a horror movie' rules."

"Stop the car!" I hopped out before Gabriel was able to pull to a complete stop. The distance from the water tower seemed right, and the moon seemed to be in the right position, but I was viewing it from the wrong angle. In his jumbled thoughts, Ray McElray had seen the lettering on the tower, "HALF-MOON HOLLOW." All I could see was "HA."

"Jane, what's wrong?"

"I think I know where to find him," I said, thankful that I'd worn my sensible sneakers while car shopping. "Come on."

"Jane!" he called as I took off running in a wide arc around the tower. "Don't you think we should call Ophelia and her team before we go chasing after Ray?" he yelled as we ducked through the trees.

"The same team that was so afraid of a little silver that they couldn't catch up with him the other night? The same team that Jamie can track with no problem and catch repeatedly?" I called back.

"Good point," he said. "So, if and when we catch up to Mr. McElray, what are we going to do?"

"No clue."

"Excellent. We're throwing ourselves into imminent danger without a plan. The usual."

"Hey, I have enough sarcasm of my own, I don't need yours."

"Jane, stop."

"I'm tired of waiting. I'm tired of cars being set on fire. I'm tired of hired guns lurking outside my house. I can't handle it anymore. You keep acting like you're trying to protect me, like I'm the one in trouble again. But you're the one he's after. You're the one in trouble. You're the one in danger. And I refuse to accept that. I saw the trailer where McElray is staying. I saw it in his head, and I'm going to find it. I am going to go find him and take his damn 'message.' And then I'm going to shove it down his throat. Now, you're either with me or you can go home."

"OK, then." He grimaced. "Now that you've explained it to me in a rational manner, let's go."

"What?"

He kissed me softly. "I'm with you, Jane. Always with you."

When we got closer, I saw that the trailer wasn't a trailer at all. It was an old school bus that had been spray-painted in camouflage. The walls were covered in gouges and rust stains. There were no lights, not even a flickering candle or campfire. A deer skull was mounted on the front fender, and cardboard covered two of the windows, which seemed to have been kicked in. There was actual Spanish moss hanging from the trees and brushing against the pressed-metal roof. I didn't even know that we could get Spanish moss this far north. Maybe Ray had bought it at a craft store and hung it for ambience.

"Holy Mary, mother of Cheez Whiz." I gaped.

This was the thing we didn't want people from outside Kentucky to know about. There are hardworking, middle-class, well-educated people living all over our fair state. People who have all their teeth, aren't married to their cousins, and have never even seen an episode of *Lizard Lick Towing*. But somehow, every time there's a natural disaster, news crews manage to track down one of these outdoorsy yahoos to interview about how the "twister came a-screamin' down the holler" and destroyed the snake farm his family had been running for generations. Frankly, I was surprised the camera crews hadn't found this place already.

I tilted my head as we studied the exterior. "You know those moments in horror movies where the two stupid teenagers are about to stumble blindly into the serial killer's lair, and you're screaming at the screen, 'No, don't go in there. That collection of creepy doll heads is not just for decoration!' because you honestly cannot believe two people could be that stupid? Trust me, this is one of those moments."

"I'll choose this moment to remind you that this was your idea. We can still call Ophelia."

"There's no reason to now. I don't sense any thoughts," I said. "No thoughts, no heartbeat. I mean, his scent is strong here, but he's not here."

"His truck is here. I can see the glimmer of the grate under that brush over there," he said. "And if I'm not wrong, this patch of woods is just a mile or so from River Oaks. It explains how he's been able to hover so closely."

"Do you think it's weird that there are no booby traps? I mean, this guy shot you with an arrow full of anticoagulants. You'd at least expect a tiger pit filled with big wooden stakes or something."

"It is a little odd."

"This is where those hired goons would have come in handy. We could send them in as booby-trap finders."

"We could go home and bring back Jamie."

"Come on," I said softly as we passed old lawn chairs and empty beer cans scattered across the ground.

The little stop sign on the side was still intact, and I used it to pull the bus door open. When that didn't make the bus explode, I took it as a good sign.

Before I hopped up onto the first step, I turned and asked, "We don't need tetanus shots, right?" He shook his head. "Good. How does someone actually live in a school bus?" I wondered as we climbed aboard. With our remarkable night vision, we didn't need flashlights to look around, which was good, because we didn't have one. "I mean, there's no water, there's no bathroom. He must have a generator or something, because how else would he—Oh, dear."

Wallpapering the interior of the bus were pictures of us—long-range shots of Gabriel and me sitting on the porch swing, of our friends helping us move Gabriel's stuff into the house, shots taken through the front window of my shop. Specs for my car's model. Line drawings of my house. News clippings from the *Half-Moon Herald* announcing Bud's death and our engagement.

"This is scarily thorough," I muttered.

I looked at the meticulously arranged cork board, which included long-range pictures of me through the shop window. A copy of my weekly schedule was pinned to the cork.

"I think it's fairly safe to assume that this is our guy. If he's pissed at you, why is all of his research on me?"

"He wants to strike where it hurts me most, by hurting you."

I cooed. "Aw, that's sweet in a sick, psychotic way. Still, I'm not the one who dropped a tree on top of his brother. I feel like I'm getting hosed here."

"Thank you for your concern."

Ray had installed makeshift counters where the bus seats used to be. They were crowded with half-emptied cans of Beanee Weenees and Vienna Sausages. Flies were buzzing thickly over the congealed contents. Empty bottles of cheap whiskey were scattered across the floor. An overly sweet, decaying scent hung in the air, with an undercurrent of vomit. Frankly, the place reminded me of my dorm's community bathroom on a Saturday morning.

"I know this is kind of a stupid question, but what's that smell?"

I looked up and saw that Gabriel's attention was drawn to a bunk bed bolted into the back of the bus. There was a dark shape huddled in the center of the mattress, covered by an old army blanket.

"Is that what I think it is?"

"Judging by the smell, I'd say it's a distinct possibility that's Ray McElray himself," he said, pushing me behind him as we crept closer. "He's human. He's definitely dead. The body has been here a few days and reeks of booze. He may have drunk himself to death after his failed attempt on you."

I groaned. "I am not calling this in to Ophelia, got it? I am sick of her snotty little jokes at my expense."

"Yes, because clearly, protecting your feelings should be our chief concern when finding a dead body."

"Shut it." I sighed as we stepped closer.

"Would you recognize Ray if you saw him?"

I nodded. "Probably. You don't forget a guy with a curly mullet."

Gabriel peeled back the blanket just an inch. I saw a head of dark curly hair peeking up from beneath the blanket. I stepped forward to get a better look, and we heard an ominous clicking noise. I looked down and saw that some sort of panel had been cut into the floor a few feet from the bed. And I'd just stepped on it. I looked more closely at the flooring behind us and saw several little panels cut into the floor. We were lucky that we'd made it this far without stepping on one.

From somewhere under the counter, I heard a tiny buzzing noise. Gabriel grabbed my hand. "I think we need to back away from the bunk bed and get off of this bus."

"I would, but I'm sort of paralyzed with fear right now," I said.

The buzzing became the blaring of an alarm clock. In a flash, Gabriel was at the nearest emergency exit window and yanking it down. He practically threw me out of the opening. Just as my feet cleared the metal lip of the window, there was a deafening roar, and I felt Gabriel's weight crashing against me as we were blown away from the blooming burst of flame. The heat prickled across my back as he turned, throwing his arms around me and cushioning my fall. I landed with a wet thump, Gabriel on top of me, and we slid across the soupy mud of Ray's yard as bits of school bus rained down on us.

Oh, and Gabriel's shirt was on fire.

Gabriel wasn't all that concerned about this as he seemed to be stunned into a coma. Coughing, I began beating on his back to put out the flames.

"Why are you hitting me?" he asked groggily as I shoved him off of me and rolled his back against the ground.

"Stop, drop, and roll!" I yelled as I rocked him back and forth in the mud.

"What?"

"You're on fire! Roll around!"

"I thought I smelled something burning," he murmured, settling his face back down into the mud.

I looked back at the flaming wreckage of the bus. "You hit your head pretty good, huh?"

"Yep. I should be OK in a few minutes."

"I'll wait," I said, carefully moving his head onto my lap. I stroked his hair. "So, is it just me, or do these pranks make Missy's and Jeanine's seem cheeky and winsome by comparison?"

"*Hmph*," he said, nestling his face against my thigh. "So, can we assume that the body in the bus was Ray?"

"It seems too much to hope for, that this whole thing was resolved by binge drinking and homemade explosives." I shrugged. "But what are the chances that he had a roommate?"

Ophelia was surprisingly gracious about the whole "we went off without you" thing, once we explained that I happened to recognize the water tower. I supposed it helped that Jamie had seen the explosion and come running, so he was standing behind me while I was explaining the predicament. She probably didn't want to look like a total shrew in front of him.

Ray's remains were collected by the human authorities. There wasn't much to collect, as the explosives had been stashed under the bunk bed. To me, that didn't make much sense. Why would anyone sleep on top of a large bomb? But Ophelia suggested that maybe he wanted to take out anyone who got that close as he slept. He didn't care whether he survived.

Sergeant Russell Lane of the Half-Moon Hollow PD, who seemed to be the only police officer on duty whenever I got into trouble, promised that they would identify the remains by dental records as soon as possible. I had the feeling that Ray didn't have any dental records, which would make identification more difficult.

"Jane, do you think you'll be able to keep yourself out of trouble for the remaining three days before your wedding, or will I need to double your guards?" Ophelia asked.

"I think I'll be fine," I said contritely.

Ophelia smiled blandly. "Well, I'll still keep them stationed outside the house, just in case. I'm sure there's more than one person interested in killing you in a splashy, public fashion."

"I would take offense to that, but you're probably right."

Gabriel's wounds healed quickly enough, although Jamie helped me load him into his car so we could drive home. Gabriel's concussion also led to his singing various Motown songs, which Jamie recorded on his phone for his own amusement.

With precious little time left before the wedding, I logged as many hours in the shop as possible, preparing it and Andrea for the week Gabriel and I would be spending away at an undisclosed honeymoon location. I trusted Andrea and Dick to take care of the business. And I trusted Jamie not to run away with the circus. But I didn't trust myself not to check my voicemail every five minutes to make sure nothing had blown up or been sprayed with battery acid in my absence.

Honestly, I was lucky to have the shop to distract me. I had very little to do wedding-wise, thanks to Iris. She'd e-mailed me an itinerary for the day before and the day of the wedding. I just had to show up at the right time and get dressed. If I wasn't marrying one of the most beautiful men on the planet, I'd have been tempted to give her a big, wet kiss.

Andrea came toddling from the supply room, struggling to gracefully move a bulky, half-constructed cardboard display.

"What are you doing?" I asked as she flipped white cardboard tabs into place and flipped the top of the display over to reveal a pair of intricately printed silver bells that read "Eternal Bliss" in a curlicued font.

"Opening us up to whole new literary market," she exclaimed, before dashing back to the storeroom. She came back with a case of books, similarly stamped "Eternally Yours." Andrea abused her vampire speed, unpacking and shelving the books with a flourish and stepping back.

"Ta-da!" she shouted.

"You've fallen completely over the edge into asylum territory, haven't you?"

She frowned. "No, you jerk, 'ta-da' as in 'Welcome to the wedding-planning section of our shop. How can we separate you from your hard-earned money today?' You would not believe how many people have become interested in vampire weddings over the last couple of weeks—whether it's because of the stories circulating in the human community about your wedding or because it just became legal, I don't know. But we've had several customers come in and request books and planners for vampire nuptials, and they were extremely disappointed that we didn't have any. So I looked up a couple of distributors online and found these. *A Novice's Guide to Planning a Charming Vampire Wedding, Elopement for the Eternal, Weddings and the Dysfunctional Undead: A Vampire's Guide to Establishing a New Family Without Killing the Old One.* They're great. Informative, thorough, and occasionally pretty damn funny."

"And you didn't think to tell me about these books while I was planning my own wedding, because?"

She chuckled. "Because the line was just launched!"

"And because seeing me drive myself crazy amuses you."

"Jane, if you'd been able to read these books, would you have felt more prepared, or would you have worked yourself into an information-overload-fueled frenzy, convinced that you could arrange the whole wedding yourself, and eventually killed one of your loved ones in a glue-gun-related mishap?" she asked, her lips quirked.

"Probably that second one," I admitted.

She hiked her fists on her hips. "OK, then, I think the words you're looking for are 'Thank you, oh newly promoted assistant manager, for finding yet another revenue stream for Specialty Books. Without you, my shelves would be empty. I would have few customers.

And my coffee would burn holes in those customers' throats.'"

"I think that was implied."

She shook her head. "No, no. I'm going to need to hear it."

"Thank you, oh—" I stopped as I heard the little cow bell over the door jingle, indicating that a customer was walking in. "Oh, thank God, 'cause there was no way I was going to really say that."

I turned to find a familiar blonde tentatively poking her head through the front door.

"Mrs. Lanier?"

I reached under the counter for the pepper spray we kept there. Andrea circled the coffee bar to stand at my right. Her face was neutral but not friendly. Clearly, Andrea believed she was the only one allowed to abuse me. Mrs. Lanier was going to have to line up behind her.

Rosie Lanier tried to smile, but her muscles couldn't seem to form the expression. She cleared her throat. "Jane."

"Is there something I can do for you?" I asked gently, although my hand was still firmly on the pepper spray.

She cleared her throat again. I reached into the mini-fridge and pulled out a bottle of water for her. She stepped back, as if she wasn't prepared to accept any sort of kindness from me.

"I can't pretend I'm happy to be here, Jane. I never thought . . ." She crossed to one of the little tables and plopped down in one of the comfy purple chairs.

I took a stool near the coffee bar.

"When I heard what happened to you, I thought, 'Oh, poor Sherry.' I never even considered that something like that could happen to my own child. I thought we were safe. We were a good family, good people," she said.

"So was my family . . . with the possible exception of Grandma Ruthie."

Mrs. Lanier ignored me as if she'd already planned her speech out in her head and any interruption would only put her off her place. "I was so angry with you when I found out what happened. I mean, it was bad enough that Jamie had been turned, but that it was by someone we knew? It felt like you should have known better, like you should have been more loyal. 'After all the time we'd spent together with her family,' I thought. 'After all those Labor Day picnics and camping weekends and New Year's Eve parties, how could she do this to us?' I hated you so much. The more I thought about it, the more you seemed to morph into this hideous monster in my head—this dangerous, vicious tramp who'd stolen my son's life away."

"I don't know how to respond to that," I muttered.

She chuckled, and for the first time in months, I saw her smile. "That changed one night when I was looking through some old albums, looking for pictures of Jamie. I found this."

She slid an old, battered four-by-six photo across the table. I groaned as Andrea swooped in, grabbed the photo, and guffawed. I glared at her.

"Right," she said, slapping the photo into my hand. "Sorry."

The picture showed Jenny, Jamie, and me during a camping weekend at Barkley Lake. Jamie must have been six or seven, his straw-colored hair sticking straight up from the back of his head like a peacock's tail. Somehow, paired with the thumb-width gap between his top front teeth, the freckles across his nose only made him more adorable. At twenty-one, Jenny was still blond, polished, and perfect and clearly humoring the both of us as we forced her to help us sing some old Oak Ridge Boys song, just because Jamie liked to sing the "oom-papa-mow-mow" chorus. And there was awkward, buck-toothed me, with the unfortunate bangs and knobby knees. I smiled goofily into the camera, with a sort of bemused confidence that this picture was going to come back and haunt me. Even then, I had a pretty profound grasp of future humiliation.

"I saw this picture. And I remembered this trip with your family. I remembered, even then, how good you were with Jamie, how you kept him out of trouble all weekend by telling him stories about Huck Finn and Daniel Boone. I remember telling your mama what a good mother you were going to make someday and how she just beamed at the thought. And I realized that girl would never do anything to put Jamie in danger. That girl, who devoted most of her adult years to helping kids learn to love books, couldn't change so drastically. That girl would give her last breath to keep someone she saw as a child safe." Her lip trembled, and her eyes filled. "It was me. I brought this down on us. It's my fault. When you were turned, I felt so sorry for your mama, for such a thing to happen to her. But all the while, I was feeling smug and superior, because it could never happen to me. Not in my family. I'm being punished, don't you see? I was so proud, so arrogant. I gave the Lord no choice but to smack me down."

"It doesn't really work that way," I said. "I wasn't turned as part of a great karmic payment plan. It just happened. The same with Jamie. It just happened. Trying to find a villain here is like trying to pin the blame on someone when a meteor lands on them." I judiciously decided not to tell her about the driver who mowed her son down and how he may or may not have tried to do further damage to members of the household. That struck me as a "need to know" sort of thing.

She bit her lip, her eyes filling as she asked, "Is he happy?"

I reached across the table to pat her hand, but she withdrew it. I tried not to let that hurt my feelings. "He misses you. He's confused, scared, but no more so than any kid who's growing up. He's a good kid, Miss Rosie. You did a wonderful job raising him. And he's the very best kind of vampire. He's just like he was as a human; he just has fangs. He doesn't hurt people. He doesn't abuse his powers. He's still your boy. And he would love to see you."

"I'm not sure if we can do that yet," she said. "I'm afraid of what I'll see when I look at him. It will break my heart if he still looks like my little boy. And it will break my heart if he doesn't. I don't know when I will be ready. I know your mama's all onboard with the Friends and Family of the Undead, but I'm not ready to march in any nighttime pride parades. It's going to take me some time."

"Please at least consider it."

She smiled, tight-lipped but sincere. "I will."

"So, you're not angry with me anymore?"

"No. I'm not going to be sending you a batch of macaroons anytime soon, but I think we're going to be OK."

"Damn, I wish you hadn't reminded me how much I loved your macaroons. But thank you for forgiving me. You wouldn't mind passing word around about our newly established peace treaty so I don't get variations of 'murdering bitch' painted on my windows, would you?"

She cringed. "I'm sorry about that. I'll admit, the first time was me. But I'll call the phone tree and cancel it for everybody else."

"That is a clear misuse of your PTA organizing skills."

"We work with what we have," she said, blushing sheepishly.

"I'll keep you in mind the next time I'm arranging a vampire carpool."

16

It's important to take time for yourself. Siring is a difficult, draining business. Set aside little treats for yourself: a hot bath, a good book, a battle to the death. A tired sire is an ineffective sire.

—*Siring for the Stupid:*
A Beginner's Guide to Raising Newborn Vampires

It was apparently the evening to resolve feelings with problematic maternal figures, because I came home from work to find that Gabriel and Jamie had helped Mr. Wainwright set up an exorcism ritual space smack in the middle of my parlor. There was a huge symbol drawn in white chalk on the hardwood, circled in sea salt. It sort of looked like a cross between a sperm and a beached sea cow. Unlit white candles were placed at each compass point. Jamie was chattering excitedly about following Mr. Wainwright's careful instructions from a book called *Spirit Rituals and Rites.*

"Mr. Wainwright found just the right ceremony. He's sure of it this time. And now, Gabe and I have to go out back and take a bath, because we're not supposed to carry the ritual objects' energy around with us. You're going to have to take one, too, before the ritual. Isn't that cool?" he cried as Gabriel kissed me.

I laughed at Jamie's puppy-doggish enthusiasm and wondered if I'd sired a closet D&D freak. I tousled his hair, and for once, he didn't complain about the gesture, instead dragging me around the room to examine all of the different crystals and herbs involved in setting up my grandmother's spiritual eviction.

In that moment, I decided against telling Jamie about his mother's visit to the shop. If she came to terms with his condition and was able to attempt a relationship with him, he wouldn't need to know that she'd needed a pep talk first. And if she decided against seeing him again, I didn't want to give him false hope. For now, he was mine. And he seemed to be thriving.

"Yes, bathing in the yard, using the hose," Gabriel deadpanned as I picked up *Spirit Rituals and Rites* and shuffled to the page Mr. Wainwright had marked. "I cannot believe the luck, especially when you consider that there are hired mercenaries watching the house who will no doubt enjoy the spectacle."

"Dude, Mr. Wainwright told you about what would happen if you entered the ritual space."

"After I'd already entered it, so the warnings were a bit of a moot point!" Gabriel exclaimed as Jamie jostled him on the way out the back door to their chilly evening toilette.

Mr. Wainwright and Jettie materialized at my elbow.

I compared the page to the symbol marked on the floor. "Mr. Wainwright, I think you have this wrong. This isn't an exorcism ritual. This is a summoning ritual."

Mr. Wainwright grinned at me. "Quite right."

"But we don't want Grandma Ruthie to stick around. We want her gone—possibly in another dimension. Are there dimensions without support hose? Because that would be sort of funny."

"Jane, have you ever heard the expression 'If you can't beat 'em, join 'em'?" he asked.

"Not from you," I said.

"I've looked in all of the pertinent books, and I cannot find a single ritual more powerful than the one that failed to, well, dislodge your grandmother. And you'll notice that while she has made several appearances here, she hasn't been able to move to different locations, although she could have caused serious trouble if she'd decided to vandalize the stock at the shop or cross the field to scare Zeb and Jolene's children. It seems as though her obsession with the family home has bound her spirit too tightly to this particular building, and as such, it will be impossible to force her to move on involuntarily."

"Well, that is incredibly depressing news . . . which, again, makes me question the whole ritual thing."

Jettie nudged me with her insubstantial hip. "If you flip the problem over and look at it from another angle, it makes more sense. If we can't force Ruthie out, what can we do to make her want to leave, not only the house but the earthly plane?"

"If the answer is burn down the house, I have to say that's a little extreme."

Jettie rolled her eyes. "No, honey. What does Ruthie hate more than anything?"

"Feminists, unruly children, long-haired dogs, certain unnamed ethnic groups, beach weddings, people who e-mail thank-you notes, and me."

Jettie gave me a pitying but understanding glance. "Being married, Jane. Your grandmother loves marrying men, and she loves burying them, but she's never been very good at anything in between. She loves the romance and the excitement of the big events, but the everyday stuff bores her to tears. Frankly, I was shocked that she spent enough time around your grandpa John to have your mother."

"Didn't need that mental image, but you make an excellent point," I said.

Grandma's interest tended to wane after she threw the bridal bouquet. She'd send her husbands off to their hobbies while she occupied herself with Junior League or the Garden Club. But the moment one of them suffered a bizarre accident, she was the consummate grieving widow, a postmenopausal Juliet elegantly distraught over the loss of her soul mate.

"We were thinking that inviting a few people here to discuss Ruthie's occupation at River Oaks might prompt her to pull up stakes," Jettie said.

I gasped. "We're going to summon all of Grandma's dead husbands?"

Jettie's lips quirked. "No, Ruthie's various exes will be

here at midnight. Gilbert and I have spent weeks talking them into coming here."

"So, that's where you've been."

Jettie continued, "The summoning is for Ruthie. We want to force her to appear and keep her here long enough to talk to her."

"Um, midnight is in about twenty minutes," I said, checking the clock on the mantel.

"Which means you need to go outside for that bath," Mr. Wainwright said, gently pushing me toward the door.

"Can't I just run upstairs and take a shower?" I whined.

Clothed in white pajamas, Gabriel and Jamie held up a ring of sheets around a metal washtub in the yard. The light of the full moon overhead lent a silvery, otherworldly glow to the unceremoniously simple bathing station. I stepped into the little tub and winced at the cold water lapping around my feet.

"You have to be cleansed outside the house, so that none of your creepy grandma's energy can affect you," Jamie said, his eyes alight and averted as I stripped down. "Can you believe all this?"

"Yes. I've spent two years surrounded by 'all this' at the shop," I told him, dutifully washing my arms and legs with the hyssop soap Gabriel had left out for me. "Mr. Wainwright was talking Loch Ness and poltergeists before the end of my interview. I've probably read every occult title available in print."

"That's what you sell at the shop?" Jamie exclaimed, although he was respectful enough not to turn and look at me.

"Yes. What did you think we sold at the shop?"

Jamie shrugged. "Romance novels. Girlie books."

Gabriel sighed. "It's been nice knowing you, Jamie."

"Romance novels!" I cried. "Why would I open a vampire-specific store for romance novels? Didn't you ever read any of the titles when you were in the store?"

"Uh, I was a little busy trying to scope out you and Andrea without Dick noticing," he scoffed. He bit his lip when he realized his admission and the fact that I was standing mostly naked on the other side of a very thin sheet. "Not that I would do that now, because you're sort of this big-sister-mother-figure for me, and that would be weird."

"Thanks." I grunted, turning the hose on and shrieking when the cold water hit my skin.

"Can I come down to the shop sometime?" he asked. "If this is the kind of stuff you have there, I'd really like to look at some of the books."

"Aw! I would love that!" I chuckled. "I would hug you right now, but I'm naked, and my big vampire fiancé is standing right behind me."

"I appreciate that," Jamie said.

"Thank you for thinking of me," Gabriel said with a snort. He pulled a brand-new set of white cotton pajamas out of a shopping bag by his feet and tossed them over the curtain. I eyed them curiously. "Mr. Wainwright said we should wear clothes that haven't been in the house yet. I know better than to try to pick out clothes for you, but I thought pajamas would be safe."

I beamed at him. "You are so the guy for me."

* * *

Suitably cleansed and dressed, the three of us entered the house just as the clock showed ten till midnight. I picked up the book and began reading the passage Mr. Wainwright had marked: "I summon the spirit of my ancestor. Ruth Ann Early Lange Bodeen Floss Whitaker, come forth from the mist. Pull back the veil and speak."

Silence. The only noise in the room was the ticking of the clock on the mantel.

"Ruthie Early!" I called. "I am your blood! I command you to come forth and speak!"

Nothing.

"Grandma Ruthie, if you don't get your see-through butt down here, I'm going to tear out the kitchen and put in a home gym! You know I don't eat, so that's not an empty threat!"

An angry swirl of red energy emanated from the center of the symbol, rising to eye level. Grandma Ruthie appeared, her silvery eyes flashing dark as she tried to hover over my head, intimidating me. I felt Gabriel and Jamie at my back, ready to shove me out of the way if Ruthie happened to have found her scissors. The symbol kept her inside the circle, unable to rise.

She glowered at me and crossed her arms over her chest. "Who do you think you are, Jane Jameson, telling me what to do in my own house?"

"Grandma Ruthie, I'm giving you one last opportunity," I said. "Leave my house now. Find some other place to spend your time. Better yet, move on to the next stage. I don't want any more ugliness between us. And I think we can agree that trying to exist in the same house will only lead to more ugliness."

"I have no reason to leave my house, Jane." She sniffed. "If anyone is going to leave, it's you."

"Are you saying that if I gave you reason to leave, you would move on?"

"I can't think of any possible motivation *you* could come up with that could change my mind." She sneered.

"Oh, I don't know about that," Jettie sing-songed as several translucent forms shifted through the walls of the parlor and hovered around the circle. We watched as they solidified into human shapes. And I began recognizing faces.

Grandpa John I only knew from pictures my mom had around the house. His face was young, handsome. He'd been in the prime of life when the truck struck him down. I had a hard time imagining this man, who was currently winking at me and grinning like a fool, ever marrying my grandmother. On purpose.

Then there was Grandpa Tom, dressed in natty picnic attire. He and Ruthie had been on their way to a Labor Day celebration when he'd sampled her famous strawberry-rhubarb pie and discovered a serious allergy to rhubarb. His airway swelled shut before the ambulance could even arrive. Grandpa Jimmy looked skittish and nervous, which was exactly what you would expect from someone who died from a brown recluse bite on the *inside* of the throat. And poor Grandpa Fred, struck down on the twelfth hole at the Half-Moon Hollow Public Golf Course, was still wearing ugly plaid pants and a hat with a little puff ball on top. I could not imagine spending the rest of eternity dressed like that.

I was glad to have Aunt Jettie out of the house with Grandpa Fred there. They had a . . . complicated history. Aunt Jettie and Grandpa Fred began dating, or what could be considered dating when one was a shade of the Great Beyond, shortly after her death. (In her defense, there weren't many men in the Hollow who hadn't been married to Grandma Ruthie. It limited her dating pool.) Through my employment at the shop, Aunt Jettie met Mr. Wainwright, who was still living at the time. They started spending time together. Mr. Wainwright died. And the next thing he knew, poor Grandpa Fred and his little puff-ball hat were all alone.

The only ex unaccounted for was Grandma's former fiancé, Bob, who'd died as the result of a Viagra mix-up the previous year. I guessed he considered his business with Ruthie concluded.

"What is the meaning of this?" Grandma Ruthie shrieked, shrinking away from the ghostly circle forming around her. "What kind of cruel, inhuman joke are you trying to pull, Jane?"

"I didn't have anything to do with this, Grandma Ruthie. But I think your former husbands have some things they'd like to say to you."

And with that, a wall of chatter seemed to crash through the room like a tidal wave. Hurts, disappointments, past arguments, resentments that each man had carried to the afterlife from his time with Ruthie. You know those British Parliament sessions they show on

C-SPAN, where everyone's talking over one another and shouting and booing, and you're thinking, *Middle-school social studies would have been so much more interesting if we got to study this*? It was a lot like that.

Grandpa John told Ruthie that the only reason he'd been hit by that truck was that he was leaving at dawn to squeeze in extra hours at the saw mill to pay off the bills she'd run up all over town pretending to be some Southern belle. And he was insulted that she'd moved on so quickly and married his best friend less than two years after he'd died. Grandpa Tom accused her of marrying him because she liked his house but not him. Grandpa Jimmy wanted to know why Grandma Ruthie banned his family from his funeral and said she had no right to hold on to the Civil War memorabilia he'd planned to pass on to his grandsons. And Grandpa Fred said that death was a "sweet relief," even if it meant getting struck by a billion volts just to get away from her nagging.

The barrage of relationship dysfunction continued for half an hour before I could get any of my former grandfathers calmed down. Jettie had settled on the couch and was gleefully watching it all play out like a tennis match, so she was no help. Ruthie's ghostly form seemed to shrink in on itself with every volley lobbed by her exes. Finally, it took Jamie sticking his fingers in his mouth and whistling for the jabbering to slow down.

"Fine, fine, fine!" Grandma Ruthie screeched. "Maybe I wasn't the best wife to any of you. But you were miserable excuses for husbands! Maybe if you'd tried just a little bit harder, life would have been a little easier for us. But it's all over now. We're all dead! I hope you all got your closure, so you can just shut up and move on!"

"But Grandma Ruthie, they're not moving on," I said, smiling sweetly.

"They're not?" she asked, her voice growing suspicious.

"Shoot, no, but they're all going to move in with us."

"What?" Gabriel and Jamie chorused.

"Yep, that's part of the summoning rite," I said. "We're going to anchor the fellas' spirits to River Oaks, just like Ruthie has managed to do all on her own. I just have to repeat this handy chant three times, and it's a done deal. It's going to be a grand old time, Grandma. Me, you, and my four grandpas. We'll be one big, happy family. Just imagine, you'll have all day and all night for the rest of eternity to devote to one another. And you'll have time for long, long conversations about how your relationships went wrong. I can see it now. The whole clan gathered around the fire. The lingering smell of Bengay permeating the air. Playing pinochle and singing campfire songs. Nothing but family time and lots and lots of togetherness."

Somehow, Ruthie's translucent face went even paler. "No. Jane, you can't do that! I won't allow it! This is my house, mine! You don't have the right!"

I raised the book, turning the page, and read aloud, "Spirits of hearth and home, hear me now! Gather those spirits present and bind them to this place!" I chanted as Grandma Ruthie begged me to stop. "By Hestia, by Hecate, I ask that you grant us an eternal home, an eternal family! As I will, so mote it be!"

"Jane, stop it!" Grandma Ruthie screeched. "Please, I'll do anything!"

"Spirits of hearth and home, hear me now! Gather those spirits present and bind them to this place!" I chanted again. "By Hestia, by Hecate, I ask that you grant us an eternal home, an eternal family! As I will, so mote it be!"

"Jane!" Ruthie wailed piteously as I started the third round. I could see her form fading, her outline becoming more and more shadowed. "Jane! No!"

By the time I'd reached the third "By Hestia, by Hecate," Grandma Ruthie had shrunk down to a tiny, pearl-sized blip in the atmosphere over the symbol. It disappeared with a faint pop, and the atmosphere in the room warmed by a few degrees.

"Did it work?" I asked Mr. Wainwright. "She's really gone this time?"

"Well, the energy coming off the symbol has sizzled away to nothing, so I'm going to say yes. Your grandmother voluntarily severed her connection to the house in order to escape to the next plane," he said. "You did very well, Jane."

"Thank you." I beamed as Gabriel squeezed my shoulders. Jettie was bent over, laughing so hard that she couldn't congratulate me. I took that as a good sign.

"So, I guess things are going to be a little more crowded around here, huh?" Jamie said as the grandpas milled around the room, talking among themselves. Grandpa Fred was giving Aunt Jettie and Mr. Wainwright a wide berth, but I was glad that he'd been mature enough to put his feelings aside and help me out. "They're not going to hang out in my room, are they? Because I sort of have a non-nursing-home vibe going up there."

"What are you talking about?" I asked.

"The grandpas, they're all moving in, right?"

"Oh, the binding thing?" I asked, laughing. "I was bluffing."

Gabriel burst out laughing.

Jamie's jaw dropped. "But the whole incantation thing and the chanting?"

"I made it up, pulled it out of thin air," I said, shrugging. "I told you, I've spent two years in an occult shop. It was bound to rub off on me. And you say I'm a lousy actress." I poked Gabriel in the chest.

"I've never said you're a lousy actress. I said you have no poker face. But I proudly admit that I am wrong. That was masterful," Gabriel said.

"But what were you going to do if she called your bluff?" Jamie demanded.

"Figure something else out," I said. "I would have kept bluffing until Ruthie admitted that the only thing that horrified her more than me owning the house is the idea of sharing it with the men she's jettisoned into the grave."

"I think the word 'jettisoned' hurts my feelings," a kind voice behind me said. I turned to find Grandpa John smiling fondly at me. "You have turned out to be a real firecracker, you know that?"

I nodded sheepishly. Over John's shoulder, I could see the other grandpas waving at me and phasing through the exterior walls, going back to their individual haunts.

I waved back, unsure of what to say besides mouthing "Thank you."

"I'm sorry I've never stopped by before, Jane. But I wasn't sure how you'd react," Grandpa John said. "I stayed around to watch your mama grow up, you know. And when she had you and Jenny, I couldn't bear to leave. I've had so much fun watching all my girls live their lives. Now that you're aware of me, I might stop in every once in a while—if that's all right with you."

"Sure."

Grandpa John eyed Gabriel and Jamie as they argued about the best way to clean up the chalk outline on the floor. "You've made this place quite the home, haven't you?"

"Despite all odds."

"I think that's why your grandmother never really got this place. She saw it as something to show off, to lord over other people, even when it was falling apart at the seams. She never saw it as a place where a family lived. You get that."

I smiled and ducked my head, only to feel the cool pressure of his hand on my shoulder.

"I'm very proud of the person you've become. I think we would have gotten along just fine, if I'd lived. No matter what your grandmother might have told you, I always liked a girl with spunk."

Grandpa John winked at me and pinched my cheek as he faded out of sight.

"Thanks, Grandpa."

17

It is vital to foster loyalty in your childe. You will need your childe someday, whether it's a year or a century from now. A loyal childe will heed the sire's call no matter where the childe is. A resentful childe will take time to make himself or herself comfortable while he or she enjoys your misfortune.

—*Siring for the Stupid:*
A Beginner's Guide to Raising Newborn Vampires

Time is a funny thing. The weeks leading up to the wedding seemed to be moving at fast-forward, what with blowing up a school bus, evicting a dead grandparent, and building relationships with dead grandpas. But somehow, walking down the makeshift aisle we'd constructed on the back lawn of River Oaks seemed to take forever.

For the rehearsal, Daddy was at my elbow, half leading, half dragging me. I'm sure that in his head, he was already compensating for the support I would need, negotiating the grass in my dress. Gabriel was waiting for me, and I just couldn't seem to get to him fast enough.

Iris was standing near the arbor that would be wrapped in flowers and ribbon while we were sleeping the next day. She was carefully reviewing the ceremony notes with Jolene's uncle Creed, who performed all marriage rites in the pack as the eldest of the clan and a justice of the peace. Reverend Neel was a good man, but his liberalities only stretched so far. And I found the idea of being married by a notary public sort of depressing. It was a special honor for a werewolf to extend such a gesture of friendship to a vampire, and without Jolene's intervention, it wouldn't have happened.

Jolene's parents were there, along with the aunties who could stomach my presence. I had to find some way to thank them for replicating my dress. And for a werewolf, that means feeding them. All of the nonvampires would be enjoying a big batch of Mama's homemade lasagna at her house while Gabriel was led to his bachelor-party doom. I think I was supposed to go to my room and pretend to be a virgin for one more night.

Mama couldn't have been more pleased with Iris's work, including the arrangement of a slightly more traditional wedding party than Jolene and Zeb had. Andrea was my maid of honor, and Zeb was my best man. Dick was the best man for Gabriel's side, with Jolene and Jenny in the supporting roles. I tried to get Jamie to serve as ring bearer, but he refused to carry the little pillow. Instead, he was the groomsman in charge of leading Fitz to the bride's family row and keeping him from chasing squirrels during the ceremony.

After sitting through countless prolonged weddings

that left my butt numb and my nerves frayed, I wanted to keep the ceremony itself short and sweet, and Gabriel agreed. I walk up the aisle, we say the vows, we walk down the aisle together. No staring into each other's eyes while soloists warble that what the world needs now is love, sweet love. No special readings from Corinthians or Shakespeare. And no unity candle. Open flames and veils tend to make vampire brides very nervous.

The good news was that this simplified the rehearsal considerably. And since everybody in the wedding party had been through the process before, they knew where to stand, where to face, and how to hold their flowers. And they knew the special "step-together-step-together" rhythm required to time their aisle walk appropriately to the processional.

If I could just get Uncle Creed to call me Jane instead of Jean, we'd be in business.

Iris considered us sufficiently rehearsed and gave us all our wedding-day itineraries. Mine said, "Show up at sunset, get dressed, relax."

"I think I love you," I told her.

She shrugged. "I get that a lot. If you'll excuse me, I have to go pry your mama off of Uncle Creed before she talks him into an altar call or something."

She scurried away, clipboard in hand, and Gabriel pressed a kiss to my mouth. "This is your last night as a single woman. What do you plan on doing?"

"Sleeping. Reading. Worrying about you and my childe and how you will be emotionally scarred by the cut-rate strip club Dick drags you to."

"For your information, we're not going to a strip club." Dick sniffed. "We're going to a casino."

"How are you going to get Jamie into a casino? He's underage!"

Dick shook his head. "You don't want to know."

"You're right, I don't. Just don't let anything happen to him, OK? Dick, I think it goes without saying that if anything happens to Gabriel to prevent him from making it to the altar tomorrow night, I will hold you responsible. And afterward, grown men will weep when they see what I've done to you."

Dick snorted and kissed my forehead. "And yet you feel the need to say it anyway."

"It's a formality."

Most of the guests had already departed for Mama's dinner. As the boys loaded themselves into Zeb's car, I bade Andrea and Jolene good night and kissed the twins. Jenny hugged me tight and promised to slip Mama a Xanax before I could rise the next night. I whistled for Fitz and went upstairs to take off my makeup and change into some sweats. The house was blissfully quiet, especially with Jettie and Mr. Wainwright off to complete some secret wedding-related task. I lay on my bed and closed my eyes, wondering if I was going to be able to sleep a wink that day.

Downstairs, I heard a soft knock on the door. Remembering the still-unidentified remains of Ray McElray, I grabbed a baseball bat from Jamie's room and crept quietly down the stairs.

"Who is it?"

"Honey, it's Daddy. Open up."

I whipped the door open to find him grinning at me.

"Grab your purse, honey."

"But I'm wearing sweatpants. Where are we going?"

"It's a surprise, and you're dressed just fine," he said, his eyes twinkling as he led me to the car. "Your mama's letting me off the hook tonight so I can have some special time with my girl before she becomes an old married woman."

"Watch it," I warned him as we pulled out of the driveway and into town.

I kept up a constant stream of chatter about my father's classes, his students, Mama's compulsive cleaning of the house as she worked through her anxieties over the wedding. Daddy pulled his car toward downtown, onto Main Street, and finally, into the parking lot of the Coffee Spot.

I gasped. The Coffee Spot had been our special place since I was little. Daddy and I would leave early on Saturday mornings under the pretense of running errands, and then we'd camp in a corner booth for most of the day, talking and eating cheese fries. Mama never could figure out how running to the hardware store and the grocery store always ended with Daddy getting Velveeta on his shirt. Of course, those cheese-fry runs got fewer and farther between when I went away to school, and even farther when Mama saw Daddy's cholesterol results. And they stopped altogether when I went on the liquid diet.

I turned to my father, who grabbed my hand and

squeezed it. "We are going to have one last shot at cheese fries."

"But I can't eat."

He grinned. "No, but you can watch me eat. And you can have one of those bottled bloods. I called ahead and asked Marjorie to stock them for you. She misses you, you know."

I sighed. "I really, really love you, Daddy."

"Obviously," he said, his eyes twinkling as we climbed out of the car.

"I'm sorry we haven't had much time together lately," I said as we entered the coffee shop.

Marjorie, who had been waiting tables at the Coffee Spot since it opened in 1956, whooped and pulled my face between her worn, bony hands.

"Look at you!" she cried, squeezing my cheeks in a death grip. Her iron-gray hair was coming loose from its top knot as she practically vibrated with excitement. "Oh, it's been so long since I've seen you, Janie! And you're getting married tomorrow! Look at that ring! I'm so happy for you."

"Thanks, Miss Marjorie."

"I can't believe it's been almost two years since I've seen you," she said as Daddy and I slid into our usual booth, with the cracked green leatherette seats. Marjorie didn't bother handing us grease-spotted menus. Daddy's order never changed from cheese fries and a cherry Coke.

"I'm sorry. You tend to spend less time in restaurants when you don't eat solids."

"That's all right, hon. Your daddy told me you like that Faux Type O. I'll grab one for you and heat it up," she said. "John, I'll get your cheese fries going. I'll be right back."

Daddy chuckled at my shocked expression. "Marjorie's always been an energetic gal."

"What was I saying?"

"You were apologizing for abandoning your father while pursuing silly things like running your own business and maintaining a relationship. Oh, and training my grand-childe to be a good little vampire."

"I'm sorry, Daddy."

"Aw, hell, Jane. I'm glad you're so busy. I worried about you before, when you were working at the library. You always seemed to be waiting for your life to start. I just want to make sure this is the life you wanted. I wouldn't want you to make a commitment to someone who didn't make you happy."

"Dad, are you giving me the Mr. Bennet premarital speech from *Pride and Prejudice*?"

"Well, you are doing a sort of theme wedding."

"Nice. Don't you think it's a little late in the game for this conversation? Are fathers of the bride supposed to get cold feet?"

"Any man standing on the verge of giving a daughter away has cold feet. When Jenny married Kent, I had to stop myself from throwing her in the back of the car and making a break for Hershey, Pennsylvania. It's nothing personal against Gabriel. He's a perfectly nice fella. I'm just saying, I know your mom has put a lot of pressure on you to settle down. I want to make sure you didn't say yes because you're afraid of being alone for the rest of eternity."

"I'm not marrying him because I'm afraid of being alone. I'm marrying him because I don't want live without him specifically. Because when I think about being without him, I feel sort of dizzy and sick, like I've been cut off from the tether that keeps me on the ground. That's about as flowery and romantic as I'm going to get."

He smiled, his eyes watering a little. "No, that was just right. Believe it or not, that's exactly how I feel when I think about losing your mama."

"That is hard to believe." I snorted as Marjorie slid piping-hot fries, dripping in gooey orange nondairy cheese food, in front of my father.

"I don't know what I'm going to do now that you're all grown up."

"Daddy, I'm thirty-one years old."

"Yeah, but I could always come here and depend on you to listen to my stupid stories and humor your old man."

"Well, you can still do that; you'll just have an extra pair of ears listening. Gabriel really likes you, you know."

"I guess I like him, as much as I could like the man who's making me give away my baby girl," he said quietly. "I couldn't hand you over to a man I didn't think deserved you, Janie."

"Thank you, Daddy." I paused, taking a sip of the warmed bottle of blood that Marjorie had dropped off at the table. "Why Hershey, Pennsylvania?"

He shrugged. "Jenny's wanted to go there since she was a little girl, ever since she heard that the streetlamps are shaped like Hershey's Kisses."

"That's sweet. What was my potential kidnapping destination?"

He reached across the table and squeezed my hand. "Right here."

I snorted. "Exotic downtown Half-Moon Hollow?"

"Well, you're a lot stronger than me. I knew I couldn't overpower you for long."

My wedding night set clear and warm, with a fingernail moon sliding low over the horizon. Jolene came bounding into my room at sunset, hopping up and down on the bed, bouncing me off onto the floor.

I sat up and glared at her. "Andrea gave you espresso, didn't she?"

"Nope!" she crowed. "But she showed me how to work the machine!"

"Augh!" I groaned, covering my face with a pillow.

"Come on, Jane, it's your weddin' night!" she cried. "Get up! Get excited! Your mama's already been outside most of the day, helpin' Iris get everything all set up. It's just gorgeous out there. Like somethin' out of one of your movies."

"Really?" I perked up, carefully retracting the sunproof shade so I could look out over the backyard. I gasped. When I'd gone to bed, it had looked like my backyard on any other night, just with lawn chairs lined up on it. Now it looked positively elegant, with a long ivory aisle runner stretched between the rows of chairs to the arbor, which was covered in fluffy green moss and roses in shades of ivory, lavender, and yellow. Little wildflowers offset the overly formal look of the roses, making it seem as though some helpful soul had just walked through the gardens at River Oaks and picked a few blossoms. The chairs were looped with ivory bows. There were little glass globes with lit candles hanging from the trees and ivory paper lanterns.

On the far side of the yard, I could see tables being set up for the reception. The rental service's employees were milling around the yard like an army of productive ants, setting up chairs, putting out table linens. Mama was in the middle of it all, conducting the chaos like a virtuoso.

"Where's Gabriel?" I asked, stretching and checking the clock. We only had an hour before the wedding. With the sun setting so late during the summer, we couldn't wait too long after dusk, or we'd be entertaining our guests well past their bedtimes. And ours, for that matter.

"You'll be very proud of them," Jolene told me as I retrieved my fancy nuptial underwear set from the dresser and ran into the bathroom. She shouted through the bathroom door as I buckled myself into my strapless bra. "The boys came home at a reasonable hour last night, mostly sober. Gabriel and Jamie crashed over at Dick and Andrea's to give you some space. Oh, and Jamie won twenty-four dollars playing blackjack. He didn't try to feed on a single human, not once."

"That's good news." I emerged from the bathroom in

my robe, because as close as we were, I wasn't going to hang out with Jolene and Andrea in my underwear for the next hour.

The door burst open, and my sister barreled into the room, wearing her bridesmaid's dress. "Who's ready to get married?"

I burst out cackling at the sight of my sister in her "biohazard suit" bridesmaid's dress. The neckline was off the shoulder, with a wide ruffle of egg-yolk yellow that gathered at the cleavage with a fabric rose, which accented the bodice's descent into what can only be described as a waist lapel. The whole effect made even my classically beautiful sister look sallow and misshapen. I laughed so hard that I tried to sit on the bed to support my shaking legs, but I missed and ended up in a giggling heap on the floor.

"Oh, good. I see that trademark charm is going to be what sustains us all night."

"I'm sorry, Jenny, this is all my fault," Jolene assured her. "I made Jane wear this dress at my wedding, and you're a victim of the fallout."

"She's the victim of fallout, all right." I giggled. Jenny glared at me. I sniffed and wiped at my eyes. "Sorry."

"Really?" Jenny asked.

"No. But look, I painted my toenails to match your dresses." I wiggled my toes in her direction to show her the neon-yellow polish. "Out of solidarity."

"Doesn't count," Jenny insisted. "Your shoes will cover them up. Now, come on and get dressed. Kent and the boys can't wait to see what kind of outfit a vampire bride wears."

I sniffed, wiping at my eyes as I rose. I managed to pull myself together, only to have Andrea come in wearing her dress, and I started giggling all over again.

Jolene left to go get dressed, while Jenny and Andrea pulled me in front of the vanity.

"Remember, neutral tones," Jenny said, dumping a shoulder bag full of cosmetics onto the vanity. "We want a light, smoky eye and a soft coral lip. And let's try to do something about those dark circles."

"Hey, that's not fair. Vampires have dark circles. Andrea has dark circles."

"Did you see them on my wedding night?" Andrea asked.

"No," I grumbled.

She preened. "Because I know how to use concealer."

Mama came bustling into the room with a garment bag over her shoulder and a mug of blood in her hand. Because there just weren't enough people in the room already. "Hi, sweetie! Are you excited?"

"So excited I may vomit at any moment," I assured her.

"Oh, you silly." She chuckled, handing me the mug of warm donor A-positive. "Gabriel said it would be better if you had something substantial in your system, so you're getting the real stuff today. Use the straw so you don't mess up your lipstick. And don't get that anywhere near the dresses! The last thing we need is you girls walking down the aisle looking like extras from *The Texas Chainsaw Massacre*."

She hustled into the bathroom to change into her

mother-of-the-bride frock. I stared after her, my mouth hanging open.

"Did Mama just hand me a cup of human blood and then make a joke about a horror movie?" I asked Jenny, who nodded, all astonishment. "Doesn't the Bible list that as one of the seven signs of the Apocalypse?"

"Well, not in the King James version," Jenny said.

"Ah!" I cried, dribbling blood back into the mug. "Don't be clever while I'm drinking. Blood spit-takes are gross!"

Andrea continued to lacquer my face, while Jenny piled my hair on top of my head. A couple of pins, a little hairspray, and I had a perfectly acceptable bun to pin my veil to. Mama came out of the bathroom in a pretty dove-gray suit and heels.

"Well, that's just beautiful, girls. You did a great job. Now, why don't you go downstairs and get that present for Jane? I'd like to help her get into her dress."

My friends were leaving me . . . alone . . . with my mother . . . right before a special occasion. I did not see this ending well for me. Maybe now was the moment to distract them all by revealing the real bridesmaids' dresses. Surely, they'd suffered enough. But then they all filed out of the room like dutiful little traitors, leaving me to the world's most awkward birds-and-the-bees talk.

No, they deserved the yellow dresses of shame.

Mama got my wedding dress out of the closet and unzipped the garment bag. "Now, Janie, did you have questions for me about tonight?"

"No, I'm pretty clear on the ceremony stuff, Mama," I said, stepping out of my robe and into the dress she was very carefully holding open for me. "I know I've been kind of a pain about this, but I really do appreciate all the effort you put into the planning."

"Oh, I know, baby. But I meant questions about later tonight."

I paused for a moment. Then my jaw dropped.

Mama continued, "It's just that after a few years, the two of you will get used to each other. And a married woman sometimes has to figure out special, um, efforts to keep her husband's interest piqued. Since the two of you will be together forever, you're going to have to work that much harder. So, if you need any advice, I'm here for you."

I stared at her blankly, unable to draw enough breath to respond.

"You know, if you need any tips—"

"What—what—Why on earth would I come to you for sex tips?" I spluttered.

She shrugged as she zipped the back of my dress. "Well, I've been married to your father for more than thirty years, and he's as happy as a clam—"

"Stop, Mama."

"Sometimes he likes it when I—"

"Oh, my God, isn't this a situation where hysterical deafness is called for?"

Jenny came into the room, carrying a little velvet pouch. When she saw the look on my face, she snickered.

"Mama tried to give you the 'wives need to learn special tricks' lecture, didn't she?" she asked, desperately trying to repress a smile. (And failing miserably.)

"I am just trying to share some wifely wisdom with you," Mama said, her hands on her hips. "Smart-asses."

"You've been branded a smart-ass. Welcome to my world," I told Jenny. She pulled a face and went to the mirror to put on lip gloss.

"Now that you're done ridiculing your mother," Mama said, eyeing me sternly, "I'm going to give you your wedding present." She opened the jeweler's pouch and pulled out a little sapphire pendant that had belonged to our paternal grandmother, Grandma Pat. She carefully draped it around my neck and clasped it. "Your grandmother gave me this to wear on my wedding day. Jenny wore it on hers. And now you're wearing it on yours. And since you're the youngest girl in the family and Jenny doesn't plan on having any more children, we'd like you to keep it."

"But what about the boys? When they get married, their wives might want this." I watched Jenny's face carefully. The distribution of family heirlooms had been a major issue of contention between us over the years. As in, she actually sued me over a family Bible. But she seemed perfectly fine with the idea of this little piece of family history remaining with me.

"Let's just wait and see if I like the girls they marry," she said. "So, that means your dress is new, and the necklace is old and blue. What can you borrow?"

"A time machine so I could go back before Mama's sex lecture and never have to hear it?"

"Oh, shush!" Mama said, slapping at my shoulder. "Borrow my bracelet." She unsnapped the thin gold bangle from around her wrist and clipped it around mine. "Ingrates, the both of you."

"She did the same thing to me on my wedding day, only we were in the church's changing room, which made it so much worse for some reason," Jenny said, shuddering.

"You couldn't have warned me?"

"Where's the fun in that?"

"I think I liked it better when you two didn't get along," Mama muttered.

Jenny and Mama scurried out to check on the groom and company and make sure they were strapped into their tuxes. Jolene and Andrea accompanied them, for the boys' sake.

I turned to look in the mirror and gasped. I actually looked like a bride. My hair gently framed my face, the chestnut color setting off the pale gray lawn of my veil. My wide, honey-hazel eyes were subtly outlined and winked out from my face like stars. My mouth looked soft and flushed. Andrea and Jenny had outdone themselves.

I stared at the mirror, unable to believe that the elegant, beautiful bride reflected back at me was, in fact, me.

"You look just gorgeous, baby doll." Aunt Jettie materialized at my side, peering over my shoulder in the mirror. "I am so very happy for you."

"Thanks, Aunt Jettie. I'm so glad you got to be here today," I said. "Even if you can't be in the photos."

"I love you very much, Jane," she said, her lip trembling. "I want you to remember that, always."

"I love you, too, Aunt Jettie. Are you all right?"

"I'm fine," she said. "I've just got a case of the wedding misties. I'm going to go downstairs and see to Gilbert before I blubber ectoplasm all over you."

She abruptly popped out of view. Frowning, I turned back to the mirror and fiddled with my veil. I wondered exactly how far I would get into the evening before I caught it on something or inadvertently set it on fire.

I heard the door open behind me. I said, "Mama, if you try to gift me with a wifely copy of the *Kama Sutra*, I will jump out that window."

I sniffed and immediately caught the scent of woods and tobacco and motor oil. I was overwhelmed with panicked thought bubbles. He had to get the female out of the house. He had to get her out without being noticed. It was pure stupid luck that he'd managed to snag one of the rental-company uniforms; now he just had to knock me out and stuff me into the bag and get out before Gabriel realized that his bride had been snatched.

I turned to find a burly man in dark blue overalls standing in my bedroom. He was holding what looked like a green canvas body bag.

This was not going to end well for my wedding dress.

I sighed. "Hello, Ray."

18

Your childe will be tempted to approach people from his or her former life, perhaps to seek vengeance for a perceived or actual wrong. Do your best to keep your childe distracted from this. Hunting, special treats, board games, hobbling—whatever it takes.

—*Siring for the Stupid:*
A Beginner's Guide to Raising Newborn Vampires

Ray McElray had had some hard days since he'd gotten out of prison. He had the same dark, curling hair, although it had been cut short from his former mullet. The same dark brown eyes, but there were now dark circles under them, and deep lines creased around his mouth. His face was a little heavier, puffed up from starchy jailhouse food.

"I don't know what you're talking about, ma'am," he said, his voice polite and even. "But I'd appreciate it if you turned around real slow."

Sighing again, I cracked my neck and removed my veil. "You can leave now, unhurt, or you can stay, and you will not walk away happy."

He reached into the body bag and pulled out what looked like a potato gun loaded with dozens of pencils. "I think I've got a better-than-average shot at it."

Dozens of freshly sharpened pencils were aimed straight at my chest. That did even things out a bit.

"Let me ask you something. When you set about to make something like that, what exactly goes through your head?"

He shrugged. "Mostly, 'boobs, beer, this will be cool, boobs, beer.'"

I bit my lip, because laughing didn't seem appropriate at the moment. "Well, you're honest."

"I don't want to ruin that pretty dress, ma'am, but I need you for something important that I have planned for your man. So I'd appreciate it if you would hold still."

"I'm bait again. Why am I always bait?" I groaned. At the very least, he was the most polite kidnapper I'd had so far.

"Kind of poetic, isn't it?" Ray asked, smiling almost proudly. "A bride goes missing on her wedding day. The groom runs to her rescue, only to be cut down himself. That's the sort of thing they used to write country songs about. Before country got all . . . sparkly."

"I don't know what you've been told about vampires, but I'm not going to just—"

He stepped closer, moving slowly and carefully. "Now, now, this has nothing to do with the fact that you're undead. Hell, I respect you as a predator. But I also know that a good predator can't be separated from its mate."

"I'm a vampire, not a timber wolf."

He pulled a capped hypodermic needle from his pocket. "Well, your fella killed my brother, and I got a bone to pick with him about it. If I have you, your Gabriel will come out into the open, without all your friends or those damn vampire ninjas you have hanging outside your house."

He stepped within an arm's reach, pressing the pencil gun right over my heart.

"Please, don't do this," I pleaded.

"Tilt your head, if you would, ma'am," Ray said, sliding that needle toward my jugular. "I'm about to stick you with a shitload of horse tranquilizers. And I don't want to splatter any arterial spray on that pretty dress."

"I really can't talk you out of this?" I asked, wincing as the needle pierced my skin.

He shook his head and *tsk*ed sadly. "'Fraid not."

My skin flushed hot as the drugs moved through my system with alarming speed. The edges of my vision blurred. And my eyes rolled up as my knees went out from under me. I felt Ray's hands catch me before I hit the ground, and the canvas bag moved over my face.

I hated being the damsel in distress.

For one thing, I was really bad at it. I was always antagonizing my captors. I would say something smart-assed and end up making them try to kill me ahead of schedule. Inevitably, I ended up with a head injury, and there are only so many concussions you can get without it affecting you long-term.

With this in mind, I woke up slowly, stretching each of my fingers, then my arms and legs. This was weird in itself, because I normally woke up with my arms tied behind my back. But it seemed that Ray was a consummate captor-host. I opened my eyes to find that I was in a squat, dirty little room, on a camp bed. My wrists and ankles were tied with bungee cords. At first, I thought that the cords were padded so they wouldn't chafe my arms, but I saw that the pads were wrapped in cheap-looking silver chains. If I squirmed or moved, the chains would tighten, slip around the padding, and burn the ever-loving hell out of my arms.

I cleared my dry throat. I squinted and looked around the bare room. I thought I might be in an old hunting shack. Deer hunters built these little shanties in the middle of the woods so they could sleep outdoors in relative comfort, then just walk outside to hunt without having to drive. Mostly, it was an excuse to get away from their families so they could go out into the wilderness to drink and belch competitively.

This particular bit of paradise looked as if it hadn't been used in quite a while. The walls were bare planks with corrugated metal protecting the exterior. There was a single darkened window on the opposite wall. The floor was covered in those sample carpet squares that flooring stores used as display, duct-taped together like a weird patchwork rug. And there was a calendar on the wall featuring Hooters's Hottest Waitresses from 1998. Charming.

The door opened, and Ray walked through. He'd shed the overalls and was wearing a pair of camo cutoffs and a T-shirt advertising the benefits of spring break in Daytona Beach. He had a pair of sparkly boxing gloves in his hands, which seemed . . . unlikely.

"Damn, I thought you'd still be asleep," he said, frowning. "Y'all must break down horse tranqs a lot faster than we do."

"Sorry to disappoint you. Why is my face sore?" I asked, stretching out my jaw and wincing at the pain.

"Well, I had you in the bag, and I was in a hurry to get you out of the house before your family noticed. And my shoulder slipped while I was carrying you down the stairs, and . . ."

"You dropped me down the stairs?" I cried.

"Well, you're heavier than you look!" he exclaimed.

"How is that supposed to make me feel better?" I grumbled. "How did people not notice that?"

"I told them you were soiled linens," he said. I balked, and he quickly added, "Look, I'm really sorry about this." He adjusted my bungee cords, being careful to stay outside of my lunging distance.

"How did you even track Gabriel down?" I asked. "How did you know he killed Bud?"

He pulled a camp chair near the bed. "As soon as I got out of jail, I went out to Bud's deer stand. I'd read the newspaper story about him dying, saw the coroner's report. I don't care what the coroner says, there's no way that kind of damage could occur from a tree just falling over on somebody. Bud and I picked that tree out ourselves when we built the deer stand. There was no rot, no weak spots. There was no way it was going to just fall over. There was obviously some sort of supernatural force at work. So, I wondered, who could be strong enough to push over a tree? At first, I thought it might be Bigfoot. But plenty of people have tried to hunt that bastard down, and it involves a lot of tracking equipment that just wasn't in my budget. It was smarter to work with monsters I could locate and eliminate them as suspects."

"I think that offends me on a couple of levels."

He ignored me. "So I went to the Cellar. I knew that it was a place where vampires hung out, so I spent a couple of nights there, kept my ears open. And before you knew it, I heard this story about some asshole vamp who pushed a tree on top of a drunk hunter." He smiled, the expression a bitter mockery of mirth. "I guess for y'all, that's right up there with flowers and chocolates, huh?"

"You don't understand—"

"I don't have to understand!" he yelled, standing so quickly that the chair toppled back. "Your boyfriend killed my brother for you, so you're going to watch him die. As he crumbles into dust, he's going to look in your eyes and know that all his vampire eternal-life bullshit has just evaporated into nothing. That you're going to live on forever without him and probably start banging some other vamp within a few months . . ." He looked down as he saw how horrified I was. "I'm sorry for my language, ma'am."

"Well, I'm sorry we blew up your bus," I said. "Though I'm pretty sure you set that up yourself."

"Don't worry about it. I abandoned that place as soon as your guys followed me from the dude strip bar. I started living here at Bud's hunting shack."

"You hoped that we would see the body, accidentally blow it up, and assume that you were dead?" I asked.

"Yes, ma'am. I took the body from the hospital morgue. You'd be amazed what people will let you do when you're wearing scrubs."

"And now I'm thankful I have no further need of the health care system." I sighed. "You know, you're holding me hostage, you might as well call me Jane. All of the other arch-villains do."

"Jane, then."

"And for the record, I won't be 'banging' some other vampire anytime soon," I told him. "I have a feeling that if you force me to watch Gabriel die, I would probably spend the next few months hunting you down and staging *your* death via deer stand."

"I won't hold it against you," he promised.

"I don't get it. I don't get how you can be so resigned to lifelong grudges. You seem like a reasonably intelligent person. What makes you think it's OK to do this?"

"Because if I don't, I'm just like everybody else. You have no idea what it's like growing up the way I did. A McElray, a charity case, a loser. My mama and daddy both went to jail before I even started school. No one expected anything good of me. Hell, the only time anybody ever treated me like I was something special was when I was playing football. But Bud was always there. When people whispered when we walked by at the grocery store, he kept his hand on my shoulder. Every single game I played, he was in the stands. And yeah, I realize that he wasn't perfect. He was a drunk and a gambler, and he hadn't held a steady job in no one knew how long. But if I let what your boyfriend did stand, then that means I gave up on him, just like everybody else did."

"Look, I know you think you're doing the right thing by Bud, but you have to understand—"

"No more talking," he growled suddenly. He pulled another syringe out of his pocket and jabbed it into my neck. I yelped as he forced the drugs into my vein, sending a burning sensation blazing under my skin.

"Asshole," I muttered as I slid under the surface of unconsciousness.

My eyes fluttered open. Gabriel was standing over me, untying my hands, his expression grim.

"Hey there, sweetie. I'm glad to see you," I slurred. "No, wait, you're not supposed to see me in my dress . . . s'bad luck."

"I dare you to try to find worse luck than ours, Jane."

"Good point," I muttered. I looked around the dingy little room. "Where's Ray?"

"Waiting for me outside. He said it would hurt me more if I had the chance to say . . . Did he hurt you?"

I shook my head and immediately regretted it. My head hurt, a lot. "Not intentionally. He's pretty polite for a kidnapper. Hates your ass, though. He thinks my dress is pretty."

"It's gorgeous, sweetheart," he assured me, pushing my mussed hair back from my face.

"Take me home."

"Right now," he promised.

"How did you even find me?"

He frowned. "Ray left me a very helpful note on your vanity. It said you were dead unless I met him at these GPS coordinates within an hour."

"You walked right into a trap? Isn't that my job?"

"It wasn't exactly a trap," he said as I sat up. It felt like swimming to the surface of a dark pool, my brain clearing the last few inches of murkiness and finally coming into focus. "And he did leave a sizable lock of your hair behind as an incentive."

"How sizable?" I asked, feeling the back of my head and finding a golf-ball-sized spot shorn to the scalp. "Damn it, Ray!"

Gabriel pulled me to my feet and steadied my elbows when I bobbled. I felt a low, heavy tug on my skirt and heard a rip. I moaned. My hem caught on a nail in the floor.

"Oh, come on!" I cried.

I turned, trying to dislodge my skirt, and gasped as the material split even wider, leaving a gap that nearly reached my cleavage. I looked up, horrified at what I'd done to the replacement dress. I doubted that I could talk Jolene's aunts into making a second one.

"We can—"

I grabbed his face between my palms and kissed him

deeply. "No. No postponements. No delays. I think we both knew this was how our wedding was going to turn out, one way or the other. I just really want to marry you."

He chuckled and kissed me. "I love you. And when you step outside, I want you to go to Dick just as fast as you can move. Zeb slowed him down a bit, but he should be here any minute. He's going to get you home. I'll meet you there as soon as I can."

I eyed him speculatively. "Do you really think I'm going to buy that and just toddle off home to wait on you like some Scarlett O'Hara wannabe?"

"Well, the dress is appropriate."

"Don't try to distract me with your intentional historical inaccuracies," I insisted. "Now, tell me what's going on."

"Ray wants to kill me."

"All right, so what's the plan?"

"I don't have one," he confessed. "This is a person who wants me dead. He wants you to watch as he kills me. And he's not going to stop until that happens. He's going to keep coming after you. I can't let that happen—"

"So your plan is to let Ray kill you?"

"Unless I manage to kill him in hand-to-hand combat, yes. And given his impressive array of improvised weaponry, I think he has an above-average chance."

I scoffed. "This is the dumbest plan I've ever heard. Zeb could come up with a better plan than this."

"Jane, I'm only trying to prepare you—"

"No! I do not accept this. No!" I yelled. I shoved past him, my ruined dress trailing behind me as I kicked open the hunting-shack door. Ray was waiting outside, his pencil gun strapped to his leg. When he saw Gabriel and me emerge, he cocked the shotgun he was holding and aimed it at my throat as I stomped toward him.

"Ray, what the hell are you doing?" I demanded.

"Jane, I know you're upset, but if you step any closer, I'll blow your head off."

"You're going to need more than that shotgun, Ray," I growled.

"It's loaded with silver shot," Gabriel murmured.

"Well, I guess that means we can't be friends anymore," I said. "Look, I know you're upset about Bud—"

"Upset? Nightengale killed my brother!" Ray yelled, turning on Gabriel. "Don't even try to deny it."

"You're right," Gabriel said, gently nudging me out of the way. "I won't try to deny it. I killed him. But do you know what your brother did?"

"It doesn't matter! It's a matter of honor."

Gabriel cleared his throat, pushing me aside even farther with a bump of his hips. "I'll try to put this in terms you understand. He killed my woman."

Ray looked to me, as if to confirm it. I nodded my head.

"Liar. You're a damned liar!" he shouted, his gun barrel bobbing precariously close to Gabriel's face. "Bud was a lot of things, but he wouldn't hurt a woman. He wasn't the type."

"No, but he was the type to get rip-roaring drunk and then do something stupid, right?" Gabriel countered. "He shot her. He was drunk. He thought she was a deer.

And he shot her. And then he just drove away and left her for dead. He just left her, like an animal, to die alone in the dark."

"You're lyin'!" he roared. "He wouldn't do that . . . well, he might. Aw, who the hell cares! The point is, you killed my brother. And now I'm gonna kill you!"

"Oh, come on, Ray!" I cried.

Ray was advancing on Gabriel. I stepped in the way, placing a restraining hand on his chest. The other hand was busy pushing Gabriel back.

"Jane, get out of the way."

"Gabriel, cut it out. He's too stupid to kill!" I yelled.

"Hey!" Ray said, his tone hurt as he scrambled against my grip.

"Ray, I'm trying to help you out here," I hissed, shoving both of them back a few steps. "Look, I'm not defending what Gabriel did to Bud. In fact, when I found out about it, I beat the absolute tar out of him."

Ray arched an eyebrow and bent sideways so he could smirk at Gabriel. "You let your woman beat on you?"

Gabriel rolled his eyes. "Have you met my fiancée?"

I cleared my throat pointedly, and their attention refocused on me. "It took me a long time to get over my part in Bud's death. I felt responsible. Please don't make me responsible for your death, too. Because he will kill you. No matter what you throw at him. No matter what you do. If you put me in danger, he's going to kill you. I get the feeling that you would do the same. Don't put more blood on my hands. Please. You don't have the stomach for this."

"How would you know?"

"Because the kind of man who would want to protect a girl's wedding dress isn't going to murder someone in cold blood. You could have killed me at the house and left a little pile of ash for Gabriel to find. Hell, even when you shot him with an arrow, you missed your mark. You've had chance after chance to kill us, Ray. Your heart, it's not in this. I'm sorry you lost someone you loved. Gabriel did what he did because Bud hurt me, because he thought he was protecting the people Bud could hurt. And really, you tried to run me down, hit a kid, and I had to turn him into a vampire. We're practically even."

"What are you talking about?"

"The old sedan that hit Jamie Lanier in front of my shop. You were behind the wheel."

Ray looked insulted. "Never happened."

"I have a hard time believing that."

"I don't give a shit what you believe," he retorted. "Nightengale killed the only family I have left. It's a blood debt, and it has to be paid."

I sighed. "Well, if that's true, then you might as well kill me, too. Because I'll just have to come after you. And on and on until everyone we love is just collateral damage to this grudge. Let it end with us, please."

"Why?"

"Because I can't handle another fight to the death. We seem to have them once a year lately, and it's not a tradition I want to continue."

"I can't just drop it now. I've tried to kill you . . . a bunch of times."

"Contrary to what the movies would have you believe, it's actually pretty hard to do," I told him, somewhat sympathetically.

"Yeah, well, I can't take that back. I can't just forget about it. What kind of brother would that make me? I wouldn't be able to live with myself if I just walked away. And it's not like vampires are known for their all-forgiving ways. Damn it, Nightengale, I kidnapped your woman. On her wedding day. Hell, even if you let me live, she'll probably kill me for that alone."

As Gabriel argued with him over my lack of desire for the usual avenues of womanly vengeance, Zeb and Dick burst into the clearing.

"Jane, would you like to know what you're getting for Christmas this year?" Dick asked as Zeb huffed and puffed beside him. "We're going to put one of those LoJack chips under your skin, like they do for dogs. It will cut down on our search time."

"I would find that insulting, but clearly, it's deserved," I grumbled. "Where are Andrea and Jolene?"

"At your place, restraining your mother," Zeb said. "We convinced them that it was the most logical use of their strength and not at all a sexist thing."

"That's Ray McElray?" Dick asked, incredulously.

"You know him?" I asked.

"Oh, sure, I see him down at the Cellar all the time. Calls himself Scooter," he said. "Heck of a pool player, but he sucks at darts."

"So, you've spent a lot of time with this guy recently?"

He shrugged. "Sure. I've mostly gone legit, since Andrea, but I still like going out for a beer and visiting Norm once in a while."

"Let me ask you something, Dick. In the course of these manly bonding activities, did you ever drink a little bit?"

"Sure," Dick said.

"Ever drink enough to tell tales about your friends?" I asked, as realization dawned on his face. "Maybe talk about this sickeningly happy couple you know who won't stop talking about the fact that the first time they had sex resulted from an argument they had about the guy pushing a tree on top of a drunk redneck?"

Dick's face went pale and almost cheesy green. "I will never drink again," he promised. "Janie, I swear, I didn't know. I wouldn't do anything to screw up my friendship with you two. You and Andrea and Spazzy McGee over there are my family. And I haven't had that in a very long time."

"I know," I said, squeezing his hand. "Now we just have to convince Gabriel."

Dick cleared his throat and stepped between Gabriel and Ray as they argued over how best to settle their debt. "How about dueling pistols?" he suggested.

I stared at him. "What?"

"You're right, Jane," Zeb conceded. "Not quite fair, what with Gabe being able to survive gunshots and all. Knife fight? Nah, still not sporting."

"How is this helping?" I demanded. "You are the worst best man ever!"

"Defusing the situation," Dick muttered, before he said louder, "You're right, Jane, a duel to the death wouldn't be fair, no matter what weapon they used. Gabriel would have the clear advantage. He's faster, stronger. Even with your pencil gun, Ray—which is awesome, by the way—you wouldn't stand a chance. So, we let you beat on each other for a couple of hours. Gabriel feels like he's suffered for what he's done. Ray defends his family honor. Everybody walks away in time for Gabriel and Jane to get hitched. Hell, the boys will probably be bonded for life by the time the fight's over. Fisticuffs have a way of doing that."

"Why are we friends?" I asked him, only to have him give me that maddening grin.

"I'm in," Ray said. "Your friend's right, it's the most honorable way to go about it."

Gabriel lifted a brow. "Really?"

"Really?" I echoed. "We went from blood debt to fist-fight?"

Ray nodded. "I know I probably don't have a chance in hell of beating you. And I can't guarantee that I won't try to stake you. But I think hitting you in that pretty face over and over will make me feel better."

Gabriel shrugged. "All right, then."

"Boys are so stupid." I sighed.

Gabriel pushed to his feet. I took his hands in mine. His mouth was pressed into a thin line.

"I really can't talk you out of this?" I asked. "I mean, we were supposed to be married, oh, about an hour ago."

"I think this is the only thing that will resolve the situation."

"Well, I'll be over here," I muttered, leaning gingerly against a nearby tree. "Trying to solve the enigma of the male ego and how it can be cured."

"No biting," Dick said, standing between the two of them like Mills Lane on *Celebrity Deathmatch*. "No unfair use of claws or fangs. No gouging. No hidden wooden objects. You fight until somebody says uncle."

Face, meet my palm.

Ray and Gabriel circled each other, cracking their necks in that weird, masculine chicken fashion that's meant either to stretch the vertebrae or to intimidate your opponent into thinking you'll throw a kiss on him without warning. They tried to be impressive, to show each other up with acrobatics and fancy combinations. Ray had obviously spent a little time at the prison gym and had built up some impressive upper-body strength. But it was still no match for Gabriel's speed and agility.

At one point, Gabriel knocked him back onto the ground, where Ray smacked his head on a rock. Gabriel made to help him up, and Ray used the gap in concentration to stab at Gabriel's chest with a broken tree branch. I shrieked in warning.

For the record, when someone is fighting, screaming his name and distracting him is not a good idea.

The branch missed its mark, sinking a few inches below Gabriel's collarbone. He yowled and dug it out and whacked Ray across the face. And then Ray kicked Gabriel off of him. Finally, they broke down to just punching each other in the face back and forth. I got bored and started trying to fix the rip in my dress.

Gabriel tossed Ray into a nearby tree trunk. "Hey!" I exclaimed. "Keep it sporting, he's only human."

Gabriel protested, "He kicked me in the—"

"That was an accident!" Ray wheezed, bending over and panting to catch his breath. "You shoved me, and my foot slipped."

"Seriously, guys, can we wrap this up? I'd like to get married tonight," I demanded. "Ray, do you feel like your family honor has been avenged?"

"Hold on a minute," Ray said, blowing out one last hard breath. He pivoted and kicked out at Gabriel, nailing him in the crotch. Gabriel grunted and fell to his knees.

"That's going to interfere with the honeymoon plans," Zeb said, shaking his head. I glared at him. He threw up his hands in defense. "Well, it is!"

"That time was on purpose," Ray told Gabriel as he helped him to his feet. "I feel better now."

"I'm so glad." Gabriel groaned, propping his hands on his knees to stay upright.

"And I've decided that we're even," Ray said. Gabriel's expression of hope was dashed when Ray added, "If you turn me."

"Beg your pardon?"

"I want to be a vampire," Ray said. "I thought about it

before. But after seeing what y'all can do, how you move, how fast you are, I want in. I don't have any family left, no reason to stay human. I want to be what you are. I figure you owe me this."

"Wow, this sounds like a great way for the Council to get really pissed at us," I said.

Dick said, "Actually, as long as Ray is entering into it voluntarily and behaves himself after he's turned, the Council shouldn't have a problem with it."

"Look at it this way, it's a life for a life," Ray implored. "You took my brother's life. You're giving me one in return."

"Your brother took Jane's life," Gabriel countered.

"Which you returned when you turned her," Ray said. "Do the same for me. Balance everything out."

"I've already got a teenager running around my house. I don't think I can handle a redneck renegade, too," I said.

"I'll do it," Dick piped up. We all turned to him in surprise. "Ray finding you, that was my fault. I couldn't keep my big mouth shut. Gabe, you know I would never do anything to put you and Jane in danger." Gabriel quirked a disbelieving eyebrow at him. "OK, fine, you know I would never do anything to put *Jane* in danger. But let me do this. Let me make up for my mistake. I can't handle you being pissed at me for another hundred years. You've got your hands full with Jamie, and I think I would be a better fit for Ray's sire, anyway."

"He has a point," I said. "If anyone could be more devious than Ray, it's Dick."

"Is this really the only way you'll consider us even?" Gabriel asked.

Ray considered it for a moment. "Yes. It's kind of poetic. I like it. And Bud would probably think it was funny as hell."

"Dick, are you sure about this?" I asked. "This is a long-term commitment. I don't want you to feel obligated because of me."

"It's the least I can do," Dick said. "And I'll keep my promise. I'll stop drinking . . . as much. No more bars. No more shady dealings with shady people."

"Dick, we wouldn't want you to do that. Shady dealings with shady people, that's who you are. We don't want to change that. Just maybe avoid talking about our sex life with random drunks at the Cellar. That would be a step in the right direction. And maybe conduct your 'side businesses' at a coffee shop or some other location where there are sober people. The Council likes using the Cracker Barrel."

"So, when are you doing this?" Zeb asked.

"Now," Ray said. "I don't want to put this off. I might lose my nerve."

"We kind of have a thing to get to," I said, jerking my head in the direction of River Oaks.

Dick patted my arm, trying to reassure me but failing miserably. "Actually, I can turn him now, drop him off at home to wait out the change, and then be at River Oaks by the time you're cleaned up and have your face back in order."

Over my shoulder, I saw Zeb and Gabriel waving their arms frantically and shaking their heads. I turned on them. "What do you mean?"

19

Never underestimate your childe's resourcefulness.
They may have skill sets that surprise you.

—*Siring for the Stupid:*
A Beginner's Guide to Raising Newborn Vampires

"It's not that bad," Gabriel assured me, putting his arm around my waist and leading me to the back of the house. We'd carefully driven around the dozen or so cars parked in front to keep our guests from seeing me (1) in the presence of my groom and (2) looking as if I'd been run through a woodchipper. Gabriel wouldn't let me look in the rearview mirrors in the car, and every time I looked as if I might catch a reflection in the window, Zeb threw his hands over my eyes from the backseat. I didn't take this as a good sign.

My worst fears were confirmed as Gabriel led me through the kitchen to find my family sitting around the kitchen table.

"What did you do?" Mama and Jenny chorused.

"I'm fine, by the way," I grumbled.

"Oh, my gosh, Jane, have you been wrestling bears?" Mama cried, rushing toward me.

"Yes, Mama, I took a little time out from my wedding prep to wrestle a few bears. I figured a mani-pedi would be passé," I said as she inspected what I suspected was a split lip and a black eye sustained when I was dropped on my face. Apparently, the horse tranquilizers slowed down our blood flow and, therefore, our ability to heal.

"Really?" Jamie asked, grinning mischievously.

Jenny took a minute to consider my snark. "Yeah, she's just fine."

"We're running about three hours late. Jolene and Andrea have come up with every possible stall story imaginable, and Iris has kept the open bar freely flowing. What should we tell the guests now?" Daddy asked.

"We could tell them she was adjusting her veil and fell out of a second-story window, but she'll be ready in just a few minutes," Zeb suggested.

"Hey!" I frowned at him.

"People who know her would believe it," Mama said.

"Hey!"

"We can convince them that Gabriel tried to ditch you at the altar, but you managed to run him down," Jolene said brightly as she hustled into the kitchen. She *tsk*ed at the damage to my dress and kissed my cheek.

"Statements like that are what got you into that dress."

"I'm glad you're OK," Jolene said, rolling her eyes.

"Revenge is what got us into these dresses." Andrea snorted. "Where's Dick?"

"He'll be here soon," I said. "Zeb and Gabriel can fill you in."

Zeb gave me a squeeze before I was pulled up the

back stairs by Mama and Jenny. "We'll give them an explanation that doesn't end up embarrassing you."

"Thank you," I said, looking over my shoulder at Gabriel. "Love you!"

"Love you!" he called as I reached the second landing.

In my room, Jenny pulled the dress carefully over my head and handed it to Jolene, who was already threading a needle with gray thread. Mama whipped a startling range of wet wipes from her purse, from stain-fighting to makeup-removing. "We can fix this."

I turned toward the vanity mirror and shrieked. My black eye and split lip were slowly returning to normal, but there was a splotch of dried blood at the corner of my mouth and a wide smear of mascara across my cheek. My hair looked as if I'd been attacked by a badger.

Mama had already started plucking pins from my hair. Jenny was dabbing at the blood, scrubbing at the mascara with a makeup-removing wipe. Within minutes, she had a fresh coat of powder and lipstick on my face and had reapplied my eye makeup.

"Jen, remember all those times I asked God why I was cursed with an evil sorority princess for a sister?"

"Vividly," she retorted dryly.

"I take it back."

Three hours late, slightly disheveled, with a discreetly mended rip up the front of my wedding dress, I was led to the garden by my father and into the hands of my future husband. Andrea, Jolene, and Jenny had been released from their lemon-colored clothing prisons and were now tastefully dressed in dove-gray gowns with empire waists and pretty beaded sashes. They were so relieved they didn't even take the time to be angry with me over the ruse.

Miraculously, Dick was waiting at the altar with the rest of the wedding party, having managed to slip into his vintage tuxedo T-shirt just in time. He explained later that he'd gotten some of Ray's blood on his dress clothes, but I knew he just liked to amuse me. Jamie was there, holding Fitz's leash. Zeb was at Gabriel's elbow, grinning brilliantly. I winked at him as I carefully walked down the aisle.

Per Mama's wishes, I'd invited all of the aunts, uncles, and cousins. And to my unending shock, they all showed, with one expected exception. Jenny told me that Cousin Junie had boycotted the ceremony "on principle." I think the principle was that I was dead, and I was still getting married before her. But the rest of my relatives waved happily from my side of the aisle, meaning that Gabriel could anticipate Uncle Dave and Uncle Junior's traditional wedding reception speech, entitled "If you hurt our girl, we will whip your ass." Only this time, they would be adding, "Vampire or not."

Daddy placed my hand in Gabriel's, and he beamed at me. He looked so handsome in his old-fashioned coat, the slightest hint of a healing bruise on his cheekbone. I wish I could say that I remember every detail of the ceremony, but all I remember is looking into Gabriel's eyes and smiling like a fool. It was a good thing we'd chosen simple vows, because I doubt I could have repeated anything beyond "I do."

Jolene's uncle pronounced us man and wife, and we practically ran back down the aisle as our friends and family pelted us with white flower petals. Near the arbor, Aunt Jettie and Mr. Wainwright clapped and shouted louder than the living.

After the ceremony, we stayed up all night in true vampire style. Fortunately, the human guests had been occupied with the planned wedding dinner while I was "indisposed," so we were able to get right to the fun stuff. The lanterns hung over the garden, their mellow light shining down on us as we laughed and drank. Gabriel and I didn't eat the cake, but we cut it for the human guests. Finally, just as dawn's pinkish fingers crept over the horizon, we were ready to go to rest for the day.

We weren't planning to go away until the next night. I wanted my first night as a married woman to be spent under River Oaks's roof. We waved from the house's front porch as the human guests departed. Unused to being up so late, Jamie went upstairs half-conscious, sure that he was going to pass out before he could get to a light-tight space. Mama practically had to be carried to the car, while Jenny was good and toasted and tried to persuade Jolene and Zeb to find an after-hours club. Or maybe a Denny's.

"And so, my lovely wife, you had a different wedding from most." Gabriel chuckled, taking me for one last spin about the porch.

"Yes, so few weddings begin with a duel and a vampiric blood-swapping agreement," I said. "Did Ray make it through the procedure?"

"Dick says he's resting comfortably at their home."

"I hope Andrea doesn't get too angry with him," I said. "She's basically going to be putting up with two of Dick."

"I have a feeling she will understand."

We turned to find Aunt Jettie and Mr. Wainwright waiting for us by the front door. They looked nervous and torn, not at all how someone attending a long-awaited wedding should appear. I carefully climbed the steps, lifting my train to prevent face-plants on the porch.

"Is everything OK?" I asked. "You two seem a little off tonight."

"Jane, it's time to go," Aunt Jettie said softly.

"Well, we're not leaving until tomorrow night, but we'll be back in a week."

Mr. Wainwright's cool, misty palm slid over my clasped hands. "No, dear, it's time for us to go."

Gabriel slipped an arm around my waist as I shook my head. "Go where?"

"Baby, it's time we moved on."

"But—but no!" I exclaimed.

Eloquent, I know.

Aunt Jettie smiled gently. "We've known for a little while that we wanted to see what's on the other side. But I wouldn't have missed your big day for anything, so we stayed. Now I've seen everything I'd ever want to see. You're happy. You're exactly what and where you need to be. And I don't belong here anymore. I'm not afraid of what comes next. I'm eager to see what's waiting for me. And Gilbert says that we'll be able to stay together if we concentrate hard enough on each other."

"Is that why you've been so distant? Why you've spent so much time away from the house? You wanted us to get used to not having you around?"

They nodded.

"But I'll miss you," I whispered as she trailed her hand down my face.

"Honey, you're a grown woman now. You don't need some silly old woman hanging around."

"No, but I want *this* silly old woman around," I protested. "Isn't that better?"

She narrowed her eyes at me and shook her head. "Oh, you're good."

"What if you get up there and the only thing waiting for you is Grandma Ruthie's vengeful spirit, preparing to annoy the hell out of you for eternity?"

Jettie shuddered. "Then we would do everything we could to find a way back."

"I really can't talk you out of this?" I asked.

They shook their heads sadly.

"You know what you've come to mean to me, right?" I asked Mr. Wainwright.

"Not nearly as much as you've come to mean to me. I love you very much, Jane. I wouldn't be able to leave this plane without knowing that you were here to care for the people and things I love."

"Does that include me?" I heard Dick's voice behind my shoulder as he joined us.

Mr. Wainwright's hands came up to cup Dick's cheeks. "Of course. I have few regrets, but one of them is not being able to spend more time with you. I hope you're not disappointed in your grandson for wanting a little rest."

"Never," Dick said. "I haven't had a lot of achievements in my life, things that I know I did right. Watching you grow up, helping you along the way, I know that was something to be proud of."

"I love you two," Andrea said. "I'll keep an eye on Dick for you, Gilbert."

"Thank you, dear," he said. "Jettie, love, are you ready?"

"As I'll ever be," she said. "Good-bye, sweetheart."

I watched as they moved across the lawn, the pinkish-blue light of dawn growing stronger. Instinctively, we moved toward the door, away from the growing sunlight. Aunt Jettie was moving farther away, fading.

"Aunt Jettie, wait!" I cried, running after her. I threw myself into her misty form. I felt her arms circle around my back as I sniffled into nothing. "I would have gone crazy by now without you. You helped me find out who and what I am. You let me know that it was OK to be myself. You gave me a place to go when everybody else in the family seemed determined to change me into something I wasn't. No matter what I did or what I was, you loved me. I just want you to know that I love you, too."

"Oh, baby girl," she crooned. "Good-bye."

"Good-bye," I said, blinking rapidly to clear the tears from my eyes.

They walked away into the distance, fading as they

moved, until they were whispers of vapor against the backdrop of morning. I moved quickly up the steps, through the protective cover of the front door.

Inside, in the foyer, Dick wiped at his wet cheeks. "Dust in my eyes."

I nodded, hugging him. "Me, too."

Andrea and Dick raced home against the rising sun. Gabriel led me upstairs to our room and went downstairs to secure the doors.

Shaken, I stood staring into empty space for long, silent moments. She was gone. Aunt Jettie was really gone. Without warning, without giving me time to prepare. I could only be grateful that she'd let me say good-bye. I couldn't believe she'd actually left me, but I understood why she did it that way. If she'd warned me, I would probably have tried to talk her out of it, made her stay.

Aunt Jettie deserved to be happy. She'd put off leaving to watch over me, to keep me happy. I was married now. I had a family. It was time for me to stand on my own two feet and be a real grown-up.

I wiped at my eyes and tried to focus on the moment at hand. I would only be a bride once, Lord willing. I didn't want to be a maudlin one.

I carefully stripped out of my dress and lay on the bed, waiting for Gabriel. He came into the bedroom, having shut Jamie's door and locked all of the other doors.

He cleared his throat. "What a disappointing groom I am. I feel like most of my work is done for me."

I propped myself up on my elbows. "Well, not all of your work. I didn't get that far."

He shrugged out of his vest and tie. "Glad to hear it. We do need to get some rest, though. We've got a very early flight tonight."

"Are you going to tell me where we're going, or am I going to find out when we land?" I asked as he crawled onto the foot of the bed, his pants and shorts left rumpled and forgotten.

He bent to kiss the delicate bone of my ankle. "I have three words for you. Hampshire. Bath. Southampton." He punctuated each location with a kiss to my calf, my kneecap, my thighs. He settled between them, tracing the line of my collarbone with his nose before nipping lightly at my throat.

"Three words that have to do with Jane Austen!" I exclaimed.

I flipped us over, straddling him, and bounced happily on the bed. Considering my position and his state of undress, this was an incredibly effective way to start the honeymoon. Gabriel shuddered under me, and I giggled.

"Sorry."

"No you're not," he growled softly. He pushed my bra aside and caught a puckered nipple between his teeth. Gasping, I ground down and tugged gently on his hair, drawing a hiss from him. His fingers tightened at my back, keeping me pinned close as his fangs dropped and worried the skin over my heart.

"You're right."

I whispered kisses over his brow, yelping softly when he ripped my panties away and rolled me back onto the bed. He hovered over me, pushing my hair away from my face. "I know we have . . . travel issues. But I wanted to do something you would find romantic. We're only going to get one honeymoon, one marriage, Jane. This is it. We're going to do it right."

And with that, he slid home, joining our bodies for the first time as man and wife. I sighed happily, and he tipped his forehead against mine.

I whispered, "I love you, Mr. Nightengale."

"I love you, too, Mrs. Nightengale."

20

Eventually, it will be time for your childe to leave the nest. You may find that you are lonely, that you miss taking care of someone. Please resist the temptation to turn another vampire immediately. You need some time to rest.

—*Siring for the Stupid:*
A Beginner's Guide to Raising Newborn Vampires

Considering our travel history, we handled the honeymoon pretty well. There was only one blow-up, and it was centered on who set up the wake-up calls for A.M. instead of P.M. We toured the villages of England. Walking along the roads at night, visiting the carefully preserved manors, you could almost imagine that time had stopped. You could see horses and carriages ambling down the lanes, imagine ladies in bonnets and gentlemen in beaver hats. I felt a connection to my favorite books that I hadn't imagined possible, just by seeing the places where they were set.

Oh, and did I mention the constant sex?

Somehow postwedding sex seemed completely new. Not to mention the fact that there were no nosy teenagers within a mile radius. We could be as loud as we wanted. We were tossed out of three hotels because of complaints from the other guests.

We returned home a week later, exhausted and pleased and burdened with a ridiculous amount of souvenirs and gifts. On the drive home from the airport, Andrea and Dick called to tell us that Jamie was waiting for us at the house. He'd been a perfect angel the whole week, Andrea swore. He'd taken care of Fitz, had run to River Oaks several times to check on the house, and had even been helpful with Ray when he rose, explaining the various perks and pitfalls of being a new vampire. So far, Ray had lived up to his word to be well behaved. He'd discovered that he didn't like bottled or donor blood but actually preferred to hunt deer and drink from them.

When I thought about it, it made a certain amount of sense.

Ophelia had already visited several times to monitor Ray's progress. And while she gave him several stern warnings about what happened to new vampires who revived old blood grudges, she was pleased that we'd managed to resolve the situation without bloodshed that she had to clean up.

We pulled onto the road leading to River Oaks. Gabriel smirked at me, threaded his fingers through mine. "We could turn around, you know. Take another few days. Get thrown out of some hotels in Nashville."

"You are ridiculously proud of that, Mr. Nightengale," I said.

"Even Dick's ridiculously proud of that, Mrs. Nightengale," he reminded me. I smiled. We'd been calling each other by our married names all week, because it amused Gabriel and had seemed sort of appropriate, considering our Austenian setting.

"Well, as sad as I am to end the honeymoon, I'm glad to be getting home. Believe it or not, I missed Jamie," I said. "It's sort of nice, coming home from vacation with gifts for our boy."

"Well, let's hope that he didn't follow the traditional teenage route of hosting a huge party and trashing the house while we were out of town."

I chewed my lip thoughtfully. "Maybe we should stop here and walk the rest of the way . . . so he doesn't hear us pull up."

"That would be . . ."

"A fun surprise?" I suggested.

Gabriel considered it. "Agreed."

We pulled over near the end of the driveway and cut the engine. We each grabbed a suitcase and swiftly made our way up the drive, moving soundlessly over the grass. From the distance, I could see Jamie sitting on the porch swing . . . and he wasn't alone.

Ophelia was straddling Jamie's lap, kissing him passionately as his hands trailed up her bare back. She groaned, grinding her hips down against his as he nibbled along her jawline to her collarbone.

"What in the name of Barnes and Noble do you think you're doing?" I dropped the suitcase.

Gabriel looked caught between confusion and horror and the urgent need to giggle hysterically.

Jamie scrambled to his feet and pulled his jeans up. Ophelia rolled her eyes and slipped back into her dress.

"Jane! I'm sorry!" Jamie cried.

"You are . . . grounded!" I yelled. "And responsible for cleaning that seat cushion."

Gabriel pressed his fingertips into his eyes, as if he could push the images out of his brain. "Jamie, what's going on here?"

Jamie looked sheepish, standing in front of Ophelia while she finished dressing. "Well, uh, see, Ophelia explained a couple of things to me. And, uh, we've been seeing each other while you were out of town. And yeah, I was wondering, Jane, whether you would be OK if I moved out?"

My eyes narrowed at Ophelia. She had the good sense to look a little uncomfortable.

"And where were you thinking of going, Jamie?"

Ophelia cleared her throat. "Jamie, darling, maybe this isn't the best time," she said.

"Phelia," Jamie prompted, his voice stern. I raised my eyebrows. "We talked about this. You'll feel better once it's out. And you owe it to Jane."

"I was the one who was responsible for your turning Jamie," Ophelia mumbled. "Indirectly."

"What do you mean?" I demanded.

She looked down at her twisting hands and mumbled. "I know who hit him with the car."

All of the blood seemed to rush through my ears, creating a tornado of sound. For a moment, I actually saw red. The edges of my vision were tinged a violent crimson, creating a tunnel that focused on Ophelia's face.

"Explain," I growled.

Ophelia nibbled on her bottom lip. "I wanted him with me. I've tried having human lovers before, and ever since the social mores regarding age difference changed, it just hasn't worked out. They age. I stay looking like a mall rat. And they eventually get questioned by the police. It's uncomfortable for everyone. I saw Jamie at the quilt festival this spring, and I just fell for him. I watched him for weeks. I watched how he behaved around other kids, how he treated girls. I knew he was just the right mate for me. He's sweet and kind but strong and resilient. He has leadership abilities that will mature as he grows older. And he's smart enough to let me have my way on occasion, but he will eventually be able to stand up to me."

Jamie frowned. "Eventually?"

"I couldn't turn him myself," Ophelia admitted. "Because of Georgie. I'm banned for centuries. But it didn't stop me from following him and talking about him constantly at home—his sports teams, his favorite restaurant, his route at work. Which was a mistake, because Georgie wanted to meet this boy I found so fascinating. She just wouldn't let it go. She asked over and over, and she couldn't believe I was actually saying no to her. I hardly ever say no to her, which is I why I think she took it personally enough to wait until I was at the Council office, steal the keys to the car I was using to follow Jamie, sneak out of the house, and drive around looking for him."

"Are you saying . . ."

"My little sister ran Jamie down with the car because she overestimated her ability to see over the steering wheel," Ophelia said, biting her lip.

My jaw went slack. It was really difficult to figure out whom to be angry with. It felt wrong to be angry at Georgie, since she was basically a child, but she was about three hundred years older than I was, and she should have known better. Then there was Ophelia, who should have at least hired some sort of supernatural nanny to keep her sister from these dangerous hijinks.

"But it all worked out, you see, because I got to meet Jamie, and we're in love, and we get to stay together forever," she said, smiling sweetly at him. "And Georgie's mistake—that's part of the reason I insisted that he foster with you. I felt responsible for what happened to him, and I knew you would treat him well. I needed someone who was a good person, who would teach him to be a good, responsible vampire but was too old for him to find attractive—"

"Hey!" I barked. "What if Jamie didn't want to be turned? Did you think about that?"

"Well, since you turned him, he'd be angry with you, not me. So that worked out, too. It's sort of perfect, don't you think?" She turned to me, grinning smugly. "You know, you're taking this a lot better than I expected you to."

I slammed my fist into the bridge of Ophelia's nose.

My hand actually smarted from the blow. She went flying over the porch rail and ass-over-teakettle into the rosebushes.

"I had that coming," Ophelia admitted. "That was your one free shot."

"Oh, hell, no, Missy, you must be losing your mind if you think that's the last of it. There will be multiple shots. I'm going to give you a twenty-one-damn-gun salute. If you're going to be dating my boy, there are going to be rules and family dinners on Sundays. Every holiday will be celebrated at my house. You can start your own traditions when I'm dead. And there will be lots and lots of digs about how you're not good enough for him."

"I think a cold chill just dislodged a disc in my spine," Gabriel muttered, shivering.

"Sort of makes you rethink that whole eternity-together thing, huh?" Jamie said, lifting Ophelia from the ground.

"You don't know what you've brought down on yourself, Cookie." I pointed my finger in her face and then turned on Jamie. "And how do *you* feel about all this?"

"Well, at first, I was wicked pissed," he said, glaring down at her without any real heat. She actually looked contrite, but it passed quickly. "But the bad part's over, right? What's done is done. And Georgie's apologized. She feels just terrible about it. Besides, it was kind of cool to hear Ophelia tell me about the whole stalking-me thing. I've never had a girl go to quite those lengths to get my attention."

"Yes, she's a regular bunny boiler."

"Are the nicknames going to stop soon?" Ophelia asked.

"No, condescending nicknames that imply that I can't remember your real name are all part of the bitchy in-law package," I told her. "And no, Jamie, for right now, I don't think you should move out. I'd be more comfortable if you stayed with me. It's not right for you two to live together right now."

Jamie shouted, "What? You lived with Gabriel before you were married!"

"This has nothing to do with marital status," I said calmly. "This has to do with your emotional maturity. And the fact that she was indirectly responsible for you being run down with a car, which implies a certain disregard for personal safety. I'm going to have to insist that you stay with me for at least another year or until you can give me a well-thought-out plan on your living arrangements, including how you plan to integrate Georgie into your life together."

"Can she do that?" Jamie demanded.

Ophelia nodded hesitantly. "It's within her rights as your sire," she said, her tone quickly becoming acidic. "Though she should realize that Georgie is none of her business, and she would be wise to leave my sister out of future arguments about our relationship. Driving incidents aside, I have never neglected my sister, and I won't start now."

"Good, you can bring her to Christmas dinner. We'll take a big family photo involving ugly holiday sweaters."

"*Augh!*" Jamie groaned. "That is so lame!"

"Well, that's me, Jane, Queen of Lame. And I'm only putting you through this embarrassment and hardship because I love you."

There was genuine delight in his smile when he heard this. He hugged me, and I felt the depth of his gratitude and affection like a humming melody from his brain. His face shifted into an expression of crafty nonchalance. "Do you love me enough to let me borrow your truck to take Ophelia to the drive-in?"

I *tsk*ed, kissed his cheek, and gave him a bone-crushing hug. "Not on your life."

"Again with the lame." His face fell. "Come on, Phelia, let's go upstairs."

"Keep the door open!" I called as they ascended the steps. Gabriel winced as Jamie slammed his bedroom door shut. "Maybe we should have stayed in England."

I shot him an amused look, wrapped my fingers around the back of his neck, and pulled him in for a kiss. "Nah, it's good to be home."

Turn the page

for a sneak peek

of the next delicious romp by

MOLLY HARPER

The Care and Feeding of
Stray Vampires

Available August 2012 from Pocket Star!

The thing to remember about "stray" vampires is that there is probably a good reason he is friendless, alone, and wounded. Approach with caution.

—*The Care and Feeding of Stray Vampires*

How did an internal debate regarding flavored sexual aids become part of my workday?

I was a good person. I went to church . . . on the "big days." I was a college graduate. Nice, God-fearing people with bachelor's degrees in botany should not end up standing in the pharmacy aisle at Walmart debating which variety of flavored lube is best.

"Ugh, forget it, I'm going with Sensual Strawberry." I sighed, throwing the obscenely pink box into the basket.

Diandra Starr—a poorly-thought-out pole name if I'd ever heard one—had managed to snag to the world's only codependent vampire. My client Mr. Rychek. When she made her quarterly visits to Half-Moon Hollow, I was turned into some bizarre hybrid of both Cinderella and the Fairy Godmother; waking up at dawn to find voicemails and e-mails detailing the myriad needs that must be attended to *at once*. Mr. Rychek seemed convinced that Diandra would flounce away on her designer platform heels unless her every whim was anticipated and met. No demand for custom-blended bath salts was considered too extravagant. No organic, free-trade food requirement was too extreme. And the lady liked her sexual aids to taste of summer fruits.

I surveyed the contents of the cart against the list. Iron supplements? Check. Organic almond milk? Check. Flavored lube? Check.

I did not pretend to understand the dynamics of human–vampire relationships.

Shopping in the "special dietary needs" aisle was always an adventure. An unexpected side effect of the Great Coming Out in 1999 was the emergence of all-night industries, special products, and cottage businesses, like mine, that catered to the needs of "Undead Americans." Companies were tripping over one another to come up with products for a spanking new marketing demographic: synthetic blood, protein additives, dental care accessories, lifelike bronzers. The problem was that those companies still hadn't figured out packaging for the undead, and tended to jump on bizarre trending bandwagons—the most recent being a brand of plasma concentrate that came pouring out of what looked liked Kewpie dolls. You had to flip back the head to open it.

It's just as creepy as it sounds, if not more so.

Between that and the sporty, aggressively neon tubes of Razor Wire Floss, the clear bubble-shaped pots of Solar Shield SPF-500 sunblock, and the black Gothic boxes of Forever Smooth moisturizing serum, the vampire aisle was ground zero for visual overstimulation.

I stopped in my tracks, pulling my cart to an abrupt halt in the middle of the pharmacy section as I recalled that Rychek's girlfriend was a vegan. I started to review the label to determine whether the flavored lube was an animal by-product. But I found that I honestly didn't care. It was 4:20, which meant I had an hour to drop this stuff by Mr. Rychek's house, drop the service contracts by a new client's house in Deer Haven, and then get to Half-Moon Hollow High for the volleyball booster meeting. Such was the exotic and glamorous life as the Hollow's only daytime vampire concierge.

My company, Beeline, was part special-event coordinator, part concierge service, part personal organizer. I took care of all the little details vampires didn't have time for, or just didn't want to deal with themselves. Though it was appropriate, I tried avoiding the term "daywalker" unless dealing with established clients. It turns out that if you put an ad for a daywalker service in the yellow pages, you get a lot of calls from people who expect you to scoop Fluffy's sidewalk leavings. And I was allergic to dogs, and their leavings.

On my sprint to the checkout aisle, I cast a longing glance at the candy aisle and its many forbidden, sugary pleasures. With my compulsive sweet tooth, I did not discriminate against chocolate, gummies, taffy, lollipops, or even those weird so-sour-the-citric-acid-burns-off-your-taste-buds torture candies. But between Gigi's worries about the potential for adult-onset diabetes in our gene pool and my tendency toward what I prefer to call "curviness," I only broke into the various candy caches I had stashed around the house under great personal stress. Or if it was a weekday.

Placating myself with a piece of fruity sugarless gum, I whizzed through the express lane and loaded Mr. Rychek's weekend supplies into what my sister, Gigi, in all her seventeen-year-old sarcastic glory, called the Dorkmobile. I agreed that an enormous yellow minivan was not exactly a sexy car. But until she could suggest another way to haul cases of synthetic blood, Gothic-themed wedding cakes, and, once, a pet crate large enough for a Bengal tiger, I'd told Gigi that she had to suck it up and ride shotgun in the Dorkmobile. The next fall, she'd used her earnings from the Half-Moon Hollow Country Club golf course snack bar to buy a secondhand VW bug. Never underestimate a teenager's work ethic if the end result is averted embarrassment.

I used my security pass to get past the gate into Deer Haven, a private, secure subdivision inhabited entirely by vampires and their human pets. It was always a little spooky, driving through this perfectly maintained, cookie-cutter ghost-suburb during the day. The streets and driveways were empty. The windows were shuttered tight against the sunlight. Sometimes, I expected tumbleweeds to come bouncing past my car. Then again, I'd never seen the neighborhood awake and hopping after dark. I made it a policy to be well out of my clients' homes before the sun set. With the exception of the clients whose newly legal weddings I helped plan, I rarely saw any of them face-to-face. I allowed my wedding clients a little more leeway because they were generally too distracted by their own issues to bother nibbling on me. And, still, I only met with them in public places with a lot of witnesses present.

Though it had been nearly ten years since the Great Coming Out and vampire–human relations were vastly improved since the early pitchfork-and-torch days, some vampires were still a bit touchy about humans' efforts to wipe out their species. They refused to let any human they hadn't met in person near their home while they were sleeping and vulnerable.

After years of working with them, I had no remaining romantic notions about vampires. They had the same capacity for good and evil that humans do. And despite what most TV evangelists preached, I believed they had souls. The problem was that the cruelest of tendencies can emerge when a person is no longer restricted to the "no biting, no using people as food" rules humans insist upon. If you were a jerk in your original life, you're probably going to be a bigger undead jerk. If you were a decent person, you're probably not going to change much beyond your diet and skin-care regimen.

With vampires, you had to be able to operate from a distance, whether that distance was physical or emotional. My business was built on guarded, but optimistic, trust. And a can of vampire pepper spray that I kept in my purse.

I opened the back of my van and hitched the crate of supplies against my hip. I had pretty impressive upper body strength for a petite gal, but it was at times like these, struggling to schlep the crate up Mr. Rychek's front walk, that I wondered why I'd never hired an assistant.

Oh right, because I couldn't afford one yet.

Until my little business, Beeline, started showing a profit margin just above "lemonade stand," I would have to continue toting my own barge and lifting my own bale. I looked forward to the day that heavy lifting wouldn't determine my wardrobe or hairstyle. On days like this, I tended toward sensible flats, twin sets, and pencil skirts in dark, smudge-proof colors. I liked to throw in a pretty blouse every once in a while, but it depended on whether I thought I could wash synthetic blood out of it. (No matter how careful you are, sometimes there are mishaps.)

And the hair. It was difficult for human companions, blood-bank staff, and storekeepers to take me seriously when I walked around with a crazy cloud of dark curls framing my head. Having Diana Ross's 'do didn't exactly inspire confidence, so I twisted my hair into a thick coil at the nape of my neck. Gigi called it my "sexy librarian" look, having little sympathy for me and my frizz. But since we shared the same unpredictable follicles, I was biding my time until she got her first serious job and realized how difficult it was to be considered a professional when your hair was practically sentient.

I used another keyless entry code to let myself into Mr. Rychek's tidy little town house. Some American vampires lived in groups of threes and fours in what vampire behaviorists called "nesting," but most of my clients, like Mr. Rychek, were loners. They had little habits and quirks that would annoy anyone, human or immortal, after a few centuries. So they lived alone and relied on people like me to bring the outside world to them.

I put the almond milk in the fridge and discreetly tucked the other items into a kitchen cabinet. I checked the memo board for further requests and was relieved to find none. I only hoped I could get through Diandra's visit without being called to find a twenty-four-hour emergency vet service for her hypoallergenic cat, Ginger. That stupid furball had some sort of weird fascination with prying open remote controls and swallowing the batteries. And somehow, Diandra was always shocked when it happened.

As an afterthought, I moved Mr. Rychek's remote from the coffee table to the top of the TV.

One more stop. I had just one stop left before I could put in my time at the booster meeting, go home, and bury myself in the romance novel I'd squirreled away inside the dust jacket for *The Adventures of Sherlock Holmes*. If Gigi saw the bare-chested gladiator on the cover, the mockery would be inventive and, mostly likely, public.

My new client's house was conveniently located in the newer section of Deer Haven, at the end of a long row of matching beige condos. As usual, I had to count the house numbers three times before I was sure I was at the right door, and I wondered how wrong it would be to bookmark my clients' doors with big fluorescent yellow bumblebees.

Entering the security code provided on his new-client application, I popped the door open, carrying my usual "Thank you for supporting Beeline" floral arrangement inside. Most vampires enjoyed waking up to fresh flowers. The sight and smell reminded them of their human days, when they could wander around in the daylight unscathed. And they didn't have to know I'd harvested the artfully arranged roses, irises, and freesia from my own garden. The appearance of an expensive gift was more important than the actual cost of said gift.

Mr. C. Calix certainly hadn't wasted any money on re-decorating, I mused as I walked into the bare beige foyer and set the vase on the generic maple end table. The place was dark, which was to be expected, given the sunproof metal shades clamped over the windows. But there was little furniture in the living room, no dining room table, no art or pictures on the clean taupe walls. The place looked barely lived in, even for a dead guy's house.

Scraping past a few cardboard packing boxes, I walked into the kitchen, where I'd agreed to leave the contracts. My foot caught on a soft weight on the floor. "Mother of fudge!" I yelped, then fell flat on my face.

Have I mentioned that I haven't cursed properly in about five years? With an impressionable kid around the house, I'd taken to using the "safe for network TV" version of curse words. Though that impressionable kid was now seventeen, I couldn't seem to break the habit. Even with my face smashed against cold tile.

"Frak frakity frak," I moaned, rubbing my bruised mouth as I righted myself from the floor. I ran my tongue over my teeth to make sure I hadn't broken any of them. Because honestly, I wasn't sure I could afford dental intervention at this point. My skinned knees—and my pride—stung viciously as I recounted my teeth for good measure.

What had I tripped over? I wondered. I pushed to my feet and stumbled over to the fridge and yanked the door open. The interior light clicked on, illuminating the dead body stretched across the floor.

Shrieking, I scrambled back against the fridge, my dress shoes skittering uselessly against the tile. I couldn't seem to swallow the lump of panic hardening in my throat, keeping me from drawing a breath.

The corpse was huge, with long, rangy limbs and narrow, highly arched feet. Dark waves of hair sprang over his forehead in an inky profusion. The face would have been beautiful if it hadn't been covered in dried blood. A straight nose, high cheekbones, full, generous lips that bowed slightly. He had that whole Michelangelo's *David* thing going. If David had been a creepy religious figurine that wept blood.

A half-empty bottle of Faux Type O lay splattered against the floor, which explained the rusty-looking dried splotches on his face. Had he been drinking it when he . . . passed out?

Vampires didn't pass out. And most of them could sense when to get somewhere safe well before the sun rose. They didn't get caught off guard and collapse wherever they were at dawn. What the hell was going on here?

I eyed my shoulder bag, flung across the room when I'd fallen on my face. Breathing steadily, I resolved that I'd call Ophelia at the local Council for the Equal Treatment of the Undead office and leave her a message. She would know what to do. And I could get the hell out of here before the hungry, wounded vampire rose for the night and made me into his breakfast.

I reached over him, aiming my arm away from his mouth. A strong hand clamped around my wrist. I am ashamed to say I screamed like a little girl. I heard the telltale snick of fangs descending and panicked, yanking and struggling against a relentless vise grip. A tug-of-war ensued for control of the arm he was pulling toward his chapped, bloodied lips. He tried to lunge for me, but the effort cost him, and his head thunked back to the floor with a heavy thud.

With my hand hovering precariously over his gaping, hungry mouth, I did the only thing I could think of—I poked him in the eye.

"Ow," he said, dully registering pain as I jabbed my index finger against his eyelid. The other eye popped open, the long sooty lashes fluttering. It was a deep, rich coffee color, the iris ringed in black.

"Ow!" he repeated indignantly, as if the sensation of the eye-poke was just breaking through his stupor.

With him distracted, I gave one final yank and broke free, holding my hand to my chest as I retreated against the fridge. I took another Faux Type O from the shelf. I popped it open and held it carefully to his lips, figuring that he wouldn't care that it wasn't heated to body temperature. He shook his head faintly, wheezing, "Bad blood."

I checked the expiration date and offered it to him again. "No, it's fine."

His dry lips nearly cracked as they formed the words, "Poisoned . . . stupid."

"OK . . . jackass," I shot back.

The faintest flicker of amusement passed over his even features. "Need clean supply," he whispered.

"Well, I'm not giving you mine," I said, shrinking away from him. "I don't do that."

"Just wait to die, then," he muttered. I had to bite my lips to keep from snickering or giggling hysterically. I was sure that crouching over him, laughing, while he was vulnerable and agitated wouldn't improve the situation.

Shouting for him to hold on, I scurried out to my car, carefully shutting the door behind me so that sunlight didn't spill into the kitchen. I had a case of Faux Type O in the back, destined for Ms. Wexler's house the next day. I grabbed three bottles from the package and ran back into the house. Sadly, it only occurred to me *after* I'd run back into the house that I should have just grabbed my purse, jumped into my van, and gunned it all the way home.

But no, I had to take care of vampires with figurative broken wings, because of my stupid Good Samaritan complex.

Kneeling beside the fallen vampire, I twisted the top off the first bottle and offered it to him. "I'm sure this is clean. The tamper-proof seal's intact."

He gave the bottle a doubtful, guarded look, but took it from my hand. He greedily gulped his way through the first bottle, grimacing at the cold offering. Meanwhile, I popped the other two bottles in the microwave. I even dropped a penny in each one after heating to give them a more authentic coppery taste.

"Thank you," he murmured, forcing himself into a sitting position, though the effort clearly exhausted him. He slumped against the pine cabinets. Like all of the Deer Haven homes, the kitchen was done in pastel earth tones—buffs, beiges, and creams. Mr. Calix looked like a wax figure sagging against the pale wood. "Who are you and what are you doing in my house?"

"I'm Iris Scanlon, from Beeline. The concierge service? Ophelia Lambert arranged your service contract before you arrived in the Hollow. I came by to drop off the paperwork."

He nodded his magnificent dark head slowly. "She mentioned something about a daywalker, said I could trust you."

I snorted. Ophelia only said that because I hadn't asked questions that time she put heavy duty trash bags, lime, and a shovel on her shopping list. The teenage leader of the local World Council for the Equal Treatment of the Undead office might have looked sweet sixteen, but at more than four hundred years old, Ophelia, I'm pretty sure, had committed felonies in every hemisphere.

Scary felonies.

"Well, you seem to be feeling a bit better. I'll leave these papers here and be on my way, then," I said, inching around him.

"Stop," he commanded me, his voice losing its raspy quality as he pushed to his feet. I froze, looking up at him through lowered lashes. His face was fuller somehow, less haggard. He seemed to be growing a little stronger with every sip of blood. "I need your help."

"How could *I* help you?"

"You already have helped." As he spoke, I picked up on the faint trace of an accent, a sort of caress of the tongue against each finishing syllable. It sounded . . . old, which was a decidedly unhelpful concept when dealing with a vampire. And since most vamps didn't like talking about their backstories, I ignored the sexy lilt and its effects on my pulse rate. "And now I need you to take me home with you."

"Why would I take an unstable, hungry vampire home with me? Do I look particularly stupid to you?"

He snorted. "No, which is *why* you should take me home with me. I already know where you live. While you were running to your car, I looked in your purse and memorized your driver's license. Imagine how irritated I would be, how motivated I would be to find you and repay your *kindness*, after I am well again."

I gasped, clutching my bag closer to my chest. "Don't you threaten me! There seem to be a lot of handy, breakable wooden objects in this room. I'm not above living out my fonder Buffy fantasies."

His expression was annoyed, but contrite. Mostly annoyed. He cleared his throat. "I'm sorry, that was out of line. But I need to find a safe shelter before dark falls. I have a feeling someone may be coming by to finish me off. No sane person would attack me while I was at full strength."

I believed it, but it didn't stop me from thinking Mr. Calix was a bit full of himself. "How do I know that you won't drain me as soon as you stabilize?"

"I don't do that," he said, echoing my earlier pronouncement, and took my bag from my hands. I tried snatching it back, but he held it just out of my grasp, like some elementary school bully with a My Little Pony backpack.

Scowling at him, I crossed my arms over my chest. "Considering you just vaguely threatened me, I have a hard time believing that."

"Check my wallet, on the counter."

I flipped open the expensive-looking leather folio and found what looked like a shiny gold policeman's badge. "You're an investigator for the Council? In terms of credibility, that means nothing to me. I've met Ophelia."

His lips twitched.

"Why can't you just call her?" I asked. "She's your Council rep. This should be reported to her anyway."

"I can't call her. The Council supplied me with that blood," he said, giving a significant look to the discarded bottle on the floor. "I can't trust the Council. I can't check into a hotel or seek help from friends without being tracked."

"I have a little sister who lives with me. I'm not going to let you drag us into your vampire bullcrap." I grunted, making a grab for my bag as his tired arms drooped. "I am not running a stop on the vampire underground railroad."

"I can pay you an obscene amount of money."

I'm ashamed to say that that stilled my hand. If anything would make me consider this bizarre scheme, it was money. My parents had died nearly five years before, leaving me to raise my little sister without much in the way of life insurance or savings. I needed money for Gigi's ever-looming college tuition. I needed money to keep up the house, to pay off the home equity loan I'd taken out for Beeline's start-up capital. I needed money to keep us in the food Gigi insisted on eating. And despite the fact that the business was finally becoming somewhat successful, I always seemed to just cover our expenses, with a tiny bit left over to throw at my own rabid student loan officers. Something always seemed to pop up and eat away at our extra cash—car repairs, fees for a school trip, explosive air-conditioning failure.

An obscene amount of money would provide enough of a cushion that I might be able to sleep for more than handful of hours per night. Mr. Calix slid to the floor, apparently drained by the effort of playing purse keep-away.

"How obscene?" I asked, coughing suddenly to chase the meek note from my voice.

"Ten thousand dollars for a week."

I quickly calculated the estimate to replace the aging pipes in my house, plus Gigi's first semester tuition and the loan payment due next month, against what the Council paid even the lowest of its underlings. I shook my head and made a counteroffer. "Twenty-five thousand."

"Fifteen thousand."

I pursed my lips. "I'm still saying twenty-five thousand."

"Which means you never quite learned how negotiating works."

It was a struggle, tensing my lips enough to avoid smirking. "How badly do you want to get off that floor, Mr. Calix?"

He grumbled. "Done."

"One week," I said as I knelt in front of him, my voice firmer than I would have thought possible under the circumstances. "That means seven nights. Not seven days and eight nights. Not seven and a half nights. *Seven nights*."

"Done."

"Excellent." I gave him my sunniest "professional" smile and offered my hand for a shake.

"Don't push it," he muttered, closing his eyes.

I sighed, pulling my cell phone out of my bag to call Gigi. I wasn't going to make that booster meeting after all.